Lady Mercy Danforthe Flirts with Scandal

JAYNE FRESINA

books
anca

Published by Sourcebooks Casablanca, an imprint of Sourcebooks,
Inc.
P.O. Box 4410, Naperville, Illinois 60567-4410
(630) 961-3900
Fax: (630) 961-2168
www.sourcebooks.com

Printed and bound in Canada.
WC 10 9 8 7 6 5 4 3 2 1

To Jenna

Chapter 1

"I HAVE ONLY ONE USE FOR AN OVERLY PROUD COCK." The old woman's black lace veil billowed with a gusty sigh. "Stewed in a pot with burgundy wine and butter. So you may put aside your pride and male vanity, Hartley. I've sent more strutting cockerels to the ax than I care to count."

In almost twenty-five years of life, Rafe Hartley had known several stubborn wenches and even met one or two who thought themselves fearless. Until they encountered him. But this one was a different matter. She could not be moved by either his charm or his temper—both of which he'd been told were considerable, reckless, and mostly the cause of his troubles.

This woman remained unaffected, impenetrable. His most fearsome scowl caused not the merest tremble of that lace veil; his deepest growl apparently fell upon closed ears. Inside that small frame, he concluded, she had nerves of steel.

"Lady Blunt, I could not take a farthing," he exclaimed. "I will not. I earn my own coin and do not look for charity."

Once again a drift of exhaled determination fluttered against the black lace veil. "This is not charity, young man." She spoke with a soft, steady voice. "This is repayment for the service you performed for my little dog, and for the company with which you have cheered a decrepit, old lady's spirits." A velvet purse dangled from a loop of ribbon around her finger. "Take it and put it to good use."

It saddened him that she expected to pay for his time. Her first few visits to his rooms had been mildly inconvenient and suffered by him out of respect for her advanced years, but he'd begun to anticipate them with a certain degree of pleasure. He never met her anywhere except here, in his lodgings, and she always wore her thick lace veil. It was almost, he mused, like a confessional. And so he unburdened his soul to a comfortable stranger and felt markedly better after each visit, his thoughts slowly untangling.

With a stiff rustle of black taffeta, Lady Blunt hitched forward in the chair, one hand curled around the silver head of her walking cane, the other still outstretched with its offering. Her breathing was labored, as if the effort of reaching, and even the weight of the purse, was too much for her. "I am a childless widow. How am I to spend my fortune before the Grim Reaper takes me? At my time of life, one can enjoy few vices."

"But surely, madam—"

"All I have are my beloved dog—which you saved from certain death under the wheels of the mail coach—and my man, Edward." She gestured with an impatient flick of her cane toward the tall, spare fellow lurking in the shadowy corner. "Edward, come here at once and tell this prideful whipper-snapper to take my money before I am forced to lose my ladylike composure."

Sometimes, when she got that imperious tone in her voice, Rafe was reminded of another woman he once knew; but that thought passed quickly, no more than a dangerous spark that spat from the fire to be crushed and smothered beneath his boot.

In response to her command, the servant ambled forward with a slanting, bemused glance at his mistress. "You would not like the lady in a temper, sir," he muttered dourly. Rafe tried not to smile, never sure whether stern-faced Edward meant to be amusing or not.

"Think of it as an endowment," she added. "Or…a prize purse, if you will."

He looked down at his scarred knuckles. When the old lady came to his lodgings, he made an effort to hide his hands, but he knew she'd seen. She'd alluded to the boxing fights in which he participated for money, although how she'd found out about them he had no idea.

She sat before him in her black widow's weeds, a figure frail in appearance—deceptively so, as he now knew—her face almost completely obscured by that veil. He saw she wore spectacles, for when she moved her head, candlelight caught on the round glass lenses. Her face, or what he could see of it through the swirls of lace, was very white, in severe contrast to the black costume. Her slate-gray hair was piled atop her head in a style from the previous century, with a few be-ribboned tails straggling over one shoulder.

"And you should know, young sir, that I have purchased your fighting contract. You belong now to me."

Startled, he looked from her to Edward and back again. "Why would...what would a lady want with a boxer?"

Rafe fought for his landlord—a sly, greedy manipulator named Catchpole—to pay off a friend's rent debt. He couldn't imagine Catchpole ever giving up his contract to another. If it was true, Lady Blunt had paid a high price. Rafe eyed her warily. What *did* she want with him?

She must have seen his expression. Abruptly she laughed. "I don't want you to fight for me or perform any other...service. Since you belong to me now, you'll do as I say. Go home to the country and make peace with your father. Heal the rift. Facing your problems is the answer. Running away from them is not."

For a long moment he wrestled with his pride.

Home. For many years he'd considered himself a wayfarer, a boy never fully belonging anywhere. But there was one place he thought of as home—a little village where he'd lived for a while with his uncle and aunt. Sydney Dovedale, a pastoral haven in the Norfolk countryside, two days' travel from London. When he closed his eyes he saw the patchwork of plowed fields as he remembered them. He heard again the soft chorus of wood pigeons and could almost smell the fresh, sweet air—so different from that of London.

"I have my own earnings, madam. Enough to get me home."

"But you will take this purse for the journey," she croaked, "and pour me another glass of that wine, you ninny."

So he finally accepted the purse. "I swear I'll pay it back with interest."

"As you see fit," she said. "We can make some arrangement later, when you are settled."

But he had another problem of which Lady Blunt was unaware. Rafe had taken on the responsibility of caring for a small family—the wife and children of his debt-ridden friend, Pyke, who currently resided in the Fleet Prison. He couldn't leave Pyke's family alone and unprotected in London, but he told none of this to the old lady. Already he'd burdened her with his problems. Why burden her with those of the luckless Pyke too?

She now used the tip of her walking cane to straighten his hearth rug and artfully flip a stray coal back over the grate. Those spectacles must give her damn good aim, he mused.

"It's time you settled down, Hartley. Marry that poor girl you mentioned—Molly, is it not? You've kept her waiting long enough. A handsome, healthy specimen should not live alone. Your cockerel goes to waste, I'm sure, on tawdry women of lapsed virtue. Think of my money as a wedding gift. Go home, invest your earnings in a bank, and marry that girl, Molly. She'll put you to better use."

Cheerful at the thought of going home, he decided to tease her. "Unless you'd accept me instead, madam." He gave her a wink. "I know I'd do you the world of good."

She chuckled at his bawdy humor. Lifting her cane, she tapped it smartly on his knee. "Knave! If I were a hundred years younger, I might be tempted to take you in hand."

"I should like to have known you when you were young, Lady Blunt. I suspect you were quite something to know."

For a moment he thought he'd spoken amiss, overstepped a boundary. Her demeanor stiffened. Those small gloved fingers spread, flexed, and tightened around the head of her cane. "Alas…we were born too far apart." An unusually pensive pause followed, interrupted by another coal falling in the hob grate. Then she added sternly, "'Twas doubtless for the best, scoundrel."

Rafe bounced up to fetch the wine jug. It was only cheap wine, but she didn't seem to mind. She always said it was not the drink that mattered but the company with which one shared it.

Behind him he heard Edward intone somberly, "One must not get carried away. Remember, ma'am, you are expected elsewhere."

Thus, his guest reluctantly dismissed the idea of more wine. As she rose from her chair, Rafe attempted to help her but was quickly shouldered aside by her manservant, who shielded the old lady's body from Rafe as if one touch of his might make her shatter.

"I must take my leave of you, young man. I have an appointment with my mantuamaker."

Rafe bowed. "Good evening, your ladyship. And thank you."

She replied as she did at the end of every visit, "Behave yourself."

He rushed around them to open the door and watched as Edward carefully steered his slow-moving mistress out into the shabby hall. Usually there would be nothing more said, but today she hobbled around to face him again—moving so suddenly and unexpectedly that she swiped poor Edward on the leg with her cane. In a grand gesture, she held out her gloved hand.

It took a moment for Rafe to understand what she expected. Then he grasped her fragile fingers, bowed over them, and planted a quick peck to the soft leather.

She was an eccentric old dear—a fact proven not only by her desire to give money to a stranger and her penchant for ribald conversation, but by the hint of a frivolous, blood-red petticoat visible under the hem of her black gown.

"That went exceedingly well, did it not?" She stepped up into the hired fly, and Edward followed, dropping heavily onto the seat beside her.

"Yes, my lady. Although I think the hand-kiss went a little beyond." He rubbed his shin where she'd hit him with her cane.

"Really? It felt right in that moment. There was a spark… I fear I could not help myself, which is most unusual for me." Tugging her veil aside with impatient fingers, she reached up to scratch under her powdered wig and knocked it slightly askew. "I believe there are fleas in his lodgings, Edward."

"I should not be surprised." He passed her a large

linen handkerchief and gingerly retrieved the cane from her lap. "I'll just relieve you of this, my lady, before any further damage—"

"The sooner he puts his stubborn pride aside and goes home to his father, the better." With a few wipes of the cloth, she removed the thick white paste from her cheeks. "He needs a good kick in the breeches."

"Like most young men these days."

She sighed, shaking her head. "I knew Rafe was not cut out for the law. He only ever wanted to work the land, but I suppose he put that aside and tried for his father's approval." Now the fool boy, having quit his studies and his post as a clerk in a barrister's office, stayed in London rather than face another bitter quarrel with his father. He'd turned to boxing, but under no circumstances could she let him continue fighting with his fists for a living. What if he scarred that fine face? Nor would she sit by and let him fall in with more unsavory company, develop worse habits, and form a taste for cheap wine. London was a treacherous pit for a generous-hearted but aimless young man with good looks and too much earthy charm for his own good. It was time he settled down.

But as they trotted along the darkened streets, her mood lifted, and she began to hum softly. At least she'd seen Rafe again, he was in good health and spirits, she had persuaded him to go home, and he still had not the slightest suspicion about her identity.

"I should like to have met you when you were young. I suspect you were quite something."

Little did he know he shared his wine and his hearth with a ghost from his past.

"Oh, and, my lady," said Edward, "I think scarlet ruffles might not have been the most appropriate of choices."

She glanced down at the hem of her petticoat, now clearly visible under the black taffeta as she swung her feet. "Well, of course I had to wear *some* color," she exclaimed. "For pity's sake, Edward Hobbs, you are my solicitor. Reserve your advice for matters of the law, not fashion."

He gave her one of his bleakly despairing looks, as if a crimson petticoat might indeed be a crime of some sort, and then adjusted the collar of his coat against the brisk chill that whipped through the open window.

"One can hardly expect you to understand, because you're a man. Naturally, you have no sense of style."

"I'm sure you are right, my lady, as always."

Smiling to herself, humming her jolly tune, she looked out on her side of the street and considered Mr. Rafael Hartley with more warmth than he deserved. Almost from the very first time they met, she knew it would be her duty to save that man. Not that he was ever grateful. *The Brat* he used to call her when he was considerably smaller than he was now.

Nevertheless, she'd vowed to straighten out his life, even if it killed her. Which it probably would.

And never knowing what she'd done for him, he would probably dance upon her grave.

Well, in her case, it would be the family vault, of course, but dancing upon a family vault would require the foresight to bring a ladder for climbing up, and Rafe never planned ahead. It would also demand a high level of balance and coordination—neither of which Rafe Hartley possessed when dancing. Curiously, he had both when swinging his fists in a boxing match, so she'd heard. But she knew, firsthand, that his dancing left much to be desired.

Far safer to think of him dancing on a grave.

"Which reminds me," she announced, "I ought to write out specific instructions for my burial. I have just the outfit in mind, and if I left such things to you and my brother, who knows what atrocity my corpse would be dressed in."

The solicitor turned his head to inspect her in some bemusement. "Fortunately, we have time enough to worry."

"Always plan ahead, Edward. Be prepared for any eventuality."

"In addition to the fact that you are two and twenty, your health is of the rude variety."

"But this fly could overturn and kill us both." She shook her head. "Our lives snuffed out as speedily as a candle flame."

"A cheering thought, my lady."

"And who will manage things when *I* am gone?"

He had no response to that, and she had not meant for there to be any. It was purely a rhetorical question. No one managed things so well as Lady Mercy Danforthe. Everyone knew it and, should they ever forget, she was quick to remind them.

"It looks like snow," she observed grimly. "I do hope, if the fly is overturned, we are killed outright. Otherwise we could be buried alive under a snow-drift and die slowly, in dreadful agony, frozen to our very bones."

"Might I observe, my lady, as I have before, that you possess a tendency to find one small thought and let it expand with many others until it no longer resembles any form of reality? Fact is too often replaced with fiction."

"And your point, Edward?"

"I rather fear that is just what you have done again," he observed tranquilly. "In fact, there are seldom snowdrifts in London, my lady."

"Even worse! The horse and driver will be unaccustomed to the circumstance should we encounter one."

Edward burrowed deeper into his collar, like a turtle. "If your brother ever finds out about this mission of yours and that you have acquired possession of a six-foot prizefighter, we shan't have to worry about a slow, painful death," he muttered. "I believe it will come swiftly for both of us."

"Six foot four and fourteen stone."

She did not have to see Edward's eyebrows to know they arched upward, like two caterpillars taking shelter under the brim of his hat. "I stand corrected, my lady. Again."

"Still," she added jauntily, returning to her previous thought, "at least if I am to die in the snow tonight, I shall be discovered in my splendid new petticoat." With that pleasing point to mitigate the tragedy of her inevitable demise, she settled back to enjoy the ride.

Chapter 2

"THE SPRING HAS GONE OUT OF YOUR BLASTED STOCK-ings, Miss Gibson. Do pull your garters up."

While this reprimand might appear somewhat harsh and a trifle indelicate for a drawing room conversation between two young ladies, it was, in Lady Mercy Danforthe's opinion, also necessarily shocking. Brevity, she always said, was a busy woman's best friend, and terms of a more ladylike nature had scant chance of sinking in when dealing with the cork-brained. Miss Julia Gibson might sew a fine seam, trot amiably in a quadrille, and fumble her way through a repertoire of songs on her mama's pianoforte, but she was not, by any means, the brightest of sentient beings.

Lady Mercy would never be observed with wrin-kled stockings, literally or metaphorically speaking. And the nervous, teary-eyed Miss Gibson must surely have realized, after a hasty perusal of her own ankles, that in this case she meant the latter. But imagery failed to relay Mercy's point. The object of her criticism assumed the expression of a spaniel pup, eager to please yet bewildered. Possibly thinking of its dinner and undoubtedly about to leave a puddle on the rug.

So much for the advantage of brevity.

With a sigh of grand proportions—the only sort of sigh one might expend while wearing a very smart bonnet lavishly caressed by a magnificent, downward-curling magenta feather—Mercy reinforced her meaning. "While I can find you a suitor, it will not assist my endeavors if all you do, whenever you see an eligible man, is burst into tears and run away."

Pausing to sip her tea, she stole a sly glance at the mantel clock and calculated a quick sum in her head. She must cut this meeting short, or she'd never make her friend's wedding on time, and that would be inexcusable. It took two days of travel along bad country lanes to reach the village of Sydney Dovedale, and she was already later setting off than she'd hoped to be. Few things annoyed Mercy more than a lack of punctuality. She could not abide it in others and was especially vexed by the possibility of her own lateness.

This was her last visit of the morning, and her feet itched to be on their way. She had already spent a grueling hour relating instructions for Edward Hobbs to keep an eye on things while she was gone. Despite her brother's decade advance on her in age, Mercy had no confidence in Carver's ability to make wise decisions, especially in her absence. Carver would be the last person she dealt with today. She'd organized her list with him at the end, because it was unlikely she'd find him out of bed before noon light streaked across his bedchamber, stung his eyelids, and woke him. Then it always took a period of half an hour at least before he was fit to be seen and could manage more than a few grunts.

Mercy checked the mantel clock again, astonished by how quickly the hands of time moved today. If Julia Gibson were not such a hapless creature in need of guidance, she would have made her excuses not to pay this visit. It was, however, a duty she took upon herself to never let anyone down. This, as she would explain patiently to Carver, was their life role—to be there for those in need, to look out for those less well placed, to lead those who stumbled. He might firmly refuse to fulfill his role, but Mercy took her part very seriously.

Miss Gibson perched on the edge of her narrow chair, possibly about to dive into the willow-pattern bowl of potpourri that sat between them. "But I can't seem to help myself, Lady Mercy. I know I must marry. What else am I to do?" She lowered her voice to a faded squeak. "Alas, I think of the horrors one must endure on the wedding night." The young woman blushed brightly, competing with the scarlet tulips nodding outside her mama's drawing-room window. "And I simply cannot look him in the eye."

"Horrors?"

"In the marriage bed," she whispered. "With…a man. And…that…thing."

Although Mercy knew very well what the other woman meant, impish fingers of mischief suddenly tickled her amusement. She feigned bafflement. "Thing?"

"A man's…private…*accoutrement*. His Arrow of Cupid." Still she waited, brows arched high, forcing her laughter down, where it bubbled away deep under her corset.

"His…" Miss Gibson tried again, squeezing out the word "appendage."

Afraid she might convulse with laughter—which would not be at all seemly—Mercy set her cup and saucer on the table and began wriggling her fingers into a pair of kidskin gloves. "The awfulness to be endured at the hands of one's husband and his trouser tentacle, my dear Miss Gibson, is nothing compared to the true agonies of this world. There are always people far worse off than oneself."

The girl looked confused again, screwing her hand-kerchief into a damp knot. It was possible, thought Mercy, that Miss Gibson knew nothing of affairs beyond her own limited existence. Some women never bothered to read a newspaper or acquaint them-selves with the larger issues. Mercy, on the other hand, poured over various lurid accounts of the world's many injustices, especially those against women. Unbeknownst to her brother, he contributed largely to charities meant to improve their lot. It was a good thing for Mercy—and for Mr. Hobbs—that Carver seldom paid attention to the accounts.

"Think of the poor, unfortunate women plying their trade in the gin shops and dark alleys," she explained. "There are almost as many prostitutes in London, Miss Gibson, as there are domestic servants. Imagine how those women suffer daily trials, strug-gling to find food, medicines, and shoes for their children. I am sure they must put themselves through great degradation to survive."

Miss Gibson opened her mouth, but this time Mercy did not wait for any sound to come out. She continued rapidly, "You need tolerate your husband's intimate company only once a month for precisely three and one-half minutes. It is hardly *The Harlot's Progress*." There, that should put things into perspective for the trembling creature. In truth, Mercy was no longer very interested at that moment in poor Julia Gibson's love life—or lack thereof. However, she considered it her mission to meddle in the lives of those she liked and to secure happy matches for her young friends most in need. People told her she was rather good at it, although, as her brother had recently pointed out, they would never dare say otherwise.

Miss Julia Gibson was, so far, her one failed project, and Mercy did not like this blot on her perfect record for matchmaking. Well, almost perfect, she thought with a frown, remembering that Carver still resisted any attempts to find him a wife. He was now thirty-three, in danger of becoming set in his ways and, as the Earl of Everscham, did not believe he should ever have to change those ways. This blinkered regard for the path ahead was a peculiarly stubborn trait he shared with his sister. Aware of this fact, she simply excused the characteristic in herself as a necessary and "clear-headed" devotion to what was proper. Mercy was the sensible one; she knew what she was doing, but the same could not be said for Carver. His obstinate frame of mind was a wretched annoyance, because it kept him from agreeing with her most of the time.

She took another, more searching perusal of Julia Gibson's wincing features. Hmm...perhaps...if she could get her two most difficult projects together, would that not make a very tidy conclusion? She dearly loved a neat solution, everything squared away, corners perfectly aligned. There was nothing so comforting as an answer found, a mission completed.

Just then, Julia struggled with a meringue and sneezed violently, sending a spray of sugar down her frock. A dollop of cream remained on her chin, but she didn't appear to notice.

Mercy drew an imaginary line through her idea. Perhaps not. Carver would chew the girl up and spit her out. He was far too critical; that was his problem.

"I'm afraid I must be off, Miss Gibson. I am expected at a friend's wedding in the country, and I still have my brother to organize before I leave, but when I return, I shall attend to this matter. Worry not."

"Oh, thank you, Lady Mercy. You are too kind."

Yes, she mused, she probably was—devoting so much of her time to girls who hadn't the gumption to find their own husbands. She really couldn't understand what they feared. Mercy had just become engaged to Viscount Grey, a gentleman she'd picked out for herself and pursued with single-minded intent until he proposed. He was away now enjoying the sights of Italy, taking benefit from the dry, warm climate that improved his health, but in a month he was due to return, and then they would make the wedding arrangements. Everything proceeded on Mercy's say-so, and just as it should be. Viscount Grey, having reached his fortieth year and survived the most trying age, would fit very well into the small space she'd allotted for a husband. He would not get in her way too much. He had coloring that coordinated very well with her favorite garments and furnishings, he was a perfectly proper three inches taller than she, and his love of outdoor sport, when health permitted, would keep him out of her hair for a good portion of the year. His wavering bouts of infirmity also gave her something to fuss over. A man in too fine a working order was often more independent than was good for him or his marriage, but Viscount Grey was just needy enough to give Mercy a purpose. And she did love a purpose.

As Julia Gibson said, a young lady must marry; there was simply nothing else to do. Far better to pick out the man for oneself, make certain he did not have any unsightly edges—if he did, file them down—and then quickly stake one's claim. All very simple.

Women like Julia Gibson fretted and whimpered as if they were being asked to scale the dome of St. Paul's. In their drawers.

Mercy stood briskly, making the last adjustments to her gloves. "I bid you good day, Miss Gibson."

The other young lady scrambled out of her chair for a clumsy curtsy, tripping over her own feet. "Lady Mercy."

It was a good thing the Gibsons had wealth—even if it was acquired merely through trade. Poor Julia hadn't much else in her favor. Fortunately for Miss Gibson, her aristocratic friend never balked at a challenge.

✒∽

Mercy swept into her brother's library without knocking. "Well, I'm off. Although it hardly need be asked—I suppose you will not come with me?"

Dealing with the daily correspondence, Carver did not look up from the letters on his desk. "Why on earth would I attend the wedding of your maid?"

"She is far more than my maid, Carver. Molly Robbins is my friend and has been my companion for twelve years. As you well know."

He gave a small snort. "You may think she is your friend, but she is your employee first and foremost. You pay her a wage. Thus, she's obliged to be nice to you."

"Carver, you have a very bitter, distrusting view of people."

"And you have an overly romantic one." He smirked at his papers. "Perhaps the less said about that the better."

Mercy strode to his desk, hands tucked securely within her muff. "Molly will be disappointed."

"Your maid can make her own silly mistakes without me bearing witness." His brow creased in a stern frown. "Marriage is a fool's venture at the best of times. Besides, does she not have ambitions to begin her own dressmaking enterprise?"

Mercy was surprised he knew that. It might have been mentioned in his hearing, she supposed, but he seldom listened to anything she had to talk about and generally acted as if Molly Robbins was invisible. Which was, as he would say, exactly how the master of the house should treat his little sister's lady's maid.

She took a hand from her muff and leaned over his desk, intent on straightening a pile of papers that were most distressingly bundled in a loose pile, so close to the edge that should the window be left open and a strong breeze blow in, they could easily drift to the carpet or be wafted into the fire.

"Her country-farmer husband," Carver went on, frowning as she fussed over his desk, "won't appreciate his wife going off to start a business. He will expect her to keep house and raise his children." Sniffing angrily, he returned his gaze to the letter he wrote, pressing so hard Mercy was surprised he didn't break his pen. "She'll be pregnant by the summer."

Seizing a large paperweight from his desk, she thumped it down hard onto the tidied pile of papers. "Don't be coarse!"

"It is a fact of life, little Sister. I believe I gave you that lecture about the birds and the bees, did I not?"

"No, *you* did not! You left it to Edward Hobbs. Unless, of course, you refer to the time I walked in on you in the stables with that flotsam, Mary Nesmith—the one with the dyed hair." She cocked an eyebrow. "That was quite a revealing lesson, to be sure." Mercy, sixteen at the time of that event, had endured an early education in certain improper matters, thanks to her brother's behavior and her own eavesdropping, but the most memorable lesson occurred when she wandered into that stable and witnessed her brother with his paramour-of-the-moment. Their harried solicitor's hasty explanation of "conjugal relations" could not possibly have prepared her for the sight of the widowed Mrs. Nesmith bent over a hay bale, her moonlike posterior exposed to the air and Carver in the process of mounting her from behind while curiously humming "The Soldier's Adieu."

He set down his pen and laughed curtly. "Ah, yes. Poor old Hobbs." He ignored his sister's remark about his old flame. It was likely he'd forgotten all about Mrs. Nesmith in any case. Many women had come and gone since then, all of them totally unsuitable and, knowing Carver, deliberately so.

As she turned away from his desk, he demanded abruptly, "What on earth are you wearing on your head?"

She swung around to face him again. "'Tis called a hat, Brother dear."

"Good Lord." He sat back in his chair, grinning. "I thought it was a drunken parrot."

"I wouldn't expect you to understand style and fashion."

"Well, I suppose it is a fittingly theatrical costume for the event."

Although she knew it would be best not to ask— far less trying on her nerves—she heard herself asking what he meant by that remark.

"This entire wedding is a farcical performance," he replied, waving his letter opener through the air. "A comedy, or a tragedy. Perhaps both. Robbins feels she must marry to please everyone else—her family and his. Even with your romantic inclinations, you must see the truth. Trapped into this marriage, she will very soon know discontent."

"I am amazed, Brother, that you can form these opinions of a situation about which you know nothing."

"Have I not witnessed that girl moping about my house for the past few months? Her lips droop every time the wedding is mentioned. Several times of late I've passed her in the hall, and her expression inspired me to inquire whether her cat had just died."

"For pity's sake, you will never understand women. A curious fact, considering your association with so many."

Carver stretched in his chair, arms behind his head. "Mark my words, little Sister, this wedding is nothing to celebrate. You've lost not only a maid, but a friend. If that's what you truly think of her."

She bristled. "What can you mean?"

"Her life travels in a new direction now. Her first responsibility will be to her husband and then her children. She will have less and less time to spare for you."

Mercy felt a swift chill that caused little bumps on her arms under her sleeves. But she said nothing, finding it necessary to straighten the window drapes instead.

"What will you do with yourself when Robbins is no more at your beck and call?"

She let his words fade out while she examined the window frame. It could certainly benefit from a sanding and fresh paint, she thought.

"You will have to discover more new projects to keep busy, Sister. I can't see your fiancé giving you much to do. He is too easily molded already."

Oh, was he *still* talking?

Mercy focused hard on the window. When she returned from the country, she would bring the chipped paint to the butler's attention. She would not let this happen in her house. Nothing should be allowed to get frayed or rotted or dusty. Or out of place. That was how accidents happened.

"But I wouldn't be at all shocked," he added, "if Robbins doesn't call this wedding off at the last minute. If she has any wits about her, she will."

Mercy spun around from the window, unable to

keep looking at the chipped paint a moment longer. "Don't talk nonsense!"

"I feel it in my bones that this masquerade won't go off without a hitch. Tell you what…how about a wager?" Carver laughed sharply, but his gaze darkened to the black of a cold, moonless midnight. "If Robbins marries him, she's making a tremendous mistake, which she will regret for the rest of her life. He is the wrong choice for her."

Mercy rolled her eyes. "Oh? And who would you choose for her? I suggest you leave the matchmaking to me, Carver. I can only imagine the disastrous outcome of any meddling in which you might find the time to indulge."

"Go then, little Sister. Won't you be late if you dally here a moment longer? Travel is so unpredictable this time of year, and they might feel obliged to delay the proceedings until the guest of honor arrives." He took out his fob watch. "Gracious! Is that the time already?"

Her pulse quickened erratically at the idea of falling behind the clock with many miles yet to travel. As he said, the country roads were unreliable at best.

"Remember, Sister, should you be apprehended by a highwayman, your wisest defense is to talk his ears off in your usual manner. Advise him on his love affairs and his diet, water down his wine, and then tell him how to dress. The tediousness of your company will surely cause him to leave you behind and take the horses instead."

Head high, feather bouncing, Mercy prepared a grand exit.

But her brother's voice stopped her midstep, yet again. "Robbins knows nothing, I assume, of what happened five and a half years ago?"

Heat rushed to her face. "Of course not. Only you and I know. And Edward Hobbs."

"And *him*."

Inside her muff, Mercy's hands tightened until her fingers hurt. A knot in her stomach began turning and twisting, much like the wretched handkerchief in Miss Gibson's sweaty hands earlier that day. "That was all a very long time ago, and Rafe Hartley was not Molly's sweetheart then."

He shrugged. "Don't you think Robbins ought to know her fiancé was married once before? To her *friend*?"

"For three hours!" Hearing her voice rise to an unladylike tenor, she fought to control it and regain her composure.

"Lucky for you, I found you both before it was consummated, or I'd have been obliged to make the rotten little bastard keep you, despite your ages."

Mercy was unwilling to be reminded, yet again, of that singular blot on her past. She stormed out, slamming his door in her wake, leaving him laughing. Carver always managed to upset the neat order of her apple cart.

The footman held the front door for her, and she marched out, down the steps to the waiting carriage, squinting against a blinding shard of sunlight. She paused for a few deep breaths of spring air until the seeds of anxiety were safely dispersed, her spirits bolstered, lifted back where they belonged. That beautiful, luxurious feather sweeping over her shoulder, visible in all its magenta glory from the corner of her eye, helped enormously.

She looked up at the sky. A recent cold and rainy spell gave way that very morning to a bright shimmer of sunlight across a cobalt background, barely troubled by a few plump clouds skipping jovially by. It seemed the weather would obey her wishes and turn at exactly the right moment for a picturesque country wedding. There would be wine and cake, orange blossoms and rice. All as it should be.

Whatever Carver said, everything would go wonderfully. With Lady Mercy Danforthe in attendance, it would not dare be anything else but a perfectly proper and divinely romantic wedding. Mercy had everything under control. Even the weather.

Chapter 3

RAFE BENT LOW TO FIND HIS PARTIAL REFLECTION IN the small, mottled, jagged scrap of mirror that rested on a shelf of the old dresser. Not bad, he thought, slicking his hair above both ears. He'd seen worse. Good thing he didn't let his friends talk him into stopping at Merryweather's Tavern too long last night. Molly would never forgive him for tipping up at the church with bloodshot eyes.

In a few more hours he'd be a married man, and he—

Uneasy suddenly, he lost his line of thought. Were his sleeves too tight? Had he put on the wrong shirt? Something felt uncomfortable. With fumbling fingers, he lifted the shirt he'd discarded a few moments ago and checked for a small tear in the sleeve, making sure he was wearing the new one. He was. Perhaps the new shirt felt odd because it *wasn't* torn, he mused.

Had he put it on wrongly? Back to front?

No. It wasn't the shirt that was inside out.

With a quick shake of his shoulders, Rafe straightened up. No point feeling his nerves rattle now, was there? Every man must wed sooner or later, and Molly was a good girl—steady, reliable, a calming influence on his life. He'd been told that many times. She'd be a wonderful mother for his children and a hardworking partner at his side. His family liked her, and he didn't want to let anybody down. It was hard to please all the important people in his life when they pulled him in different directions, but at least this marriage was the one thing they all agreed upon, the one thing that made everyone content. For once.

At least, unlike his old school friend Pyke, he had not found himself married with three children before he was five and twenty—drowning in debt.

Rafe trailed fingers over his newly shaven chin, and those wings in his belly began to beat even faster. The taking of a wife, his uncle lectured him last night, was a considerable task to assume. Soon there would be children.

Responsibilities of that nature had very nearly been the end of poor Pyke. Rafe had taken Lady Blunt's purse to pay some of his friend's debt, only to find Pyke had escaped the Fleet Prison and run off, leaving his wife and children behind in Rafe's care. There was nothing he could do but bring them with him into the country.

For now, Mrs. Pyke and her children were housed at the Red Lion Inn in Morecroft—about an hour's ride away—until he could find a more permanent place for them. Molly knew nothing about it. Yet. She would not be pleased at the burdens he shouldered for another man. Having met Pyke once, she'd declared him "sly and silly." Molly had no time for people who couldn't look after themselves.

"You're too easily taken in, Rafe," she'd said to him once. "Your generosity is abused by others. When will you put your needs first?"

"I will," he'd replied, "when I know what they are."

"Well, if you don't know by now, Rafe Hartley, you never will. You're too soft."

Molly could be quite sharp at times.

But after a few cross words, she would let the matter rest. She didn't try to boss him around. She didn't quarrel with him at every turn. Molly was smart as a whip and steady as a rock. And penny-wise. Most importantly, reliable Molly Robbins would never abandon him.

He broke off his thoughts again, trying to see his full reflection in the window. Why the devil was this shirt pulling on his shoulders? He couldn't possibly have grown since he was last measured. But it definitely felt as if he wore another man's clothes today. Glancing at his old shirt, he thought, somewhat wistfully, that he'd wear that one if he could get away with it. If it wasn't stained in the front, where it showed. He'd never hear the last of it from his father.

Rafe required something to steady his nerves, temporarily abandoned the process of dressing, and stepped into the cool larder for a tankard of beer. As long as he didn't arrive at the altar stinking of ale, nobody could begrudge him a little jug today. He took a long gulp of beer, and some spilled from the corners of his mouth as he tipped his head back a little too far and too hard. Better. Now emboldened, he approached his new waistcoat—a fancy, printed silk of the sort he would never have worn if he wasn't talked into it by a very persuasive tailor. He slipped it over his shirt and tackled the buttons with hasty, fumbling fingers. Again he checked the shadowy reflection in his crooked mirror. Not bad. Slight resemblance to a trussed-up Christmas goose, perhaps. If anyone laughed, he'd just laugh harder. Molly wouldn't, of course. She'd already warned him that he'd better keep a straight face in church.

He cast a wary eye around his small farmhouse and wondered, as he often did lately, whether Molly had grown too fine for him now. Would life as a farmer's wife be dull and tedious after her time as a lady's maid, living in that grand house with Mercy Danforthe in London?

Damn and blast! Don't think of The Brat today.

Lips pursed in a whistle that was more volume than tune, he slipped the last waistcoat button through its hole and tucked certain thoughts away likewise.

"Rafe?" His father was at the open front door, tapping with his knuckles.

Caught up in restless thoughts, Rafe hadn't heard the carriage and horses. "Come in," he shouted as he still fussed with the linen neckcloth which felt as if it might strangle him.

James Hartley, impeccably dressed as always, stood in a wedge of sunlight, one foot on the doorstep. Two more different men could scarcely be found, and Rafe occasionally wondered whether James really was his blood father or if there'd been a mistake. After all, they had only Rafe's mother's word for it, and she, a housemaid with whom James had a brief affair, died within a few hours of his birth. According to the tale

Rafe was told, he came under his uncle's guardianship immediately after his mother's death because his father was unaware of his existence until years later. Now his father tried to make it up to him.

He'd been trying to make it up to Rafe for twelve years. Sometimes Rafe wished he wouldn't try quite so hard. It chafed to be reined in suddenly when he'd been free to run wild most of his youth.

"Well, Son, are we ready?"

"As ready as I'll ever be to don the shackles," he replied jovially.

His father did not crack a smile but looked Rafe up and down with a stern, critical perusal.

"Do I pass inspection, then?" He should, he mused—he'd spent an hour just polishing his boots that morning because he couldn't sleep.

"I'm glad you had a new suit of clothes made. Should have gone to my tailor in Norwich, however."

"Aye, well, Jammy Jim was cheaper."

"Evidently." His father exhaled the word gravely. "And I suppose there is no point reminding you of my offer to pay."

"When a man fills out his breeches, he ought to be able to pay for them himself, sir." He laughed, trying to lighten the mood.

"Yes, well...when you're ready, the carriage is outside."

"I told you I can walk to church, Father. There was no need to bring the chaise."

But James Hartley insisted. "No son of mine will saunter to church on his wedding day."

"Does it make a difference if I go on wheels, hooves, or feet?"

His father was looking around the farmhouse, inspecting it. Finally his cool gaze returned to Rafe. "Yes, it does."

Apparently his wedding day was no time for a sense of humor. His father looked as tense as Rafe felt inside. "Like what I've done with the place, sir?"

"You've made it very comfortable. I'm sure Molly will be happy here." It was, Rafe suspected, what his stepmother told James to say. She very much wanted the two men to put past quarrels aside and find peace, but with differing opinions on what Rafe should do with his life, they had some distance to bridge. "I am, naturally, disappointed with your decision to abandon the law and any hope of working for the family business in order to take up farming instead…" He cleared his throat. "But this is perhaps not the day to discuss the matter."

"Perhaps not." Rafe gave up trying to make his father smile, and shrugged into his new blue superfine tailcoat.

"I hear Lady Mercy Danforthe plans to attend the wedding," said James suddenly.

Well, there went his chance of getting through the day without using a curse word. Of course that interfering, bossy-mouthed girl had to come, didn't she? "Aye. Every silver lining has a cloud."

His father clearly saw her attendance today as a social coup—if such a thing might be had at a small, unfashionable country wedding. "Molly is fortunate to include Lady Mercy as a friend. I hope you won't be rude to her today."

"As long as she says naught to me, I'll have no cause to say aught to her, shall I?"

His father sighed. "For Molly's sake, hold your temper. Don't spoil the day."

"Like I said, Father, if The Danforthe Brat keeps her opinions to herself for once, I'm sure we can tolerate each other for a few hours."

"Yes, well… See that you make an effort. And stop cracking your knuckles." His father did not come any farther inside but hovered uncertainly in the door frame.

"Are we late, sir?" Foolish question. It always felt to Rafe as if he was never on time for anything. No matter how hard he tried, too many obstacles and distractions got in his way.

"We shall be, if we dally," his father confirmed. "Don't want to keep the young lady waiting."

"I'll just take a last look around and make sure everything is as it should be. For when Merc…Molly comes." His nervous stomach had started again, and his fingers felt fuzzy. He needed a few moments alone to compose himself without his father's stern gaze watching and reading his face. For some terrible reason, he couldn't stop his thoughts from wandering down the very worst of paths—one that led him through knotted and scratchy brambles. Somewhere down that mysterious lane in his mind, over the treacherous ruts and wayward tree roots, there lived a chattering, obnoxiously proud pixie with curly copper hair.

As soon as James stepped outside, Rafe grabbed his tankard and drained it.

It didn't help much. He burped.

One last look around. Damn. He should have

picked some flowers and put them in a vase for the mantel. He'd meant to do it and forgot, but he was never one for fancifications, and Molly knew it. She would probably have looked at him with her big doe eyes and said, "Flowers? For whose approval did you do all this, Rafe Hartley? Not for mine, to be sure."

As if there could be anyone else on his mind.

So this was it.

Resuming a tuneless whistle, he grabbed his new hat from the table and followed his father out into the sun.

❧

As Mercy exited the carriage, her foot had barely touched the ground when she was descended upon by two anxious women: the groom's stepmother and his aunt.

"Thank goodness you are here," they chorused almost in unison.

Gratifying as it was to be greeted so eagerly—for it was not always the case in Lady Mercy's life—she sensed at once that theirs was not an exclamation of delight but rather one of relief.

"What is it?" A dark foreboding quickly settled over her as she recalled her brother's teasing words. "What has happened?" She barely had time to straighten her bonnet—a much more modest affair today, gilded straw scattered with dainty primroses—before the two women shuffled her speedily through the lych-gate and down the church path. "Am I so late?" she muttered.

They assured her she was not late and, once at the door of the vestry, they halted, both gathering their breaths with grateful sighs and finally allowing her boot heels to touch the ground.

"Don't you look lovely!" Rafe's stepmother exclaimed with a false sort of jollity. "What a fresh shade of yellow—so springlike. And your hair has lightened to such a pretty gold. I remember when it was almost copper, a fiery lion's mane. But now it is much softer."

Mercy frowned, skeptical of this excessive and unlikely flattery. "Is something amiss, madam?" She'd endured two days of uncomfortable travel, worrying the entire time that she might be captured by a bloodthirsty highwayman or—even worse—that she could be late. The last thing she wanted now was to be waylaid by these two ladies, infamous for their love of a good prank.

"Amiss?" Rafe's stepmother had wide violet eyes that seemed in a perpetual state of amusement, even in moments of dire emergency. "Goodness no. Just a little…a slight delay in the proceedings."

"A delay?"

The two older women looked at each other, and then Rafe's stepmother confessed in a breathless whisper, "Molly has changed her mind."

"She will talk to none other but you," his aunt added, clearly annoyed with the bride-to-be.

Mercy's heart fluttered up into her tight throat. "Changed her mind? After all these years?"

They shrugged haplessly, gesturing at her to go in. She took a breath as deep as she could muster after that shocking news, then opened the vestry door and entered.

In one step, she left the bright spring sun behind. Her skin pimpled, swept by the coarse brush of a grave-like chill, the cold, damp mustiness of ancient stone closing her in. One shaft of light filtered in through a narrow, arched window, and there Molly stood, wringing her hands, gazing out wistfully. She might have been posing for a portrait in watercolors.

It struck Mercy suddenly how so much had changed in the twelve years since she first met Molly here in Sydney Dovedale. Not that the village had changed hardly at all, but they had. Together they'd grown from girls to women. Mercy liked to think she was much more sensible now, although she still had a tendency to assume the world would turn the way she wanted it to. And why shouldn't it? Did it have anything better to do?

At the sound of the heavy door creaking open and closing again with a solid thunk, Molly turned and ran into her friend's arms. "Oh, what have I done? What have I done?"

"I can't imagine," Mercy replied drily. "What *have* you done?" She couldn't, for a moment, believe her old friend was prepared to turn her back on Rafe Hartley. Mercy was not about to let it happen after all she'd gone through to bring this wedding forward. It must simply be a case of last-minute nerves.

Weddings, of course, were emotional events. Not that hers would be. Mercy knew how dreadful she looked with a red nose and eyes, so she always did her weeping in private, under the bedcovers. If only other ladies were so prudent, she thought as she surveyed the tattered, mournful exhibit of womanhood wilting before her. Apparently here was another girl whose stockings had lost their staying power at the prospect of a wedding night. "Do pull your garters up, Molly." She withdrew a silk handkerchief from her muff. "Now, blow."

Obediently, Molly blew into the handkerchief but could not stem the tide of tears falling in lush droplets down her pale cheeks. "He will never forgive me, I know."

"Forgive you for what?"

"For not marrying him. But I can't. I just... can't..." Molly descended into more sobs, louder ones this time that shook every inch of her slender form and disturbed the neat arrangement of her chestnut hair. Petals of orange blossoms fell like snowdrops to the stone floor of the vestry.

Mercy steered her friend back to the light of the window and tried straightening the bridal headdress. "Molly, do cease these dramatics, which are so unlike you. How many times have I heard you say how much you look forward to being married?"

"I have not said that for a long time. I suppose you have not noticed. I hardly realized it myself, until this morning as I was being dressed." Molly looked down at her wedding gown—one of her own creations—and shook her head. "Quite suddenly I realized I hadn't felt that way for months, perhaps even years. It just became something I was accustomed to saying out loud. Without thinking."

"This is merely a case of matrimonial nerves, Molly Robbins. Now, where does the parson keep his wine?" Mercy began searching the cupboards and shelves. "Gracious! What happened to cleanliness is next to godliness?" she muttered, swiping at the dusty shelves with a folded altar cloth and setting a stack of tumbled prayer books back upright.

Behind her, Molly blew her nose again, the disturbed dust quickly worsening her red-eyed state. "When someone claims they love a person, the other has no choice but to return the sentiment, do they? Otherwise it seems so dreadfully rude and unappreciative of the compliment."

After a brief, bemused glance over her shoulder, Mercy continued her search for wine. Always in control of her own wits, and never having her opinion swayed by another, she couldn't quite comprehend the notion of agreeing for the sake of courtesy. Honesty might be brutal in some cases, but it was often kinder in the long run. As they now had evidence.

"I do care for him, but I don't... I'm not *in love* with him."

"Aha!" Mercy found a crystal decanter. She lifted the stopper and sniffed. "Not bad." A further search for drinking vessels turned up empty-handed. "Here," she said, passing the decanter to her friend. "You'll have to swig it."

Molly wrinkled her nose and shook her head at the offered decanter. She folded her arms. "I don't want to be a wife. Not yet, in any case. I want to start my dressmaking business. I have some capital now to start, and I...I have a lease on a small room in a building near—"

"Molly Robbins!" Mercy was astonished that so much could have been done without her knowledge, and especially without her advice. "I always told you I would lend you the money, if you wanted it, but I thought *this* was what you wanted."

"I thought so too. I thought marriage and children were what I *should* want. But this other need has crept up on me. It is so strong now that I cannot deny it. Not any longer."

There was something about the gentle way the other girl spoke, even through half-contained sobs, that suggested her mind was made up. As if she knew that when she turned at this crossroads, the path she'd walked before was lost for good. She did not want to search for it. She had her eye on a new horizon now, her mind set on it.

"I intend to be a businesswoman, Lady Mercy. I have the talent to design dresses, and I am a skilled seamstress—"

"Where did you get the capital?" she demanded.

The other girl looked away, evasive suddenly. "I saved all the money I've ever earned. You've been very generous to me."

"Did my brother give it to you?" Her anger mounted quickly as she thought of Carver's laughter when she last saw him in London—his scornful comments about this wedding and his teasing suggestion of a wager.

"No."

"Don't lie to me, Molly Robbins. He gave you money to start your business and not marry. Oh, Molly! Don't you see? Carver insisted you would never marry Rafe Hartley. Now he's made certain of it, because he cannot stand to be wrong!"

"Well, he wasn't wrong, was he? I won't marry. I can't. Rafe thinks I'll stay here, in Sydney Dovedale"—her cheeks colored—"and have a baby every year. If I do that, I can forget all about *my* dreams."

The words she spouted were painfully similar to Carver's remarks. Obviously he'd put these ideas into her head for his own motives, although what they could be puzzled his sister. He'd never liked Rafe Hartley, but he would never be so cruel.

He could, however, be thoughtless. Knowing Carver, he might even assume he'd done a good deed. With no experience in helping others and having never shown the slightest inclination to begin, Carver now used his power, but not at all in the way he should. Of course, the fool would not confer with her first, even though Molly was *her* friend. Oh no, he just had to step blithely in and make this enormous, arrogant blunder. Mercy's irritation with her brother almost overflowed, but when she considered how upset Rafe was about to be, her heart ached for him, and sadness tempered her mood.

"Rafe would never force you to do something that makes you unhappy. Have you told him your dream?" She knew the young man had his faults, but surely if he was aware of his sweetheart's plans, he would support her.

Molly's mind, however, was set against sharing her dreams with the man she was supposed to marry. Apparently she thought he would never understand her ambition, and she wouldn't give him the chance to try. "I always thought we would live in London once we married, but now he declares he must be a farmer and never leave Sydney Dovedale again. That fine education was wasted on him. I wish I'd had that opportunity, but no—I had to go into service." This last was said with a shot of bitterness that surprised Mercy. Molly had never looked down on Rafe before this. Neither had she suggested she was unhappy as a lady's maid or that she longed for permanent escape from that little country village where she grew up.

Mercy was greatly vexed to witness her tidy plan falling apart. It seemed that by trying to help Rafe find happiness, she had actually made him a less appealing prospect to her friend. "There is nothing wrong with a man who chooses to work the land, Molly."

"He refuses to take another penny from his father. And I know how he earned his coin while he was in London. The coin he's using to rent the farm. The coin he's invested in shares at the bank. Coin of which he's so proud." She raised her fist, fingers crumpled around the borrowed handkerchief. "His knuckles, Lady Mercy. That's how. Bare-knuckle fights. Boxing." Her expression was one of disgust. "Gentlemen wagered on the fights, and that's how he made his money—beating six bells out of other men and getting it beat out of himself too on occasion, I daresay. What sort of a dignified life is that?" Molly shuddered, handkerchief pressed to her damp cheek. "He must have parted from his proper mind to refuse his father's help, and resorted to brawling for money. He could have been killed! Just like you always said, my lady, he's got too much misplaced pride. He never thinks anything through, but changes his mind in an instant. He thinks he's ready to settle now, but how can he know that? How can I? He takes nothing seriously. I wouldn't be at all surprised if his brain's been knocked loose in his skull. Not that it will matter much, since his grand university education will all go to waste anyhow."

"Molly! What has come over you to speak of him with such a sharp, unfeeling tone in your voice?"

"If you like him so much, you marry him!" Having shouted this at the top of her lungs, Molly promptly burst into more tears. It was not like her to be so hysterical, but then this was developing into a very odd day indeed.

Mercy turned away and took a swig from the decanter. She needed it now. Oh, Lord, she needed it. Some women just didn't know a good thing when they had it.

"I'm sorry!" Molly moaned into her borrowed handkerchief. "I don't know why I'm being so horrid to everyone. I feel positively wretched and hate myself. I wouldn't blame you all if you never spoke to me again."

What could she say? A bosom friendship of a dozen years could not be undone over a few cross words. Before she might be tempted to drink more, or accuse the other young woman of being ungrateful, she set the stopper back in the decanter. After she'd given it a good polish with the altar cloth.

"Molly, you simply must tell Rafe about your desire to open a business. You should have shared all this with him long before now. The two of you can——"

"It is too late. I cannot discuss it with him. I don't want to." She snapped her lips shut in a very stubborn line.

"You are not being fair to Rafe."

Molly drew herself up like a flower unfurling, gaining strength. "You always say men are thick-headed and know nothing. A man, you said to me once, is less use and more expense in the long run than a sturdy, well-made piece of furniture."

Mercy laughed uneasily. "Yes, but—"

"You said 'tis better for them if they *don't* know what goes on in our thoughts most of the time."

"True, but I did not mean—"

"You said we should know our own minds, be well-informed and capable of making our own deci-sions. Women are more logical than men, you said."

There was nothing she could do when confronted with her own words. She itched to pick up the wine decanter again, but somehow she restrained herself. "It is true that Rafe often lives for the moment, but that has always been the case. It is nothing new—"

"I'm fond of him, but we're not in love. We never were. There's long been something in the way." Molly shrugged, a quick, irritable motion of her slender shoulders. "A shadow of some sort between us. It's almost as if he doesn't see me at all when he looks at me. I used to imagine"—she exhaled a wobbly laugh—"that he had another woman on his mind."

"Oh?" Mercy fumbled along the shelf and began rearranging the prayer books in order of most wear and tear.

"But everyone expected us to marry for these past few years," Molly was saying. "It just seemed easier to float with the tide than swim against it. I daresay it was the same for him as it was for me."

There was a long silence. Finally, with the last, most dog-eared book placed in line, Mercy felt she'd done her best for the parson's shelves, and now the dank stone walls of the vestry closed in again, made her nauseated. She needed the warmth of the sun. "So," she exclaimed, "what are we going to do about this? We can't leave him standing at the altar interminably."

Molly blinked away a last tear. "I...I hoped you might take the news to Rafe."

"Me?" Under her layers of clothing, Mercy's skin rippled with another wave of goose bumps. "Surely his father, or his uncle—"

"No! I can't face them to tell them."

"Then, I'll tell them, and they can—"

"Please." Molly grabbed her sleeve. "Please tell him yourself. It will be better coming from you."

"Not from you?"

"Oh, no. I couldn't."

The girl looked so pitiful in her shattered bridal garland, her nose all red and her eyes puffy, it was hard to refuse her anything. But even so... "Rafe Hartley despises every bone in my body. Why on earth would it be any better coming from me?"

"That's just it. Don't you see? It would break his heart if he heard it from someone he loved. Hearing it from you, he'll just be furious."

Mercy could only stare, her lips falling open.

"I daresay he'll throw a few things—perhaps even directly at you—but you're such a strong person, my lady. You're so brisk and sensible, he can't possibly make a dent, no matter how he curses and insults you. You're very quick at ducking."

She began to think she would never get her lips back together again. They seemed stuck in their current startled O. So this was why they'd all waited for her arrival with such eager anticipation. They wanted Mercy to be their messenger, because no one else dared face him. She was the sacrificial lamb. Not one of those anxious people waiting outside knew of her past entanglement with the groom. They knew only that he hated her, and therefore she was, in a sense, disposable.

Rafe Hartley was about to kill her—would probably shoot her with the same gun he used to hunt rabbits and pheasant. She sincerely doubted even her own speedy skill at "ducking" would allow her to evade a bullet.

Chapter 4

HE PACED IN THE CHURCHYARD, HAT IN HIS HANDS. When Molly was half an hour late, he'd thought she must be ill or some tragedy had happened to keep her from getting to the church. But as time wore on and he saw his stepmother's face and then his aunt's peering fearfully at him around the corner of the chapel tower, he knew this was not the case.

Finally, here came Mercy Fancy-Breeches Danforthe, picking her way daintily over tussocks of grass. Trust this damned woman to be in the thick of it.

It was some time now since he'd seen her this close, but there was no avoiding each other today. Rafe readied himself, gathering the memories of all those things she'd done to him, all the pain she'd caused. It was because of this woman that Molly went off to London and developed a fancy for finer things. Molly's experience of life in Town had been very different from his, of course. The side of London she saw was clean and shiny as a newly minted penny.

"Well, say what you've come to say," he exclaimed

as Mercy drew near. "Give it to me straight. I can take my punches."

She looked up. "So I hear, Mr. Hartley." A flare of bright sun lit her wretchedly pretty face, and a sharp spur of anger burned in his gut. The opinionated wench was more beautiful today than he remembered. Stunning. The sight of her sent his mind into a furiously spinning vortex from which it could not rescue itself. His temper traveled rapidly likewise. He supposed she was satisfied now, having ruined his wedding day. Again. Ruined his life, for the second time.

It was five years, five months, one week, and three days since The Danforthe Brat persuaded him, in a wild moment of stupidity, to run off with her to Gretna Green. It shocked Rafe that he knew the exact number of days, for until that moment he hadn't realized he was counting. Her brother, the Earl of Everscham, would never tolerate the match, of course. Their marriage was declared void within hours, because they were both too young and neither had consent. Good thing too, Rafe could say now with hindsight.

Slowly she untied the ribbons of her bonnet, lingering over her message.

"What are you waiting for?" he grunted impatiently as he shifted from foot to foot.

Mercy slid the bonnet from her hair, and when she tipped her head to one side, another brilliant glimmer of sun caught on her curls. She squinted. "I'm sorry—"

"I'll bet you are."

He saw her straighten her shoulders and wrap her bonnet ribbons tightly around her fingers. "I may as well tell you without preamble."

"I'd be grateful," he snapped. *"My lady."*

She exhaled sharply. "Molly says she can't marry you. Not today."

"Does she indeed?"

"She's confused. Afraid. It's just nerves."

Rafe looked away for a moment, curbing the instinct to curse out loud. The temperance wouldn't last long, he knew. Good manners were never his strong point.

"I'm sure she'll come to—"

"Why can't she tell me this herself?" he demanded.

The woman stepped closer, taking shelter under the dappled shade of a yew tree as if that might protect her, not only from the sun's rays but from his wrath too. "It seems there is much the two of you have not discussed."

"What business is it of yours?"

Even in the shade of the tree she glowed. Her buttercup-yellow gown held on to the sunlight, as did her hair. "Molly is very upset. Distraught."

"What the bloody hell do you think *I* am?"

She nodded, her full lips pressed tight.

Rafe wiped his brow on his jacket sleeve. "Content now, woman?"

Her eyes widened. They were a very light shade of green, inquisitive and watchful. Like cat's eyes, Rafe thought. He never did like cats much. "Me?" she replied. "Why should I be content? I don't like to see my friend in tears."

"She's not your friend. She's your servant, and *you* tell her what to do. You never wanted her to marry me."

"That's not true." She was too steady, too calm. The superior little witch stood before him as if butter wouldn't melt in her pouty mouth.

Humiliation soared within Rafe. That she, of all people, took it upon herself to play messenger. She probably could barely contain her amusement. In that moment he forgot all about his own doubts and fears regarding this marriage. All he knew was that he'd been made a fool before his family and the entire village. And before this woman who already looked down on him, just because she was the daughter of an earl. Just because one of her ancestors, back in the dark ages, probably murdered and cheated his way into land and a title. That made her imagine she was above him, that her existence was somehow more worthy of life's breath than that of the men who worked her brother's land, the women who dressed her every morning, or the man who shoed her horses. Or him.

The flames of a hot, tinderbox temper consumed any last sensible thought he might have had, and all the resentment he held against folk of her class came quickly to the fore. She was the symbol of everything he despised.

Why did she have to be there? Why did *she* have to come with the message?

"Liar." He pointed at her with his hat. "Smug, self-satisfied *liar*! Always spouting your damnable opinions. Think you know best. I suppose you've told her that she doesn't need me. That she can do better."

He saw her glance slyly at his rough knuckles with the same sort of morbid curiosity that led a child to peek at slugs under a damp stone. Unable to stand there looking at her a moment longer, he swung away and marched for the lych-gate. He knew she followed. He heard her panting as she hurried after him in the midday heat. When he reached the shadow of the gate arch, he stopped and snapped at her again. "Leave me alone." He jabbed a finger at her. "Damn you, *my lady*."

But she wouldn't give up, and he might have known that. She was like a fly spinning around his head. Her boots tripped forward over the dewy spring grass, and while his clumsy fingers fumbled with the gate latch, she slipped, almost falling against him under the arch. With a slender, gloved hand on the top bar of the gate, she righted herself. "Rafe Hartley, control your temper! How dare you speak to me as if this is my fault!"

Because who else's fault could it be? It could not be Molly's fault—she was an honest, loyal country girl whose head had been turned—he caught his breath and stared down at the creature in the fancy yellow gown—turned by *her* and the life of idle luxury she led in her grand London house. A life that gave her too much time to play puppeteer with the lives of other folk.

"Slink off back to London now," he muttered. "Your work here is done."

"Put your dislike of me aside for two minutes, you great, bumbling seed ox, and listen! You must stay and talk to her. The two of you have much to discuss."

Rafe glanced over her head toward the church. If he stayed, what would he say? How could he talk Molly out of her fears when he had not been thoroughly capable of doing the same to himself? His courage that morning had come from a mug of ale and the desire not to hurt anyone's feelings, not to let anyone down.

He never imagined he'd be the one rejected. Again.

Confused, hot, and humiliated, he fidgeted with his hat, looked up at the cloudless sky, at the trees nearby, and then down at his feet. During the course of its restless, searching route, his gaze returned continually to Lady Bossy-Breeches Danforthe and her pursed lips.

"Get out of my way, wench. For a little bit of woman, you take up a lot of damn space."

"Rafe Hartley, you will come back at once. This matter must be fixed now before the wound is left to fester."

"The day I need guidance from you, harpy, I'll be in my cold, dark grave." Leaning over her, he stamped his booted foot hard in the grass and narrowly missed her toes. "Right here," he bellowed, "in this ground."

His tall form cast a shadow over her face as she blinked up at him. For all the disparity in their size, her expression remained fearless. "How like a man," she exclaimed, eyes gleaming with mild amusement, "to use his ears only when it's too late and they're rotting in the dirt, along with the rest of him."

"And how like you to still be working that tongue after you put me there."

"Now I am culpable for your future demise too?"

"I've no doubt, woman, that you'll have a hand in it." With that he replaced his hat, plucked her fingers off the gate, and walked through it at speed.

❧

Mercy watched her carriage set off for London with Molly Robbins tucked safely away inside it and wondered if perhaps, as Mr. James Hartley had suggested, she should have gone too. But she was so angry with her brother for meddling in this manner that she could not, just yet, trust herself to look at his face without wanting to slap it. There was also the fact that she'd been blamed unjustly for these unfortunate events, and Mercy did not stand mutely to be accused by anyone. Especially not by that insolent young man, for whom she'd gone to great lengths. She thought of him stamping his foot in the churchyard, trying to frighten her. She shook her head. Men, like dogs and horses, should never be tolerated in bad habits, or else, before much time had passed, those traits would be thoroughly ingrained. It was far kinder to the creature if proper training began at once.

No one, unfortunately, had corrected Rafe Hartley's faults; instead, they were indulged. In an excess of well-meaning, he'd been left largely to his own devices and was still prone to boyish displays of temper. It may be too late for positive change, but Mercy's spirit was not in the least subdued by the odds set against her. The prospect of a challenge was, as always, irresistible. So she decided to delay her return to London a while longer and be of service here, where she was most needed.

Once things had calmed down tomorrow, she would visit Rafe and put him straight. She didn't like leaving the matter unresolved and him thinking her the villainess. Again. In truth, she did suffer a pinch of guilt about taking Molly with her to London to be her lady's maid and companion. Perhaps it *was* selfish of her to need Molly's friendship so much that she took her away from the village in which she grew up. But it had never occurred to Mercy that this would make her friend dissatisfied later with the future Rafe offered.

Mr. Hartley's wife kindly invited her to stay at their fine house in Morecroft, the nearest market town to Sydney Dovedale. The Hartleys' two little girls, nine and eleven, were delighted to have the company of Lady Mercy, who allowed them to try on her bonnets and her jewelry while they rifled through her trunk. The eldest girl, Jenny, showed early signs of the beauty she would undoubtedly become, while her little sister, Elizabeth—called Lilibet—was very much a hoyden, apparently having found that naughty behavior was the only way to get attention when one's sister was already labeled "the pretty one." Their bedchamber and nursery were across the hall from Mercy's guest room, and after she had shown them the contents of her trunk, they insisted on showing her all their toys and dolls. Lilibet's, she noted in amusement, were all separated from their heads. Several of her sister's dolls had been served likewise, although Lilibet claimed to have no knowledge of how it happened.

On that first evening, before the girls were put to bed, Mercy played three games of fox-and-geese, exhausted herself in a lively and rather noisy round of hide-and-seek, lost abysmally at charades, and posed for a silhouette. By the time the girls were sent up to their supper in the nursery, she felt as if she'd been trampled by a coach-and-four, but it was very pleasant to be part of a larger family, even temporarily.

She sat down to dine with Mr. James Hartley,

his wife, and his ancient grandmother, Lady Ursula Hartley, who lived in her own quarters on the third floor of the house and, Mercy was told, deigned to join the family for dinner only if there were guests in whom she took an interest. It would have been a subdued meal if not for the old lady, who apparently neither knew nor cared about the day's events, her own curiosity and needs far outweighing anyone else's. Mercy estimated her age to be nearing ninety, perhaps more.

Lady Ursula was hard of hearing yet too vain to bother with an ear trumpet. "So you're Everscham's little gell," she bellowed down the length of the table at Mercy as the first course was served. "How is your father?" Giving Mercy no chance to reply that her father had been dead thirteen years, the old lady continued at a brisk pace. "I remember when he was a wild young rascal, always getting himself into trouble. I hope you don't take after him."

"Indeed, no, Lady Ursula. I've always been most sensible," she replied so sternly that no one had any choice but to believe her. "Although I'm afraid the same cannot be said for my brother. He is very like our father, so people say."

"What's that?"

"My brother—Carver."

While the old lady frowned quizzically at her, Mr. Hartley explained, "Lady Mercy's elder brother is the current Earl of Everscham, Grandmama."

"Eh?"

"You met him once or twice, Lady Ursula"— Mercy raised her voice—"I believe he attended a ball here once at Hartley House."

The old lady shook her head. "You've got your mother's coloring, however. Your father is very dark, as I recall."

"Yes, my brother takes after our father in looks, as well as character."

"And how old are you, gell?"

There was a brief, startled silence following this brusque question, but Mercy was amused rather than offended. It made a refreshing change to be asked outright instead of having the question nibbled around like a piece of cheese in a mousetrap. She was, of course, a great believer in brevity and getting to the point.

"I am two and twenty, Lady Ursula."

"What's that?"

"Two and twenty."

"Gracious! It's time you were married, gell."

She smiled. "I shall be soon, Lady Ursula. I am engaged to Viscount Grey."

"To a what?"

She spoke louder still, fearing she might dislodge the footmen's wigs. "Viscount Grey. The Earl of Westmoreland's son."

"Ah, good. He'll keep you on the straight and narrow, I daresay. Every young gell needs a husband, and the sooner the better. Marriage is the only obstacle to sin."

Even further amused, Mercy smiled wider. "Oh, I quite agree."

Lady Ursula seemed very pleased to have her statement concurred with so eagerly. "And where is your beau now?"

"In Italy, Lady Ursula. I expect him back soon. By the end of the month."

"Italy? Indeed! And why, pray tell, do all these young men need to travel about like gypsies these days? To be sure, there is nothing in those wretched foreign places that cannot be seen at home, if they open their eyes more often."

Mercy sighed, heaving her shoulders. "My sentiment exactly."

Once again, Lady Ursula looked surprised to have an ally. Mercy suspected the old lady was usually disagreed with in that house.

"Oh, we are acquainted with Viscount Grey and his father," exclaimed Mrs. Hartley. She looked at her husband. "You must remember, James, when we were at Lark Hollow last summer, they visited friends nearby and came to our garden party."

Mr. Hartley's face showed no expression one way or the other. "If you say so, my dear." Evidently, Mercy's fiancé had made no impression upon him. No surprise. Carver called the viscount "The Grey Shadow," which actually made her fiancé sound exciting and mysterious, so she never complained.

"Yes," Mrs. Hartley continued, "I remember he has property in Surrey, does he not?"

Mercy agreed that he did.

"Surrey is a pleasant enough place," pronounced Lady Ursula. "But I much prefer Norfolk and always shall."

"You never go to London, Lady Ursula?"

"Indeed no. I favor the country. In London, one is more likely to meet foreigners. I have quite had my fill of foreigners." As she said this, she glanced at her grandson's wife, whose greatest sin was being half-American. In Lady Ursula's mind, she might as well have been a cannibal from the jungles of Brazil.

"I have a fondness for the countryside," agreed Mercy. "And Norfolk in particular is one of my very favorite places."

Now that she'd found a like-minded companion at the table for once, Lady Ursula threw out a little attempt at flattery. "I must say, I never did care much for red hair, but it is quite becoming in your case, my dear. I can look at it and not feel the glare too harshly."

"Thank you, Lady Ursula."

Mrs. Hartley added her kindly opinion. "Perhaps with the light of the fire behind you it has shades of red, but I think it is more autumn wheat now than red."

Mercy smiled. "I have never seen anyone with hair even remotely the same shade, and I would be most upset to lose this fiery tint completely." After a slight pause in the conversation, she added casually, "I think I shall pay a visit to your son tomorrow. May I borrow that smart little curricle I saw today?"

The Hartleys exchanged anxious glances.

"Perhaps it might be better to let sleeping dogs lie," Mrs. Hartley ventured.

"Nonsense. Dogs who sleep too much get fat," Mercy replied. "They need exercise."

Down the table, Lady Ursula heartily agreed, adding that she knew a good deal about dogs, having kept a great many.

"My point being," explained Mrs. Hartley, "that

dogs, while sleeping, are quiet. When woken, they make a vast deal of noise."

"Oh, I knew what you meant." Mercy smiled. "But Rafe's noise has never frightened me. That is why I was commissioned to give him the bad news, is it not?"

"I must apologize for that, Lady Mercy." Mr. James Hartley looked at his wife, who was suddenly very interested in her roast beef and horseradish. "Had I been conferred with in the matter," he said emphatically, watching his wife stab her cutlet with gusto, "I would certainly never have sent you into the fray."

"Mr. Hartley, I was happy to be of service. Think nothing of it. Sometimes, after all, a woman's touch is best." She paused, reaching for her wineglass. "Especially when the touch is that of a flat palm wielded with speed and force against a saucy cheek."

His wife looked up and laughed openly, while even Lady Ursula appeared to suppress a chuckle.

Mr. Hartley, however, remained somber. "If you must visit my son, I would suggest waiting a day or so. Poor Rafe was in a very difficult temper today. At such a time, he might not take kindly to—"

"What I have to say must be said, whether he wishes to hear it or not," Mercy interrupted. "Forgive me for speaking plainly, sir, but I will not go away again while he holds me responsible for what happened." Of course he blamed her, because the upper classes, in Rafe's eyes, were the root of all evil. He had yet to reconcile himself with the discovery of his own father being a gentleman of wealth and consequence. Sometimes Mercy suspected he would have preferred that his sire turn out to be a chimney sweep. It would certainly have made his life choices easier. "Soon Molly will return to him," she continued. "I will put everything back in order. You'll see."

Mercy was determined. Rafe's father, seeing this and having some familiarity with her stubborn character, eventually agreed that she may use the curricle, but he wanted her to take an escort.

"Why?" she replied, half laughing but as politely as possible. "I travel almost everywhere by myself. I am accustomed to it." Her brother had been a lax guardian, to put it mildly. A procession of nannies and governesses had come and gone, making little impact, and the most constant companion she'd had for years was Molly Robbins. Eyebrows might be raised, but the idea of taking a chaperone with her to Rafe's house was, in her mind, patently ridiculous. "What's he going to do to me? Eat me? No, no, I am quite capable of going there alone."

Mercy had known Rafe since he was twelve, and she'd watched his relatives try to compensate for everything—his birth out of wedlock, a motherless childhood spent in poverty, and then the sudden revelation of his father's identity. As a result, there were a lot of allowances made for Rafe, and he was cocky enough and wily enough to make the most of it. Since he'd returned to heal the breach with his father, everyone was on their best behavior, keeping the fragile state of peace. No one wanted to cross swords with Rafe or give him any cause to run off again. Even his father, with whom he had fought the most often, was apparently reined in.

Poor Rafe indeed! He worked on his family's sympathy, but underneath it all he was just what her brother called him—a street-toughened ragamuffin with no need for anyone to stand up for him. Only to stand up *to* him, perhaps.

"Please do not fret. You'll see. I shall put everything back to rights. Before we know it, Molly will come to her senses, realize she's in danger of losing a wonderful man, and then she'll return posthaste. And we shall have that wedding after all." She set down her glass and picked up her knife.

Mrs. Hartley was looking at her in a very odd fashion.

"What is it now?" Mercy asked.

Mr. Hartley remarked quietly, "It seems you have it all under control then, Lady Mercy."

She detected a faint wry tone, which she chose to ignore. It was hardly the first time anyone doubted her organizational abilities. But she'd show them all. Let them sit around waiting for that overgrown boy to finish throwing a temper tantrum. She had an orderly plan to keep and no time for tiptoeing around, waiting for Rafe Hartley to apologize to her.

"I remember the first time we met, Lady Mercy," said Mr. Hartley suddenly, his eyes so like Rafe's but assessing her with greater warmth. "You were on the back of a galloping pony, racing across Hyde Park, and I followed, thinking you in need of rescue." He chortled. "How wrong I was."

Mercy remembered that day in London too, when handsome rakehell, James Hartley, became the hero of her childish romantic dreams. She'd embarked upon a campaign of love letters immediately, fastening herself to him like a piece of sticky goosegrass. Eventually she'd run away, chasing after him into the country, and that was the first time she came to Sydney Dovedale, met Molly Robbins and Rafe. It all felt like a very long time ago, which, indeed, it was.

Although James Hartley assumed she had never really needed rescuing in the park that day, he was wrong. Mercy had been in a state of great panic, on a horse out of control and, as usual, her brother was inattentive. When James rode to the rescue, she was in his debt far more than he knew. At the first opportunity she would repay the favor with a dozen years' interest, she decided.

❧

As it turned out, she did not visit Rafe the very next day after all. Awakening to a rainy, gray morning, she delayed her journey to Sydney Dovedale. Better wait until the sun shone again, she told herself, for nobody could be cheered up when it rained. It was nothing to do with losing her gumption or needing more time to plan her speeches. Nothing at all to do with that.

She wrote letters that day instead—one to her brother, admonishing him severely for his role in all this, and another to Molly, advising her to spend her time away thinking very carefully about her choice. Then, having run out of people to lecture by pen for the time being, she spent the afternoon reading a very melodramatic romance to Lady Ursula and the young Miss Hartleys, with occasional pauses to explain exactly where the heroine went wrong and where her lover's behavior might have been improved.

The following day it rained again, giving her another reason to delay the visit to Rafe. She had expected to see him arrive at his father's door, looking for sympathy, tea, and crumpets. But he did not come. At last, on the third day after the abandoned wedding, a weak sun reappeared. Mercy took Mr. Hartley's curricle to Rafe's farm, carrying with her a hamper of food prepared by his stepmother and, of course, many carefully rehearsed lines about stiff upper lips, patience, and love withstanding trials.

For the outing, she selected one of her best muslins with a tiny pattern of flowers so small they seemed no more than dots until one examined them closer. The haberdasher, when she purchased the cloth, had assured her the shade was called "Mystery of the Orient," but Molly Robbins had somewhat annoyingly referred to it as "orangey." One of Mercy's reasons for purchasing the material in the first place was to rescue much of it from the tacky clutches of her old nemesis, Cecilia Montague, who had also been eyeing the bolt of cloth from across the shop and would have made something atrociously gaudy, given half the chance. Mercy could not stand to see such a stunning color wasted on that painted, coarse-mouthed hussy, and thus it was purchased for what Molly Robbins scornfully declared to be an "outrageous" amount of money. As far as Mercy was concerned, it was worth every penny. Dressed in this bold color, she felt equal to whatever the day held. It gave her Danforthe courage that extra boost that a softer, pastel shade could not have achieved. She buttoned over it a matching spencer and topped the entire effect with a velvet-trimmed bonnet and a partial veil in ruby lace. There! No one—not even Rafe Hartley—would dare argue with her today.

As she came down the stairs, Mrs. Hartley met her in the hall and stopped to admire the outfit. "Goodness, that is very…bright, Lady Mercy. We certainly shan't lose you in that color."

Mercy chose to take that as a compliment. She'd been told before that her taste in fashion was very bold, but she saw it as another of her duties in life—to lead others in the matter of style. Few people had her eye for taste, and even fewer, as Molly Robbins once said, had her gumption.

Alas, although she could control everything about her appearance that day, she could do nothing about the changeable temper of Mother Nature. The country lanes were in an atrocious state after the previous two days of rainfall, and it was not conducive to the picturesque jaunt she'd imagined. Instead, the ride was rough, the curricle wheels lurching in and out of deep ruts filled with muddy rainwater. By the time she finally pulled up before the farmhouse gate, sprinkles of rain began to fall again and the temperature dropped rapidly, causing her to regret the lack of a coat that was practical rather than decorative.

A quick assessment of Rafe's cottage suggested it was deserted. The windows were shuttered, the yard empty but for a few hens, not a sign of human life anywhere. Surely he hadn't gone chasing after Molly? That would be the worst thing to do.

It was a pretty cottage, with dimpled pebble-and-flint walls, the windows framed with redbrick. Two dormers peeped through the fringe of a thatched roof, and a stout brick chimney coughed out slender wisps of smoke—proof that someone was home. Mercy clambered down from the curricle and shouted for assistance, but no one appeared, although one of the plow horses looked out of his box and whinnied a greeting. She unlatched the wide gates and marched up to Rafe's front door, where a few stout raps on the weathered wooden planks were also ignored. After trying the door handle in vain, she checked the building by peering in through cracks and knotholes. At last, she discovered a pair of window shutters unlatched, nudged them farther open, and looked inside, where she searched through a curtain of ashy fog.

There he was, slumped over the table. Panic squeezed around her heart with cold fingers until her searching eyes adjusted to the dim, smoky light and she saw the pewter jug beside his head. Mercy exhaled in relief. Unless he'd cracked himself over the head with it, he was merely drunk. That she could deal with, thanks to experience with her brother. Since no one else was brave enough to beard the beast in his lair, the task was up to her.

She hitched up her skirt and petticoat, climbed onto the brick window ledge, and swung her legs into the room. It was an action no proper chaperone would have condoned, but Mercy could never be kept out of somewhere she intended to be.

The shutters fell back against the wall with a clatter, causing Rafe to jerk upright in his chair as if roused by cannon fire. He swore loudly, holding his hands to his brow, and then she watched his gaze tracking the pale morning light where it cleared a path through the ashen gloom. Stiffly, he turned his head, and a pair of furious, hot blue eyes burned into her, scorching her fine gown.

When he spoke, his voice cracked, and the way he set each word down like a heavy burden was more menacing even than the manner in which his eyes raked over her. "My Lady Bossy-Breeches...what the blazes are you doing here?"

She brushed dirt from her frock and checked that her bonnet remained in place. If she was going to face this man, eye to eye, and deal with the business for which she came, Mercy needed all her parts in order. This was a man who earned money by fighting with his fists, and she knew he had a hot temper. However, she thought with a sudden sly smile, he was her property now, was he not? Rafe Hartley's boxing contract was in her hands. With this pleasing thought in mind, Mercy ran her wondering gaze over his wide shoulders, down his chest to his narrow hips and thick, hard thighs. Her eyelids grew heavy; her pulse quickened. Her teeth dug into her lower lip, and she forgot—for just a moment—what she'd gone there to do.

"Well?" he barked as he jerked to his feet and the chair fell back to the flagstones with a bang. "You'd better have a damned good reason for coming here, woman."

It did not escape her notice that this was the second time he'd said "damn" in her presence. He not only said it, he relished the word.

Mercy's gaze fastened on the abused chair. Someone ought to pick that up before it was tripped over, she thought.

"Well?" Rafe demanded.

Back to the business at hand. "I'm here to set you straight, Master Rafe Hartley. Apparently no one else has the courage. Your father thinks you should be left to your own devices until you stop sulking. But I have no time to wait around on your whim. Oh, and I'll take an apology, too, for those things you said to me in the churchyard. I understand I must make certain allowances for your temper in the heat of that moment, but I would like an apology nonetheless."

"Don't hold your breath for one, meddlesome harridan."

He stood before her, shoulders braced, fists at his side—a man ready to chase her out. She might as well be ten again and guilty of aiming an egg at the back of his head. Mercy could almost see the yolk dripping down the side of his neck, as it did back then.

Assessing him slowly, inch by inch, Mercy was just as astonished by his height today as she was every time she saw him since he turned fifteen and shot up almost overnight. It never ceased to shock. Rafe Hartley continued stretching north, and his shoulders were, she was certain, wider than some doors.

His eyes were still as blue as cornflowers, his hair as black as a crow's wing. And that sizable chip remained on his shoulders, possibly growing in unison with their width.

Chapter 5

RAFE STARED AT THE SCARLET TRESPASSER. DIDN'T SHE know it was dangerous to wear red around a bull? Standing in a shaft of rain-streaked daylight, once again she glowed. Like an angel. No, he quickly corrected himself—not an angel. Like an evil pixie. A demon of some unholy nature.

She observed him slowly, and then her gaze turned to the pewter jug on the table. Her fine eyebrows arched high. "So your first reaction to a little setback is to drink yourself unconscious?"

A little setback? Yes, that is all it would be to her. Nothing ever ruffled her pristine feathers. Naturally the woman assumed he was drunk. In fact, he'd fallen asleep reading last night, but she was prepared to imagine the worst. High-and-mighty people like Mercy Danforthe had their preconceived notions about "common" folk like him. He wouldn't bother disabusing her of the idea. Hands behind his back, he quietly closed the open copy of *Bell's Weekly* upon which he'd slept most of the night. "Come to gloat over my misfortunes, woman?"

She passed slowly through the beam of light to stand within his reach—either brave or stupid to put herself that close. It had to be the former, because he knew she wasn't the latter. She was too outspoken for her own good. Always had been, and he'd known her since she was ten, when she was all bronze curls, big green eyes, and busy mouth.

"Why are you still here?" he demanded, fists clenched at his sides.

Ignoring the question, she stooped gracefully to retrieve his chair from the floor. Her sweet, soft scent wafted up into his nostrils, and his heart slowed. The steady thumps in his chest seemed to thicken, grow heavier. He opened his fists, shook out his fingers.

Don't think about that sort of thing now. Not with her *here. The Danforthe Brat.*

He groaned and pressed his hands to his head.

"Sit down before you fall down," she exclaimed. With her hand on his arm, she forced him down into the chair. Even when she took her hand away again, he still felt her firm touch though his rolled shirtsleeve. Bloody woman. Why couldn't she leave him alone? She'd done enough damage. Perhaps she had yet more planned. Through narrowed eyes, he watched her opening shutters, sighing extravagantly, and tut-tutting at the mess he'd made in his bachelor solitude over the past few days.

"We can't have Molly coming back to this, can we?" Mercy exclaimed.

"What makes you think she's coming back?"

"It was matrimonial nerves. They happen all the time."

"Matrimonial nerves?" This was rich coming from

her, he mused. The girl who once changed her mind and abandoned him on their wedding night to run back to London with her brother. "Becoming a pattern, isn't it?" he muttered sourly.

"I beg your pardon?"

"The second time a wife has abandoned me." He hadn't meant to raise the subject, but there it was. She'd stirred the matter out of its dark, uneasy slumber by coming here to his house, forcing her way in.

Mercy's eyes were two calm pools of verdigris that shone confidently through the little bit of lace that decorated her bonnet. "Let's get the matter straight. We were two silly children, carried away in a moment of foolishness. You were nineteen, and I was seventeen. What you and Molly have is a proper match, quite different."

Yes, he thought grimly, different in so many ways.

"Why aren't you back in London by now?" he demanded again, since she'd not answered him before.

"I'll help you write a letter to Molly, and she'll be back before you know it." Although still not a direct answer to his question, the statement was delivered with her usual air of unshakable conviction.

"You think that, do you?"

"I'm quite sure." Of course she was never wrong. In her mind. Now she had the gall to smile as if there was anything in the world to feel gladness about today. He watched morosely as two dimples appeared in her cheeks. Old acquaintances, not forgotten.

His stomach hurt. "Mayhap I don't want her back," he snapped.

"Nonsense." She briskly pulled off her gloves. It

was a "taking charge" gesture, and something else he'd seen before many times. But not for a while. "Water?"

He jerked a thumb over his shoulder. "Scullery. Pumped some from the well yesterday."

She took the empty jug into the little room, and a few moments later he heard water pouring. "You'll forgive her because you love her," she shouted. "And she loves you."

Love? He snorted. What did this wretched woman know of love? She didn't have a heart.

He propped his elbows on the table, clutched the back of his neck, and let his head hang forward. His skull ached. Did the meddling menace have a cure for that? When footsteps returned, he raised his head and glared hard at her, putting every grain of effort into it. Calmly disregarding his expression—which he'd meant to be very fierce—she filled his cup. "Here. It'll help the dry mouth."

In fact, he *was* thirsty, so he took the cup from her hand. Their fingertips briefly touched. Water splashed up over the rim of the cup, and he thought he caught just a slight coloring of her cheeks. She strode quickly to the other end of the table and wiped her hand on her skirt.

Of course. She wouldn't want his dirt marking her dainty, smooth skin. Now she ran that hand over her bonnet and her ringlets, as if to check they hadn't let her down. God forbid any part of her neat attire should come "undone."

"You think I told her not to marry you, but you're wrong, Rafe Hartley," she said. "I want you both to be happy. I'm very sorry about the way things turned out, but I am not the culprit."

He stared at her skeptically. She must have had a hand in Molly's sudden change of heart; everyone else was in favor of the marriage and keen to see him settle. It was too much coincidence that this woman arrived on the scene and, immediately, Molly changed her mind. Rafe swallowed a mouthful of water, relished the cooling liquid on his tongue and parched throat. "Something made you come here today," he said. "Must have been a guilty conscience. Unless it was a hankering to see me again." He was surprised at how quickly he fell into teasing her when he'd meant to stay angry.

She met his gaze and held it steadily, but little pricks of bright pink appeared on her cheeks. Her reply was terse, resorting to an old childhood insult. "I told you—*Cloth-Ears*—that Molly will come back."

He shook his head and swilled the water around his mouth. Now he'd made her blush. Good.

Mercy paced before the window. "She'll realize it was a mistake, letting you go. She must."

"Was it a mistake, then?"

She stopped to look at him, and her eyes sparkled brightly through that pointless half veil of lace. "Of course it was. How could she let *you* go?"

Rafe stared at her mouth as it faltered. Her tongue hastily dampened her lower lip.

"I mean to say, you are perfect for Molly," she continued. "She'll see that, and then she'll come back."

Somehow his warriors regrouped, returning to formation, shields raised. "What if she doesn't? What then, clever-drawers?"

"If she does not come back, I'll personally find you a bride."

His throat dry and hot, Rafe gulped down more water so fast that it spilled from the corners of his mouth and trickled over his rough stubble.

"There, see." She looked smug. "You shall not go without a bride, whatever happens. I will put everything straight, just as I promised."

He choked. "You're going to find me a wife? You, Lady Bossy-Breeches, mean to play matchmaker for humble Rafe Hartley?"

"There is nothing humble about you," she replied drily.

He held his cup to his chest and leaned back. "What makes you so concerned for my welfare?" He laughed low. "I suppose since you once ran away like a coward and now you talked Molly into doing the same, some might say you owe me a bride." Now he teased her again. It was all too tempting, and his mood was much improved already. Perhaps it was the bright color of her frock. It was hard not to feel his heart cheered when the sun—in the guise of this little woman—came right into his cottage, filling it with light and warmth. Pity the sun, in this case, had to bring a lot of noise too.

"Are you still in your cups, Hartley? I owe you nothing. I do this because I don't care to be unjustly accused of meddling."

"You must be at loose ends, m'lady. I wish I was so in want of work to fill my days." Rafe sighed deeply. "But the embarrassment of two runaway brides is quite enough for me. I'll give marriage vows a miss from now on, if you don't mind."

"Oh, the martyrdom." She rolled her eyes. "Still playing for sympathy, I see."

"And you're still as irritating as a fleabite." One he was forbidden from scratching.

"Well, I suggest you give it some thought. My matchmaking services are at your disposal, should Molly not return." And then she added hurriedly, "Although I'm certain she will."

There was new experience in her face now, he realized, more knowledge and wit apparent in her eyes, intriguing depths in the shimmering layers of green that gently twinkled beneath her copper lashes. He'd never known another woman quite like her. Most women let Rafe get his own way. This one didn't. He'd often thought she must enjoy the argument, because she always came back for more.

If their marriage had stuck, he mused, they probably would have killed each other by now.

As she stood before his window, soft morning light framing her curves, he was forced to acknowledge his first wife's surface attractions. Didn't mean he was happy about it. And yes, even if that marriage was void in the eyes of the law, he could think of her still as his first wife. They'd said their vows before God, hadn't they? The laws of man only complicated things and were always changing. God never changed. God knew what He'd heard, just as He knew what was hidden in a man's heart.

Rafe set his cup down and cracked his knuckles. "Why don't you go home?" he muttered under his breath. Her perfumed presence was more hindrance than help in his current overheated, frustrated mood.

"This place needs a woman's touch, and since no one else dare disturb your brooding isolation, you'll have to make do with me. For now." Before he could protest, she was removing her bonnet. "Perhaps you could see to the horses and the curricle? I'll make a start on the fire."

Short of picking her up and bodily tossing her out, there was nothing he could do. She wasn't leaving.

"Just one thing I must know," she said suddenly.

He waited, scowling.

"Are you quite certain this is what you want? This life of a farmer? You will not change your mind again?"

"It's what I always wanted," he replied crossly. "As a wise lady told me recently in London, a man can never be content if he spends his life pleasing others. This is my choice."

The hint of an odd, relieved smile seemed poised to claim her lips and soften them, but she quelled it and gave a brisk nod instead. "Very well."

Accustomed to folk questioning his choices, he was unprepared for that simple reply. "I suppose you think I should wear a starched shirt every day and work for my father's business."

She answered very certainly, very calmly. "I think you should do what makes you happiest."

"Do you give yourself the same advice?"

"Always."

But he knew her to be a proponent of "duty first." If he questioned her further, she would probably say that duty made her happy, and thus they would descend into another quarrel.

Finally Rafe got to his feet. He scratched his rumpled head, glanced through the window, and saw his father's curricle by the gate. She must be staying at

Hartley House then. Did her wretched ladyship have nothing else to get back to? Or no one else? He'd spent more time than he should, on dark, cold, lonely nights, wondering what this annoying pixie was up to and who she was with. He couldn't ask Molly, and she volunteered very little, assuming he didn't care to hear about her mistress—the woman he made no secret of despising.

When he looked over his shoulder, she was bent before the fireplace, getting soot on her fine frock, her pert posterior high in the air.

"Do you know how to tend a fire?" he grumbled, slightly breathless as he watched her hips sway. "Don't you have servants to do that?" She probably had one to tend every fireplace in her house.

"Worry not," she muttered distractedly as she examined the tinderbox with a wary eye. "I have it all under control."

Rafe was glad someone did. He often felt as if he'd never get his life settled and straight. The harder he tried, the more tangled it became. As he paused in the doorway, he thought about going to help her with the fire, but since she insisted she knew what to do, he decided to leave her to it. She already had a dot of soot on the end of her prim nose, a sight that cheered his spirits more than might be expected under his current circumstances. In fact, it was suddenly expedient that he get outside quickly or else risk bursting into laughter and thus alert her to the presence of that smudge.

It was truly astonishing how quickly the quarrelsome creature's company lifted him out of his doldrums.

❧

When at home in London, Mercy considered herself in charge of her brother and ran his household with a firm hand, but Carver tolerated her attempts to manage him because he was the lazy sort. The same could not be said of Rafe. He accused her of being there only to "pry" into his "things," not being specific about what they were. She briskly ignored his muttered complaints and sent him into the scullery to wash his face and hands before he ate.

There was great satisfaction to be had in seeing his small house put back together, a good fire in the hearth, food on the table, floor swept with a damp mop, window ledge dusted. Now if only the man himself could be so tamed, but there seemed little chance of that now Molly Robbins had left him, taking her calm, steadying influence with her. He would doubtless use that excuse as long as possible to vindicate any bad behavior in which he felt inclined to indulge.

Mercy hoped the exertion of cleaning his house hadn't flattened her curls or made her face too pink, which would clash horribly with her "Mystery of the Orient" frock. Finding a shard of mirror resting on the dresser, Mercy took a moment to check her reflection. A fingertip-sized black blob darkened the end of her nose. Hastily, she licked her handkerchief and rubbed at the offending mark.

On the shelf beside the mirror fragment, there rested a burgundy velvet money purse. The rich color stood out among the pewter plates and chipped pottery jugs. She recognized the purse at once as being the one she'd given him in London while she was disguised as Lady Blunt. Mercy ran her finger over the soft nap of the velvet and felt a little pang deep in her heart. Their meetings in London had been few yet special. She missed sitting with him in that small room, dispensing advice while he was, for once, listening.

"Now I know for sure you have a guilty conscience—doing all this for me, Bossy-Drawers."

Mercy jumped like a little girl caught with her finger in the jam jar and almost dropped the mirror. She set it back on the shelf beside the velvet purse and turned to look at him. He was in the scullery doorway, shoulder propped against the frame while he dried his hands on a cloth. Water dripped from his dark hair and fell upon his shirt. Quickly his gaze moved beyond her to the shelf.

"What are you doing with my things, woman?"

There it was again, she mused, his precious "things." As if he had a great many. As if she was ever likely to do anything but tidy them, whatever they might be.

"That's a very fine purse," she muttered, hands behind her back. "I was just admiring the soft velvet."

After a moment's hesitation, he replied, "It's not mine."

"I thought it must not be."

"A lady gave it to me." He flipped the hand cloth over his shoulder.

"A lady?" She raised her eyebrows. "Would this be your wise lady friend in London?"

"That's right. A benefactress."

"A benefactress?"

"A good, kind lady I knew there."

"Perhaps I know her."

"I doubt it," he answered curtly. "She's not one for your Society parties and balls. She's too sensible to be caught up in all that foolishness."

Oh, she wanted to laugh. It actually hurt her stomach. She took a steadying breath. "Does Molly know you have a *benefactress*?"

"No." There was a pause. "And why the tone?"

She walked around his table, rearranging the food she'd set out. "It's just that you needn't pretend for me. I know about the ways of men and the world."

"Men and the world?"

"And their fancy women. Call her whatever you wish. She's your paramour, I suppose. Your mistress, your floozy, your *bit of petticoat*." Hiding her smile, she added, "If Molly knew, that could be the reason why she left you at the altar. That's why I asked." When she finally looked up, Rafe hadn't moved an inch. Arms folded, he watched her from across the small width of his cottage, making no attempt to correct her.

"Anything else you want to ask about my life in London, Lady Know-all?" Even narrowed, those blue eyes could cause severe damage to their target. "Since you think you're so entitled to meddle."

With great effort, she kept her countenance. "No more questions. For now. Come to the table and eat." Apparently his sustenance for the last few days had consisted solely of the liquid variety. No one else dared approach the house to see that he ate, so it was a very good thing she was there. "You won't be much use to Molly, or any other woman, if you don't stay healthy and keep your strength up."

Rafe sauntered to the table. Drops of water gleamed

like diamonds caught in his lashes, made them seem
even darker, and that, in turn, made his eyes shock-
ingly blue. He must have noticed the vase of wild
flowers and herbs she'd hurriedly picked from the
overgrown garden while he washed his hands. A little
twitch of censure lifted the right side of his mouth.
She remembered he never was one for what he called
fancifications. But perhaps it was time he learned to
appreciate a few pretty things here and there. Molly
might have stayed if she had some little hope left for
his improvement.

"Lavender," he murmured, pointing at the purple
stalks.

"Yes. I love the fragrance, but the flowers make
me sneeze."

"Ah." He scratched the back of his neck as he
looked at the table of food.

"Please sit," she said and gestured at the chair.

"Will you eat with me?"

This offer was unexpected. Cautious, she looked
at the food on the table. "I really should return to
Morecroft before they send out a search party."

"But since it's your fault that I have no companion
at my table today, you'd best stay and sup with me.
How do you know I won't take up the ale jug again
once you're gone?"

Although she could have argued again that this was
not her fault, he had cleverly tossed the second remark
out to distract her from the first. She knew he did it
deliberately, but he was right about the ale. In his
current swamp of self-pity, the man might let all this
food spoil while he dove back into the barrel. What

else could she do but stay? Only a while longer. Make sure he ate to line his stomach.

Before she might change her mind, Mercy pulled up a chair and sat, carefully moving the vase of sneeze-inducing flowers away from her. It may not be proper to dine alone with a bachelor, but this was merely a favor for an old friend. Nobody could honestly imagine anything untoward if she stayed another half hour, could they?

She suddenly decided she was hungry after all and reached for a slice of bread and the butter. Rafe filled his mouth quickly with a large bite of pork pie and chewed greedily, his doubting gaze riveted to her face, until she thought he must have counted every freckle. "What did Molly tell you in the vestry? If you didn't talk her into it, what reasons did she give for running off?"

Finally he was ready to listen sensibly, she thought with relief. "She spoke of her intention to become a modiste and open a dressmaking business in Town."

He kept chewing and staring at her.

"I know she will have a good clientele in no time. Most of my friends are mad with envy whenever I go out in one of her unique creations."

His gaze steadily raked her up and down, but he was silent.

"Did she never discuss it with you?"

At last he swallowed. "No."

"If you did not know that about her, it would suggest you know less about Molly than even my brother knows."

"Your brother?" A crumb of pastry flew between

them and landed on her sleeve. His eyes burned hot with a quick flame of newly ignited anger and old rivalry.

Oops. Mercy didn't want to get Carver in trouble. One should be loyal to one's brother, even if he was an ass who had meddled where he had no right. She could say what she liked of her own brother, but woe betide anyone else who said the same. "Molly has lived with us for a few years now, and *we* were aware of her ambitions."

He glowered at her. "What does that have to do with Molly leaving me?"

"She feared you would not support her. That you would want her to raise babies instead."

Confusion darkened his eyes. Mercy had seen that look before, when too many thoughts crowded into his mind and he didn't like any of them. "I thought that was what *she* wanted."

"For some reason, she was afraid to discuss the matter with you." She spread butter on her slice of bread, making sure to get it to the very edges, leaving no portion unbuttered. "Did you never talk of plans beyond the wedding?"

"I would have kept that wench happy," he shouted and banged his fist on the table. "I spent the past few months making this farmhouse comfortable for her to live in it. Now I know I wasted my time, because she didn't want this. Or me."

Mercy remained unmoved by his angry gestures, which were, she suspected, all show. He wanted her to tell him he was right and that he'd been treated abominably. Other people in his life would say that, just to alleviate the menacing darkness in his eyes, to comfort and reassure. To remain on his good side. But Mercy knew it was too late for that in her case. She hadn't been on his good side for years; therefore, she had no fear.

"So the answer is 'no,'" she said calmly. "Clearly the two of you never discussed the future and what you truly wanted."

Ignoring her comment, he stared down the table at some invisible foe. Suddenly he burst out, "Where would she get the coin to start her own business venture?"

Now she paid even greater attention to the bread she buttered. "Eat your pie."

The intense heat of his gaze burned the side of her face. "You gave it to her."

"No, I did not." She sneezed. It came upon her too suddenly to prevent it. Angry, she pushed the vase of lavender farther away.

"Then your damnable brother did." He shoved back his chair and stood. "Of course. I should have realized. Carver bloody Danforthe was always very quick to throw his coin around to get his own way. He threw it at me once too, didn't he, when he wanted me out of your life?"

"Why would my brother interfere in this—?"

"Because he never liked me. He wants to see me suffer. I stepped beyond my boundaries with you, and he continues to punish me for it."

"That makes no sense."

"Oh, it makes a great deal of sense, *my lady*. Can you look me in the eye and tell me he was in favor of my marriage to your maid?"

When she didn't immediately respond, he flung his plate and the remnants of pie across the room.

"So much for sitting down together and sharing a peaceable meal." She set down her butter knife. "Now I understand why Molly was afraid to face you, if you fly into this temper at the slightest provocation."

"The slightest—?"

"You are reacting quite unreasonably."

"Unreasonably?" He stood with fists clenched, knuckles resting on the edge of the table. *"Unreasonably?"* He swore in words that would make most women wince, or perhaps even swoon.

"Apologize to me at once, you uncouth boor."

"Apologize to you, Fancy-Drawers? Never! You and your brother were in this together, encouraging her to run off and leave me at the altar. Do you enjoy playing chess with simple folks' lives?"

It hurt that he still blamed her, but of course he couldn't know what she'd gone through to encourage the marriage to Molly, or how she'd helped him. He didn't know how much she cared for him. And he could never know. "If it is anyone's fault," she said, carefully holding her own temper in check, "perhaps we should all take a share of the blame."

He snatched her plate up, and she watched that spin away too, parting company with her slice of bread.

"And there goes luncheon." She stood swiftly. "It seems I outstayed my welcome. I won't dally here longer."

But before she took a step, he grabbed her sleeve. "You weren't welcome in the first place, but you pushed your way in, didn't you?"

"Let go of me at once!"

He hauled her to his side, and she felt his breath

disturb the ringlets by her cheek. "You and your wretched brother filled Molly's head with fanciful ideas. You pushed your opinions on her, just like always, until she couldn't bear to stay here with me, couldn't stand to marry a simple, common fellow like me."

She stamped hard on his foot, and he released her arm. "You are far from a simple fellow, Rafe Hartley. If you did not know what Molly felt, I suspect you did not want to know it. Like all men, you turn a blind eye to the inconvenient facts while remaining steadfast to those that serve your own purpose." She reached for her bonnet where she'd set it on the window ledge. "It seems Molly was right, and the two of you were drifting along with the tide. At least she had the gumption to halt the proceedings before it was all too late."

"You've got a nerve, woman, coming here and telling me—"

"Yes, I have a backbone and a head on my shoulders, and I'm not afraid of you. You're all hot air." Spinning around on her toes, she poked him in the chest with one sharp finger. "You, Rafe Hartley, are a storm in a teacup. I don't know why all these usually intelligent women like your aunt and your stepmother are so afraid to tell you the truth. Instead, they spoil you, dote upon you, and tiptoe around you."

"Spoiled? *Me?* A fine accusation indeed, coming from you, Brat."

She poked her finger into his chest again. "You have an uncle who adores you and is always there to advise you, a father who cannot do enough for you and is constantly looking to make amends for past neglect—although, I admit, he does not always know the best way to go about it. As for the women in your life, you have all shapes and sizes at your disposal, it seems. But they let you get away with whatever you want. Spoiled"—*poke*—"Spoiled"—*poke*—"Spoiled!"

Mercy had not known, until that moment, how deeply she'd felt the lack of family in her own life. She was envious of those who had relatives around them, people who genuinely cared, and not because they were employed to do so.

"You're an ungrateful, thickheaded…*boy*. You don't need a wife. You need a nanny."

He was staring at her pointing finger where it still contacted his chest. Then he looked up, his jaw squared, mouth tight, knuckles resting on his hips. "Take that back, wench."

She tipped her chin up. "Never."

There was a short, thick silence. Even the hens outside were quiet for once. Mercy turned away and took one step toward the door, but he grabbed her around the waist. He was never one to worry about the rules of propriety, of course—the strict code of behavior that should have prevented such physical contact. The brazen man actually lifted her off her feet to prevent her leaving. When he set her back again, she stumbled against the table, righted herself, and glared at him.

"Prepare yourself for some truths, Master Hartley," she said. "Since no one else dare lay them before you, I suppose it falls to my lot yet again. I'll say my piece whether you like it or not." She raised her chin again. "Then punch me on the jaw and see if I care."

"As if I'd ever strike a woman!"

"I suppose you're afraid I might hit back."

His eyes suddenly lost much of their anger. It was as if someone tossed a bucket of water on the flames, reducing the fire to smoldering sparks. "Why don't you take the first swing then, Frosty-Bottom?" He put his hands back on his hips, set his feet apart, and squared his shoulders.

For a moment she was actually tempted to aim a fist at his taut stomach. She was angry enough after all his unjust accusations.

He taunted her with a cold laugh. "Not so brave after all, eh?"

"Courage, Master Hartley, is not the same thing as stupidity. I see you still confuse the two. Why would I be afraid of you? You're naught but a pair of breeches and a big mouth."

"Don't forget the balls. I've a pair of them too, my lady. And a good-sized picklock for that fancy box of jewels you keep under your petticoats. Give me half an hour, and I'll have you undone. But that's what you're afraid of, is it not?"

Mercy flung her arm back, gathered a tight fist.

But as she swung forward, he simply reached out one hand, fingers splayed, and pressed it to her startled face, holding her at arm's length while she punched the air inches from her target. Before she knew what had happened, he'd picked her up by the waist, spun her around, and trapped her against the stair rail. His angry face loomed over her.

"You're a thickheaded, cloth-eared oaf," she exclaimed, breathless. "I wouldn't let you near my *jewels* if the alternative was a hanging at Tyburn."

His arms penned her in, his hands gripping the rails on either side of her shoulders. "Take. That. Back. Wench."

"Never." She raised her chin for a third time, meeting his gaze without blinking. "I will not take it back. Not a word of it. Because it's true—you're a boy."

"A boy?"

"One should learn to admit one's faults," she added smugly, "or else one might never improve."

Rafe bowed his head very slightly. She felt his moist, warm breath on her lips. His broad shoulders surrounded her, his thighs brushed up against her skirt, and his hands reached a little higher to rest on the oak banister behind her head.

"You'll be sorry," he muttered, his voice low, deep, every breath heaving his shoulders.

"For what? Pointing out the blasted facts, you great, stupid brute?"

"For pushing my temper, yet again, with your unwanted opinions, wretched harpy."

She tipped her head back even farther. "You, Rafe Hartley, are all bark." With each word, her lips almost touched his chin. Her throat was dry, her pulse pounding. "All hot air."

"Oh, I'm hot, all right," he whispered. "Better that than be frigid—cold as an icehouse."

"I'd rather be cold. One can always wear more clothes if necessary, but there is a limit to the number of layers one can remove in Polite Society."

"Good thing my society is never polite."

As he slid closer, her fingers lost their grip on her bonnet, and she grabbed onto his shirt. Her lips parted, ready to administer a word of warning.

But it was vanquished, smothered, the breath stolen from her as his hard mouth closed upon hers.

Chapter 6

HE DIDN'T MEAN TO DO IT. WITH HER REFUSAL TO STEP down and admit he was right, she pushed him to the edge. Her challenge to his manhood sent him over it.

His tongue found hers, fought with it as if they were two swords in a duel. Why did she have to taste so sweet? Smell so damn good? No woman this mouthy and stubborn should feel so soft and tempting. It wasn't right. Wasn't fair.

He let his knuckles brush her silken ringlets, but he wouldn't unfurl his fingers. That would be too dangerous. Putting his hands around her waist had been a daring move. Not many men would venture into that treacherous territory with this haughty madam, but he couldn't let her leave with the last word. Rafe decided to kiss her until she lost the will to argue. But he knew that if he touched her again the way he wanted to, he would forget himself completely. *Her* fingers, meanwhile, seemed to have no such quandary, no such reserve. They clung to his shirt and then spread, boldly sweeping to his shoulders, then his neck, finally losing their tips in his hair.

Groaning softly, he leaned his body to hers, devoured her lips, ate the shocked sounds off her tongue. His arousal sprang to life, aching with raw need. The yearning was more than he could bear. Yes, he now knew for sure what he wanted from life. The one thing too far out of his reach.

Suddenly she pressed her hands to his chest, gentle but insistent.

Their lips parted enough to allow speech, even if it was of a slightly hoarse variety.

"How dare you?" she gasped.

"How dare you?" he demanded, his voice gruff, terse. More so than he meant it to be. He wanted to touch her, put his hands all over her. Instead, he wrapped his fingers around the stair railings again, keeping her trapped.

She lowered her lashes. His body still touched hers, and he felt every breath squeezing through her in a halting pattern of shattered sighs. At last he'd unsettled the wench. There were few things more satisfying in life than getting her to bite. Despite her attempts to retain control, she never could resist the bait he dangled, and she'd get caught on it for a while, until she wriggled free. He wished he could reel her all the way in.

Rafe leaned closer, wanting more, but she ducked under his arm to escape. "That's quite enough of *that*, young man. You know where a kiss took us once before."

Yes, he mused, all the way to Gretna Green in the middle of the night. One heated, forbidden kiss had been all it took to turn his world on its head five and a half years ago.

Now she was aloof again as she retrieved her bonnet from the flagstones and looked for her gloves. Back to the ice princess.

"Was that meant to be your apology for the bride you cost me?" he demanded, arms at his sides, hands trying to stay out of trouble. "Twice."

"I did not come here to apologize. Only to set you straight."

Oh, she'd set him straight, all right. Straight, tall, and hard as marble. Now, apparently, the rotten tease was leaving. Again.

While she tied the ribbons of her bonnet, she lectured him about making sure he ate some food and got some sleep, but he noticed she couldn't look him in the eye. "I'll come back tomorrow, when you are in a more sensible frame of mind, and help you write a letter to Molly."

He scowled. "She can write to *me*. She's the one who left."

"You'll do as I say, Rafe Hartley, and we'll have no more of this nonsense."

"You don't own me, woman."

"Oh, yes, I—" She stopped short. "I know what's best for you and for Molly. I came here for a wedding, and there will be one."

The bossy wench didn't like her plans spoiled, or things falling out of place. Years ago, at his uncle's harvest party when they were children, he'd watched Mercy spend half an hour organizing a pyramid of apples on the sideboard, patiently picking up each one that fell, polishing it again on her silk kerchief, and setting it carefully back in place. Naturally, he'd waited until she was done, then walked by and removed an apple from the bottom layer, causing her neat arrangement to tumble all over the room. He'd received a slap 'round the ear for that from his uncle, but, as he'd protested at the time, it was her fault for tempting him with the opportunity.

She'd begun pulling on her gloves, but her fingers fumbled and, if he was not mistaken, her hands trembled. Even so, she kept her tone curt. "You see, this is why you need my help." One of her gloves fell to the floor because she was too rattled to keep control of it. "You're a male," she added, stooping to retrieve the fallen item, "oblivious."

Rafe wanted to be annoyed but couldn't; he was too amused by her funny, nervous little gestures as she tried to ignore what just happened between them, tried to maintain her customary frosty edge. "And you're a woman. Fickle."

She dismissed the statement with a shake of her head and a wrinkle of that prim nose. Her lips appeared darker, fuller, as if his kiss had stung them.

Mayhap he'd test the waters a little further. He cleared his throat. "Well, if you do come back tomorrow, woman, don't come too early, and make sure you knock this time."

"I certainly—"

"This *oblivious male* might have company. Of the pretty and shapely female kind."

Her gaze sharpened, finally lifting to meet his.

That tumbled her apples, didn't it?

"Such as?"

He shrugged. "There's a couple of milkmaids with their

eye on me. I'll saunter down to Merryweather's Tavern later and pay them a visit on the way home. See if I can't tempt them into joining me here for a jug of cider."

"How quickly you forget about Molly," she muttered.

"Just as you forgot about me."

She stilled, her plump bottom lip disappearing beneath the upper.

"Didn't you?" he pressed.

No answer. The woman held her emotions in so tightly that he couldn't even see her breathing. Only a very slight gleam in the corner of her right eye proved how great an effort she made and how much she kept imprisoned within.

He hoped the memories plagued her. For the last five years he'd fought to push this desire down, to drown it, smother it. Now she reappeared in the flesh, dredging it all up to the surface again. The feelings were still there, much as he might have tried to deny them ever since.

"I suppose you're too proud, my lady, to admit you made a mistake once."

Silence again. He watched the gleam grow more evident in her verdigris eyes, the heated temper she tried to control.

He folded his arms high over his chest. "Why did you ask me to run away with you that night?"

She pursed her lips, and when they parted again, her words shot out to pierce him like arrows. "It was your idea. Not mine."

He let that pass for now, although it was a blatant lie. "So why did you go with me?"

Her eyes shone brightly now with that stifled

temper as more oozed out, freeing itself from her hold. "I thought it would be an adventure."

"And then you changed your mind and left me." He shook his head. "Brave Lady Bossy-Breeches got scared."

Again her lips gathered in a tight pout, as if she was done with the conversation.

Well, he was not.

"Always giving out advice, aren't you, woman? Never like to think you might have been wrong, even once in your life, eh?"

She ran the tip of her tongue along her lower lip. Made it shine. Suddenly she said, "Yes. I made a mistake."

Rafe stopped rocking on his heels. At the suddenness of her confession, his pulse became irregular, too rapid. "Now you're sorry you left me?"

"No. My folly was agreeing to marry you in the first place when you are so far beneath me."

At those brutal words, his heart stumbled, like a horse changing its mind at the last minute before a looming hedge and leaving him to fly over it alone.

"Molly is the one for you." Adjusting the veil over her eyes, she walked to the door. "And Molly will come back. This is a temporary problem, nothing more."

Thus she left him standing in his kitchen, alone again.

Dear God and all the saints in heaven! She'd just let Rafe Hartley kiss her on the mouth.

That kiss with Rafe had started a very strange sensation inside her, not unlike being caught out in a storm—a thrilling sort of anxiety that went spinning and bouncing through her until she couldn't catch her breath. It made her think of her fiancé. Not because it reminded her of him, unfortunately, but because his kisses had *never* felt like that. She'd been waiting a long time to have her desires met in that regard, but her fiancé was every bit the gentleman he should be and never did more than kiss her lightly on the cheek or hand.

Tomorrow, when she returned, she would bring his stepmother along. It was the proper thing to do, even if she could, strictly speaking, handle him herself without assistance. Lady Mercy Danforthe had an irreproachable reputation, and it must remain unbesmirched. So what if Rafe made her admit, out loud, that she once made a mistake? The error in judgment occurred when she was only seventeen. He was two entire years older and should have known better. She hadn't realized, until he held her against the stair rail and she succumbed to his forceful kiss, how much of a danger he was. Still.

Mercy ruefully pondered the difference in his attitude toward her when she was dressed in the guise of old Lady Blunt. He was much sweeter to her when she wore that gray wig, a thick layer of face powder, and heavy black widow's weeds. When he thought she was that bent, frail old lady, his mysterious "benefactress," he was quite receptive to her advice. Truly it was astonishing, the change in Rafe Hartley, when she stood before him as herself and he hadn't one solitary pleasant thing to say to her. But then her own words today had lacked considerable finesse, because he got her in such a temper.

You are so far beneath me. Oh dear. Another thing

she probably should not have said to him. She hadn't meant to be cruel, but sometimes the truth was harsh, and it was always necessary. And she had, in that moment after his kiss, been in a state of panic that made her less than tactful. For both their sakes, it was important to remember their places in life. No good could ever come of forgetting the proper order of things. Thus leads the way to chaos.

Driving the curricle back toward Morecroft, she was soon slowing the horses until they moved in an ambling walk rather than the usual brisk trot she favored.

What if he did go to Merryweather's tavern, drink too much, and stumble home through the village unguarded? Eligible bachelors were scarce in the area, so Molly had told her. Young girls who'd waited for their chance at handsome Rafe Hartley would surely take advantage of the fact that his bride-to-be had run off. Especially if he played for sympathy with those terribly blue eyes—the way Mercy knew he could.

Surely, as Molly's best friend, and in her absence, it was up to Mercy to stop Rafe from doing anything foolish. It was not on her own behalf that she worried. No, it was all for Molly. After that shameful kiss, she felt even more determined. It was guilt, she supposed. A guilty conscience was a terrible thing indeed.

So she turned the curricle around and steered the horses back into the village. She would visit Rafe's aunt and uncle, the Kanes, at their farm nearby. Indeed, it would have been impolite not to visit them while she was there. Later, when she drove back to Morecroft, she could ride by the tavern on the common and make certain Rafe was not drinking too much or gambling.

If he was there, she would give him a ride back to the farm. And a piece of her mind.

A piece of one's mind could safely be given from arm's length. She ought to know, since she was a frequent giver of such pieces.

Clearly surprised to see her, his aunt and uncle nevertheless welcomed Mercy into their busy home, where she was instantly surrounded by the noise of three young boys and two little girls. It was somewhat overwhelming to be leapt upon from all angles, and her head soon ached as if it had been struck with a mallet repeatedly, but Mercy kept her composure under the lively assault.

"I do hope Molly returns before it's too late," said Rafe's aunt Sophie while wrestling a carving knife from the youngest daughter. "She could be a stable influence in his life, and I fear her sudden desertion does not bode well. I wouldn't want that boy to involve himself with the wrong sort of woman, and there are plenty here eager for their chance. He's always had a slightly unpredictable quality. And many admirers."

"Yes, so I hear." It was a good thing she was there, she thought again, to keep him on the right path. Men should not be left untended for too long. Especially men like Rafe. Look what happened the last time he made a spur-of-the-moment decision about his love life—he ran off to Gretna Green with the first girl willing. "Don't worry. I'm quite sure Molly will come back."

Rafe's uncle looked up from his newspaper. "That girl doesn't deserve my nephew. She's broken his heart. If he takes her back, he's a fool."

"I have put off paying him a visit," Sophie exclaimed, finally falling into a chair, looking exhausted. "I know how he is when in a temper, and at such a time, he is best left to his own devices."

Mercy decided to say nothing of her visit to the jilted groom, for they would only ask her what had happened, what sort of state he was in. Neither question could be answered without causing her to blush.

"Will you stay long in Morecroft, Lady Mercy?"

"I'm afraid not. My fiancé returns from Italy in a month." She faltered. "But I can stay a day or two. I hate to leave with everything so…undone. I am determined to put everything in order again before I leave."

"It is good of you to help," his aunt whispered. "But that girl made up her own mind. The best we can hope for now is that she changes it back again. For Rafe's sake."

"Well, I hope she stays away," his uncle snapped as he shook out his newspaper with an angry rustle. "Humiliating that boy before the whole village. He ought to find a good woman, a steady woman with her feet on the ground. Someone content with what he has to give, not a girl always looking for something better. Tomorrow I'll visit the lad, talk sense into him. There's many a young woman in these parts that would jump at the chance to wed our Rafe, and he needs a wife now, a companion to help him with the farm."

Mercy's heart had a very erratic beat that day and now it almost lost the rhythm completely. This was very bad. They needed time for Molly to return, more time to settle this in a calm, organized manner. If Rafe's uncle stuck his oar in, that fool boy just might grab the nearest willing female to save his wounded pride. That, naturally, would infuriate his father, who still had hopes of Rafe following Molly to London, where he could make use of his education in some profession. Everyone had plans for Rafe, and they all thought they knew what was best.

Rafe's aunt got to her feet again, having sat still for no more than a few minutes. "Would you stay and take tea, Lady Mercy? Goodness! Where are my manners that I didn't ask you earlier?"

"Oh no, that is quite all right. I called in only to—"

The lady suddenly tipped forward, her face drained of color. She caught hold of the table edge to right herself, and Mercy rushed to her aid. "You look very ill, madam. You should sit."

Her husband dropped his reading and hurried over. "Sophie, the doctor told you to rest more."

"I am perfectly well," she stubbornly declared, when it was quite evident that the opposite was true. Rafe's uncle, whose skin was of a naturally swarthy tone, turned almost as pale as his wife. His strong, work-roughened hands trembled as he eased her down in her chair.

Mercy fetched a woolen shawl from the rack of clothes drying before the fire, and he wrapped his wife in it, muttering, "Now rest. Put your feet up."

"Put my feet up, indeed. I've been through this seven times before. I think I know what I'm doing by now, don't you?"

Rafe's uncle shook his head, his lips set firm in silent disagreement, his forehead lined with anxiety. Mercy had not realized the lady's condition until that moment, for no one had mentioned it to her, of course. She was surprised, knowing the lady to be in her early forties and therefore beyond the average age of childbearing. No wonder her husband was so concerned. Ah, but was it not also his fault that she was in this state?

Now there was even more for her to worry about. Women in this state were so fragile. It made Mercy extremely nervous just to be around them.

Men, thought Mercy with a hearty sigh. They were always unmindful of the trouble they caused until it was too late.

Chapter 7

WHEN SHE DROVE MR. HARTLEY'S CURRICLE BACK through the village, softened sunlight had just begun its descent, lowering shyly behind the white blossom sprigs of the proud horse chestnut trees along the common. It was a mellow, pleasant evening, the sort that made her wonder why Molly Robbins should be in such haste to leave the country behind forever.

During her visits to Sydney Dovedale with Molly—visits that stretched over a dozen years of her life—Mercy had come to know the place very well. Most things never changed, but there were a few new developments of note, one being that the village shop was no longer managed by the very solemn Mr. Hodson. It was now run by his much livelier son, a tailor of questionable skill, known to the village inhabitants as "Jammy Jim," not only because of his predilection for the sweet comestible, but also because he was well known for the talent of talking himself out of sticky situations. From his father he inherited the ability to sell milk to a cow, but while old Mr. Hodson had used this convincing chatter to run a successful business, Jammy Jim used it mostly to argue with his wife—a very pretty and hot-tempered young woman he'd talked into marrying him a few years ago. Much to Mercy's amusement, when the couple were not fighting, they were wildly in love, and there was not often a great deal of time elapsed from one kind of passion to the other.

This evening, as she rode by in the curricle, Jammy Jim was cleaning his upper windows while his wife held the ladder.

Mercy slowed the horses to view the display in the bow-front window—an old habit. She did love to discover a good bargain and felt her inner huntress on high alert whenever passing a well-designed shop front. The young Mrs. Hodson, recognizing her as she trotted by, forgot her husband's ladder to run into the lane and tell her all about some new silks and summer muslins available in the shop and, most importantly, a millinery counter recently enlarged and under her sole management.

"I shall be trimming bonnets myself to order," the lady explained earnestly. "All the latest styles can be had now here in Sydney Dovedale."

Mercy promised to return soon and sample her fashionable wares. Meanwhile, Mr. Jim Hodson's ladder began to waver precariously in the corner of her eye. "Madam, perhaps you had better—"

"And I have just the thing for you, Lady Mercy! A peacock-feather muff I know you will adore! Mr. Hodson was just saying yesterday that he wondered why I thought such an item as a peacock-feather muff might be needed in Sydney Dovedale. He inferred that I made a mistake"—she raised her voice so he would hear—"that no one would wish to purchase it, and that it would gather dust on the shelf. But I said to him, it is just the thing for a discerning customer of fashion—the very sort of customer we should court. It should arrive direct from Paris in a day or two. And here you are, Lady Mercy. Conjured up like a genie, just in time!"

Behind the young woman's head, her husband's ladder swayed. Dropping his bucket, he looked for her in some understandable alarm. "Cathy!"

She dropped a hasty curtsy. "Do excuse me, your ladyship."

"Please go and save your husband."

Jammy Jim clung to the thatched edge of his roof and bellowed for his wife in tones that startled several nesting doves above his head. As they fluttered up into the sky, he gave a high-pitched shriek and almost lost his footing completely. Somehow he stayed on as the ladder tilted first one way and then the other. Perhaps, mused Mercy, his feet were as "jammy" as the rest of him.

As she drew the curricle around the village common, slowing for the geese that crossed the lane in no particular hurry, she looked to her right and assessed the front of Merryweather's Tavern. A few weathered benches were set outside, filled with farm laborers who enjoyed a pint pot after a hard day of spring planting. No sign of Rafe. Good.

Several men watched her pass, and those who knew Mercy from her previous visits to the village— particularly those familiar with her generosity toward anyone who opened and closed a gate for her—doffed their hats respectfully. Suddenly one of them jumped up and trotted alongside the curricle. "Milady, good eve to you." He tipped his dusty old cap. "I 'ope you don't mind the liberty, ma'am, but I think someone should step in like and put a stop to it, afore young master Rafe gets 'imself in trouble."

She drew back on the reins. "What has he done now?"

"Gone and got 'imself into a game o' cards, ma'am, and losing money as if there's a hole in 'is pocket. We all know yon lad's had a tough time of it—what with young Moll Robbins running off like that, but some folks will take advantage, milady. There's some fellows who never held much liking for young Rafe, and reckon he's too big for his boots. Now's their chance to kick the lad while he's down. If thee knows what I mean, milady."

"Yes, I see." He did have a habit of rubbing folk up the wrong way, because he was so fond of speaking his mind. She glanced over at the open door of the tavern. Raucous laughter spilled into the mild, sweet evening air. "Is he in drink?" she demanded.

"Not yet, milady, but I daresay the lad's fair on the way to it."

"Please go in and tell him I wish to speak with him." She settled the horses and waited while the old man lurched inside. The wait stretched on, and the laughter continued unabated. Finally, the worried fellow reemerged and hobbled over to the curricle once more.

"Well?" she demanded.

"Master Rafe says if you want 'im, milady, you'll

'ave to come and get 'im yerself, if yer please. Beggin' your pardon, milady."

And that, she thought, was probably not all he said. Or how he said it. Rafe Hartley never cared about the words he used, or how, or when.

Mercy exhaled a hefty sigh. If she rode on, she would fret all night about Rafe and any lack of judgment he might suffer under the influence of too much ale. He could end up with the wrong woman that evening. He might trip and fall in a ditch, or encounter a poacher's trap if he wandered off the path. Well, she was there to help, was she not? This was no time for her Danforthe nerves to fail. Once again she seemed the only one capable of dealing with the wretched boy. "Lady Blunt" would certainly not let anyone stop her from entering a tavern once she got the idea in her head.

"Here," she said, "will you hold my horses for me, my good fellow?"

"But, milady, a young lass—*lady*, like yourself, shouldn't—"

"I am not afraid, I assure you." She climbed carefully down and straightened her skirt. "How bad can it be?"

She soon found out. Marching boldly through the door of the tavern, riding crop in both hands, she was hit at once by the thick odor of stale ale, wood smoke, rotten apples, and masculine sweat. It almost swept her back out again, but she gathered her courage to push her way through the mob. Men's faces turned in shock, the laughter cut off as if by a scythe. Some hats were lifted; many were not.

"Rafe Hartley," she shouted.

He was at a corner table, leaning with his bared forearms on the pitted wood, cards in his hand. He blinked several times in disbelief when he saw her. "What do you want, woman? Come to continue our quarrel? I thought I was rid of you."

Someone tittered and then yelped as they were abruptly silenced. Mercy waved a hand before her face, clearing a spot through the dense smoke that belched from the fireplace. "It's time you went home. I'll take you."

He leaned back, watching her with those intense blue eyes, one arm hanging over the back of his chair. "I'm in the midst of a game, *your ladyship*, and I'm not inclined to leave it unfinished. Unlike some folk"—his eyes darkened meaningfully—"I finish what I start."

He might not be drunk yet, but as the old man had said, he was on the way to it. Someone had just bought him another filled mug. She walked up to where he sat and urged him again to get up and go with her. There was a pile of coins in the middle of the table, and right at the pinnacle sat Rafe's gold pocket watch. She knew it was his—a present from his father three years ago when he turned one and twenty. Molly had told her about it.

"I can't go yet, you see." He grinned up at her. "Got to win my watch back."

It was quiet enough now in that tavern to hear a moderate-sized pin drop.

"You sit here next to me, your dainty ladyship," Rafe drawled, patting a stool at his side. "Mayhap your fine, aristocratic"—he eyed her up and down— "*presence* will bring this poor country boy some luck, eh?" He snorted with laughter, but none of the other men around the table joined in, too in awe of the uncommon stranger in their midst.

She sat hastily, almost lowering her backside onto his hand. "As you wish. I'll wait here until you're done, and then I'll take you home." She swung her gaze to the face of each man around that table. "While I'm here, I'll see that no cheating occurs." Mercy might not know the rules of their game, but she could tell a guilty expression a mile away, and several of his opponents had very suspiciously shaped ears. For instance, Tom Ridge, the blacksmith's son, was, in her opinion, a sly, untrustworthy fellow and an opportunist. She treated him to one of her most forbidding frowns.

Rafe reached for a newly filled tankard, but she beat him to it, determined to keep him at least partway sober. "I'm thirsty," she exclaimed when he glowered at her.

"It's strong scrumpy. None of your ladylike sherry, my lady."

"Thank you for the warning. I can assure you it is not necessary." Her brother always said she had hollow legs and tin innards. So to prove herself to Rafe and all those who watched, she lifted the small veil of her bonnet and downed the tankard of cider in one long gulp. "Quite refreshing." Ooh. Yes, it was certainly refreshing. If that was the word for it. For a moment she thought it had removed the surface of her tongue.

"Watch yourself, my lady."

She gave him an arch smile that already felt slightly looser and wider than usual. "And you do the same."

The game progressed, and she tried to follow, but cards had always bored her, and she knew only solitaire. Even that she seldom played, for in her opinion, games of chance were an utter waste of time. She preferred chess, something where real skill and planning was involved and it didn't all depend on how the cards were shuffled.

It surprised her that Rafe would be so careless with his coin and valuables, but he always had a surfeit of self-assurance that was often more hindrance than help. Tonight it remained unwavering, despite a succession of bad cards. When he continually failed to win back his pocket watch, Mercy saw a shadow dim the merry light in his gaze, but he acted as if it was a mere trifle. Only she was aware of his knee bouncing anxiously beneath the table.

It was very odd to be seated there beside Rafe while wearing her very fine "Mystery of the Orient" muslin. She certainly had not expected this when she set out that day in her bright garments. The other men at the table were considerably quieted by her presence, on their best behavior and not very happy about having their evening spoiled in this manner. Some stared at her in curiosity. Most carefully avoided her eye. Rafe continued in his usual bold way, teasing her, laughing, and joking as if his opponents joined in. He pretended not to notice the general discomfort that dropped over the room, and he acted as if it did not matter at all whether she left or stayed.

Another tankard was brought for him, and she drank that one too. Then a third. He watched her with guarded amusement. "I drink like that only when

I want to forget something. What are you trying to forget, precious primrose? Some scandal in your past, perhaps, milady?"

"I am merely passing the time until you're ready to leave, country bumpkin."

If he was concerned about the amount she imbibed, surely he would want to leave soon, she reasoned. It was the only way to get him out of there before he lost the shirt on his back, because she certainly couldn't carry him over her shoulder.

"Perhaps"—he leaned closer to whisper, pretending to show her his cards—"you're hoping the scrumpy cider will help you forget that kiss you gave me earlier."

He meant to shock her, of course. He did like to make her blush while he played the "humble" country lad. "You gave it to me," she corrected him crisply.

"You started it."

"I most certainly did not. It was thrust upon me." She swigged another mouthful of cider, growing accustomed to the burning sensation and then the numbness that followed until the next gulp. "In any case, what does it matter?" She flicked her hand carelessly, almost knocking the cards out of his grip. "It is already forgotten." She finished the contents of the third tankard. Or was it the fourth? Her body felt very warm now, her mind pleasantly drowsy. "Your kisses are not that memorable, Hartley." *Oh, what a lie!*

"What would your brother have to say if he saw you here like this…with me?"

Carver, she mused, would probably laugh and make a wager on how many pints she could drink. He'd always viewed his little sister as an irritating burden, the charge of which had been forced upon him by unlucky fate. He would much rather have had only himself to worry about. When she was seventeen, running away with Rafe, she'd almost expected her brother to let her go. But she had discovered Carver did have some limits. She'd often thought, since then, that the evening of her elopement was the first time Carver realized it too.

It was the only time *he* took charge of *her*. The only time she'd ever known her brother cared.

Rafe was looking hard at her, unblinking, giving his full attention to the woman at his side instead of the cards in his hand. Mercy, vaguely aware of the other men watching them impatiently, could not take her gaze from Rafe or fail to concede, again, that he was darkly handsome. Attempting to convince herself of his utter unattractiveness was a hopeless endeavor.

He had discarded an old, patched coat at some point in the evening, and it hung over the back of his chair. Of course, a gentleman should never remove his coat in public, but what did he care? Now he wore only a white linen shirt with the sleeves rolled up, a frayed waistcoat, and stained buckskin breeches that might benefit from the application of a buffball. If he possessed such an item. Or a valet to draw it to his attention. All his garments were, no doubt, thrown on without a thought, and most of them clumsily sewn by Jammy Jim, yet he still managed to be very pleasing on the eye. As much as he thought he blended in there, he stuck out among all the other men in that tavern like a tall beeswax candle accidentally left in a box of tallow stumps. Imagine, she thought, how he would look if he actually took any effort over his clothes. If only he was hers to manage.

"It's not mine," she muttered.

"What isn't?"

She licked her lips and tasted the tart apples of the scrumpy. Oh, why did these wildly irregular sensations come over her in his proximity? It was most unfair.

"What isn't yours?" he repeated.

"The fault for your misfortunes." She struggled to remain very solemn. As long as she maintained the appearance of being in control, no one could possibly accuse her of otherwise. "The fault isn't mine."

"Of course it isn't. It never is." He shook his head and reached for the empty tankard she gripped in both hands. "I reckon you've had enough. Some folk don't know their limits."

That reminded her... "Your aunt is having another baby," she whispered, trying not to sound so shocked or disapproving. Failing on both counts.

"You don't say," he replied drily.

"But what can your uncle be thinking?"

He lifted one shoulder in a loose shrug. "Extra hands on the farm as they grow older? Free labor in the fields."

She stared, tying to focus on his rugged profile while he played his next hand. Sometimes it was hard to tell whether Rafe was teasing or deadly serious. "Your cousins may not wish to be farmers."

"Why wouldn't they? Are we not all supposed to stay where we're born? That is what people like you, your brother, and my great-grandmama believe, is it not? We are all born to a life we should never try to change. Things should stay the way they are. Anyone steps out of line and rebels, they must be punished."

"I'm sure I never said such as that."

"But it's ingrained in the way you think. Now, my lady friend in London"—he smirked at his cards—"she did not think that way."

"Your *lady friend*?"

"She," he said proudly, "wanted me to make something good of my life. Said I shouldn't waste my talents."

The men at the table chuckled into their scrumpy.

"She didn't believe in holding a man down."

"The only thing holding you down, Rafe Hartley, is yourself," she exclaimed. He'd meandered through life, more intent on enjoying himself than making serious plans. Until recently. "I always thought it was a jest for you to study the law. *You*—who has always sought to break it."

His fellow players laughed again, many agreeing with her. Rafe good-naturedly smiled too. "Aye. I was not cut of the right cloth for that profession. I thought to please my father."

Surprised to hear him admit it, Mercy kept her gaze riveted on his smile as it turned to a contrite grimace. Rafe worked hard at trying to please everyone in his life—his father, his uncle, Molly… Most of the time pleasing one meant disappointing the other. No wonder he was confused and could not find his direction for so long.

She knew hers, of course. Had always known it. Was born to it. Marry well for the sake of the family name and provide at least one heir. Host parties and balls, manage household staff, visit the poor and infirm, write letters of thanks, sympathy, and felicitations. Arrange flowers. Most importantly, keep oneself above scandal. That was her purpose.

There was no profession for her to worry about, only a strict, unswerving duty.

And here she was, in a tavern full of men, unchaperoned, slightly drunk. None of this was in her plans. Where did she go wrong that day? At what point did it all go amiss?

Studying Rafe's lips, she felt forlorn, overwhelmed, out of her depth for one of the few times in her memory. It was a rare occurrence for Mercy.

Fingers of sunset reached in through the tavern windows, which were left open this evening, and Rafe's quizzical eyes reflected tiny sparks of gold that fizzled, like fireworks dampened by rain, smothered before they could show their full glory. Watching for them drew her in until she felt that deep, velvety blue all around her.

She hiccupped. "You should not have kissed me," she whispered.

He swore under his breath. "And you should never have come back here."

"Yes, I should. Someone had to put things… put things"—*hiccup*—"in our proper laces. In *their* proper…places." Oh, she couldn't think what she was saying. "And you should not curse in the presence of a lady." There, that was better.

"You bring out the worst in me," he replied, shaking his head, dark hair falling across his brow until he swept it back with his fingers. "'Tis dangerous, my lady, for me to be around you."

"On the contrary. I will keep you out of trouble, young man."

He licked his lips as they curved in a slight, weary smile. "Too late. Like my uncle says, you *are* trouble."

"Well, I must say," she exclaimed, "that's most unkind and definitely uncalled for."

"My uncle is a wise man. I only wish I could be the same."

"Wise indeed! A wise man would know when he had enough children."

The last thing she remembered with any clarity was his low, sultry chuckle as he finally extracted the tankard from her fingers. "Let's get you home, Bossy-Buttercup," he whispered.

❦

Rafe drove the curricle back to his farm and unloaded the giggling woman, lifting her in his arms and taking her inside. Only then, as he sought somewhere to put her down, did it occur to him that he'd brought her to *his* home—not hers. He should have driven her back to Morecroft, but it was dark now, the drive another good hour at least, even at his usual reckless speed.

"Mind my bonnet," she exclaimed as he carried her into his house. "And I hope your hands are clean. I don't want my new gown spoiled. It's mystery of the…something… I forget."

"Oh, it's a mystery, all right," he muttered. Only Mercy Danforthe could lecture him while she was inebriated. But there was something almost human about her in this state. The ice queen was melting. Amused as he was by her current unraveled condition,

she would not want this messy inkblot spoiling a page
in her very proper ledger. He was shocked that she
entered that tavern to find him, risking her reputation
just to save him from losing all his money. On the
other hand, The Brat was brazen enough to imagine
she might carry it off without castigation.

He tried to sit her up in a chair at the table, but she
kept wilting to one side. Finally, he carried her upstairs
and laid her on the bed. At once she rolled over,
closed her eyes, and appeared to fall asleep. He shook
his head, crouched at the foot of the bed, and removed
her boots, struggling over the laces and breaking one
of them in his fumbling haste. The only other thing
he removed was her bonnet, which he laid carefully
on the little bedside table. She looked disgustingly at
peace and at home, sprawled across his bed, drooling
into his bolster.

They'd have to make the best of it now, he
reasoned. At first light, before he began work, he
could get her up and sneak her out without anyone
knowing she spent the night there. Although he had
no idea what she could tell her hosts in Morecroft
tomorrow. He'd leave that up to her. He had his own
problems to deal with. Besides, he never asked her to
come there, interfering, putting herself in his house…
in his way.

"It was all because of you," she murmured, her eyes
closed, bronze lashes twitching against her cheeks.

"What was?"

"You talked me into it."

Rafe's temper, usually so quick to flare, was napping
this evening, like an old dog lying in the shade of a

tree on a sunny day, unwilling to rouse itself and bark. Could it be that he was simply tired of fighting with her? He never thought that was possible before. "Yes," he replied. "If you say so."

What would it matter, since she was unlikely to remember his concession come the morning?

"I need a peacock-feather muff direct from Paris," she whispered. "It is just the thing. I cannot be married without it."

Following that curious remark, there was nothing but a gentle snore. He sat, just a moment, on the edge of the bed. It was improper, but Lady Know-All was not awake to remind him.

Now what? Anyone might pass his yard and see that curricle. Best get the horses into the stable and pull the curricle out of sight around the side of the barn. He might not have invited her in, but she was there now. His responsibility for a few hours at least.

Rafe's heart was beating very fast, not just from the exertion of carrying her up the stairs. The more he tried to calm the pace, the worse it became. He hadn't felt this much excitement since the night of their elopement. After the hurt of her desertion, he hadn't expected ever to feel his heart leaping like this again.

Chapter 8

MERCY WOKE WITH A JOLT, SURPRISED TO FIND HERSELF lying flat in all her clothes. Where the blazes was she? Her skull felt several inches thicker than usual, her tongue stuck to the roof of her mouth. Moonlight sifted through knotholes in the wooden shutters. She was definitely on a bed, but not the soft mattress to which she was accustomed.

Very slowly she hauled herself upright. Her sight adjusted to the dim shadows, and although she didn't recognize the chamber, she guessed where she was now. All was silent but for a low owl hoot. There was her bonnet beside the bed. But where were her boots? Her toes were cold in only stockings.

Mercy sat on the bed for a few minutes, and events came back to her like scenes visible in parts through a windblown curtain. The tavern and the card game. His gold watch sitting on the pile of coins. Her intention to keep him sober and sensible at all costs—to keep guard over that man for Molly's sake. She sincerely hoped Rafe Hartley realized she went to these lengths for him and his fiancée. No other reason. Tonight, thanks to the scrumpy, she had possibly made a fool of herself. Not that she could quite remember what she said. Or did.

Eventually she climbed off the bed, grabbed her bonnet, and tiptoed into the narrow hall. Her head ached dreadfully. As she put one shaky foot before the other, it felt as if the back of her skull dragged behind her on the floorboards. Her mouth was dry, her tongue gritty. The thought of a long journey on dark roads all the way back to Morecroft did not make her feel any better, but she could hardly stay at Rafe's farm all night. That would be beyond even her brazen sangfroid.

There was only one other door above stairs, and she assumed he was behind it, asleep; thus, she decided to make her sly retreat and save them both a great deal of awkward conversation. But as she crept down the staircase, she heard a sound—a soft creak and then the crunch and crackle of coal being tossed into a fire. He was up. So much for getting away while he still slept.

Best foot forward then. Even in her stockings.

Rafe sprawled in a chair by the fire, legs stretched out, hands behind his head. "Sobered up, have you, menace?"

"I thought you were abed."

"There is only one bed. You were in it. We don't all live in mansions with a lot of empty bedchambers."

She wondered if the sizable chip on his shoulder would ever get too heavy to carry. "Where are my boots?" she croaked.

His gaze slowly drifted to her feet. "I know not. Wife."

"Wife?"

He scratched the stubble on his cheek and stared at the fire. "Slip o' the tongue."

Oh, he liked his jokes. "Most amusing." She winced, one hand pressed to her forehead, inside which an angry miniature blacksmith currently pounded a vicious little hammer, using her brain for an anvil. "Where are my boots?" she repeated. "You must have taken them off me."

He shrugged his shoulders against the chair. "What does it matter? You can't travel in the middle of the night. Not on these country roads."

"But I cannot stay here until morning. There will be scandal."

The corner of his mouth bent in the trace of a smile. "I don't see as we have any choice. Should have thought of that before you followed me into that tavern and drank a skin's worth o' strong scrumpy."

"I did that to save you, ingrate!" Yes, she should have given more thought to her actions earlier, but unfortunately her need to help this villainous cad was greater than her duty to propriety. So it occurred to her, in a moment of sudden horrified realization.

"I don't need saving," he replied. "Your favors are better spent on others who can't think or act for themselves. Your *friends* and tame pets, for instance." He swept a hand across his mouth as if to straighten it. "Those who hang on your every word and obey your rules."

"You will tell me where you put my boots," she hissed. "This is not amusing in the slightest."

His hand dropped to his knee, and he stretched slowly in a casual, lounging pose. "Seems damnably droll to me, my lady, that you—always so in control—should forget yourself over the scrumpy."

She dare not ask him what she'd said under the influence of that foul drink. Instead, Mercy quickly surveyed the candlelit farmhouse. "Give me my boots."

"I don't know where they are. Wife."

Exasperated, she looked down at his feet. "Very well then. I'll take *your* boots." But as she made a lunge, he sprang out of the chair, grabbing her before she stumbled sideways into the fire.

"I told you, there's no point putting boots on your feet, because you can't leave. Not now. Not until it's light out." His fingers were tight around her arms as he held her close. "Don't make me take more drastic measures to keep you here, Bossy-Buttercup."

Her heart's rhythm echoed too loudly in her ears. Although she was dressed, her shoeless state seemed… naughty in his presence. Some of her curls had come loose, her hairpins lost as she slumbered on his bed. In her peripheral vision, one strawberry curl unraveled against her cheek.

And Rafe's stormy gaze followed its progress down the side of her neck, all the way to her shoulder. "It's rare to see you so undone."

She thought of the last time she'd been "undone" in his presence. In a small bedchamber, under the wind-pummeled slate roof of an old inn, on their wedding night. Just before her brother found them and rescued her.

"Pity," he said quietly.

Did his thoughts wander along the same dangerous path? He did not let go of her arms. In fact, his fingers tightened further, holding her with a degree of possessiveness that seemed more than improper. Frankly wicked.

Mercy swallowed hard. "Molly will return." A reminder for them both.

Her face was reflected in his warm irises and those widened, velvety pupils. It was so unfair for a man to have eyes like his. Or lips like his. Or any part...

"You can't kiss me again," she said.

"I wasn't planning to."

"Indeed you were."

"Was not."

"Liar!"

"I never plan." He raised his right hand to her chin and ran his thumb along her lips. "You know how reckless I am. If I wanted to kiss you, I would, whenever the feeling came upon me."

Her lips tingled from the contact of his broad thumb. "Without permission?"

"Permission? I am not your servant. I am your husband."

"For the love of all that's holy..."

"I'm glad you mentioned that. We said our vows. Before God."

"That marriage," she replied tightly, "was void, as you well know. I shall run out of breath from telling you."

"Promise?" He chuckled.

Exasperated, she pushed with her palms flat to his chest, trying to make a more proper distance between them.

"If you want me to kiss you," he remarked as he

watched her struggle fruitlessly against his strong arms, "you only have to ask."

"So I have to ask, but you don't?" Mercy frowned. That didn't come out quite the way she meant it. "Kindly remove your filthy hands from my person, before they spoil my gown."

He finally released her and fell back into his chair.

She waited a moment and then tried again. "May I have my boots?"

"No," he growled. "You'll stay here until it's light. Have you ever tried driving through the night out here in the country?"

It was not a prospect she relished, but some attempt had to be made to avoid scandal. "I could take a lantern."

"Haven't got one to spare."

That, she knew, was a rotten lie. What farmer wouldn't have a spare lantern? More than one, in all likelihood. But the horses could stumble, fall lame when she was halfway to Morecroft. What would become of her then?

"Go back to bed," he grumbled, sour, staring at the fire.

How could she? Too many thoughts spun inside her head, and she might as well try to sleep in the midst of a barn dance. "Perhaps I can help you write your letter to Molly?" she offered hopefully, rubbing her arms where he'd held her so tightly moments before. A letter to Molly would give her mind something else to dwell upon. His too.

He shrugged one shoulder in that familiar lackadaisical gesture, his gaze on the hearth.

Mercy looked around for a writing box. When

she searched the dresser, she found again the velvet purse. She checked over her shoulder and saw he was still absorbed in watching his fire, so she slipped her finger through the silk ribbon drawstring of the coin purse and lifted it. Time to have a little fun with Master Hartley.

"Your mistress must be a wealthy lady. Although *lady*, perhaps, is not the right word."

That got his attention. "What are you babbling on about now?"

She strolled to where he sat, swinging the purse on her finger. "What is her name?"

He glared at the purse and then at her. "Why would I tell you, Bossy-Drawers?"

"You need not worry. It is doubtful a woman like that would move in the same circles as I."

"A woman like what?"

She spun the purse in a wheel around her finger. "A trollop."

"She's no trollop." He frowned angrily and sat up, reaching for the purse, but she put it behind her back. "She's a fine lady. With a heart, unlike you."

"How did you meet her?"

He would not reply.

"I am not naive, Hartley. I know most men have mistresses, so there is no need for this secrecy. Where did you meet her?"

He turned away to study the fire again. "I performed a service for her."

"I can imagine."

"Can you?" He shot her a dark look from the corner of his eye. "I doubt it."

Mercy walked around his chair, playing with the purse again. "Tell me what she looks like. Is she very beautiful? Is she slender? Plump? Blonde? Brunette?" She chuckled. "Or is she silver-haired?"

"Why? So you can compare yourself to her?"

"Tell me." She was amused to find him so tight-lipped. If she did not know all about Lady Blunt and that their relationship was completely innocent, she supposed she might indeed have felt more than a twinge of jealousy. Entitled to it or not.

"You are most fond of her, I see," she teased.

He would not answer, but pinched his lips tightly together.

"How often did you meet her?"

"Often enough."

"You do not care to marry her? Or perhaps she is not free to marry?"

She saw his jaw twitch where he ground his teeth. "Marriage is out of the question between us. The arrangement we had suited us both." He leaned back, folding his arms.

"And she gave you gifts." Mercy held up the purse again, dangling it from her finger. "You must have been *very* good company."

He sprang out of his chair and snatched the purse away from her. "Only folk like you think it's all about the coin."

"What was it about, then?"

"Friendship," he snarled as he dropped to his chair again and held the purse in his fist. "Kindness and... conversation." Rafe shifted in his chair and grumpily stared at the hearth. "And yes, she's very beautiful and obliging and was appreciative of what I had to give her, unlike some wenches. So now you know."

"Indeed." Mercy turned away to hide another smile and resumed her search for the writing box, but the beat of her heart bumped along an uneven lane and made it difficult to focus on the task. So he had thought of her as a kind friend—had genuinely liked her. How shocked he would be to learn the truth about his benefactress.

"I will pay her back, every shilling she gave me."

"Does she expect you to?"

"I told her I will, and I keep my promises." He sniffed. "Unlike you."

"Me?"

"You made a promise to me once," he reminded her, stern.

Mercy resumed her search for writing materials. "I was seventeen," she murmured.

"That's no excuse. Seventeen is not a child. You were a woman already, and you knew what you wanted then."

"You tricked me," she declared. "I was an innocent."

"Innocent?" He chortled.

In a huff, she continued her search for paper, and eventually, with no guidance from him, she found some sheets inside a ledger of accounts. A pot of ink and a pen were both located in a dresser drawer. She set these items on a small table by the fire and brought over a chair to sit across from the surly, silent young man.

"Shall I write to Molly, or will you?"

At first she thought he would not answer, but he sat

up, tucked his feet under the chair, and snatched the pen from her fingers. "I'll write. You tell me what to say. Surely, you'll like that."

"I can give you some ideas of proper phrasing," she replied. "But I will not put words in your mouth. Any woman will know if the sentiment expressed is false. You tell me what you would like to say, and I can advise you on the placement of the words."

"In a straight line," he muttered. "I think I know that much." He dipped his pen in the ink and then paused, ready to make the first mark. "So?"

"Well, what do you want to say to her? The first thing you want her to know."

Rafe stared at the paper for a long moment. Finally he put down his pen and relaxed in his chair, leaning back out of the fire's glow so only wisps of light traced his expression.

"Perhaps a man is better off proving his love with actions than with words," he said. "I know my words have often failed me."

"But words, once written, are permanent testimony." Mercy picked up his pen and ran her fingers along the goose feather. "The written word is used to record facts. Actions can be forgotten if they are not written down. As a student of the law, you should know that."

He snorted. "Trust you to compare a love letter to a legal notice. I suppose in your life 'tis one and the same. All the points of agreement written down, along with the penalties for failure to comply. Neatly signed by both parties."

"There is no occasion to mock me. I'm trying to help."

"I wonder, my lady, if you even know what love is."

"Of course I know."

"How does it feel, then?" Leaning forward, he stuck out his jaw, a readiness to challenge visible in the very square set of his shoulders.

"Why ask *me*?"

"You mean to say there is something you don't know?" He laughed scornfully. "An answer you don't have? Ah, but people like you don't have feelings. Of course I knew that. If your heart is a fortress of ice that has never been breached, how can you advise me, or anyone, in the matter of love?"

"I do not care to discuss my feelings. It seems you forget we are talking of Molly."

He was silent, very still.

"I am trying to help you." She wanted him happy and settled. Seeing him sad and alone was very hard. Even if it were true—as her brother said—that there were some things in this world she could not fix, she would not let Rafe be one of them.

"But you insist none of this is your fault."

She sighed and shook her aching head gently. "Perhaps we are all a little to blame in our own way. Even Molly, because she did not share her dreams with you. But does it matter where the fault lies? There is little good to come from pointing an accusing finger. Write in a calm temper. I know too well how brusque you can be." A university education had not filed down his rough edges.

Mercy couldn't see his eyes. The top half of his face was in shadow still, but she knew he stared; she felt the intensity of his searching gaze. "Go to bed," he muttered. "I'll write my letter. Don't you worry. I'll manage without fancy words and your advice, even if Molly has formed a taste for finer things and a disdain for my plain manners."

There seemed no other choice now. Her head still ached, and her feet were freezing. "Will you sleep there, in that chair? It cannot be very comfortable."

He leaned forward into the light, and those thick, dark eyelashes lifted as he perused her face. "I've slept in worse places, Buttercup. Now take your cold feet and your precious orange gown upstairs out of my sight."

Mercy backed away toward the stairs, informing him proudly that it was not orange. "It's 'Mystery of the Orient.'"

"I stand corrected, rebuked, and chastened." He grinned slowly, and firelight caressed the side of his face. "Get up those stairs, Buttercup, my patience is far from infinite."

Well, she knew that already.

Hovering on one foot, then the other, she looked at Rafe sprawled in that chair beside his fire and felt a hollow ache in her stomach. He was more out of that chair than in, being too large for it. But somehow his size made him seem more sad and alone. And tempting. No one ever had this effect on her, making her forget the things that should be important.

"If you're sure," she murmured, her tongue suddenly too thick for her mouth. "If you don't need your own bed."

He scratched his unshaven chin. "It's not as big as the one you're used to, I daresay."

"It's very comfortable."

"Not as comfortable as it could be. It's hard. Very…hard."

She watched his fingertips trail slowly over the dark stubble on his cheek. "I don't mind," she said. "A firm bed is often better."

"I like something soft in mine." Swift blue darts of fire shot from his eyes and arced across the distance between them.

Mercy swallowed, reaching behind her for the newel post. "Oh."

"Yielding under me," he added quietly, unblinking.

"That's…nice."

"It would be. Very."

A coal fell from the fire and onto the hearthstones. It woke Mercy from her trance, and she hurried up the stairs without another word.

Reaching his bed, she fell face-first upon it and inhaled a deep, hearty breath of his manly scent where it clung to the quilted cover. It was a good thing, she thought then, that he had Molly to wait for and she had the viscount. Without those barriers, who knew what might have happened that night on a foolish whim they would later regret? She snuggled against his bolster, arms tucked around it. He had no idea how much unrequited passion she held stifled in her own soul.

But he liked her gown, she thought sleepily, remembering the way he'd looked her up and down, his gaze trailing over her like warm, wanton fingertips. He approved her gown. She'd only ever been looked at like that once before. By him. On their aborted wedding night, when she wasn't wearing anything but a corset and chemise.

That, of course, had been her most impulsive, disorganized flight ever. Veteran of several escapes from her elder brother's lackadaisical caretaking, she'd never previously failed to pack all the right clothes and accessories for adventure. It was her belief that one should always be well shod and fashionable, no matter what the occasion. But at seventeen, embarking on a spontaneous, midnight elopement with Rafe, she'd left behind her best lace nightgown. Handmade Alençon lace too. When the item was discovered missing from the neatly folded clothes in her trunk, she'd exclaimed in distress at her absence of mind, but Rafe had merely laughed. He'd asserted, with a cheery wink, that she had no need of it on that night. He would keep her warm enough.

But it was not fear of a chill that had kept Lady Mercy, still in her corset, fretting over the contents of her traveling trunk for a quarter of an hour. It was the fact that, without the aid of a lady's maid when she packed her trunk, she'd forgotten a nightgown. This was unusual for her, and therefore a bad omen. The entire order of her evening was subsequently destroyed. That, she realized now, was where her courage went on that fateful night.

"Come to bed." The young man's blue eyes, so startling and heated, had watched her from beneath a coal-black fringe of hair. "If you don't come to me, I'll come and get you."

He was a very tempting, distracting fellow, and one could almost disregard the importance of proper order when he was around to dismantle everything. That, perhaps, was the trouble—the reason why she forgot

her lovely, gossamer lace nightgown. Rafe Hartley
was scrumptious enough to make a girl forget her own
mind. It didn't matter how levelheaded a person was,
if the head itself was left behind where it could be of
no use in such a time of crisis.

She couldn't understand her feelings for that young
man. Neither could she fight them.

Only the evening before their mad flight, she'd
been in London at a winter ball hosted by her brother.
Of course, the staff had their own dance on the same
night, and when Molly learned Rafe was in town with
his father, she invited him to attend. Unfortunately,
Rafe, not content with remaining below in the
servants' hall, invited himself to the ball above stairs
instead. Not that he had any intention of dancing.
He came there to cause trouble and talk Mercy into
running off with him. They'd shared their first kiss,
and the next thing she knew, they were on their way
to be married, fleeing into the chilly November night,
their laughing, excited breaths crisply outlined against
the dark sky.

But it was never consummated. Mercy, finally
assured that her absent nightgown would not be
missed, had just taken two steps toward the bed, when
the door crashed open and there stood her brother,
along with the startled innkeeper.

Just in the nick of time. She'd begun to think
she would never be rescued from Rafe Hartley. Or
from herself.

Five years later, here she was again, letting herself
fall into a scandalous situation with the same man. She
was still entangled in his life, had put herself back into

it when she dressed in the black taffeta and wrapped her face in a shroud of lace, looking to help him in some way. Needing to.

Ah, if only Molly hadn't lost her nerve, none of this would be happening, she thought peevishly. He couldn't still tempt *her* if he was safely married to another woman, could he? Perhaps Carver hadn't believed that. Perhaps he hadn't wanted Rafe to marry her lady's maid because it would make a permanent connection between them.

And perhaps she'd wanted him to marry Molly for that same reason.

She and Carver were both guilty of interfering in their own way.

Mercy couldn't be sure how long she lay there on his bed, drifting in and out of her drowsy thoughts that were not quite dreams. It was some considerable time later when she heard a loud creak outside the chamber and then the rusty complaint of old hinges. The door opened.

"I changed my mind."

Her eyes flew open. She held her breath. Had she imagined that voice?

No.

Somewhere behind her, he cleared his throat. "I'm sorry, my lady, but I need my bed after all..."

Mercy rolled over and pushed herself up on her elbows. Rafe stood in the open door of the bedchamber, a mere shadow, his features hidden.

"And the woman in it," he added.

"We can't," she protested feebly, heart drumming hard in her ears.

"I've been told there's no such word."

"Then we musn't." But she was losing the breath to speak. And the will to argue. "We shouldn't."

"I don't care about shouldn't." He stepped into the chamber and closed the door behind him, masterful and arrogant. "You came here to put things right. So put them right. Give me what you denied me five years ago."

"But I...we..."

"Unfinished business, my lady. You owe me."

Chapter 9

HE'D TRIED, HADN'T HE? THE TEMPTATION SHE OFFERED, putting herself in his path again, was more than any flesh-and-blood man could withstand. One knee on the bed, he stretched slowly over her form as she lay propped up on her elbows. If she meant to run away again, now would be the time to do it.

But she stayed. Didn't move an inch.

Just as well, because he had a feeling he couldn't let his slippery catch off the hook this time.

He knew what he was doing when he carried her inside his farmhouse that evening, and when he hid her boots so she couldn't leave. He'd told himself it was for her own benefit, but he wasn't a good liar.

Strips of silver moonlight trickled in through the leaded windows, casting a pattern of distorted diamond shadows across the bed and her sprawling form. She half lowered her lashes, and her lips parted. He could hear her breath, could feel it now too as his hand swept from her waist to her bosom.

The material of her gown was warm under his palm, soft, but the flesh beneath it was firmly corseted.

How could she sleep in that discomfort? Answer—she simply couldn't. Good thing he was there to help the ice queen out of it, then.

His lips caressed hers slowly, parting them. He expected a word of protest, another reminder about Molly, but there was nothing, just a gentle yielding of that sweet-tasting mouth as she sank down on her back and his body covered hers, his hand on her breast, his fingertips trailing over the swell of flesh above her bodice.

He'd waited five years for this. For her. Not that there hadn't been other women, but there were none like this one, and he knew it the first time he saw her, when he was twelve. Then, looking for some way to get the strange redhead's attention, he'd lobbed a ball at her head and knocked her bonnet off, directly into a puddle. She promptly called him an "ignorant peasant," and thus he'd decided she wasn't worth his notice anyway. Fate had seemed determined to keep them on opposing sides of every argument from then on. Everyone thought he ought to be with Molly Robbins, until even he began to think it. Molly was a part of his world, and this woman never could be. When he was sensible, he knew that.

Tonight, he wasn't being sensible.

She wriggled under him, guiding his hands to her breasts, but their lips never broke from the kiss. It turned hungry, greedy. Her hands came up to pull on his shirt, ripping it in her haste. When he felt that eagerness, sheer pleasure raced hot through his blood. On their wedding night she was hesitant, using any excuse to delay joining him in bed. Tonight she was eager, a wildcat. He knelt astride her while he opened the fall of his breeches and she lay rumpled under him, her hair pins all lost, her clothing half-undone.

"Rafe," she murmured as her moonlit gaze followed the path of his busy fingers. "What are we doing?"

"You're putting things right, remember?" Breathless, he tugged his breeches down and then tipped forward again to slide her petticoats upward. "Making it up to me." Her fine silk drawers were soft and warm under his suddenly trembling hands. "After all this time."

He heard her sigh as his fingers touched her intimately through the slit in her drawers. "We must have lost our wits," she whispered haltingly. But even as she spoke, she moved her hands to explore. When her fingers touched his erection, it grew another inch at least. Desire lay heavy in his loins, and each gentle caress of her soft hands threatened to bring him beyond the brink.

Moonbeams were caught, trapped under her lashes, gleaming like flashes of light caught on a lazy stream.

"You *are* sober?" he asked carefully.

"I don't know," she replied on a hitch of breath. "Am I?"

He bent to kiss her lips, then her chin, then her throat. It seemed a shame to him that she worried so over her costly silk garments, when the skin beneath was far more exquisite, a material made from cream, honey, and molten gold, woven by creatures from another world. Why cover it at all? he mused. If he had his way, she would never wear another stitch of clothing. Except when he wanted the pleasure of removing it.

"Yes, I am sober," she sighed, "but we still shouldn't. Should we?"

"Oh, yes." He inhaled a deep breath of her fragrance as his mouth traveled lower, over the swell of her breasts. "We'll find our wits in the morning," he managed, hoarse. "If we want them back again." She arched, moaning softly, but not in any manner that might be mistaken for complaint. His lips sank into her sweet, delicious flesh again, sucking and nibbling gently.

It was too late for shouldn't. Clearly they both knew that.

His finger entered her slowly through the slit in her drawers, and she gasped. At the same moment, her hand closed tightly around his swollen, thickening manhood. "It is warm," she muttered, sounding surprised.

"Full of life," he agreed. His pulse quickened and seemed to start somewhere in the root of his cock, traveling all the way up his spine to thud away in his temple.

If he wasn't careful, he would spend too soon. So he drew back a little and teased her with his finger, withdrawing it until she squirmed and complained. Bossy-Drawers. She was hot and moist, pushing herself into his hand. "It's awfully distracting to have you and this"—he added a second finger and moved them together, slowly, in a circular motion—"preying on a man's mind."

Her eyes widened. "Yes…I can…see…how…how it would be—"

It still wasn't enough to silence her, but *this* would be. Sliding his fingers through her dewy entrance,

Rafe sought the magical pearl that would transport her away from her doubts and fears, beyond her blessed self-control. As he worked it with just enough pressure, he kissed her again. His tongue delved deeper, digging for the capacious cries of wanton desire now blossoming inside her, seeded by his targeted caress.

Not so icy now, was she? Excitement pulsed a maddened rhythm in his heart, sent his blood quickening through his veins. He wanted her more than he'd ever wanted anything in his life. And tonight— just for tonight—she was his.

❧

"You are my bride," he whispered huskily. "Mine."

In that moment, she agreed utterly. The heat and strength of his body over hers completely swept all other considerations out of her mind. His hair smelled of wood smoke from the tavern, but underneath that it was all Rafe. The scent of masculinity. She gazed at her pale fingers in his dark, dark hair, and then looked up at the pattern of moonlight over the cracks in the low ceiling.

His tongue tasted of mint leaves, and when he broke the kiss, burying his lips in her hair, his rough cheek grazed the side of her face. She didn't mind it in the least.

"Tonight," she murmured. "This once."

"Yes."

All those quarrels had to lead somewhere. This was it. In a sense, she mused, it was inevitable that they should find themselves in bed together. Their arguments had always felt like mere preparation for the grand event. He was a whetstone for her temper, yet he sharpened other things too—something for which she had no name. Something wicked but irresistible.

Mercy could hear her own breath, gasping out with sheer need in a most unladylike fashion. It was almost a laugh. Joy and the excitement of adventure swept through her. She thought suddenly of squeamish Miss Julia Gibson cringing in fear at the idea of a man's "appendage."

Rafe must have felt her trembling, and a quick check of her expression revealed the cause. "Think this is funny, woman?" he grunted, licking the side of her neck.

She arched like a contented cat, and more curls dripped loose down her cheek. "Yes. I am consumed with the hilarity." Consumed with him, she thought, as those rapid tingling waves still lapped through her, tickling in every corner, every nook and cranny. Especially the most intimate places. With only his fingers, he'd taken her up into the clouds to the gates of heaven. What could he possibly do next?

He kissed the inside of her wrist. "Glad to amuse."

Was it like this for other couples, she wondered, this sense of delicious anticipation and wanton curiosity?

Rafe stripped off his own clothes with alacrity, tossing his buckskin breeches aside as if they were on fire. Moonlight honored his fine form, highlighting those broad shoulders, dripping down over the hard planes of his chest, and caressing his strong, powerful thighs. And there was that very proud cockerel, raised up, thick and tall. Below that, if her eyes did not deceive, were two plump goose eggs. She stared. Her pulse fluttered.

"Good Lord," she exclaimed.

"Something amiss, m'lady?" He waited with his knuckles resting on his hips.

"I very much doubt it. Everything seems to be in its place."

"Then we may proceed?"

Mercy turned so he could struggle with her corset laces. "Hurry!" she demanded as she looked over her shoulder. Her gaze still traveled hungrily over his nakedness, absorbing every inch now on display before her. And growing.

It was his turn to chuckle. "Patience, Bossy-Drawers."

Before she was entirely free of the corset, Mercy grabbed his hand and pulled him down onto the bed beside her.

"You're eager, m'lady wife," he whispered, grinning, moonlight shining on his teeth.

Eager was not quite the word for it. Yearning might have been more accurate. Wriggling out of the last bindings, she threw herself atop his supine form and felt his large hands close over her buttocks, his fingers spread, squeezing. The need inside her grew in leaps and bounds. Her core was overheated, and she was dripping with molten lust. His cock lay hard between them, ready to claim her maidenhead. "If we only have one night, best get on with it, country boy."

"As you wish, m'lady," he purred, reminding her of a tiger at the zoo. She felt the rumbling tremors through his body as he lay beneath her. He slid her up his chest until her breasts came level with his mouth. "But I don't want to rush my prize."

Mercy gasped as his lips closed around her nipple and a rush of white-hot desire flooded from that sensitive spot, down through her belly, to the apex of her thighs. She was still afire there from his previous attentions to that hidden core, and she suspected it would take no more than one thrust of his splendid organ to make those flames pulse high and wild again. With his hands on her bare bottom, his fingers digging into her skin, she was lost to the wickedest of unladylike needs. And she wasn't sure she could wait to have every one of them fulfilled. Loose strands of hair already stuck to her neck as the heat of passion glazed her skin with a thin layer of perspiration. She was aglow with this craving for a man who was forbidden to her.

God help her, but she cared not for the consequences. It was very freeing to feel the care and concern slip through her fingers. Perhaps she should advise Miss Julia Gibson to indulge in the occasional mug of scrumpy.

Suddenly, she laughed again; it burst out of her.

Rafe's lips left her nipple damp, swollen. "This amuses you?" He sounded bewildered. "Not quite the effect I hoped for."

"No." She shook her head violently, and more loosened locks dripped to her shoulders. "It's just that..." How could she explain? At this moment of her undoing, she'd thought, most strangely, of Julia Gibson's fearful face, covered in meringue, as the girl whimpered unhappily about a bride's fate on her wedding night. If Miss Gibson saw her now, she would surely faint into her teacup. As would anyone who knew Mercy Danforthe, painfully prim and proper on the outside.

She pictured a series of Hogarth-type sketches detailing this amorous escapade. *The Wanton's Progress. Lady Mercy Danforthe, Careening Fearlessly Toward Her Ruination.*

"Rafe! Rafe!"

That was not her voice.

He stilled, hands cupped around her bottom, his face nuzzling her breasts, the crest of his manhood pressing at her entrance.

"Rafe!" Outside, in the yard, his father knocked loudly at the front door.

Mercy's laughter faded.

"Oh, tell him I'm not here," she whispered as she sank down and her lips touched his rough, warm cheek. "Tell him I died. Anything."

But she knew it was too late. Once again, fate intervened.

❧

Rafe threw more coal on the smoldering, neglected fire, avoiding his father's searching perusal for as long as possible. "She'll be down momentarily. It seems she was fast asleep."

"This could put Lady Mercy in a compromising position. Did you have no thought of her reputation?"

"But it was late," he snapped, frustrated beyond measure. "I meant only to save her from riding back to Morecroft in the dark, in her state."

"Her state?"

Rafe thought quickly. "She was unwell." He finally looked at his father and saw concern. Those eyes—which Rafe had been told were very like his own—darkened to a navy blue.

"She was not ill when she left Morecroft yesterday morning." Although it wasn't said, Rafe could almost hear the accusation: *What have you done to her, boy?*

"Must be something she ate," he muttered.

Rafe glanced through his window and saw streaks of pale dawn breaking across the sky already. He'd lost track of time with dire consequences. "Why could you not have brought her back yourself?" his father demanded.

Because she's my wife, and I want her to stay. But of course, he could say nothing. "Well?" His father's booming, angry voice finally brought Mercy down to join them. She skipped down the stairs in her stockinged feet, feigning innocence, her gown refastened, her hairpins all in their place—or so it seemed at brief glance.

She greeted his father with a bold smile and a bold lie. "I was taken dreadfully ill, and I'm afraid I was forced to impose on Rafe's hospitality. It came upon me quite suddenly, but it's gone now." She beamed, her face gleaming with confidence, far too healthy for a young woman recently seized by a mysterious, unnamed ailment.

But she was poised in the face of calamity; Rafe had to give her that much praise. A woman familiar with deception, perhaps. He jabbed at the fire with a poker and ashes fell to the hearth. Like pieces of his heart. Why did he put himself through the agony with her again, when he knew the outcome would be the same? She'd claim it was all his fault, and then she'd leave.

You are so far beneath me, she'd reminded him yesterday.

She did not fit in his world, nor he in hers. Still, the churning heaviness of thwarted desire remained.

Why had she burst into laughter in bed? Was this hapless peasant's lust for her ladyship so damned amusing?

"My wife was most distraught, Lady Mercy, when you did not return before dark," his father said. "I'm sure Peter from Merryweather's might have been dispatched to Morecroft with a message, as he is whenever a doctor is needed or there is some emergency."

"Oh, please don't blame Rafe, Mr. Hartley. I would not let him disturb anyone. It was my idea entirely." She laughed lightly.

Rafe didn't realize he was cracking his knuckles until his father looked at his hands and scowled. "We'd best make haste, Lady Mercy, and get you back to Morecroft before the more curious residents of the village are up and about. I should hate for anyone to see you in the same dress you wore yesterday."

Rafe hadn't thought of that. Of course, he wasn't thinking of anything much beyond his base needs that night. He cast her a quick, sideways glance and saw her flush. Unfortunately, that bright orange gown couldn't easily be forgotten. His thoughts traveled swiftly to the tavern and all the folk who'd seen her there with him.

His father spoke firmly. "My wife will be relieved to know you're safe. I shouldn't like her to worry longer than she has already."

Looking slightly crestfallen, but bearing his father's disdain bravely, Mercy slipped into her spencer and tied the ribbons of her bonnet under her chin. She whispered to Rafe, "My boots?"

If his father's eyes were not ~~boring holes in the back~~ of his scalp, Rafe would have pretended he forgot where he put them. Then she'd have to stay a few more minutes. But their moment was gone. Other people intruded. He strode over to the dresser and, as if it was the most natural place in the world to keep shoes, reached up onto the top shelf, lifted down a flour jar, and took out her boots. He went through the motions mechanically. No one said a word.

Mercy quickly put them on, making no comment about the broken lace. There was a brief moment when her gaze caught on his, but he couldn't read her thoughts. Suddenly she spied the folded sheet of paper on his mantel, where he'd set it last night before he went upstairs. Now, before he could stop her, she reached for it. Although there was no address written on it, she assumed it was the letter they'd discussed.

"I'll see this gets to Molly with the next post," she told him softly. "I'm glad you wrote to her. I'm sure she'll come back as soon as she reads this."

He grabbed a corner of the folded note. "No. It's not…"

She held fast to it, her thumb less than an inch from his. "We both know it's for the best," she whispered. "*This* cannot be." Apparently she was resolved to bring Molly back to him, and their impassioned encounter on his bed was to be ignored, forgotten, labeled another regrettable mistake.

Glaring at her, he let go of the folded note. If that's the way she wanted it, so be it. He'd tried to thaw her out before and ended up with frostbite, hadn't he?

"It is the least I can do to help." She closed the

small square of paper in her gloved hand, pulled the half veil of lace over her eyes, and swept out. When she passed through his door, it felt colder and darker in the house, as if the fire had gone out. He heard the coachman opening the carriage door and then her muted thanks as she stepped up.

Poised with one hand on the door, his father spoke softly, discreetly. "I trust you have not forgotten you are a gentleman's son."

Rafe wanted to remind his father of a certain other illicit coupling between classes that once took place and resulted not only in his birth, but his mother's young death. His father was certainly not without sin. Instead, he replied, "She remains intact."

This response, although forthright and direct, clearly did not wholly satisfy his father, but there was no time to continue the conversation beyond a few more terse words. "Lady Mercy has a fiancé. You knew this, I assume?"

A cold draft blew in through the door his father held ajar, and Rafe's shoulders stiffened against the chill. "She didn't mention it." Damned Brat.

Slowly his father nodded and then replaced his hat. "Now you know. Perhaps you should follow Molly to London and persuade her to return with you."

"I don't know about that," Rafe replied. He shook his head, hands on his hips. "I have my pride to consider. You're always telling me I'm a Hartley and should act like one. Would a Hartley charge after a woman who left him at the altar?"

Lines deepened in his father's brow. "There are a great many things a Hartley would not do, but that doesn't appear to trouble you unduly. Still, you wrote to Miss Robbins at least. That is a start."

Two seconds later, Rafe was alone again.

But he had not written to Molly. Last night he wasn't thinking of Molly Robbins at all, because he understood now that what she did on their wedding day was merely something he had not possessed the courage to do himself.

No, there was another woman on his mind. Another wife.

She thought him so far beneath her, yet on that bed upstairs there was no inequality. For once, they were on the same plane.

Now she'd left again. She had a fiancé, which she conveniently forgot to mention, and she had a full life, many worlds removed from his, carefully run by those rules of which she was so fond. Rules he would never follow.

Damn her then, he thought crossly. Let her think that note was for Molly. Let her send it.

He was the lady's fool, making her laugh. Falling for her again the moment she let down one inch of her guard.

Later, when he went upstairs, he discovered she'd left her corset behind. Must have been unable to tie the laces herself, of course. He lifted it to his face and inhaled her scent. Ah, he could lie with it crushed beneath him; he could imagine it was her; he could treat it in an ungentlemanly way and get some relief.

At least he had a part of her, he mused. But, as he soon found, that was worse than having nothing. Expending his excess vigor on whalebone and linen was like trying to scratch an itch with a feather.

Chapter 10

MR. JAMES HARTLEY ESCORTED HER BACK TO Morecroft in his carriage, and a groom drove the curricle behind. They were almost clear of the village and in safer territory when they passed Mrs. Flick, the most notorious gossip in Sydney Dovedale, out for one of her notorious "early morning constitutionals," which was really just an excuse for her to spy on the comings and goings of her neighbors. The old lady hobbled onto the verge as they passed rapidly along the lane. She stared hard through her spectacles at the flying carriage, and there was no doubt she observed the little curricle following along in their wake.

"Well, that's put a cat among the pigeons," Rafe's father exclaimed under a rush of terse breath. "The world's oldest surviving gossip will soon get her teeth—or rather her gums—into this item of news." He smirked coldly through the window on his side of the carriage. Although his face was turned away from her, Mercy caught the steely chill of his expression reflected in the glass.

"You mustn't blame Rafe, Mr. Hartley."

"Mustn't I?"

"No. It was entirely my doing." Father and son clearly had a strained relationship, and she would hate to be the cause of any further problem. Someone ought to step in and put the two obstinate men to rights. They had already missed out on many years they might have known together. Would they let their pride—for they were really far more similar in character than either believed—get in the way of a future relationship? "Your son is really a good man, sir. He is a little wild and rebellious, but he means no harm, and he is trying to settle down. I...I believe he is."

James Hartley scowled at her floury boots. Nothing about her person was perhaps more suspect this morning than the state of her boots. She might have got away with her bold bluster, but there was really no excuse for Rafe putting her boots in the flour jar other than to hide them and keep them out of her reach. Explaining why he thought that necessary would require a confession she was not prepared to give. Even as a woman with a measure of independence, it would not be easy to admit she'd imbibed too much cider and become so wayward and insensible that Rafe Hartley took those extreme measures for her safety.

Mercy fiddled with the buttons on her gloves. Oh dear, she'd really made a mess of things, and that was not like her at all. Now she was on the verge of becoming a drunk *and* a harlot. "I meant to put everything straight," she mumbled.

"That boy cannot stay away from trouble. I would have thought, at his age——"

"But it was my idea not to send anyone to

Morecroft, Mr. Hartley. I thought if I could rest a moment I'd feel much improved and then be capable of returning in the curricle. But I fell asleep. I suppose Rafe didn't want to wake me."

Yes, it was a reasonable excuse, but it still did not explain the boots in the flour jar.

Thanks to his seductive qualities and a certain weakness in her own character, she was a few silk petticoats removed from a gin-shop hussy.

On their return, Mrs. Hartley was very solicitous for her health after yesterday's sudden "illness." The ancient Lady Ursula insisted it was something in the air.

"Spring is a dreadful season for spores, my dear," she explained as they sat down to breakfast. "The less one goes out and allows oneself to be bombarded by them, the better, and sunlight is very bad for the complexion."

"I fear you are right, Lady Ursula. I am quite freckled enough already."

"I shall lend you Dr. Swithun's Elixir. You will find it quite beneficial." The old lady glared at her grandson's wife. "Although some creatures in this house stubbornly refuse to recognize the benefits."

"The best thing for a complexion," Mrs. Hartley assured Mercy with a knowing smile, "is love. I daresay you're missing your viscount."

Mercy quietly nibbled her toast, but she had no appetite and merely went through the motions. She could think only of her secret former husband eating his breakfast alone at the farmhouse. By now they could have been lovers. They could have been eating breakfast together beside his fire.

Not once had she thought about a nightgown, she

realized. Neither had she thought of the betrayal they committed—to Molly and Viscount Grey. She had not cared about anything except being in his arms.

❦

Seated at the dressing table in her room, Mercy still felt his kisses on the pulse at the side of her neck, sometimes fluttering like butterfly wings, other times more insistent. Again she remembered the sweet friction of his rough cheek against her soft skin, the unique sensation of his tongue lapping over her nipple. And savage, unfulfilled lust—until then something she'd assumed to be entirely the province of men—burned through her like a flaming arrowhead. Nothing could extinguish it.

Mercy touched her cheek and found it quite warm, although she was not blushing despite the winding path of her thoughts.

It was so very wrong to let these ideas cut their way through her mind like a scythe through wheat. She should be on her way back to London by now, awaiting Grey's return, making her wedding plans. Instead, she sat there, daydreaming in her chemise and drawers.

If only Rafe could be kept like a special trinket in a secret treasure box. She shook her head, amused, imagining his face if she ever suggested he submit to being a kept man.

Solemn again, Mercy rested her elbows on the dresser and thoughtfully traced her lips with her warm fingertips. It was almost a pity, she mused, that his father came when he did. By now she would have known what it was like to be a complete woman.

Rafe was eager to make her one. His desire was rough, primitive even. He wanted to claim her, like a prize of war. Why? To get his vengeance on her brother, perhaps? To get his vengeance on her?

You owe me, he'd said.

A quick shiver lapped over her skin, as if a draft found its way into her bedchamber. Her nipples hardened under her lacy chemise when she thought of his rough hands on her body, caressing her so intimately, taking what he wanted and giving at the same time. Pleasure of a kind she'd never known.

Oh…another shiver rippled over her skin, and her lips parted against her hand so she could feel what Rafe must have when he kissed her. She'd touched the tip of her tongue to her fingers and sighed. No, she was not confused, even if he was. She'd had all her senses about her when they lay together on his bed. In fact, she'd become aware of some senses she never knew she possessed until then.

Glancing at her bedchamber door, she checked that the key was turned in the lock. Then she slid her hand down her stomach to the juncture of her thighs. She closed her eyes. It was not the same as when Rafe touched her, but it felt very pleasing. Closing her legs tightly on her stroking fingers, she bit her lip and swallowed a moan of part excitement, part despair. She placed her other hand on her breast and cupped it though the soft lace of her chemise, picturing Rafe's lips on her nipple again. The fire he'd begun in her loins, never fully smothered, quickly gained strength, heat, and density again. She gasped at the trickle of dew against her fingertips, where she blossomed and throbbed with unremitting tension. Mercy rubbed harder, biting her lip to keep from crying out.

At the moment of her peak, she opened her eyes to witness the wanton hussy she'd become. Her curls—sporting a new luster this morning—fell loose over her shoulders, her lips looked very dark and full, and her brown nipples pricked through the delicate, ivory lace with unabashed impertinence.

Nothing about her expression looked sorry, she realized. If anything, the woman staring back at her looked relaxed, content as a cream-thieving cat. An entire basket of naughty kittens, in fact.

Perhaps, as Lady Ursula said, it was all the fault of fertile spring air—pollen and spores invading her body, making her flustered.

She mouthed at her reflection in the mirror, "Do pull your garters up, woman."

It simply wouldn't do to let herself lose control this way. Rafe Hartley was a mischievous, lusty young man who took ungentlemanly delight in unsettling her nerves. She should put him out of her mind at once. Never again could she let him kiss her. Never.

There was just one more thing she must take care of before she left for London.

❧

Spring was a busy time on the farm. Rafe barely had a moment to think of anything beyond the routine of work. Each morning he rose with the dawn to go out into the fields, and at night, soon after supper, he fell asleep quickly—a blessing. When the first opportunity arose, he traveled with his cart to Morecroft and called upon Mrs. Pyke at the Red Lion, anxious to make sure she was comfortable there. It was his hope that Pyke would soon show his face again and relieve him of this burden, but until then, he'd promised to keep the family safe.

A bosomy woman with no refinement but a great deal of natural cunning, Mrs. Pyke had spent her blossoming spring on the stage—which was how she caught Pyke's eye—and her summer living in a style her husband could not afford. Now, having born three eternally crying children and suffered an autumn in penury, her formerly pretty face sagged like an empty wine sack. Since her life with Pyke had not turned out at all the way she expected—or her husband had promised her—Rafe supposed she was entitled to some pity, although her temperament, which was needy and querulous when not kept content, made her very trying to deal with at times. His patience was challenged when she presented him with a list of complaints about her new surroundings. The other guests at the Red Lion Inn, she said, looked down on her, and the innkeeper asked too many questions. She thought they would be better off in other, quieter lodgings, away from prying eyes.

"I'm quite sure Mr. Pyke wouldn't want us to stay 'ere. There's a vast deal o' drunken rowdiness at night, and I must lie awake wondering what might become of us in such a den of ill repute."

"I can assure you, Mrs. Pyke, it is a respectable place." Far safer than the lodgings in which her husband had previously left them, he thought.

But she was adamant that the Red Lion would not

do for them. "Truth be told, me 'ealth suffers since we came 'ere, and our littlest one 'as such a cough. I daresay an afternoon in the sea air wouldn't go amiss. Yarmouth is not far, so I 'eard."

"It is not, Mrs. Pyke, but it would be an expense for all four of you to travel there."

Her lips squeezed into a plump pout. "To be sure, I do miss my Pykey."

"Indeed. We all miss him." *And wonder where he ran off to in such haste, leaving his family to the care of another.*

"'Ere I am, all alone without 'im. Me and the little 'uns, left to manage in the cold, cruel world."

Rafe attempted to cheer her spirits. "You have me, Mrs. Pyke. You are not alone."

"I wager ol' Catchpole is fair miffed." She swung the youngest Pyke onto her hip and jiggled him so rapidly his sobs turned to hiccups, giving Rafe a brief respite from the noise. "To lose 'is best fighter and two tenants, all at the same time. Serves 'im right for being cruel to my Pykey, sendin' 'im off to the Fleet like that."

The fact that Pyke owed a vast amount of money to Catchpole, and many other tradesmen besides, made barely a dent in her awareness. Everyone was always against them, and it was never their fault. "You are my Pykey's oldest pal and particular friend," she'd said once. "Who else should stand up for us if you did not?"

And who else would pay her bills if Rafe did not? With her husband disappeared off the face of the earth, if not for Rafe's support, she and her children would have been in the gutter, begging for food.

"Mayhap you should take up fighting again, if money's short," she said with a loud, wet sniff.

"I have put that behind me, madam," he replied.

"Seems a shame to waste the talent."

"I hope I have other avenues to success."

Being a woman who looked always for the easiest, fastest route to coin, she had no comprehension of patience or the potential reward of slow toil. She screwed up her face in confusion, until a sudden thought occurred to her.

"Your pa lives here, don't 'e? A right fancy gent, so my Pykey said. Mayhap your pa can 'elp us."

Under no circumstances did he want his father meeting Mrs. Pyke. "I will see what can be arranged for your accommodations, but I'm afraid, for now, the Red Lion will have to do."

Peevish, she grumbled at the child to stop pulling her hair. "At the very least we'd be able to get out more, if I 'ad proper shoes to walk in."

He looked at her feet. Clad in a worn pair of boots, they looked perfectly normal to him. "Proper shoes?"

"These are winter boots, ain't they? I need slippers for fine weather, and wooden pattens for when it's wet and muddy. Like the other ladies I see walking about. Otherwise I stick out, don't I? Since my Pykey went off to the Fleet, I've made do with these boots, but folk 'ere will notice."

Rafe sincerely doubted it was her footwear that made his friend's wife stand out, but he did want her to blend in as much as possible. Reaching into his coat pocket, he drew out another banknote.

〜❧〜

Old Mrs. Flick wasted no time informing the general populace about Lady Mercy "sneaking" away from the village at first light in her "fancy orange frock, just as brazen as you please!"

There were also, of course, several witnesses to her presence at his side that night in Merryweather's Tavern—in the same brightly colored frock. Rafe told anyone who asked him that she was taken ill and she'd had to wait at his farm for his father to fetch her. Then he left it at that. Whether they believed him or not was up to them. As his aunt Sophie said, there was always gossip of some sort in a small village. The less kindling thrown upon it, the less stirring and poking it received, the quicker it fell to a smolder before dying away to ashes that would disperse when the next wind passed through.

His uncle suggested he find another bride quickly. "Don't wait for Moll Robbins to come back, lad. She gave you up and doesn't deserve your patience," he said as he sat in Rafe's cottage and warmed his hands at the fire.

Naturally, his father and his uncle were on opposing sides in this issue. Although never close friends, the two men had tentatively formed what his stepmother called a "laissez-faire attitude," but while each sought privately to advise Rafe, their opinions seldom coincided. Rafe's choice was never clear, for he worried about offending one or the other. The only point on which his uncle and father agreed was that he should marry. This had been their one, unequivocal, united decision. Now that Molly had run off, they privately retreated to enemy corners again on the matter of whom he should marry.

That was the good thing about his elderly bene-factress in London; she had no side to take, no bias, and thought only of him. She listened as no one else ever did and encouraged him to do what was best for himself, with no concern beyond that.

"Oh, I'm not waiting for Molly Robbins," he assured his uncle.

"Good lad. Move on and look ahead, not back."

Leaving his uncle by the fire, Rafe stepped down into the scullery to wash his hands and forearms. He wondered whether Mercy would open that note she took from his mantel, for he'd be surprised if her boundless curiosity would let her send it off to Molly unread.

His uncle shouted from the other room, "There's many a local girl trying to catch your eye."

But he wasn't interested in them. He'd spoken to Mercy about two dairymaids only to get some reaction from her. It worked too, he thought darkly. It caused her to ride by Merryweather's and see what he was up to. Even made her follow him inside the place, endan-gering the reputation in which she took such pride.

"Your aunt suggested you might have some thought of Lady Mercy Danforthe," his uncle said suddenly, startling him out of his reverie. "I told her she was a fool to imagine that."

"She's engaged," Rafe muttered glumly as he stared at his hands in the water and watched the grime of another day in the fields float in clouds to the surface.

"So I hear. Some viscount from Surrey."

His heart suffered a hiccup. How could she kiss him like that and be engaged to another? But was the fault not with him too? He was supposed to have married Molly Robbins a few days ago, and here he was dwelling on the lips of another woman, wishing they were his to play with just a while longer. Of course he wasn't perfect—never claimed to be. He had his faults, his weaknesses. Mercy Danforthe, he realized now, was one of them.

"I told your aunt," his uncle continued, "our Rafe would never take a fool's fancy for a troublesome petticoat like the Danforthe girl."

Rafe shook his head, winced, and reached for a dry rag. Odd that his uncle should say something like that, when he'd pursued and won a woman from a higher class, a wife the rules of Society told him he couldn't have. Perhaps it ran in their blood, to reach for something forbidden. Did his uncle regret it? Not likely. He had a fine family now—one still growing—and Rafe occasionally knew envy when he saw his aunt and uncle laughing together, both so transparently happy it made his teeth grind.

He recalled suddenly how he and Molly had walked home from church one Sunday, following his aunt and uncle, observing the older couple holding hands and laughing together like young lovers.

"Not every wedded couple can be as fortunate as them," Molly had murmured wistfully.

At the time, Rafe simply took it as a passing comment on a cool Sunday afternoon, and he was more concerned with making sure she didn't walk in a puddle than he was listening to her conversation.

Now he realized what she'd tried to say.

Yes, he was jealous too when he watched them

together; today he could acknowledge the emotion. His aunt and uncle were never very circumspect when it came to showing their devotion to each other. As a boy, it had made Rafe groan with embarrassment. As a man, if he was in a good mood, it amused him; if he was in a bad mood, their displays of affection annoyed him. He'd never paused to examine the reasons why. Until today.

He was lonely. He wanted a companion, his own family. For years he'd thought that was something he'd never have, wasn't even sure he wanted it. Now he knew he did. Very much.

Rafe had spent a childhood moving from place to place, never quite belonging. His uncle had done the best he could, but he was absent for most of Rafe's early years, trying to earn a living, going into the army and forced to leave his little nephew in the care of others. Then, after his uncle married and settled there in Sydney Dovedale, he brought Rafe to live with his new family. It took a while to adjust, much as it would for a stray tomcat to become a domesticated pet. A few years later came the discovery of his real father—James Hartley. So yes, there had been a great many changes in his life, a vast sea of ups and downs that sometimes threatened to swamp his little boat completely. But he rowed on. Did his best. Rafe knew he was still finding his way, his place. One day he hoped to reach smooth, tranquil waters so he might unwind his sails and take a break from rowing.

He liked it here in Sydney Dovedale, and he'd even become a shareholder in the Morecroft and Norwich Bank. He knew he could settle here. All he missed was a woman at his side.

Molly could have provided the steadiness his boat required. Mercy Danforthe would probably overturn it completely.

Better remember that and not think of her again.

Even if she would look good wet all over. Perhaps begging for his clemency and grateful to him for saving her from drowning.

He smiled as the pleasant fiction grew in his mind. She would offer him her kisses without complaining later, without accusing him of stealing them. Cupping his palms through the basin of water, he imagined her breasts in his hands, her soft clean flesh delicately scented, his for the tasting.

Heavy hooves clattered across the yard and shattered that glorious fantasy, and likewise his mood. Stepping out of the scullery, he saw Tom Ridge, the blacksmith's son, lumbering back and forth in the light of the open doorway.

His uncle greeted the new arrival. "Mornin', Tom."

The tall fellow didn't come in but hovered nervously, gesturing that Rafe should come outside.

What was it now, he wondered, another rumor?

He followed Tom into the yard.

"I'm to give this back to ye," the big man muttered, reaching inside his old, dusty coat. A gleam of gold shone through his grimy fingers, and Rafe glanced hastily over his shoulder to make certain his uncle was still indoors.

"But you won it—"

"It were wrong o' me to take advantage when you were so lovelorn." Tom gave a wink and a gap-toothed grin. "This feller's conscience won't allow 'im to keep it."

Assuming his fiercest scowl, Rafe snatched his pocket watch from the other man's fist. "I was not lovelorn." He'd known Tom for enough years now to know the man had very few scruples that troubled him.

Tom chuckled saucily, replaced his cap, and mounted his horse. "I 'ope, for your sakes, Rafe, young Moll comes back soon. Shouldn't like you to get into worse trouble."

He had a sense they were talking of more than his watch.

"She'd be none too 'appy to find what you been up to while she was gone, eh?"

"I'll thank you to let me worry about Molly Robbins."

Tom merely laughed as his carthorse set off for the gate in a swaying amble.

Rafe looked down at his watch, relieved to have it back again. Its absence would have taken some awkward explaining to his father. But why would a grumpy fellow like Tom Ridge bring it back to him? Any concern about Molly Robbins, spouted from a mouth unaccustomed to kind words, was unconvincing to say the least.

His uncle came out into the yard. "Well, I'd best go home and make sure Sophie isn't doing too much again. Just wanted to give you a little nudge, my boy. No point sitting about waiting for that girl to come back. Plenty more ripe berries in the orchard."

"How is Aunt Sophie?"

"Tired. But she will not listen to me and keep her feet up more often."

Rafe nodded. "Stubborn creatures, women."

"Aye. But the world would be a much duller place without them in it to quarrel with us. I had my pick of village girls back in my day, young Rafe, but I had eyes only for my Sophie. She didn't make it easy for me, of course."

He tried not to laugh. "I thought you told me once that she leapt from a balcony into your arms." Although that was the romantic version of the story, he'd also heard that Sophie actually advertised in the *Farmer's Gazette* for a husband, and that was how his uncle came to Sydney Dovedale. Rafe still wasn't sure which tale to believe.

"Don't let too many weeks pass, Rafe my boy. Spring is the season for love. Bring home a wife before harvest. Another pair of hands will never go amiss around here. There's a few young girls the parson's wife would like to introduce at tea after church, if you come with us next Sunday."

Polite conversation and tea after church? He could think of nothing more painful.

Alas, the net of well-meaning attention closed in.

Rafe shrugged and then bowed his head to study his feet. "I can't consider another lass just yet. After all this…" He rubbed one hand across his brow and let his lips droop. "Can't change direction so fast."

"Of course." Sounding very sorry, his uncle placed a firm hand on Rafe's heaving shoulder. "You take your time. Just not too much of it, eh?"

Finally raising his head, Rafe watched the other man stride off down the lane and smiled thoughtfully. A gentle breeze ruffled his hair and carried the sweet fragrance of blossoms across the yard from the apple and cherry trees along the border of his rented property.

Spring is the season. Plenty more ripe berries. His smile faded.

If only life was that simple. If only he'd never laid eyes on Mercy Danforthe and been so distracted by her—the wrong woman. Not all berries were sweet. Some grew among prickles to discourage his fingers.

Rafe looked at his watch again, snapped it shut, and rubbed a smeared fingerprint from the engraved case.

He knew The Brat was behind it. Who else would pay Tom Ridge's price, which was no doubt high. Not to mention persuade the hard-hearted bugger to return it. She could debate the hind leg off a donkey.

He shouldn't read too much into it.

Should he?

Chapter 11

"MY DEAR GELL, I WON'T HEAR OF YOU GOING BACK TO London already," Lady Ursula complained loudly one morning in the drawing room where the ladies gathered with books and needlework. "You have only just got here. Why must you be dashing about the country? Can no young people be settled in one place these days for more than a few hours?"

"I was supposed to stay only for the wedding," Mercy replied. "My brother will expect me back."

"Wedding? What wedding?"

Seated on the couch beside Mercy, Rafe's stepmother wearily explained, "Your great-grandson's wedding."

But Lady Ursula had never acknowledged Rafe as a Hartley. The old lady closed her ears to anything she did not care to hear, and as she grew deafer, this trick was ever more convenient.

"You must stay a while longer, my dear gell, and keep me company. I am in need of a companion, since I have no one here who cares about me."

When Rafe's stepmother joined in with a gentle, "Please do stay, Lady Mercy. The girls enjoy your company, and you are a great help to me in keeping them entertained," Mercy eventually conceded that she might impose upon them a little longer—until the end of another week, perhaps. That would bring her visit to a full fortnight.

Mrs. Hartley went on to say how much Rafe's aunt had appreciated her visit recently. "Sophie is so overwhelmed with all those children. I have offered to have them here until after the new baby is born, but she will not hear of being parted from them. I even suggested sending Mrs. Grieves, the girls' nanny, to help her out, but she will have none of it. Her stubborn nature will not allow her to accept anything she views as charity. Her husband is much the same." She shook her head. "They struggle along in that drafty old farmhouse, living from harvest to harvest. I do worry for Sophie."

"But they seem very happy."

"Oh, yes, they are happy, of course. Two people in love can be happy anywhere as long as they are together. But I do wish they would accept help when it is offered."

Lady Ursula piped up with her shilling's worth, "As they brew, so shall they drink. The fault is their own. Lust is no basis for a marriage. In my day, folk married where they were told, and happiness did not come into it."

Mrs. Hartley laughed lightly. "Ah, the good old days."

Lust. Mercy stared at her hands in her lap and thought how eager those fingers were to caress Rafe Hartley's naked body. Only a week ago, she'd assumed that lust was a sin suffered only by men. How wrong she turned out to be. Her cheeks, she mused, must be scarlet. Or "Mystery of the Orient." That sounded far more romantic.

"When I was young," Lady Ursula grumbled, "there was none of this marriage betwixt classes. Everyone knew their place and stayed where they were put. These days, there is too much traveling about, too much laxity, too much dancing and music."

The eldest Miss Hartley exclaimed in horror, "There was no music when you were young, Great-grandmama?"

"There was music, of course…"

Mrs. Hartley whispered in Mercy's ear, "Banging on rocks with sticks."

"…but it was regal, and the dancing was dignified, stately. There was none of this hurling of one's body about. None of this public caressing." Lady Ursula shuddered. "That obscene dance they call a waltz would never have been allowed in the ballrooms where I made my debut."

"How did you dance with a gentleman then, Great-grandmama?"

"One held hands," she replied sternly. "But only when necessary."

The two little girls tried valiantly, but without success, to smother their giggles.

"It is such a pity the Red Lion no longer hosts monthly assemblies," their mother remarked. "That would have enlivened your stay considerably, Lady Mercy. When I was a flighty young girl, I looked forward to those balls until I could scarce think of anything else. In those days, they were held in a large room on the second floor of the inn, directly above the coach entrance on the side of the market square."

The eldest daughter gave a forceful sigh, looking up from her sewing. "Oh, I do wish we still had monthly balls in Morecroft."

"You would be too young to attend, Jenny," her mother replied.

"In a few more years I won't be."

"A few more years can last a very long time when one wishes too hard for something," said Mercy. "I would advise you not to anticipate your coming-out so eagerly, or the time will feel endless."

The younger sister puffed out her cheeks, collapsing backward in her chair and swinging her feet. "It's bloody inconvenient to be too young."

Her mama exploded. "Elizabeth Anne Hartley! How many times have I told you not to use that word?"

"Our brother says it all the time."

"Rafe ought to mind his tongue around you, but even so, that is no excuse for your behavior, young lady. No need to repeat everything you hear. I know you think you are nineteen, but you are in fact only nine, and if you continue to push your father's temper as you do, it will be a miracle if you reach your first decade. Which reminds me—no more experiments with theatrical blood, young lady. Your father's valet almost had an apoplexy when he discovered you yesterday, lying on the hall tiles beside that ghastly puddle, and thought you'd fallen over the banister. Poor Grieves, I have never seen him so pale."

Lilibet erupted in giggles. "My death scene was most realistic."

"You are fortunate Doctor Sharpe was not called out and his valuable time put to waste. Poor Grieves could not hold a glass, he was shaking so terribly after the shock."

"He still downed the brandy though, Mama. Two snifters full. And I apologized to Grieves later. He agreed the scene was most impressive."

Mercy got up and went to the window, her pulse suddenly very uneven. She too had seen Lilibet's theatrical performance yesterday, and it had brought back memories of another accident, many years ago when Mercy was a child. Memories of her mother's blood in very similar puddles on hall tiles at the foot of some stairs. Real blood. And of a small wooden ball Mercy had left out on the landing after playing skittles where she was not supposed to, and then forgetting to put it away.

As if it was only yesterday, she heard the house-maids whispering of the child her mother had miscarried after the fall down stairs. Guilt slowly tore another hole in her heart.

She stopped, looked at the music sheets on the pianoforte, and tidied them with trembling hands.

"If there were assembly balls," Jenny intervened, apparently eager to resume a more interesting and useful topic than that of her little sister's misbehavior, "Lady Mercy could go and tell us all about it. That would be almost as good as being there ourselves."

Both girls looked at their guest with wide, hopeful eyes. Mercy managed a smile. "It is indeed a pity there are no monthly balls here," she agreed, having listened only partially. In her mind, she picked that stray wooden ball up from where it had rolled halfway down the stairs after her mother tripped on it, and with her pudgy, five-year-old hands, she put it away in the toy box with the skittles, where it should have been, and snapped the lid shut on her memory again.

"Do you suppose the landlord at the Red Lion could be persuaded to reopen the room for dancing?" exclaimed Mrs. Hartley. "To be sure, Lady Mercy, you could talk him into it, if anyone could."

"Well, I—"

"You always have the most reasoned arguments for any case."

Vanity flattered, she broadened her smile. "I could try, certainly." The idea of a new project improved her mood. It would do her spirits good to spend more time in the countryside, before her obligations forced her home again, and if she could find worthwhile causes while she stayed, even better. Causes to keep her busy. Her mind already moved quickly onward, leaving that reopened box of bad memories behind. For now. "If I embark on an endeavor to resurrect the dances, madam, you must help me. You will know how everything used to be. I could not have a better partner in the scheme."

"The Morecroft assembly rooms were no more than a hothouse for criminal behavior," Lady Ursula intoned somberly, shaking her head.

Mrs. Hartley transparently struggled to keep the corners of her mouth from turning up, and the strain probably almost did her in. "Of course I will make myself at your disposal, Lady Mercy."

"Splendid. We shall form a planning committee."

"It might be a very good idea. The more I think of it, the more I like your suggestion of reviving the monthly dances."

"You would," Lady Ursula huffed from her chair. "Any chance for debauchery and wild exhibition."

Although it had been Mrs. Hartley who put the idea in her head, Mercy was now forced to take all the credit. "How clever of you to think of it, your ladyship. There is so little opportunity here for young people to meet those beyond their small society. A ball is exactly what we need in Morecroft, and folk can attend from all the surrounding villages, just as it used to be when I was a girl spending my summers in Sydney Dovedale."

"Laying a trap for my grandson," Lady Ursula grumbled. No one paid her any heed.

The two little girls immediately resumed begging for a chance to attend, only to be reassured, yet again, that they were much too young.

Mrs. Hartley raised her voice above her daughters' whines. "Do tell us about your viscount, Lady Mercy. Usually young women chatter incessantly about their beaus, but you have been quiet on the subject." She gave Mercy a teasing smile. "Perhaps you do not like to share him, or you fear blushing before us."

"There is not much to tell."

But Mrs. Hartley insisted on hearing all about Viscount Grey. "I met the gentleman on only a few occasions last summer and had little opportunity to observe him closely. Had I known of his connection to you, Lady Mercy, I daresay I would have paid

greater attention and questioned the fellow unrelent-
ingly, as all sweethearts should be interrogated."

The room fell quiet, every ear listening. Even Lady
Ursula reached for her ear trumpet. Mercy struggled
to find something interesting to say about her fiancé.
"He has just turned forty years of age."

A gasp of horror escaped Jenny Hartley's lips before
she looked at her mother and clamped them shut.
Lilibet exclaimed, "Why, he's nearly as old as Papa!"

"An older man has much of an advantage," Mercy
explained, quite wounded by their reaction. "He is
experienced in matters of the world without being
arrogant. His temper is under good modulation, and
he is not prone to sudden irrational decisions."

Mrs. Hartley made much of searching in her sewing
box for a new thread, Jenny's fingers inched across the
table to reopen her book, and Lilibet yawned loudly.
Lady Ursula wanted to know if he was tall.

"He is medium height," Mercy replied. "Medium
everything, really." That was what made him just right,
of course. He was neither too much nor too little. "He
has brown hair and eyes. He is a man of good practical
sense. Very…steady, frugal, and reliable."

Lilibet rested her elbow on the table and leaned her
chin in her palm. "What's frugal? Is it like fat-headed?"

"It means miserly, silly," said her sister.

"No, it does not," Mercy cried. "It means he never
spends lavishly or unwisely. He keeps his accounts most
prudently." She paused, her temperature rising. "Why,
pray tell, would I describe my fiancé as fat-headed?"

Lilibet shrugged. "Mama said he is."

She looked at Mrs. Hartley, who hurriedly corrected

her youngest child. "I said *fastidious*!" Chagrined, she glanced at Mercy. "The things children say! The word I used to describe him was fastidious, I assure you."

Mercy got the distinct impression that the lady was choking back her laughter. Wounded again, she straightened her spine and put her chin up. "He has a manor house in Surrey, as you know, Mrs. Hartley." She reached desperately for more items of interest. "Twenty acres of arable and woodland. He keeps three coaches." Her voice drifted off, and she let it go, suddenly feeling as if it was too loud in the room.

The eldest Miss Hartley demanded to know whether he liked dancing, and Mercy replied, "He does not care to dance much." In truth, she'd danced with him only twice during the span of their acquaintance and, when she remembered those occasions, the clearest thought was of the gown she was wearing at the time and the degree of envy on Cecelia Montague's face.

The girls looked at each other, the eldest plainly disapproving of a man who was not in love with dancing. The younger sister, often the mouthpiece for the elder and not yet having the presence of mind to hide the first thought that came to her, blurted, "Lord above, is that all? He sounds a bit of a dry biscuit."

Mrs. Hartley quickly admonished her with another forbidding frown, and Lilibet sulked, slouching in her chair, kicking her heels against the slender mahogany legs which already showed signs of similar abuse.

"He rides and enjoys hunting, outdoor sports, etcetera." She stopped again, and her gaze circled the room. She expected comments or more questions. None came. The Miss Hartleys were now pinching each other in boredom, and Lady Ursula seemed about to put her ear trumpet down.

Bravely, Mercy soldiered on. "His name is Adolphus." Oh dear, now she reached for facts. There were few names less inspiring. Her main fear, when she first learned his name, was that he might expect their firstborn son to be christened likewise. To ensure this didn't happen, she'd decided upon a careful exercise in Thought Adjustment to commence as soon as they were married. It would involve constant repetition of other male names until they became lodged in his mind, replacing any unpalatable ideas he might have. It was a method she'd found quite useful when it came to steering him in the right direction. In this subtle way, she'd encouraged him toward a proposal of marriage, and angled him artfully into the purchase of a splendid pair of pearl earrings—which she picked out and wrapped for herself. Thought Adjustment had also recommended to Adolphus the services of a new tailor, in an attempt to bring his attire up to the modern style.

"You said you met him last summer, Mrs. Hartley," she prompted, keen to know what else her hostess had thought of him. Hopefully, there was more than "fastidious" to come.

"Yes. He attended a garden party at Lark Hollow. That was once my family's manor house, you know, in Buckinghamshire. My stepfather was in danger of losing the place when I married, so my husband purchased the house for me as a wedding gift. We spend the summer months at Lark Hollow and return there again for Christmas. The girls love the old place." She paused, leaning back to study the embroidery stretched over her tambour frame. "Viscount Grey was rather quiet, as I recall. Solemn and studious. A very proper gentleman."

"Oh yes," Mercy hastily agreed. "He is very serious. Very proper." And he never argued with her, never raised his voice. If she told him to wear a warmer coat, he did, without hesitation. She no longer had to remind him to use the boot scraper before he came in after riding, and he always folded his paper away or closed his book to give her his full attention when she had some news or instruction to impart. His training was coming along admirably. Mercy knew she could be of help to Adolphus, advise and guide him well. He needed her; she was quite sure of it. In fact, what would he do without her?

Suddenly, she began to feel hot, choked, cornered. "What a lovely day it is. Perhaps Lady Ursula would enjoy a walk in the park?"

From the expression on all their faces, she'd just said something quite earth-shattering.

"Great-grandmama does not like the park," Lilibet explained with the ponderous gravity that only a nine-year-old, with a certain flare for the dramatic, could manage.

"Really? Yet there is so much to see in a park, and it is much better to be walking through it than to be watching from outside the painted railings."

Lady Ursula tossed her ear trumpet aside with a grand gesture. "If Lady Mercy cares to wheel me in the chair, I should enjoy a little fresh air for a change. As long as it is not too much."

"But what about the spores in the air, Great-grandmama?"

"Huh! At my time of life, spores are the least of my troubles. Let them hasten my end if they can, since I am no use to anyone these days. Come, Lady Mercy, fetch the chair. We shall take a turn about the dreadful park."

The old lady's fussy company was just what Mercy needed to take her mind off other things. Absorbing herself in the management of another person would soon help her forget her own troubles.

After that day, she took Lady Ursula out for a stroll in the park every afternoon, once any callers had left and as long as the weather permitted. Aware he was busy with spring planting, she did not expect to see Rafe for the remainder of her stay. According to Mrs. Hartley, he did not come to Morecroft above twice a month and, despite repeated invitations, never stayed to dine at Hartley House. With all this in mind, she felt safe and easy in her decision to extend the visit.

❧

Rafe strode briskly along, raising his hat to the occasional cluster of ladies who, although they pretended not to see him, smiled anyway. They swayed and shimmered in the sun like buds opening, and he admired them easily, frankly, never paying much heed to the rules of propriety. Certainly not giving those conventions more than a passing thought today. It was beautiful weather, the air thick with the fragrance of blossoms. Adding to his merry mood, Rafe's pockets were full of notes from the trade of several sacks of fleece at the market. Two-thirds of his earnings would go to Sir William Milford, of course. Some money he'd left with Mrs. Pyke to purchase summer worsted for clothes. With the rest, he would make a deposit at the bank before he returned to the village.

Since he was in Morecroft anyway, may as well pay a visit to his father. He turned the corner with his long stride, whistled a favorite tune, and glanced to his left, making a quick survey of the park across the street. Cherry trees bloomed with heavy clouds of pink blossoms, and below them, little children ran around the black-painted railings, tapping on them with sticks. The pavement here was much better maintained, for this was the finest street in Morecroft, and Hartley House, a tall white building embraced in the midst of the elegant curve, was the grandest residence in the town. It was almost too grand for Morecroft, in fact, and Rafe often felt the house knew it. Sometimes, when the light caught upon it from a certain angle, the front of the building looked scornful of its surroundings, particularly that little park. Those tall, elegant windows glowered down with crystal-clean disdain upon all they surveyed. He'd never liked that house and rarely visited, despite repeated invitations. Fortunately, as an illegitimate son, he was not in line to inherit the wretched place. That burdensome honor would eventually go to his half sisters, for most of his father's estate was to be split between them in a fee simple, as opposed to an entail. Rafe knew some provision would be made for him—his father had insisted. But he wanted nothing, expected nothing, and asked for nothing. His own savings at the bank were steadily growing and a great source of pride.

When he arrived at the house steps, he paused. Surely Mercy would be gone by now, back to London. If not, how would he react to seeing her again? He laughed at himself. They were both grownups, capable of meeting each other in public without making an exhibit. If she was there, he would bow politely and ask her how she enjoyed her stay. They would speak of the pleasant weather, and that would be that.

Shaking off any whisper of caution with the ease of one well versed in the art, he bounced up the grand sweep of steps and rang the doorbell.

❧

Rafe stayed a while to talk with his father in the library, but as he crossed the hall on his way out, he collided with his stepmother, who rushed in from the garden with a basket full of freshly cut flowers, to ask about his aunt.

"I have not called on her these last few days," she exclaimed upon hearing of the lady's ill health. "I must take her a tonic."

He replied that he thought that was a very good idea, and then took another step across the hall, only to be halted again by her hand on his arm. "Your sisters will be most upset if they find you were here and did not stay to visit with them."

Rafe waited while she called to the girls who were, it seemed, at lessons with their governess above stairs.

"Perhaps a glass of lemonade?" his stepmother suggested. "So refreshing on a day like today."

He declined the offer politely, and eventually she

shouted again for her daughters. Finally the girls appeared, tumbling down the stairs to greet him joyously, as if it was years since they last met. Rafe suspected their excitement stemmed more from the prospect of an abandoned French lesson than at seeing their half brother, but he was very fond of the girls and loved to tease and torment them.

"Miss Jenny and Lilibet Hartley, what can be the meaning of this unladylike dashing about? Is the house on fire? Only hoydens show their ankles by running." He mimicked their great-grandmama so well that they burst into peals of laughter. There was, he saw with a strange mixture of relief and regret, no sign of Lady Mercy and no mention of her. He was right, then; she must have returned to London by now. Deciding it was safe to stay a while longer, he allowed his little sisters to drag him into the drawing room.

"You have had no word from Molly Robbins?" his stepmother inquired.

"She must have much to take up her time in London." In truth, he wished her the best of fortune. If only she hadn't left him to be mocked by the villagers, severely wounding his pride, he could have told her all that. Then they would have parted as friends. All those years they'd been close, and yet they hadn't really known each other at all.

He thought of the note Mercy took from his mantel the morning she left the farmhouse. What, he wondered, would Molly make of that when she read it?

Good thing The Danforthe Brat was back in London, where she belonged. But just as he thought this and as he was spinning his youngest sister around his head like a bird, the woman who had played a mostly willing role in his spirited dreams for the past three nights walked into that parlor, wheeling his great-grandmama in a chair. Lilibet Hartley almost fell to the carpet on her tousled head and remained suspended for a few seconds, upside down, his hand gripped around her ankle.

"Ah, Lady Mercy, there you are," his stepmother exclaimed merrily. "Look who came to visit."

Chapter 12

Mercy stopped abruptly, bringing Lady Ursula's chair to a bouncing halt. "Mr. Rafe Hartley," she exclaimed, her gaze going immediately to the little girl currently suspended upside down by one foot.

"Good gracious," cried Lady Ursula, "what can be the meaning of this display? Has the revolution begun? Take my jewels, you vagabond, but leave the children."

Belatedly remembering his little sister, he swung her the right way up and set her carefully down on the carpet. "Lady Mercy." He gave a stiff bow that might have been the very definition of reluctance. "I expected you to be back in London by now."

She couldn't think of a blasted thing to reply, certainly no explanation for her remaining in Morecroft. Her brother, if he were there, would be amazed to see her struck dumb. It was not merely the shock of finding him there in his stepmother's parlor. The sight of Rafe with his little sisters—laughing, tender, and playful—further knocked her heart out of rhythm, made her breath catch in a hiccup. He was the stray left on her stairs, too easy to trip over and tumble for.

"I was just lamenting the lack of entertainments we can provide for Lady Mercy," said Mrs. Hartley. "Now, Rafe, you are always promising to join us for dinner. I insist you come tonight and help entertain our guests."

Mercy expected the man to make some excuse, but he merely stared at her while his sister tugged on his sleeve, pestering for another flight around his head. "Guests?" he mumbled. She watched his lips, imagined them gently kissing her bosom.

You owe me.

Her palms were disturbingly moist, and it felt as if the rigid bones of her newly purchased corset were the only things keeping her upright.

"Your father has invited Sir William Milford," his stepmother was saying. "He will bring his sisters, I fear, and that leaves my table setting quite dreadfully unbalanced without another man present."

"Oh." Rafe looked down, finally releasing her from his wicked gaze. "I see."

At last Mercy caught a proper breath, but she perspired to such an extent under her chemise that she feared melting away in a gooey puddle on the carpet.

"I'm sure Lady Mercy and Sir William's sisters will oblige us with a few lively airs on the pianoforte," that good lady continued, "and we shall have cards. Yes, it will be a cozy evening. Shall we say seven?"

He reached for his watch and checked the time. Mercy had paid Tom Ridge handsomely for the safe return of Rafe's watch, but it was worth the expense.

Still holding his watch in one hand, he suddenly looked up and caught her eye.

"Very well," he said softly. "Seven o' clock this evening."

Mercy retrieved the last stray pieces of her scattered wits, but the man who had shredded them remained only a few minutes more, then made his polite adieus and left.

The awkward meeting was over. If he did come for dinner that night, she felt capable of seeing him again now without any remaining embarrassment about their intimate encounter on his bed. If he *did* come. He might yet make some excuse at the last minute and send his regrets. So there was no cause to get herself in a flurry.

His younger sisters begged to be allowed to stay up for dinner, but their mother calmly refused. "You will have supper in the nursery with Mrs. Grieves and go to bed at the same time as always. We are not savages in this house."

Lady Ursula mumbled under her breath, "Could have fooled me." Louder, she enquired, "Who is that tall, unmannerly young fellow with the hair of a gypsy, and why does he come here to fling my great-granddaughters about like rug beaters?"

Mrs. Hartley rolled her eyes. "You know very well who he is."

"Indeed I do not," the old lady protested, nostrils flaring, gnarled hands banging her stick on the carpet. "I have seen him a half dozen times in this house, and no explanation is ever given. He has the look and speech of a vile revolutionary. Since he is allowed shocking liberties with your daughters, I am surprised you do not let him throw me about the room too."

"Next time I will," Mrs. Hartley assured her pleasantly.

Mercy told herself, several times over, that he would not come to dinner. His greeting to her in the parlor had been stiff and formal. They might have been complete strangers, if not for the sultry and rather mischievous gleam in his eyes when he looked at his watch and then at her. It left her heart spinning like a bobbin.

She dressed cautiously for the dinner party, anxious not to appear as if she fussed over her appearance. Naturally that required even more care than usual. Then she scorned her reflection in the mirror and chastised herself for worrying about what was very probably nothing at all.

It was wrong of her to have these skittish, silly feelings for Rafe. It was irresponsible to act the way she had with him. She should be ashamed of herself.

Tonight, therefore, she would allow no gesture or expression to give away whatever turmoil yet remained in her heart. She would be perfectly at ease, friendly, polite, gracious. From a distance. All her emotions would be safely packed away where they could do no harm.

Sir William Milford arrived promptly with his younger sister, Miss Isabella Milford, and the widowed elder sister, introduced as Mrs. Kenton. The ladies were elegantly attired in an understated fashion. Miss Milford might benefit from a little more color, Mercy thought, but not everyone could be expected to have *her* sophisticated eye for style and fashion.

Although he purchased property in the area some years ago, Sir William was seldom in residence. Recently he had returned to the country, probably to oversee the renovations on his house, and now he brought with him his sisters. What they found to do while installed in their brother's damp, unprepossessing ruin of a castle on a hill overlooking the sleepy village of Sydney Dovedale was anybody's guess. The invitation to dine with the Hartleys must have been a huge relief.

Miss Milford was a plump, pretty creature with large, sad eyes. The sort of eyes, thought Mercy, that any romantic heroine ought to have. She was agreeable and expressive without being overly demanding of attention. She appeared modest, answered questions with just enough information—never too much—and since her politely uttered remarks never once offended Mercy's views, she was speedily established as a potential new friend. Added to her other advantages were her age—being seven and twenty, and therefore five years older than Mercy—and her status of being unattached, unengaged, in clear need of a suitor. A woman who might be helped. Mercy was soon planning new outfits for Miss Milford, as well as a much more flattering arrangement for her unimaginatively dressed, dull brown hair.

The other sister, Mrs. Kenton, was harder to endure. It became plain, very quickly, that she saw herself as a matchmaker—of all the ridiculous things—and had decided, prior to their arrival, that

Lady Mercy Danforthe must be set upon and secured for her brother. As an expert in this field herself, Mercy was irritated by the efforts of an amateur.

"How delighted I am to make your acquaintance," the stout Mrs. Kenton exclaimed, sinking in a slow curtsy which, while it possessed the air of one rehearsed many times, quite failed to be graceful or very respectful. Once down, she was in too much hurry to get back up again and resume her speech. "I cannot tell you what an honor it is to meet you at last, your ladyship. I hear so much about you, and I must say, you are far handsomer than I expected from report." She laughed gaily, while her younger sister blushed and her brother cleared his throat.

"Thank you, I'm sure." Mercy was amused to know she was a pleasant surprise in person.

"We have all been on tenterhooks to meet you, especially dear William. Have you not, Brother? As soon as we heard you were here, I said to William, *we must pay our respects*. Society here is much less diverse than that to which we are accustomed. We have been desperate to meet any new face just to stave off the boredom. Almost anything will do for company to get us out in the evenings."

For the first half hour, Mrs. Kenton's odd comments were vastly entertaining. Although often obliquely insulting, she seemed completely unaware of it. Her poor brother's throat must have been sore from the clearing of it, but even that caused her only to look at him worriedly and exclaim that she hoped he was not getting a cold.

Sir William was a nice enough fellow, although

rather quiet. His conversation, when left unprompted by his sister, revolved around a new carriage he'd just purchased and the fear that he might have trodden in something unsavory on his way between that carriage and the steps of Hartley House. Repeated assurances of no foul odor emanating from his foot did nothing to appease the fellow, and he shuffled self-consciously about the room like a guilty man around the corpse of his murder victim. Mercy tried putting him at ease by asking about renovations made to the drafty, incommodious, old fortress he'd purchased in Sydney Dovedale. This was a project undertaken several years ago and still not progressed far. According to Molly Robbins, it was something of a joke among the villagers, although the amount of coin sunk into the property must be far from comedic for Sir William.

"How intensely satisfying it must be," she said to him, "to indulge one's creativity in restoring a fine, ancient structure like that fortress. A great project indeed!"

"Yes."

She waited, but there was nothing more forthcoming.

Mercy tried again. "I understand the flint tower has graced that very spot since the Norman conquest."

Sir William scratched the side of his nose. "Yes."

"And the stone was ferried here from the mouth of the river Yare, where it was once used in a Roman lookout tower."

"Ummm." He smiled uncertainly and then glanced shyly at his foot. Mercy began to think he cared nothing about the history of the place he'd purchased. The ruin, however, had always fascinated her. Carver said it was the fault of her romantic sensibilities that she should find anything appealing about that damp, mossy, unprepossessing pile of old stone.

At this point, Mrs. Kenton took over the conversation, as was clearly customary. "When William first announced an intention to purchase property in the country, I suggested Buckinghamshire. It is a place in which I lived many happy years with my dear husband, God rest his soul."

"Oh?"

"My husband was the curate at Hawcombe Prior, the village near Lark Hollow, the Hartleys' country house. Did you know?"

"Indeed, no." Neither did she particularly care. The woman's dead husband could not be of any interest to her, since he was permanently beyond helping. She searched for something else to say. "You have been widowed long, Mrs. Kenton?"

"Three years this month." The lady sighed and blinked as if she tried to squeeze out tears. Her eyes remained dry, clear, missing nothing that went on around them. "I still have many friends in Hawcombe Prior and visit often. I do like to keep abreast of matters. I see it as a duty to my husband's memory that I remain in contact with the families of the neighborhood—his *flock,* as he liked to call them. There is little that goes on there without my knowledge," the lady added proudly. "I have my ear to the ground, my finger on the pulse."

"I'm sure the parishioners are most grateful for it," Mercy muttered.

"The current curate is sadly not up to the standard set by my dear husband. Neither does he appreciate my assistance. But I press onward with my good works, continuing my dear husband's efforts as he would have expected."

"Very admirable, indeed." After this, Mercy turned her attention to the younger sister, ignoring most of Mrs. Kenton's chatter.

When the drawing room door opened, Mercy looked over Miss Milford's head, fully expecting the footman to enter with a note of apology from Rafe. Instead, there was the man himself. He came.

Mercy completely forgot what she'd been in the midst of telling Miss Milford.

"Goodness," Mrs. Kenton muttered. "Well…"

Well, indeed, thought Mercy. Apart from his recent wedding day, she'd never seen Rafe make so much effort over his attire. Frequently, it seemed to her as if he deliberately played down his good looks. Tonight he did not. His clothes were clean and free of patches, not a stain or loose stitch in sight. She recognized the blue tailcoat he'd worn on his wedding day—must be his best coat. Rafe Hartley would not look out of place in a London drawing room, she thought with surprise.

Ah, but he would. Pretentious members of the *ton* would sniff him out as an imposter. That quick temper and wild spark in his eye would give him away, even if his crude tongue, the moment he opened his mouth, did not. Rafe wouldn't pretend for anyone, wouldn't hide his thoughts, however improper and contrary to popular opinion. Worse than that, even, the way his presence filled the room was not…gentlemanly. It was too hot, too dangerous—revolutionary, as Lady Ursula had said. And that was a terrifying word in aristocratic circles. People would be unsettled, not knowing whether to admire or fear him.

He greeted his stepmother, who steered him across the room to introduce him to the Milfords and Mrs. Kenton. Lady Ursula, although safely situated by the fire, well away from his trajectory, clutched the diamonds at her throat and slid fearfully into the corner of her chair.

To Mercy's relief, Mrs. Kenton's attention promptly unfastened from her and switched to Rafe. Having already learned that woman's ideas on everything from parliamentary reform to removing stains on lace, she was certain there could be no topic left for their discussion. As for the lady's beloved village of Hawcombe Prior, Mercy now knew the layout of every lane, the distance of every walk, the age of every tree, without ever having been there or nursing any intention of going.

As only the "natural" son of James Hartley, Rafe might have been a person unfit for the Milfords' notice, other than as a charity cause. But his illegitimacy had not held him back. He was openly acknowledged by his father's family—except for Lady Ursula, of course—and he'd known the benefit of a Cambridge education. However, his preference to work with his hands rather than assume the mantle of "gentleman" made his status somewhat puzzling to Mrs. Kenton. But however unconventional she might regard his appearance in that drawing room, she must be canny enough to realize that Rafe held a certain position in his wealthy father's life. He was also, it could not be denied, positively breathtaking to look upon, rendering the ladies in the room quite short of the required air just by walking through it.

"I heard you recently suffered a great disappointment, sir," said Mrs. Kenton, barely lowering her voice, discretion apparently being a stranger to her.

"A disappointment?"

"Your canceled wedding, Mr. Hartley." She moved a step closer, head wedged far back on her neck in order to assess his face as it looked down from miles above her.

"Ah, yes. *That* disappointment." His tone was unusually restrained, mellow. "But perhaps it was as well the young lady changed her mind before the vows rather than after. It saved us both a great deal of trouble, I daresay."

Mercy was impressed. He held his temper and showed generosity of spirit toward the girl who'd jilted him. He also managed to look extremely fine while doing so.

Oh, Molly Robbins, you foolish, foolish girl!

Mrs. Kenton was ready to pity him. "The girl must have been undeserving."

"I'd like to think so, madam, but I'm sure we all have our faults. I am not such a wondrous catch for any woman. I've been told I try people's patience." His head hung slightly forward, and he gave a morose sigh. "That I've been spoiled and get away with too much. To hear some people say it, I need a nanny, not a wife. They would not share my company if the alternative was a hanging at Tyburn."

Mrs. Kenton absorbed every word. "Goodness, Mr. Hartley, what a dreadful thing for anyone to say.

I am most distressed to hear how unjustly you've been treated. I do so hate to hear of a sweetheart's betrayal. There is nothing worse, to be sure."

"Nothing worse than a mind changed and a wedding broken off?" Mercy exclaimed. "I think you enlarge the matter, madam. There are many tragedies in the world that far outweigh this one."

"Lady Mercy has never had a broken heart," Rafe said solemnly, one hand raised to his chest, pressing on it and wincing as if he felt severe pain. "She cannot know what I suffer."

"Shall I get you a shovel, Mr. Hartley?" she suggested with an arch smile.

"A shovel?"

"To help spread the cow manure?"

The remark went over Mrs. Kenton's head. "Poor Mr. Hartley, you have been ill used, but I shall see to it that this doesn't get you down with a fit of the blue devils." She raised her finger with a flourish. "I, Augusta Kenton, shall personally ensure your spirits are lifted. You need merry company to heal your heart and make up for that other flighty creature."

"Flighty *and* sharp-tongued," he muttered.

So much for his forgiving spirit, thought Mercy darkly.

Mrs. Kenton assured him not to worry. "I shall erase her from your thoughts before too long, sir. I shall take you under my wing and find you another young lady to soothe your wounds."

"Please do not trouble yourself, madam, just to help me. I daresay I can manage tolerably alone. It is not…" He paused and took a deep breath. "…not so very hard."

When Mercy gasped in irritation, Rafe looked at

her and smiled. If it were possible, she thought, for a wolf to smile.

"Miss Milford"—she turned quickly to the woman beside her—"do you play at all?"

Chapter 13

THE DANFORTHE BRAT ALWAYS ASSUMED THAT BY playing loudly she could hide all her skipped and improvised notes. It was much the same method by which she argued with him for the past dozen years. Bright plumage and a great deal of noise were her shields, meant to distract other people from seeing her faults.

At the end of her song, Miss Milford applauded with an enthusiasm that caused Rafe to wonder if the young lady was in her employ or simply hard of hearing. Mrs. Kenton, he noted, prodded her brother to respond likewise, and Sir William eventually found his feet, sauntered wearily to the pianoforte, and offered to turn her music, therefore giving Rafe's stepmother a rest. She came over to where Rafe sat in a corner of the drawing room.

"Before you comment to me on how well Lady Mercy looks this evening," he muttered quietly, "I will agree and dispense with that line of conversation." He'd always been able to read his stepmother like a wide-open book. With very large print.

She perched beside him on the sofa and spread her fan, using it to hide her lips. "A conversation cannot be ended until all participants are satisfied."

He sighed heavily and leaned into the corner, elbow resting on the rolled arm of the sofa. "I refuse to compliment her on her playing. Yes, she *looks* quite beautiful. That is as far as I can go with any degree of sincerity. It is no more of an achievement to be beautiful than it is to be rich, when one was born thus." Pity Mercy Danforthe didn't have a softer heart and a little kindness in her soul, he thought. She was so busy pushing people around to do her bidding that she gave no thought to their feelings.

Mercy could take a lesson or two from Lady Blunt, who had offered her advice in such a kindly way that he took it without feeling bombarded and bullied. He could respect the old dear, of course, for she was a woman of advanced years, and there was none of that unfortunate sexual attraction to get in the way between them. He missed their conversations, he realized. Despite their age difference, the old lady had touched a chord in him. He meant it when he said he wished he'd known her when she was young.

His stepmother eyed him above her fan. "I see you made an extraordinary effort with your own grooming this evening, Rafe."

"Yes. I do manage to scrape the dirt of the farmyard off me from time to time."

"Just for us. We are honored."

"I hope so," he replied tightly, his gaze focused across the room on the pianoforte. "Lady Mercy does not appear in any haste to return home. Odd, is it not?"

"Not especially. She enjoys the country."

Enjoys meddling, he thought.

"And her company is most entertaining. Don't you agree, Rafe?"

He snorted. "Like a public hanging. Morbid curiosity makes it impossible to look away."

"That's a fine way to talk of an old friend."

"Friend? We do naught but quarrel. Her view of the world is the very opposite of mine. We agree on nothing."

His stepmother laughed in her easy, infectious way. "Exactly. If you were not dear friends, you would never bother to argue. It would not be so important to make the other person understand."

He squared his shoulders against the back of the couch. "She's a menace."

"Your father used to say that of me."

"She gives me a headache."

"Poor Rafe." She beamed over her fan. "I daresay it's the...tension."

"Tension?" He didn't like the sound of that, or the pause before it.

"Better stock up on the apothecary's powders, because I suspect she means to stay a while yet."

He winced. "God help me."

Miss Milford now took over the entertainment, and Rafe's stepmother stood quickly, beckoning to Mercy as if she had something to say. The young woman walked over, smiling expectantly, poised to hear whatever urgent message Mrs. Hartley had to impart, only to discover that she merely meant to give up the seat beside Rafe.

There was no time to escape the proximity for either of them.

Mercy, cornered, sat tentatively and folded her hands in her lap. His stepmother, meanwhile, fanned herself rapidly and gestured to the footman for some wine. "Is it just me, or is it dreadfully warm in here?"

"It's just you," the two younger people replied sternly in unison.

Mrs. Hartley persisted. "You look a little flushed, Lady Mercy. Are you sure you do not feel the heat?"

Rafe stole a glance at Mercy and saw her face glowing with a tint of pink. "Quite sure," she answered softly. The slight vibration of a copper ringlet by her cheek was the only thing that moved, apart from her lips.

"We were just talking of headaches, Lady Mercy," said his stepmother wickedly. "Rafe seeks a reliable cure. Do you know of any?"

"Our housekeeper makes an excellent elderberry wine," came the cool response. "Although, as I advise my brother, refraining from the known causes of *his* headaches would be more beneficial than any cure."

"There, Rafe, see? I knew Lady Mercy would have a cure for what ails you." Having amused herself, Mrs. Hartley wandered off, leaving them alone together.

Although Miss Milford showed herself to be an accomplished performer on the pianoforte, no one paid her much attention. Her brother had evidently assumed the task of turning the music only because he wanted to please Lady Mercy, and now that she had abandoned the instrument, he was forced to stay and serve his sister instead. Mrs. Kenton, while making a show of being interested in her sister's playing, astonished Lady Ursula and Rafe's father with a soliloquy in favor of gaslit street lamps and various other modernizations that were now common in London but had yet to reach towns like Morecroft. In her eagerness to prove herself conversant with new developments, Mrs. Kenton wildly misjudged her audience, for Lady Ursula was a woman happiest if nothing around her ever changed. In her opinion, good folk had no cause to be out in the dark, so why would they need reliable lighting? Only for the easy accomplishment of criminal deeds, she assured Mrs. Kenton gravely, leaving the other lady with nothing immediately to say.

Rafe, meanwhile, glanced at Mercy and saw her lips pressed tight, her chin lifted, her eyes determinedly focused across the room. While she was this close and they were separated from the others by a good distance, he felt the urgent need to make her talk to him. If he did not, the moment would pass. Always someone or something intervened.

"You left an item behind at my house, Lady Mercy."

"I believe I did," she replied hesitantly.

"When will you retrieve it?"

"That will not be possible."

"Lost the use of your legs?"

Her lips barely moved, her reply little more than a ruffled breath. "Only my wits. Briefly."

"They are recovered, then?"

"Quite robustly recovered," she assured him firmly.

He was disappointed to hear it, although it was no less than he expected. A few nights ago, this woman had lain on his bed, exploring his body with eager hands, her warm laughter tickling his cheek. Now she was cold marble again, a statue in a museum or a grand house, something to be admired from a distance. No touching. No trespassing.

In his peripheral vision, he watched each deeply troubled breath lifting the sweet mounds that peeked shyly above her jade-green bodice. Her stiff demeanor was betrayed by that clue—a hint of vulnerability. His hunger quickened, pulse pacing like the paws of a caged tiger. "I suppose I can make use of what you left behind."

She drawled wearily, "As you wish."

"I'll put it on my scarecrow. That should scare the blackbirds from my seed beds."

He watched her feign a yawn, but she could not hide the indignant flame in her eyes at the idea of her corset being used in such a manner.

"Miss Milford plays very well," he said, swallowing a chuckle.

"I suppose she does."

"I *suppose* it was lucky you played first. Miss Milford would be a hard act to follow."

She tapped her closed fan against the palm of one hand. "Do you infer that my skill is inferior?"

"I merely point out that she is very accomplished."

"At the pianoforte, certainly."

"She is also a young lady with humility, and has a very sensitive way about her."

"How observant of you to know this already."

"I find her conversation light and civil, her manner pleasingly demure."

"You spoke to her for five minutes. I daresay that

was not quite enough time for her to disagree with you on any point."

"Some women could learn from her example."

The tapping of her fan quickened.

"Perhaps you don't like my honest opinion, my lady?"

Her delectable breasts, enticingly flushed, rose and fell ever more rapidly. He wondered if they might spill out with a little more encouragement. His stepmother was right, he realized; it was a form of tension he felt around her. A tightening of all his nerves and tendons. It couldn't be healthy to let it continue without relief of some kind.

"I'm sure I don't care one way or the other for your opinion, Rafe Hartley."

"No. But everyone must always care to hear yours."

Her lips moved, ready to argue.

"One should learn to admit one's faults," he added, reminding The Brat of her own words to him just a few days prior. "Or else one might never improve."

To his surprise, she was silent. Even seemed to shrink slightly. Had he made a dent in her armor? He stretched his fingers over his knees, before they might feel tempted to start cracking knuckles. Or reach for her hand.

But suddenly she changed the subject. "You have not heard from Molly?"

He formed his reply with care. "I know she is not returning to the country. I am resigned to it."

A slight frown passed over her expression, but she still watched Miss Milford. "Then you have had a reply to your letter?" she persisted.

"Whether or not I have had any communication

from Miss Robbins is beside the point. I do not need a *letter* to tell me what is in her heart. She made that plain by her *actions*."

"I think you—"

"The matter is over and done with. I have decided to look elsewhere for a wife. As you suggested recently, Lady Mercy, you might be of service to me."

"Service?" she murmured, her lush, green-eyed gaze fixed on the pianoforte.

"In the acquisition of a bride. You did say you have had some success as a matchmaker."

"I have."

"As a working man, I am too busy to find a bride myself, and even if I had the time at my disposal, I would likely make a poor choice. I possess something of an unfortunate habit in that regard, as I'm sure you agree." When she finally looked at him, it was Rafe's turn to stare at Miss Milford across the room. He smiled as she finished the final notes of a well-executed, rather gloomy melody. "Unless, of course, you don't feel up to the task. For personal reasons."

"I accept the mission, Mr. Hartley. Please do tell me what you look for in your future wife."

Apparently emboldened by Rafe's smile, Miss Milford began another tune, this one much happier, her expression more animated. "A woman who minds her own business, does not try to tell me mine. Someone quiet and still, not prone to wander off."

"A mute in leg irons, perhaps?"

He wanted to laugh, but curbed it. He also wanted to put his arm around her. What would she do, he wondered, if he leaned over and kissed the side of her neck here and now? Perhaps it was his imagination, or wishful thinking, but he thought she'd just moved her frosty drawers an inch closer.

"What I desire, your ladyship, is a gentle woman to entertain me in the evenings after a long day in the fields. Someone musical, whose voice does not remind me of fingernails on slate and whose approach does not startle me like carthorse hooves over cobbles." He returned his gaze to her. "A woman who is not *too proud* to work beside me and does not mind a little dirt on my skin after the day's toil."

Her slender brows arched gracefully; her lip quirked. "Is that all?"

"She must not lecture me about my manners and never think it her place to quarrel or question me."

"She sounds a saint…or a fool."

"Perhaps it is beyond you to find me such a woman."

"I would advise you, Mr. Hartley, to consider your list of requirements most carefully. Marriage is a solemn undertaking that cannot be undone. It should not be approached as a jest."

Amazed she could preach to him on that particular matter with a straight face, he stared. "*Cannot* be undone? Interesting you should say that. For once we are of the same opinion, you and I. A vow once made should be kept."

Her lips tightened, eyelashes half-lowered. If she had anything to reply to that, apparently she chose to stifle it. Another first.

"I wonder why you did not mention *your* fiancé to me when we were last together, Lady Mercy. Perhaps it was the scrumpy that erased him from your mind."

Rafe rose swiftly from the couch. "I look forward to reviewing your selections for my bride. May they improve upon my own." He strode over to the pianoforte, hands clasped behind his back. There, he thought, that told *her*.

❧

She flapped her fan with as much elegance as she could muster. Rafe Hartley, she thought crossly, was behaving like an ill-tempered boar while attempting to dress it all up in a fine new coat.

And he'd dared to suggest she never listened to anyone else's opinion. She was still reeling from that remark.

There were several moments when she felt the urge to let him know he belonged to her, that she'd paid good money for him, and he should, therefore, do whatever she bade him. Would that not add some excitement to the party?

But when her temper calmed, she knew it was better that he never know she was the woman behind Lady Blunt's veil. It would be only another excuse for Rafe to accuse her of meddling, to shout and rail at her in that wearisome manner.

The seat cushion lowered beside her, and there, alas, was Mrs. Kenton. Mercy hid a groan of despair behind her fan.

"Such a well-favored young fellow. I confess myself surprised to find him in possession of good manners. When I heard he was a farmer, I expected Mr. Hartley's son to be a little more...rustic."

Mercy managed a thin smile, lowering her fan. "Oh, there is plenty of the rustic about Mr. Rafe Hartley, but he shows proper manners when he chooses. Beware, however, he is just as likely to choose not."

"He is extremely handsome, and surely more than six foot tall in his stockinged feet."

"Six foot four." She felt her cheeks flush. "I would imagine."

Mrs. Kenton drummed her fingers on her knee, keeping time with her sister's playing. "Mrs. Hartley tells me you have been acquainted with the young man since childhood."

"Yes," she muttered wearily. "Our paths have crossed on numerous occasions."

The lady nodded, and her feathered headdress bobbed. "He has been most fortunate to move in high circles of Society."

"He would not see it as fortunate. For the most part, he spurns Society. I was surprised to see him here tonight, but he is keen to please his father now that he has returned."

Mrs. Kenton, she sensed, was barely listening but picked up on the few words she found important. "The prodigal son, as Mrs. Hartley calls him. Now that he is settled, I am sure whatever wildness he once possessed will give way to maturity. Doubtless he will benefit from his father's consequence." Mrs. Kenton's gaze circled the elegant parlor as she admired aloud the hand-painted wallpaper and elaborately carved, classical motifs of the marble chimneypiece.

Across the room, Rafe gave Isabella all his attention, and she had already fumbled several sheets of music, dropping them to the carpet in her haste to find something that might please him. Rafe had that effect on women—caused a grievous amount of disorder. Unfortunately, he knew it.

"Mr. Hartley the elder has no other son by his marriage, Lady Mercy?"

"He has two delightful daughters."

"Splendid! Splendid!" Mrs. Kenton remarked distractedly, eyeing Rafe again with very evident approval.

He laughed loudly at some self-effacing remark Miss Milford made about her playing. Although unable to hear the words, Mercy saw the other woman's expression of modesty and the hand gestures, all made so that Rafe could have the opportunity of rebuffing. An opportunity he took.

"Your sister plays beautifully," said Mercy, setting aside a sudden twinge of jealousy. "I'm afraid she puts my attempt quite thoroughly in the shade." Although difficult to admit any young lady could have more skills than she, sadly it must be acknowledged.

The older she grew, the more she was forced to face facts. There were, she supposed, a few things she might have improved upon—things at which other ladies had time to excel. Of course, she was always too busy managing her brother, his household, and other people who fell under her care. But Rafe had known Isabella for all of half an hour. It was no wonder she seemed so accomplished to him. He did not know many single, eligible ladies of that caliber. Besides, she thought peevishly, any woman could pull the fleece over a man's eyes for half an hour.

"Isabella has come out of her shell tonight," Mrs. Kenton announced, "and I am glad to see it, for she has been low in spirits these last few months. I hope we all become better acquainted, Lady Mercy. Perhaps you will honor us with a visit soon. We are always in want of company. There are days when I am so excessively bored out there that I would gladly take tea with anyone."

Mercy was so preoccupied by her thoughts that she almost forgot to take offense at the idea of being a last resort.

Chapter 14

At dinner, Mercy watched Miss Isabella Milford's sorrowful aspect and became increasingly convinced she'd found another worthy project. It could be that Miss Milford was crossed in love. She had not mentioned any beaus, and her sister surely would have wasted no time giving all the details if there were any to be had. No, Miss Milford was in danger of becoming a wallflower. It would be a kind mission to take her in hand, brighten her up, and find her a suitor.

Rafe was very solicitous toward the lady, asking how she liked her soup and even gesturing for a footman when she dropped her napkin or her wine-glass needed refilling. Mrs. Kenton's hopes, begun while she watched them together at the pianoforte, expanded prematurely, like a bulging marrow under hothouse glass.

"You studied law, Mr. Rafe Hartley? Yet you do not practice in Town? Such a pity."

"I doubt Town regrets my absence."

"But you would look most dashing in a barrister's robes."

"I much prefer the country, madam. The life of a farmer suits me better than a horsehair wig."

His father said, "Rafe thinks a man must work with his hands in the soil or else his is not a worthwhile occupation."

"I never said that, Father."

"Hmph." Mr. Hartley senior glowered at his soup.

"I said no other work would suit *me*. Whatever makes a man content should be his to decide." He shot Mercy a quick glance. "My opinions are *mine*. I do not expect everyone to agree with me."

"Quite right, Rafe," his stepmother exclaimed. "We should all be free to make our own choices."

Her husband looked up. "One wants what is best for one's children."

"These young men and their ideas," exclaimed Mrs. Kenton. "Just like William buying that decrepit fortress in which we are forced to stay. He could not wait until something more suitable became vacant. Now we suffer in discomfort because he would not heed my advice and lease a place in less need of refurbishment."

"I did not want to lease, Augusta," said her brother quietly. "I wanted to buy."

"Hence we have a place falling down around our ears because it was all you could—" She stopped herself when he glared at her. "All you would look at."

Mentioning money troubles would have been indelicate, to say the least. Mrs. Kenton, showing herself not entirely without prudence, seemed to realize her tongue had run away with itself, and she reinstated her focus on Rafe.

"Well, if you ever do come to Town, Mr. Hartley, you must call upon us there."

Rafe smiled.

"I know Isabella will be pleased to see a fresh face," she added.

Her sister flushed prettily, and Mercy's annoyance with Mrs. Kenton increased several notches. If there was any matchmaking to be done, it was her province.

"I extend the same invitation to you, Lady Mercy," the eager woman continued, switching her attention abruptly. "My brother is equally in want of sensible company. We did not meet with more than half a dozen young ladies of tolerable wit last Season, did we, William? There were evenings when I said to myself, where are all the interesting ladies? They do not have to be beauties, but at least let them have something to say for themselves. I've always considered beauty to be overrated," she added with a condescending nod of her head at Mercy, "and superior intelligence to be much more useful. After all, beauty is never lasting, but one seldom outgrows stupidity. I much prefer ten minutes of conversation with a lady of quick wit, like yourself, Lady Mercy, to half an hour in company with a great beauty."

Although guessing she was meant to be flattered, Mercy was far less amused by Mrs. Kenton's faux pas now than she was at the beginning of the evening. She was no longer so certain they were unconsciously done. It didn't seem possible that one boring woman could make so many in a row.

"Lady Mercy is engaged," said Rafe suddenly. "Has she not told you? Be sure to invite her fiancé too." He refused to meet her eye above the candelabra, and his lips formed the slight curve of a semisneer before he put them to his soupspoon.

"Oh." Mrs. Kenton adjusted her expression hastily. "To whom are you engaged?"

"Viscount Grey." Silently, she prayed there would be no further questions about him. She'd had her fill of inquiry from Mrs. Hartley and her daughters. To endure even less subtle prying and poking from Mrs. Kenton—and in front of Rafe—would be unbearable.

Mercy need not have worried. Mrs. Kenton's eyes fogged over, but she pasted on a vague smile, congratulated Mercy, and returned the subject to Rafe. But he was not done with the topic he'd begun, and after curtly answering a few more of the lady's questions, he said, "I am surprised the viscount did not come with you into the country. He has important business elsewhere?"

"He is in Italy."

"And he left you to your own devices?" Rafe chuckled softly, and the tall, elegant candle flames flickered between them. "I would not be so careless as the viscount. I would not let you out of my sight."

Mercy decided it was folly to join him in any further debate, for he was evidently in a teasing mood.

"He is not afraid you might change your mind in his absence?" Rafe pressed again. "Find another sweetheart? Some ladies are of a changeable nature."

"As are some gentlemen." Oh dear. There went her determination not to play his game.

Distantly, she heard Mrs. Hartley asking Isabella Milford how she liked her soup. The lady claimed only a very little appetite and finished no more than a few mouthfuls before setting down her spoon. But she quietly assured her hostess that there was nothing amiss with the taste or temperature of her portion.

"I suppose you think of the young lady who jilted you." Mrs. Kenton tossed a pitying glance at Rafe. "But not all our gender are so untrustworthy, Mr. Hartley. You must not let that incident taint your view of us. Or of romance." She beamed around him at her sister.

Isabella, her face very pale, delicately lowered her lashes and smiled apologetically. He would like that, of course, Mercy thought crossly; he would enjoy Isabella's humility, her quivering meekness, and feminine frailty.

She was suddenly feeling quite ill. For a woman with a strong constitution, it was most unusual. Perhaps there *was* something amiss with the soup.

❧

Rafe began to enjoy himself about halfway through dinner, when he spoke at length on the heartlessness of some women, while observing the little signs of his ex-wife's mounting irritation across the dining table.

"I suppose my runaway bride must serve as a lesson taken," he remarked to Mrs. Kenton. "Although the loss caused me great pain, the sun still rises every morning and sets every evening. Life goes on, as must I."

"How brave you are, sir," the lady exclaimed. "And how strong, to pick yourself up and strive onward, even with a broken heart." She looked around him again at her sister, who picked listlessly at her turbot.

Rafe sighed, one hand to his heart. "It is my lot in life to carry the burden of a sensitive soul."

Across the table, Mercy covered her lips with a napkin. She was perhaps a hair's breadth from rolling her eyes, but kept them hidden behind her bronze-tipped lashes. Rafe knew she was dying to look up at him and snap out some sharp remark. If not for the guests, she would have.

"Good things, so I was recently assured, come to those who wait," he said softly, reaching for his wine-glass. "The woman I lost might yet return to me."

Mercy's lashes lifted only slightly, and he couldn't tell whether she looked at him. She, too, reached for her wine, and as her lips met the rim of her glass, Rafe sipped from his own. It was the closest he could get to kissing her at that moment, so it must suffice.

Suddenly her gaze swept up, and she caught him in the brilliant twinkle of gold-and-emerald dust. He felt like a crab finding its claws trapped in a fisherman's net. She spoke. "I thought you were quite certain she will not return, Mr. Hartley. Were you not prepared to struggle valiantly onward with your broken heart? Even find another love to mend it?" Of course she assumed he spoke of Molly when he mentioned his runaway bride.

"I make the most of the hand I am dealt," he replied. "I am a man of action. There is little point daydreaming of what might have been."

"Quite true. Nothing good can be gained by drowning in one's sorrows. Or the ale barrel."

"And yet"—he paused and set down his wine-glass—"if she returned, I would hold no grudge." He stared at her lips. Darkened by the wine, they seemed fuller, even more kissable than usual, and he forgot about every other person around that table. "My feelings never changed. If she comes back to me, we can find common ground—a way to meet both our needs."

"Sometimes the disparity is too great," she said, her eyes avoiding him again.

Stubborn wench. He wanted her to look at him. Really look at him. "Our differences make life interesting."

"Perhaps she does not see it that way."

"I know our differences scare her. While uncertainty and unpredictability cause her anxiety, they are the very things that keep me alive."

Now, when her sharpened gaze finally sought his through the dancing candle flames, he knew she realized he spoke of them. Deep in her emerald irises, sparks flared into flame.

"Some people speak of regrets," he added. "I have none. No game is ever lost until a man throws down his cards. But I daresay you're not a gambler, my lady?"

"Certainly not. I don't believe in games of chance."

"You would never place a bet for the thrill? Never take a risk for something you wanted?" The urge to reach across that table and take her by the arms was almost enough to lift him from his chair. Tonight, a dam broke inside Rafe. He had to make her understand that she needed him. She was headed for a life of duty and despair, too afraid to step outside that plan.

When she threw him a warning glance, he knew she'd felt the tremor of his passion. As usual, she blocked it, put up her shields. "Thrills of that nature are vastly overrated."

"How would you know, my lady, if you've never had any?"

"One doesn't need to have the experience to understand it."

Like love, he mused. She thought she knew it all without ever having felt it herself. She thought she knew all about everything.

Soft amber candlelight played over her features, accentuated her graceful neck, and gilded her high bosom. Every unsettled breath she took drew his gaze to those fine bubbies and—may his father forgive him—they almost made him forget he was a gentleman's son.

"I wonder if you ever had any thrills, my lady," he muttered.

Her reply was smug. "I am thrilled every day when I wake to see the sun, or hear birdsong through my window." She smiled sweetly at the other guests around the dining table. By Christ, he wanted to kiss that mouth. To possess it. Make it cry out his name.

"No offense to Mother Nature, but apparently you mistake *thrill* for an everyday occurrence," he replied drily.

"No offense to rebels, revolutionaries, and reckless rogues, but I prefer my kind of thrill to yours."

We'll see, he thought.

His father intervened, bringing their debate to an abrupt end. "Miss Robbins is merely a nervous young lady. I have no doubt she will soon realize her error and come back to my son."

"Let us speak of something more cheerful," his stepmother exclaimed. "Mrs. Kenton, I know you will be most excited to hear of Lady Mercy's idea to resurrect the local assembly room balls, and I am certain she will invite you to join her planning committee."

Thus the subject changed, focusing on more of The Danforthe Brat's meddling ways. It seemed she found plenty to keep her busy while she remained in the country.

Rafe planned on doing his part to make certain she wouldn't become bored.

❧

After the maid helped her dress for bed, Mercy sat up for quite a while composing a letter to her brother. Her temper was decidedly more forgiving now than it had been earlier regarding his interference in this affair. The wedding he prevented—if indeed he had a hand in it—would have been a farce, it seemed, just as he suggested.

Rafe had not outgrown his wild streak, and he was more intent on flirting with her than he should be if he truly suffered a damaged heart. As for Molly, since she hadn't bothered to contact Rafe with even a short letter…

But there was still much here to be fixed, much more to be put straight than she'd ever imagined—and Carver should not expect her home until all was resolved. Fate sent her here for a reason. As Lady Mercy Danforthe, she had a duty to those whose lives were less orderly, less well regulated. Her brother would understand why she stayed.

She blotted her letter, folded and sealed it. There. That had bought her another week at least.

Blowing out all but one of her candles, she turned to the bed and pulled back the tapestry curtain that was drawn around it.

There lay Rafe Hartley, on his back, ankles crossed, arms behind his head. His boots, she noted, were not removed, but his tailcoat was. She almost dropped her candle, and the flame sputtered wildly, caught in the startled whirlwind of her breath.

"Never realized it took a wench so long to ready for bed," he said.

"What do you think you're doing here?"

"I had a wine stain on my coat," he replied as he sat up partway, rested on his elbows, and grinned drowsily. "Grieves, my father's valet, offered to take care of it for me, so I needed somewhere to wait."

Her candle shook. "You cannot stay here. Get out at once. What if someone saw you enter my chamber?"

"Well, that's the thing, you see. I was actually looking for my sisters' room. I meant to poke my head in and say good night to the little minxes before I left, but I found myself in here by mistake. Then I heard people in the hall, and I was forced to hide. Couldn't risk leaving again and being seen, could I? It was like Vauxhall Gardens out there—folk milling about constantly."

She didn't believe a word of it. "I'm sure you've never been to Vauxhall Gardens."

"True, but I'm not completely ignorant of all the places gentlemen take their ladies for an illicit fumble in London."

Naturally, he would be most interested in those sorts of places, rather than art galleries and museums, places of cultural entertainment.

He yawned and dropped back again, his head on her pillow. "Now *this* is a comfortable bed. I almost fell fast asleep."

He must have been there for an hour at least, since the Milfords left, and she thought he had too. In that time, he'd lain there, making up this ridiculous story. In all likelihood, he'd watched her through the bed drapes while the maid undressed her. To her distress, a prickle of wicked excitement blossomed in goose bumps over her skin. He could have been caught there at any moment before she came to bed. The maid might have pulled back the drapes and found the man lying there. That idea did not make the prickle go away. If anything, it grew worse.

She remembered what he'd said at dinner about taking risks—basically, that he took them to be sure he lived.

Mercy shoved Rafe's boots off the bed and straightened the counterpane with brisk slaps and sharp tugs.

"You may take all the risks and enjoy all the thrills you desire," she said breathlessly as she pummeled the pillows with unladylike violence. "But I don't appreciate your dragging me into it, sharing the risk with me."

He said nothing, but looked up at her, openly admiring. Mercy felt her taut nipples rubbing on the lace bodice of her nightgown. Her breasts were heavy, and the heat had begun again, lower down, causing her thighs to squeeze together, her breath to break in her throat.

"Where is Grieves with your coat?"

"Below stairs, I expect. Working on the stain. He's a good fellow. Most obliging."

"You should have taken your stain home with you." She eyed his dirty boot heels now endangering the carpet.

"Grieves insisted he knew the very thing to get it out, and that it should be immediately attacked."

Somewhere in the house a door closed with a low thud.

"Soon, everyone will be abed," he added, eyes twinkling.

"Grieves," she pointed out crisply, "knows you are still in the house."

"But he doesn't know where."

"You think he won't look for you, Rafe Hartley? I very much doubt he would leave you to wander about while he goes to his own bed, unconcerned."

All he said was, "I like to see your hair down. Makes you look like a milkmaid."

She currently wore it in a long braid that hung over her shoulder and reached almost to her waist. As he spoke, his gaze dripped down the length of that braid and all the way back up again. Slowly.

"If you give me one kiss, milkmaidy, I'll be a good boy and go."

Mercy studied his countenance and saw that he tried very hard to keep it straight. "I don't believe you."

"Kiss me, maidy." He sat up and grabbed the end of her braid. "Come down here and kiss me."

So now it wasn't just a kiss. She had to get down on the bed with him to give it. There was always something, she thought. Give a man an inch, and he'd take a mile.

"Otherwise, I'll stay here all night," he added with another of those wolfish grins.

Mercy shook her head, tugged her braid free of his hand, and took her candle to the door. "I'll go and find Grieves."

He was up off the bed and striding toward her in the next breath. She tripped, fell with her back to the door, and Rafe Hartley kissed her. He kissed her like a man who'd been waiting all night, all day. All his life.

And Mercy gripped that candle as if it was a plank of wood and she was shipwrecked in the midst of the Atlantic. One free hand was not enough to push him away. She let that be her excuse.

"I'm not ready to throw down my cards," he whispered against her lips. "This game is not yet lost."

"I am engaged to another," she reminded him, terse, but annoyed with herself as much as with him.

"You were mine first."

Mercy groaned in true despair. "Go home. Please." She needed him gone before temptation overwhelmed her again.

"But I've not had my dessert yet." Slowly he kissed down her neck to her bosom.

"You said one kiss," she protested, not very convincingly, her back still pressed to the door.

"Just one more," he whispered, his breath hot and wet through her lace.

"Very well then. One."

He slid farther down her body, and then she felt his hands lifting her nightgown. "I mustn't waste it." He

cursed softly at all the lace ruffles impeding his progress, and then, for a moment, he made her wait. Her
breath almost snuffed the candle flame that wavered
fitfully before her.

"Your viscount should know," Rafe muttered, on
his knees, fists bunching her nightgown up above her
hips, "that this common man doesn't defer to titles.
This man doesn't hand over his property without a
fight." His lips ventured between her thighs where he
kissed her directly on the sensitive spot that throbbed
and ached, causing her so much anguish. "And I don't
treat poachers leniently when they trespass, so he'd
best beware."

She was too shocked to speak, and if she could form
words, what would she say?

Stop seemed most unlikely.

Please continue seemed dangerously possible.

His wet tongue darted out, and the curled tip swept
teasingly over her furrow. Once. Twice. It left her
quivering, hot, yearning.

He blew on her roused flesh. Gently. Wickedly.
Deliberately increasing the waves of need flowing
through her, making her hips move a fraction toward
him in silent plea. But he let the ruffled hem of her
nightgown fall back into place, where the lace stroked
her from thigh to ankle. Then he stood. "My stepmother was right. You do have a cure for what ails
me. And I have the cure for what ails you. One day
you might realize that. Come to me when you do."

"You have nothing I need," she replied tightly.

"Give me one night to prove you wrong."

"Never." Accustomed to getting whatever he

wanted with one blue-eyed wink, now he meant to
treat her like a naive dairymaid or some giggling light-
skirt. She was Lady Mercy Danforthe, not Fanny Hill.

"Does your viscount know about me?"

"Why would he?" she demanded, imperious.

He cupped her chin in his palm and kept her face
turned up to him. "If my future wife had another
entanglement, I'd want to know."

"You and I are not entangled. We never were."

"On the contrary." His gaze was on her lips again,
heated and lusty. "We will never be free of each other.
I, at least, have the good sense to realize it."

"Again, let me remind you, it was not a marriage.
It was void by law."

"I was too poor and common for your brother."

"There were many reasons why that marriage could
not be."

"Tell me what they are again, then. I need a reminder."

"Why waste my breath? You may be rash and reckless, but you are no simpleton. If you did not know
what the rules were, you would not be able to bite
your thumb at them as you do."

"Jabber, jabber, jabber. Plain terms, woman, if
you please."

"Very well, then." She paused, looked up into his
eyes, and then said, "Our worlds are legions apart."

For practical and logical reasons—not to mention
their own sanity and health—they were better off
apart. Better off with partners from within their own
spheres. By an accident of fate they'd been thrown
together in the past, chance and mutual acquaintance
making an introduction when they should probably

never have met. Certainly should never have shared a kiss.

Mercy was suddenly conscious of gazing too long into his hungry blue eyes. For such a cool color, they were remarkably hot tonight. She quickly closed her eyelids tightly, saving herself from the heat, but when she sank into that darkness, her mind showed pictures she would rather not have—of a huge, overgrown bramble hedge looming, and the horse under her galloping for it while she clung on. She felt her seat lifting, control ripped from her by the powerful horse. So she opened her eyes again and looked at Rafe.

"I wish you were coming home with me," he said, his voice low. "I am envious of the time you spend in anyone else's company. Even when we argue, I would rather you quarrel with me than any other."

She did not know what to say. This was another difference between them. Rafe never feared to show his feelings. He opened himself up to be hurt, left his heart vulnerable. Her Danforthe courage balked at that. It was the only time it failed her.

"I'd like to see you every day," he added. "To wake and see you there beside me. Or, if I could not have that, to know at least that I would see you at some time in the day."

It was as if he left his words on ribbons of silk that wrapped around her heart. She could not get free of them.

"My lust for you has not decreased, Bossy-Drawers. What are you going to do about it?"

There, he did it again. Saying things he should not, blasting the rules.

"What is your answer for that?" he demanded. "How will you solve my problem?"

Our problem, she thought. *Remain calm*, she warned herself. Nothing must show on her face. "As Lady Ursula says, a relationship begun out of lust is a mistake."

"Do you suppose she knows anything about lust?" Amusement trickled from his voice like gentle summer rain through leafy branches. "I believe you and I know more about that."

"Rafe Hartley, you shall not be young and handsome forever, and then ladies will no longer be so ready to forgive you for speaking improperly. I hope you realize how much you get away with already."

"Ladies who don't like plain speaking would never be in my company."

"Since you asked me to find you a bride, it is my duty to guide you in these matters. Do make some attempt to conform."

He stared, incredulous. "You still think to find me another bride?"

"Of course. Why not?" Even as she spoke, Mercy felt another surge of nausea, and now she knew what caused it. Nothing to do with the soup at dinner.

She couldn't bear to think of him with another woman. She was shocked by the intensity of her inner protest. Her body railed against the injustice, while her mind tried to regain order.

As long as she knew things were in their place, there could be no accidents. No tragedies.

But Rafe was a man out of place, and he refused to stay in the box where she put him.

"For you I am like lavender. You like the scent of me—can't keep away from me—but I make you sneeze." He was almost laughing at her, but there was still fire in his eyes. "You can't understand why you have those desires for a common fellow like me. You've chosen to pretend they don't exist. Your heart"—he placed his hand over her left breast—"is not accustomed to doing anything but pumping your blood around. Apparently it takes objection to any other task."

Her nipple, already alert and primed, swelled further under his heavy hand. He cupped her breast. His thumb brushed over the sharpened peak, teasing it lightly.

Finally she pushed his hand away and stepped aside. "Get out," she hissed, her breath forced out in a desperate rush. How dare he touch her that way and put his mouth on her, reduce her to a trembling jelly?

"Have it your way then," he snapped, all humor gone from his tone. "Find me that bride as soon as possible and send me a bill for your fee, won't you?"

"Certainly." To her horror, tears threatened. She blamed it on her heightened emotions, the shock of finding him on her bed and then the recent, vivid return of painful memories.

The dreadful hollow ache in her heart.

And with all these sensations carved into the memory, there was the cool, smooth surface of the ball she held in her chubby hands just before she dropped it into the box of toys and closed the lid.

With no more to say, Rafe opened the door and passed through it into the dimly lit hall. No one, fortunately, was about.

Mercy closed her door and sank against it, eyes shut tight, breath scratching at her throat. She thought again of her mother, this time wearing a riding habit, being carried into the house on a stretcher. She heard her father's anger: *"She should never have taken the hedge. I told her to go by the gate, but she was laughing, determined. Reckless woman."* She saw her mother's pale face, her eyes closed, brambles caught in her hair, mud streaked across her skirt, a limp, gloved hand falling over the side of the makeshift stretcher.

Another accident. The last her mother had. Not Mercy's fault that time.

Or was it? Certainly, it could be argued that if not for the miscarriage caused by Mercy leaving her ball out on the landing, her mother would not have been out riding six months later. She would have been preparing to welcome a new baby into the world instead of joining the hunt that day, taking hedges at full gallop just to feel the thrill.

Mercy's recall of these tragic events had been nudged violently by Lilibet Hartley's prank the previous day. Every moment came back to her again now, flooded in. Her mother's cry as she slipped on the wooden ball and tumbled. The halting, painful pattern of her own fearful, guilty pulse when she realized her carelessness had somehow caused her mother to lose a child—a little sister, according to the gossiping housemaids.

Then the riding accident and her mother's death, which had just assuredly been the end of her father's life too, although he lingered on for five more years. She was now forced to relive moments in her youth, when being left in the care of a wayward brother made her feel exposed, vulnerable again. Carver was not quite twenty-one when he inherited his title on the sudden death of their father. He was still bent on his own pleasures, not ready for responsibility. In the gasp of their father's last breath, all changed. From then on, they had only each other, and Mercy felt as if she was rattling around in a runaway coach with no driver at the reins. It was an unsettled period that further reaffirmed what Mercy first learned on the night of her mother's miscarriage; that the world is only as certain as one can make it. The best a person could do was try and be prepared for any eventuality. To have a path laid out and keep to it.

Since then, the only giddy moments she'd known had happened in Rafe's company. When she was seventeen, and then, more recently. The rest of the time she kept to her path and tried to keep other folk to theirs. She was so busy concentrating on straight lines that her childhood had passed quickly after her parents' deaths.

Rafe, on the other hand, preferred curves and circles. He was free to wander about, blithely chasing pleasure without a thought for duty. He was unorganized and unpredictable. A wandering stray. Dangerous.

Sadly irresistible.

Do pull your garters up, woman. And put your toys away.

Chapter 15

WHILE SHE SAT WITH A NAPPING LADY URSULA THE day after the dinner party, Mercy attempted to write a list of potential brides for Rafe. As much as her mind wandered from the task, he had thrown the gauntlet down last night before he left her chamber, and Mercy never refused a challenge. Perhaps he'd said it only to taunt her because he was angry at her rejection. What did his reasons matter? Men seldom knew their own minds when it came to relationships, but the sooner she found him a bride, the better for everyone. He would realize it too, eventually.

Time to immerse herself in business before any sneaky desire for pleasure reared its wicked head again.

The memories of her mama had surely come to warn her. Take the gate, not the hedge. This was no time to be careless, or someone could be hurt. Already he'd tempted her to flirt with scandal, and it simply could not happen again. He *said* he wanted a bride. She would find him one and, in so doing, prove to herself that she could give him up with equanimity.

Mercy had some familiarity with the local flock of

young ladies and knew a few by name, others only by sight. Since Mrs. Hartley was out, she could not appeal to her for help, but when Lady Ursula woke after a particularly loud snore and sat upright, demanding to know what list she was writing, Mercy decided to seek the old lady's assistance.

With her ninety years of amassed knowledge, and a memory that could be surprisingly thorough when it chose to be, Lady Ursula turned out to be a fount of information on the eligible women of Morecroft. Curiously, she could not remember who Rafe was or how he was connected to her, but she knew the lineage of every bonneted maiden they saw from the parlor windows, and the secrets of every married lady too.

"Now there—in the ghastly pink—that is Miss Croft-Hawley. She has a most unpleasant laugh, shoulders fit to pull a plow, a wart on her neck the size of a shilling, and her mother is a greengrocer's daughter, common as muck. But her father does well for himself in some form of trade, and she will have a good dowry, being an only daughter. I daresay she would do for that gypsy. Indeed, he should be grateful for the opportunity of such a bride."

Mercy carefully wrote the name on her list, and next to it a brief description of the young woman—a much kinder one than that given by Lady Ursula.

"And Emily Prescott walks with her. The Prescotts are from Yarmouth and, sadly, it shows. A family of fishermen, I fear. Her posture makes one wonder if she should be ringing the bells at Notre Dame, and there are a great many long-sounding *r*'s in her speech. But it cannot be her fault that she was never corrected."

Mercy dipped her pen in the ink pot. "Yes, I always say that children should not be held responsible for the sins of their parents."

"Ah, just alighted from that phaeton, there you see Catherine Dawlish. Widowed. Has two young children. Her husband was in the militia and quite a cad. Her father raised pigs, and her mother made very good sausages, as well as plum cake, which she used to bring to me every Christmas." She paused and raised her lorgnette to study the woman through the window. "She dresses most inappropriately for a widow. Her bonnet is much too young, and her bosom far too exposed. I heard tell of an affair with a farrier in Norwich. Wouldn't put it past her. No woman's hair can possibly be that shade of yellow naturally. Neither are one's cheeks in a constant state of flush without the aid of too much garish paint. Now, a modicum of powder and rouge is acceptable to help the complexion, but there is a fine line between sophisticate and strumpet. As I must constantly remind my granddaughter-in-law."

Having started to write the name Catherine Dawlish, Mercy now drew a strong line through it. A flirty widow in too much rouge was the last thing Rafe needed.

"That blowzy woman there with the flock of untidy children, I do not know. I have seen her pass this way several times lately, but her name escapes me. I've seen no man in her company, although to be sure there is one."

"How can you tell? Apart from the children, I mean, for she could be a widow out of mourning."

Lady Ursula explained, "She goes to such effort with her own appearance—new shoes, I should not be surprised, for they pinch, you see." As if on cue, the woman walking by the park stopped, lifted her foot, and stuck her finger down the heel of her slipper. "That is the third time she has had need to adjust them. And, there, see how clean they are, despite the mud in the street?" Lady Ursula raised her lorgnette again. "For all the care she takes over her own garments, her three children are less well shod. Her hair is always curled, and yet the children's do not seem to know contact with a comb. Definitely a man in her life who can afford to buy her shoes, but he may not be the father of her children. She has no time for her offspring and likely resents their very existence. See how angry she is with the one who lags behind."

"You are most observant, Lady Ursula."

"One does not get to be ninety without keeping one's eyes open. Especially in this house of flibber-tigibbets and marauders." Lady Ursula rose from her chair, leaned over Mercy's shoulder, and turned her lorgnetted gaze to the list on the writing desk before them. "I cannot think why you go to all this trouble for that black-haired gypsy revolutionary."

Mercy replied boldly, "Do you not feel some interest in the woman your great-grandson will marry?"

There was a pause. The old lady stiffened, dropping her lorgnette so it dangled from the beaded chain.

"After all," Mercy ventured onward, "one day his children will carry on the Hartley name. Your name."

Lady Ursula returned to her chair and tripped back-ward into it as if she just received a punch to the jaw.

"It may be an uncomfortable fact to face, but Rafael is the last male Hartley and, in all honesty, madam, it is unlikely your grandson will sire more children." She did not know this as a certainty at all, but why give the old lady any lingering hope? Far better for Rafe to be seen as the last male of the line. "You must learn to make the best of it. As women, we face many hard-ships, Lady Ursula. Sometimes it is up to us to keep the family from disaster. I know this, as my brother would be quite lost without me. Now, to the matter of your great-grandson…"

"A by-blow," the old lady finally exhaled. "A bastard child. Son of a housemaid. That the family should come to this."

Mercy sighed. "Quite true, but he is your blood. One must be practical about these things. Don't you think?"

"I always knew my grandson would do something foolish. Never content to let me choose a bride for him. Insisted on being *in love*! As a result, we end up with this sorry state of affairs. An illegitimate boy, born of a housemaid, and two surly, loud, and disobedient girls, product of my son's marriage to a half-breed—an American, for pity's sake."

"Your great-granddaughters are turning into charming young ladies. You should be very proud."

"Charming?" She huffed. "They cannot wait to see me in my grave, to be sure. Just like their mama."

"Nonsense."

"The little one leaves sketches of guillotines about

the place for me to find. Warnings. I have no doubt she plans to take my head from my body as I sleep one night."

Mercy chuckled. "Lilibet does have quite a gruesome fixation, but I suppose that is due to her age. Were you never like that, Lady Ursula?"

"Certainly not. I behaved as all children should. I was seen and not heard. And I was seen only when I was clean, well groomed, and sent for to be looked at. Children these days run about willy-nilly, unsupervised, and not in the least respectful." The many lines and folds of her face falling in a grim, weary languish, she shook her head, the lace lappets of her cap almost reminding Mercy of a bloodhound's ears. "Could my grandson have disappointed me more with his offspring? My ancestors must be turning in their graves to see what has become of this family. All because he could not allow me to choose his bride."

"Precisely. Men are dreadful at making important and logical decisions. That is why I offered to help Rafe Hartley." Brisk and efficient, Mercy blotted her list. "At least you and I can help prevent another disaster, Lady Ursula, because who knows who the last remaining Hartley would pick without your guidance."

When he passed Hodson's shop, Rafe noted his father's curricle outside. Naturally, The Danforthe Brat was incapable of staying long in the area without visiting Hodson's. She was an incorrigible shopper.

The little bell above the door announced his arrival with a pert tinkle, and Rafe's stepmother looked over.

Although caught up in the assessment of some lace, she smiled and waved. He removed his hat and smiled back, hoping the slight tremor of disappointment wouldn't show on his face. But as he strode across the creaking wooden floor, he heard a voice he recognized, and thus his mood improved, as did his day. His instincts were right. *She* was there.

In a pensive temper last evening, he'd pondered his feelings for Mercy, comparing her effect on him with that of Molly Robbins. He concluded that while Molly was soft, quiet, and reflective as a summer Sunday morning, Mercy Danforthe was the brisk, heart-stopping cascade of thunder and refreshing rain that came out of nowhere late in the day and lingered afterwards in a brilliant but transient rainbow. Beautiful, yet untouchable. Her beginning and her end indefinable. Impressed with his poetic turn of mind, he'd even thought of writing his ideas down. Fortunately, the desire passed.

"I am most disappointed, Mrs. Hodson," the rainbow complained. "I had plans for that beautiful peacock-feather muff you described to me."

"It was purchased out of the window almost as soon as it was put in. My husband was sadly unaware I meant to reserve it for you."

The shopkeeper's wife appeared around a display of watering cans, and Mercy followed close behind, her expression vexed as she compared two muffs, one on each arm.

Rafe bowed to the ladies and waited until Mrs. Hodson was occupied with his stepmother. "How lucky that we should meet, Lady Mercy," he said.

"Is it?" she muttered churlishly, not looking up from the items she studied so intently on her arms. He couldn't tell whether she was in a temper with him or the muffs. Likely both.

Hands clasped behind his back, keeping them out of trouble, he said, "I hope you gave some thought to the matter we discussed."

Finally she looked up. "Ah, yes. Finding you a bride."

That was not what he meant, of course. Frustration twisted through his body, every muscle and sinew reacting to her smug, superior expression. "You still mean to go through with that?"

"Of course. I told you I would."

Very well, if that was the way she wanted to play this game. "I await your expertise, Lady Mercy. Don't let me down."

She smirked, her head tilted. "You may trust that I have it all under control."

"Because, of course, if you find yourself over-whelmed with the task, Mrs. Kenton is most willing to help."

At the mention of that lady, her eyes flared and her lips forgot their self-satisfied twist. "I'm sure I can manage."

"She invited me to tea, you know."

"How nice." Now her smile turned glacial.

"It is always good to make new friends."

"I wouldn't be too flattered. She told me herself that she is usually so excessively bored here that she would invite practically anyone to tea. Now I see she spoke truthfully."

Rafe scratched his bowed head, hoping to hide his

expression of amusement. "Mrs. Kenton seems most earnest in her desire to help mend my broken heart."

"Well, if you decide her matchmaking abilities are greater—"

"Would it not improve my chances to have both of you at work upon the matter?"

"No," she snapped. "Mrs. Kenton has her own methods, no doubt. She has strong views on everything."

Rafe feigned surprise. "You did not take a liking to the lady?"

She studied the muffs on her arms again. "I have no opinion one way or the other. You must do as you please."

Laughter spilled out of him before he could restrain it. "You have no opinion? Good Lord, has the sky fallen in? Is that...is that Richardson's old sow flying by the window?"

Mercy turned her back and tossed both muffs onto the counter. "I'll take them all, Mrs. Hodson."

"Very good, my lady!"

"Perhaps you don't approve of Mrs. Kenton," he whispered, stepping up behind her, "simply because she's just like you."

She rounded on him. "How dare you? She is nothing like me."

"On the contrary. Mrs. Kenton is you in another twenty years or so. Unless someone takes you in hand by then and curbs your meddling. I sincerely doubt that Viscount Grey is capable."

A small, tight sound escaped from somewhere inside The Brat, but her jaw tensed, and her lips shut firmly.

"If he was capable," he added, "you would never have agreed to marry him."

"Unlike you, he doesn't think I require *taking in hand*."

"He must not know you so well as I do."

"Oh…just…just go away." That, it seemed, was the best she could do.

"The purchase of a new muff brought you to Sydney Dovedale?" he asked. It was an odd place to come for the latest fashions, and she would not have much more use out of a muff until autumn.

"I was buying a gift for your aunt," she replied reluctantly. "We are on our way to her, and Mrs. Hartley wanted to purchase lace for a christening gown she's making."

Rafe glanced again at the muffs. "My aunt will have few occasions to use those. She is a farmer's wife, not a lady of fashionable leisure. She has no time to sit around thinking of ways to interfere and generally create havoc. I daresay *her* hands are too busy to get cold."

"These are for your sisters. The gift for your aunt is already bought and wrapped." A heavy sigh drifted over the downward curve of her lower lip. "Sadly, neither of these muffs are quite what I had in mind for myself. I was rather sold upon the idea of peacock feathers."

"I suppose it's seldom you encounter something you can't have. Unlike the rest of us." He stared at her petulant lips. "But those would warm hands just as well as one made of peacock feathers. Perhaps even better."

"That is beside the point, Hartley. Peacock feathers would have been splendidly dramatic." She sighed again, visibly frustrated. "I cannot expect you to understand, of course. You know nothing of

fashion." Her sultry, willow-green gaze turned to
his muddy boots, then traveled slowly upward, over
his much-worn, much-stained, but very comfortable buckskin breeches, and finally to his favorite
old waistcoat. "You clearly get your style tips from
the *Pig Breeders Gazette*." She closed her eyes and
shook her head, disdain oozing from every hair on
her head.

"I don't have coin or time to waste on fripperies
and trivial nonsense," he muttered as his hands tugged
on the labels of his patched coat. "I work for a living.
I'm a man of the soil, not an idle toff. I don't have
other folk to do things for me, freeing up my day so
I have plenty of hours to do naught but worry about
peacock-feather muffs."

His stepmother came over, arms full of packages.
"Lady Mercy and I were just discussing with Mrs.
Hodson the possibility of donations for the assembly
room, Rafe. Remember, I told you about Lady Mercy's
plans. Perhaps you would volunteer your services."

"What on earth could I contribute?" he muttered,
not seeing much to be excited about at the prospect
of monthly balls. He was no dancer. He'd sooner be
tortured on a medieval rack.

"We could make use of a strong, able fellow like
yourself to hang new curtains and replenish a little
paintwork. The room above the Red Lion is in a sad
state of disrepair."

"Oh, but Rafe is always very busy," Mercy
exclaimed, her tone weary, lips pouting. "He must
work for a living, unlike some of us. We cannot ask
him to take time away just for our *trivial nonsense*. To

be sure, we can find other men willing and able. He need not put himself out for us."

He ignored her and directed a reply to his step-mother. "I'll do what I can to help."

Mercy turned away to discuss her purchases with the shopkeeper's wife, and he stared at the back of her bonnet. He thought about ripping it off her head, turning her around. Making her kiss him.

"Rafe, do help me with these packages."

He tore his gaze away from Mercy's bonnet, took some of the heavier parcels from his stepmother's arms, and followed her outside. The curricle was soon so loaded down with presents that there was barely room for a driver, let alone a passenger too. "Oh dear," his stepmother remarked, finger to her lips, "I hope we haven't overdone it. Sophie will be most annoyed." She swung around as Mercy came out of the shop behind them. "Lady Mercy, I fear there is no room for you in the curricle. Dear Rafe must bring you in his cart."

In the next breath, his stepmother was in her seat, gathering the reins and smiling down at them.

"I'll see you there. Make haste." And she was gone.

Mercy looked over her shoulder. She hoped stupidly for some other form of transport to make itself suddenly available. But there was only Rafe's cart and horses.

"You'll have to make do with me, Dainty Breeches," he muttered. "Despite my lack of sartorial elegance."

"So it appears, you big brute."

As the last word left her lips, he raised his hand to her face. Not knowing what he meant to do, she went very still. Her pulse raced like a rabbit from a hound. He stroked one large finger along her cheek and moved a curl of her hair.

"What is it?" she exclaimed, fraught.

"You had a hair out of place. Can't have that, can we?"

"For pity's sake, let's get this over with."

He offered his other hand to help her up into the cart. It was a large hand. Everything about him was too large. Her own hand looked like a child's doll in comparison.

Just as she raised her foot to the step, Mercy realized they were being watched from across the lane. Mrs. Flick had caught them in the rays of her prim, bespectacled glare as she exited the cobbler's. She quickened her hobbling pace across the village common, chased by a flock of swans that had wandered up out of the nearby lake.

"Lady Mercy Danforthe! You remain *still* in the neighborhood? I thought you had returned to London. Something most pressing must have kept you here."

Mercy slid her fingers from Rafe's enormous fist and prepared her most nonchalant face to greet the old gossip. "I decided to stay a while longer, Mrs. Flick. I trust you are well." Certainly the ancient crone—usually reliant on a walking stick—managed to move with surprising alacrity on her own two feet when she was afraid of missing an ounce of good scandal.

"And you, Hartley. No word from Moll Robbins, eh? I thought you would have gone after the girl, but now I hear you have other company at the Red Lion to occupy your time."

Mercy looked at him, wondering what the Red Lion had to do with anything.

"Molly Robbins does not want me to chase after her," he said.

The old woman leered at Rafe. "'Tis just as well. Young men today. Not to be trusted." Her small, mean eyes grew bored with him and now inspected Mercy's appearance. "Tom Ridge tells me *you* enjoyed yourself at Merryweather's Tavern not so many nights ago. Indulging in the demon drink. With young Hartley here at your side."

She felt her heart drop. Most folk in that village treated Mercy with respect, as befitted her status, but old Mrs. Flick considered herself above paying deference to anyone. At her age, she clearly saw no reason to hide her venomous fangs. Sinking them into surprised quarry was probably her one remaining pleasure in life.

"You and your fine scarlet frock," she added with a sneer.

Mercy drew a quick breath. "The color is 'Mystery of the Orient,' Mrs. Flick."

"Is that what they call it these days in London? A popular color for sin, I'm sure. You were always a wicked child with too much to say for yourself. The rod was spared with you too oft, that much is plain."

Rafe seized Mercy's hand again, and she feared he meant to crush her bones. "Let's make haste. They expect you at my uncle's house, Lady Mercy."

"With no parents to guide you," Mrs. Flick

continued, "I suppose you've been left to make your own mistakes. I hear your brother is scandalously ill behaved. The filthy rich, of course, do not care how they sin. But all that coin will not pay your way into heaven, young lady."

Rafe had moved around, his other hand placed lightly on her waist, his tall frame sheltering her from the old gossip.

"I saw you leaving this young man's farmhouse in the small hours. Illness, indeed. There was nothing amiss with you that morning. I saw with my own two eyes, you in that same scarlet hussy frock."

Guided by his hand on her waist, guarded by his comforting body heat, Mercy stepped up to the seat in front of his cart. "Once again, Mrs. Flick, the color is 'Mystery of the Orient.'"

The old woman grumbled under her breath. Her wrinkled face crumpled even further with disappointment now that they were leaving before she could conclude her lecture with more tales of damnation.

Rafe leapt up beside Mercy, and the cart wheels bounced into action, carrying them away down the lane. Another unfortunate item for gossip, of course. She should not be riding unchaperoned with a man.

For a few moments, they said nothing. Eventually the lane turned, and the horses slowed as they started uphill. Catching her breath, Mercy looked at Rafe. "I'm afraid there will be a scandal." Since several days had passed with no one making mention of her dawn exit from Rafe's farmhouse, she'd happily and somewhat foolishly concluded it was forgotten. Or else people believed the story of her falling ill.

He shrugged easily, expression unchanged, eyes on the road ahead.

"Do you not care?" she demanded as she wondered if the fool even heard what she said.

"What worries you most? That she'll spread the story of you spending the night with me, or that she'll get the color of your dress wrong?"

"I did not *spend the night* with you. Kindly refrain from describing the incident as such."

"Yes, you did," he replied smoothly. "You were in my house, weren't you? With me? All night. Don't expect me to lie for you. That would be perjury, and I'm an honest soul."

She gripped the edge of her seat as the lane evened out again and Rafe's horses picked up speed. The verges whipped by, and her head began to spin.

"Worst comes to the worst," he shouted above the clip of hooves and rumble of wheels, "you'll just have to marry me, won't you? Again."

This was impossible, she thought irritably. Typical Rafe. Thank goodness for men like Viscount Grey. She knew where she was with him. There were no surprises, no puzzles. Life with him would be smooth, predictable, neat, and tidy.

They bumped over a hard rut, and Mercy almost slid out of her seat. His cart was far less comfortable and safe than any vehicle she'd ever ridden in before. "Slow down, knave!"

He slowed the horses to a walk, much to her relief and a measure of surprise. She stared at the passing verges and plowed fields beyond them, finding comfort in the neat lines of rolled earth and the trimmed hedges separating fields in a quilt-like pattern. "What did she mean about the Red Lion and company there to occupy your time?"

"Who knows?" He snorted. "The old hag is half-senile."

Just then an open barouche appeared around a bend in the lane, heading toward them. Rafe pulled his cart aside to let it pass and tipped his hat when they saw it was Mrs. Kenton, her sister, and Sir William.

"Good day to you!" Mrs. Kenton called out as they trotted by. It looked as if she appealed to her brother to stop the carriage, but he was lost in his daydreams, and in the next instant they were gone. It had been just enough time for Mercy to see the large peacock-feather muff in Mrs. Kenton's lap. The gall of that woman!

How could Rafe say she was just like her? It was an outrageous insult. She swiveled on the little wooden seat to stare straight ahead, teeth grinding.

"Miss Milford looked very pretty today," he observed.

"Miss Milford looks pretty every day. The very moment she awakes, I'm certain, her face could launch a thousand ships."

A rumble of laughter shook the wooden seat on which they both sat. "Envious, my lady Bossy-Drawers?"

"Not at all. I like her." In truth, she wished she did not like Isabella Milford. It would have been far easier and much less confusing to dislike her, since Rafe was so enamored.

But then he said, "Do you not think there is something about her...almost an air of grief. Her heart has been abused, I think."

Mercy was pleasantly surprised to find him that perceptive. It never occurred to her that he would take time to look beyond Isabella's pretty surface. "I thought so too."

"Sakes, we agree on something for once." Then he sighed and hunched his great shoulders. "Obviously, I can detect the fellow sufferer of a broken heart."

It was hard not to smile when he resorted to fishing for pity, but she managed nonetheless. "Perhaps you can suffer together then. You have a bond already. You can share your tales of lovelorn woe." She didn't believe his heart was in the slightest way injured, although his pride must be a different story. "Miss Milford is a very good sort of girl, and she likes you."

"And you are a very wicked sort of girl who despises me." Quickly abandoning the dour, sad expression, his lips lifted in a crooked grin. "I must be a glutton for punishment. Surely you understand, your ladyship. To me, you are that peacock-feather muff."

Reminded of that item in Mrs. Kenton's possession, Mercy seethed inwardly and glowered at the horizon.

"What did I say now?"

Ha! As if he didn't know exactly how to get under her skin.

"Can't you even smile at me today, Bossy-Drawers?" he asked silkily. "Show me your dimples."

"No."

"Would cost you too much, I suppose, to bestow any kindness on a lowly peasant like me."

"Precisely. Since you know that to be the case, I wonder why you ask. And you are not lowly." She thought of the night at Hartley House when he breached her bedchamber and threatened to stay if she did not meet his demands. "You are dreadfully forward, impertinent, and presumptuous."

"And your coldhearted, haughty manner makes you the most irritating creature I ever beheld, but I have difficulty keeping my hands off you nonetheless."

She reflected a moment on his peculiar talent for surprising her. Insults would tumble freely from his mouth and then turn, quite suddenly and unexpectedly, into a form of reluctant flattery. It meant that she never knew which part of his statement to correct first. "I'm sure 'tis a fascination that will pass."

"Why? Because you say it must? I know you like everything in its proper place, all tidy and under your command. If only I obeyed your orders, but I make things untidy for you."

"When things—and people—are in their proper places, life is predictable and calm."

Rafe drew the cart to a halt. "Predictable and calm? Is that all you want out of your marriage? Out of life?"

He said that as if there was something wrong with an orderly world. Perhaps because he'd never known one.

Too many things had occurred in Mercy's own young life to knock her tidy world askew, forcing her to scramble and restore order. She still recalled the gentle crackle of coals in the hearth, the methodical tick of the mantel clock on the night her mama died. Her nanny, old Mrs. Potts, sat nearby, sobbing quietly into her handkerchief, and no one spoke to Mercy of what happened at the hunt, but she overheard plenty and was aware of everything changing around her.

Her father's voice rang throughout the house, cursing wildly. "Why did she take that hedge instead of going by the gate like everyone else? Why did she not heed my warning and take the safer route? Foolhardy! Reckless, headstrong woman!"

In all the chaos, Mercy was exiled to the nursery with Potts, instructed to fill the afternoon and then the evening cleaning out the shelves in her nursery and refolding her clothes, deciding which might be given away to charity. Once that was done, she'd sat by the fire to play with her dolls while the gentle and steady sound of the mantel clock kept rhythm and order among the madness.

Five years later, when her father died of a fever and—so she romantically liked to think—a broken heart, Mercy took her comfort again from that nursery mantel clock. After her brother came to relate the bad news, she ran not into the waiting arms of her governess, but to the fireplace, where she stared at the clock and watched the smiling moon face above the number twelve. Then she changed into the heavy black-crepe mourning clothes and set about tidying her shelves and cupboards, arranging her shoes and boots in a straight line.

Order must always be kept.

"Well?" Rafe Hartley demanded impatiently, eyes narrowed as he stared at her, elbows on his knees, reins slack between his fingers. "We both know what we want. We knew it when we were on my bed together and you put your ladylike hands on my—"

"Never mention that lapse again. Yes, I do know what I want, and it is not you. I will take the gate, not risk my life over a hedge when I can't see what's on the other side."

He blinked at her in a confused manner.

"Never mind," she exclaimed. "Now please drive on."

He dropped the reins, shifted closer on the wooden seat, and clasped her face between his large, warm palms. "First, I'll take my fee for giving you a ride."

Mercy grabbed his thick wrists and tried to pull his hands away, but he was too strong and determined. His lips found hers, forced them apart. She weakened. It horrified her to find this softened center beneath her cultivated barriers, but there it was. He knew it was there and teased it out of her, remorseless, ruthless. His tongue swept hers, curled around it, drank her startled moan. Thank God no one was in the lane at that moment, she thought. It might not matter to him if she was painted a scarlet hussy, but it did to her. As soon as his lips set hers free, she demanded that he remove his hands from her person.

"Are you intent on scandal?"

"If there's to be rumor in any case, may as well make it worth our while."

"Rafe Hartley, that is the wickedest thing you've ever said." It was also not far removed from what she'd thought the morning after their escapade, when seated at her mirror and still suffering the fluttering ache of want.

"So you just used me when you had a fancy for a bit o' rumpy-pumpy that night, my lady." His voice was getting louder.

"I must ask you to stop compromising me at every opportunity. I am not here to be your plaything."

Mercy climbed down from the cart. "I can walk the rest of the way. Thank you, Mr. Hartley. Good day." Lifting her petticoats out of the mud, she marched onward, heading for the farmhouse gates. It was suddenly very difficult to catch her breath, but she would not stop and look back at him. She could not.

By the time she reached the gate, his horses were following her.

She lifted the rusty latch, and the gate squealed open. Finally she felt composed enough to face him again. "Was I not clear enough?"

His expression was faintly amused. "Clear as crystal."

"Then I would thank you not to trail after me."

"I come to visit my aunt and uncle, ma'am, not to trail after you."

"Oh." She swallowed. "Very well." She could hardly stop him from paying a visit to his family, could she? "As long as you don't get any more of your silly ideas," she added as she held the gate open to let him through.

He rode by at a brisk clip and laughed down at her. "Best make haste and find me a bride, woman, or I might take matters into my own hands, eh? Get her for myself."

It was increasingly difficult to catch her breath and focus her mind. She kept seeing a looming hedge full of thorny brambles directly in her path as fast hooves carried her toward it. A loud rushing sound filled her ears, as though the wind tore at her. Why didn't her mother take the gate?

Rafe was still talking, chattering away. "Might decide to take the wife I want by any means, whatever she has to say about it." He leapt down from his cart.

Mercy gathered a breath at last, and forced the vision away. "Then I suggest you invest in a stout pair of manacles and a scold's bridle if you hope to keep her." Quarreling with Rafe was safe territory, familiar. It kept her from dwelling on those dark, unhappy thoughts. Strangely, she always felt better after a good fight with Rafe.

"I was thinking that very thing. Should have had them for my first wife," he said.

"Be still my heart. That medieval view of romance certainly aligns with your thickheaded male chest-thumping."

"Romance? I've no time for that."

"Evidently."

He scratched his head. "I need a woman to feed me, clothe me—"

"Why don't you appeal for a housekeeper?"

"—and provide comfort on long, cold winter nights."

"I would advise a woolen nightshift and a bed warmer."

He grinned. "A bed warmer. Just what I had in mind."

Rolling her eyes, she skirted him quickly to walk on into the house. "Do excuse me. I must get away from your irritating presence. I have surely put up with it long enough today." And she felt the danger of it all too deeply. His mischievous company had certain addictive qualities.

Suddenly he caught her fingers. "Let's call a truce."

"A truce?"

"If you don't plan to be here long, let's not be at war the whole time."

Wary, she studied his countenance, and for once she could not immediately read his intentions. "I've played enough games of chess with my brother to know that men give up only when they know they can't win. Calling a draw is one way to save face."

"But who'd want to save this one?" He laughed easily, pretending he didn't know how handsome he was. "I promise not to try kissing you again. I'll be sensible from now on. Friends?"

Mercy looked at his hand and thought of it on her waist earlier, gently guiding her up into his cart, rescuing her from Mrs. Flick.

"Very well then," she muttered. "A truce." No doubt she'd discover, soon enough, what he was up to.

"Now we are friends, we needn't die alone and miserable," he chirped. "I'll visit you and make you laugh. We'll have tea and scones together."

Amused by the picture, she chuckled softly. "If we have teeth left with which to eat scones."

He considered it, head on one side. "I'll make you some wooden ones."

"Lovely. And I'll knit you some hair, because I daresay you will have lost all yours."

"Splendid. See, we *can* be friends." He gave her his arm, and after a brief hesitation, she took it. They walked into the house together.

Chapter 16

HE FOUND TOM RIDGE, IN HIS LEATHER APRON, standing outside the forge, taking a midday break.

"I'll thank you not to go spreading tales about Lady Mercy Danforthe," Rafe said as he strode up to the big fellow.

"What's this, Hartley? No pleasant good morn? No gentlemanly greeting?"

"I do not care to hear her name on your lips ever again."

"I spread no tales. I just tell what I see." The man was smug, his sweaty face lined with dirt. "If other folk make their own conclusions, I can do naught about that."

Rafe's anger quickened, but he tamed it as best he could. He didn't want trouble here, and had hoped to leave all that behind. "Then from now on, I suggest you keep what you see, in regards to that lady, entirely to yourself."

There, he thought, that was polite, surely?

Tom croaked with laughter. "Lady, eh? In name only."

"Watch your tongue, Ridge!" In Mercy's presence,

he'd shrugged off the gossip for her sake, not wanting her to see how it affected him.

"We all know what you were up to with her in that cottage. I don't know why you try to deny it when 'tis a feather in your cap. There's hope for us poor fellows after all, eh?"

Well, he'd tried. With no further warning, he swung his fist into the man's belly, and as Tom doubled over, falling forward with the air gushing out of him, Rafe brought his second punch up under that broad, square jaw. Tom stumbled, weaving to and fro, and clutched at his bloodied mouth where he'd bit his own tongue.

"You young bugger. You'll pay for that!"

"I warned you, Ridge."

"That was a sneaky, underhand punch," the man growled, humiliated because his father emerged from the shelter of the forge and laughed at him.

Rafe straightened up. "Next time, you'd best be prepared then. I hear one more word of gossip about Lady Mercy, and we'll do this properly."

Tom eyed his fists and spat upon the ground. For all his bluster, there was no way the man would chance his luck against Rafe.

The blacksmith looked at his son. "What's all this? You'll not speak badly of that lady. If I hear of it again, you'll answer to me too."

"Why?" Tom wiped blood from his lip. "She's just a haughty madam. What do you care? Does she pay double to get her horses shod?"

"I care, lad, because when your ma died, Lady Mercy Danforthe brought us cooked food and clothes

for the little ones. She consoled me with kind words
and memories of your ma, when I didn't even think
she knew us by name. She attended the funeral and
paid for a stone on your ma's grave, because I couldn't
afford it. And why did she do all that? Just out of the
goodness in her heart. She knows every family, every
face in this village. If she were asked, I daresay she'd
know every name too. Ours is not the only family to
benefit from her kindness in hard times. Now you
wash those insults and that filthy gossip out of your
mouth. That lady deserves respect, and I won't hear a
word against her."

Throughout this impassioned speech, Tom stared
dumbfounded at his father, in whose stern eyes a fine
mist of tears now formed. Rafe was equally surprised.
He had no idea that Mercy ever did those things.

He'd been so caught up finding fault with her bossi-
ness, he'd never acknowledged the good side of that
"take-charge" nature.

Back at his cottage, he thought more about Mercy
Danforthe—the facets of her life that he seldom
considered. Duty was very important to her, and she
would, no doubt, think it part of her obligations to
take an interest in the lives of people like the Ridges,
but perhaps she did so with genuine concern too. Rafe
knew she was capable of throwing herself wholeheartedly into an idea when it came to her, and not only
did she like things in neat order, but he sensed that
she also wanted folk to be happy. That was often her
driving force.

When the blacksmith spoke of her with such
warmth and admiration, it made Rafe feel proud that

he knew her, counted her as a friend. He also knew that whatever her thoughts on the matter, she would always be more than a friend to him. The regard in which he held her grew higher every day, and there was nothing either of them could do about it.

⤫

Tiresome as Mrs. Kenton's chatter could be, Mercy was soon reluctantly obliged to admit gratitude for the lady's help. She certainly threw herself, wholeheartedly, into the renovation of the dusty, old assembly room, donating several yards of material for new window drapes and a box full of beeswax candles. Unfortunately, Mrs. Kenton's opinions on paint color clashed with Mercy's. She was also very adamant on the best way to polish a floor, the most flattering way to place lighting, and how many instruments ought to be hired to play for a public dance. It seemed she was an expert in everything.

"I do realize," Mercy huffed in Mrs. Hartley's ear one afternoon, "that being a lady nearing forty, Mrs. Augusta Kenton is entitled to her opinions and should be treated with respect, but I confess myself extremely weary of her vast compendium of knowledge."

Her companion laughed. "Mrs. Kenton means well."

Mercy arched an eyebrow. "I always think that when a person's actions need to be explained as *meaning well*, they have obviously failed in their intentions."

"It is just her way."

"Yes, that's another comment along the same lines."

How on earth could Rafe suggest she was just like that woman? There was no resemblance whatsoever, as far as she was concerned. Unfortunately, Mrs. Kenton's company had been forced upon her more times than she cared to count since her arrival in the country and Mercy's stay kept being extended. Now that work on the assembly room had begun, she felt it necessary to see the project through to completion. She could hardly leave things under Mrs. Kenton's management and let her take the credit, could she?

Fortunately, Isabella Milford had amiable qualities that compensated for her sister's tendency to offend, making her presence as welcomed as Augusta's was dreaded. Apparently keeping no strong opinions on anything, she agreed with Mercy on every point. At least, she did so when Augusta was not close enough to hear the betrayal, and when Mercy was able to pin her down. Isabella often seemed more fearful of Mercy's friendship than she was eager for it. The lady was as nervous as a cat in a thunderstorm.

Another welcome addition to her Planning Committee was the enthusiastic and cheerful Mrs. Hodson, who offered her assistance and brought any odds and ends that could be spared from her husband's shop. Eager to keep Lady Mercy's valuable custom, she could be counted upon to raise her flag squarely on Mercy's side in any debate. Often without even knowing what it was about.

Pestered by his stepmother, Rafe brought his bag of tools to mend a few floorboards and a hole in the musician's podium. The moment he entered the ballroom, Mercy felt the atmosphere change. He was instantly the center of all attention, and naturally he basked in it, teasing the ladies and good-naturedly taking more of Mrs. Kenton's ever-ready advice. This annoyed Mercy more than anything—that he could submit to that woman's advice and yet never heed hers. He was quick to take Mrs. Kenton's side whenever she appealed to his judgment. As if he knew anything about decorating a ballroom.

"He merely appeases the lady," Mrs. Hartley assured her in a whisper.

"I'm glad he feels it necessary to appease *her*."

"I'm surprised that you would want merely to be appeased by Rafe. I always rather thought you enjoyed the argument."

When Mercy turned to look at her, Mrs. Hartley was already walking away at a smart pace, eager to check on Isabella's progress with the covering of some chairs.

Rafe stood beside Mrs. Kenton, listening with rapt attention to the old busybody, who attempted to secure his promise of attending the first ball. "I hear, Mr. Hartley, that women far outnumber gentlemen here in Morecroft and the surrounding villages. You simply must come! We can't have ladies standing up together. That would be a shocking waste of all our hard work."

"I doubt it will be wasted. I always thought ladies needed something to keep busy." He glanced over at Mercy. "Keep them out of trouble."

If she was a woman of less self-control, she would have stuck out her tongue, but then she remembered their truce and held her temper.

"Oh, Mr. Hartley, you cheeky young fellow," Mrs. Kenton simpered. "Now tell me, sir, do you prefer a stately but dull minuet to open a ball, as is the old-time tradition, or would you favor something unusual and lively to begin? A Scottish reel, for example? Something to get the blood up?"

Mercy ground her teeth. This had been a subject of debate earlier that day between herself and Mrs. Kenton, but she doubted Rafe even knew the difference between the two dances.

"I prefer a plain country jig, Mrs. Kenton. I like it even better if I am not expected to take part. I can look foolish enough without exposing myself to ridicule deliberately."

"Now, now, sir! You tease! You must not turn shy on us. I shall not allow it. So you do prefer something less traditional."

"Madam, I am always in favor of the untraditional. I am not a great one for rules of any kind. Especially since I am never applied to in their making, they are generally never to my advantage, and I am always forced"—he winked at the lady—"to break them."

Mrs. Kenton tittered stupidly. "Oh, Mr. Hartley, the things you do say!"

Mercy marched over to his bag of tools, took a hammer, and returned to the stray nail she'd been trying to pull out of the wall for ten minutes at least. She had intended to pull it out using the hooked end of the hammer but changed her mind. With one hearty bang, she crushed that stubborn nail firmly into the wall.

Mrs. Kenton was still talking, no loud noise enough to stop her once her tongue was set in motion by a new idea. "Mr. Rafe Hartley, you have put me in mind of a scheme to raise more donations." She danced in a circle, fingers waving over her head.

"Have you been bitten by a spider?" Mercy asked politely, almost hopefully.

"No, no! But I have come upon a splendid idea to benefit the ballroom, which is still in need of funds to repair the old chandelier and those broken windowpanes."

Mercy had already offered to pay for all the outstanding items, but neither Mrs. Hartley nor Mrs. Kenton would hear of it. She was told she had contributed enough already. "And as you are not local," Mrs. Kenton had added once, "it would not be fair to take more from you, Lady Mercy. After all, you will hardly ever reap the benefit. I cannot imagine you will come often, if ever again."

She was tempted to respond that if she was not "local," then neither was Mrs. Kenton, strictly speaking. But she chose not to engage the dreadful busybody on that occasion. There were plenty of other points to quarrel over.

Now the woman enthused over her sudden thunderbolt of an idea, as if it was a remedy for wrinkles and age spots. "We shall have a bachelor auction to raise funds and donations!"

Mrs. Hartley was interested immediately. "A bachelor auction?"

"There are so few about—we suffer from a paucity of single males here, as my sister observed. I'm sure ladies will bid handsomely for a partner like Mr. Rafe Hartley."

Still holding the hammer, wishing she had something else to knock into the wall paneling, Mercy muttered, "I do not like the sound of it. Would it not be rather…demeaning?"

Mrs. Kenton looked at her blankly. "It is all in a good cause. I'm sure the young fellows here about will be pleased to participate."

"To be auctioned like cattle?"

"But it will be lighthearted fun, Lady Mercy. The ladies may bid with coin or perhaps the offer of supplies for the refreshment table. They might donate sewing services, or carriage rides to those without. After all, we have not asked for an entrance fee or subscription, and musicians must be fed and paid for."

"It would be very community spirited," Mrs. Hartley offered gently, smiling at Mercy. "I cannot see anything amiss with the idea."

Mercy still did not approve, but she was outvoted when Rafe exclaimed merrily, "Count me in. I do like to be fought over by the ladies!" He looked at her with laughter in his eyes.

"Oh, Mr. Hartley," she muttered, "the things you do say."

❧

Printed leaflets announcing the "Bachelor Auction" were posted all over Morecroft. Young men, and quite a few elderly widowers too, signed up to take their places on the podium and be bid upon. Much to Mercy's surprise, even the ladies were eager to participate. No one but she, it seemed, saw anything tasteless in the event. Even her appeal to Lady Ursula fell upon deaf ears. Literally and figuratively. The old lady was just as excited by the prospect as anyone a quarter of her age.

Mrs. Hartley, after some pressing, did agree that all

bids would be secretly made and sealed. It was a small victory, but at least Mrs. Kenton, who had envisioned a rowdy, marketplace atmosphere, would not get everything her way. The sealed bids would be opened by Lady Mercy and her planning committee at the end of the day, and the highest bids for each partner then written on his dance card in order of value.

"Now you mustn't spend all your coin on me," Rafe whispered, walking up behind her one day as she studied a leaflet pinned to a tree by the park railings. "Save some of me for the other ladies. 'Tis only fair."

She glared at him over her shoulder. It seemed he visited his family in Morecroft much more frequently than Mrs. Hartley had led her to believe, for here he was again, leaping out at her. "Have you forgotten I'm engaged?"

"So?"

"I will not be bidding on anyone. It would not be proper."

He shook his head somberly. "Of course not. How dull you are these days."

Startled and more than a trifle annoyed at his tone, she spun fully around to face him. "Dull?"

"There was a time when you were quite fun to tease. When you would throw eggs at me, and I'd chase you around a haystack until I caught you." A wistful look came into his blue eyes.

"Yes, well, we all have to grow up sometime."

"True." He sighed. "My lady friend in London said much the same to me."

"She sounds very wise." Mercy patted his arm.

"Shall I give you advice on your dress for the auction? So you might fetch a good price?" If he wanted teasing, she'd give it to him.

But he straightened his shoulders. "I never needed help of that nature before," he assured her. "I always manage to catch ladies' attention."

"If that's true, Hartley, why is that you seek the services of a matchmaker to find you a bride?"

His answer was swift, smug, and one she should have seen coming. "Never had a problem finding women—only a wife that stays put."

Rather than discuss that topic further and risk their tentative peace pact, Mercy asked him if he was going to visit his father.

"I am," he said, holding out his arm. "Perhaps you will walk with me?"

It was very odd to hear him being so polite, particularly to her, she mused. But she took his arm, and they crossed the street to Hartley House, where his stepmother exclaimed upon seeing Rafe, "Goodness, we have never been so often graced with your company as we have of late."

He muttered an excuse about having been on the way to his bank when he ran into Mercy, and his stepmother's eyes twinkled merrily as she reached up to pat his cheek.

"And freshly shaved," she exclaimed. "Just to make a deposit at the bank."

❧

When the day of the auction arrived, it was not Mercy's intention to go, but Lady Ursula insisted on observing the proceedings and would have no other companion at her side. Forced, therefore, to attend, she could do nothing but suffer as Rafe took his turn on the podium in the dining room of the Red Lion, showing off with his usual flair, making a jest of it, encouraging the audience with his most dashing smile. Mercy looked around at the furiously scribbling ladies, all eager to outbid one another. Her fingers itched to reach for her own pen. It was worse than shopping, she mused sadly. Just as she could never pass a well-designed shop window, she struggled to pass up the chance to bid on these hand-some offerings. Perhaps it was, as her brother had suggested, a sickness.

Somehow she restrained herself. Now no one could suspect her of having a particular and inap-propriate preference for Rafe Hartley. Once he was dancing with all those other eager ladies, it should nip any dangerous rumor in the bud forever. Mercy only hoped she could witness it all with composure, because she had just discovered a very unfortunate streak of jealousy in her heart, and try as she might, it was yet to be vanquished by any reminder of his utter unsuitability.

By the time the last man took his turn, Lady Ursula had drifted off into a nap and Mercy was about to walk her home, when a woman approached in a rather sad-looking shawl and a bonnet that seemed to be made up of several different ones all ripped apart and put back together by someone with more enthusiasm than taste.

Her ringlets were very yellow and her face very pink. As she drew near, Mercy remembered her as the woman she and Lady Ursula had watched through the parlor window several days ago. The woman with the shoes that pinched.

"Excuse me, yer ladyship." She tilted sideways and then forward in a precarious curtsy. "Lady Mercy Danbridge, ain't it?"

"Danforthe," she replied sternly. The closer the woman came, the stronger the smell of cider.

"You and me share an acquaintance. I don't think 'e would mind us making friends." The woman gave a toothy grimace. "The name's Pyke. Abigail Pyke."

Mercy had never known another woman to walk brazenly up to her in that manner, completely uninvited. Her first instinct was to make a brief but polite remark and then walk quickly away. The forward stranger, however, came closer, penning her in between Lady Ursula's chair and the wall paneling.

"I'm a particular friend of Mr. Rafael Hartley—like what he says you are—and since the feller ain't seen fit to introduce us, I thought I'd take matters into me own 'ands."

Mercy took her in with more care now and noted a grubby string of pearls around the woman's throat. Pearls *in the afternoon*? Imitation, no doubt. There was more bosom on display than could possibly be required in broad daylight at any hour. It was a very good thing Lady Ursula slept and could not witness the vulgarity of her great-grandson's "particular friend." Whatever that might mean.

The crowd in the room began to disperse. More than a few faces now observed her talking with the strange woman. No sign of Rafe. Not knowing what to look at first—not wishing to study any of it for too long—Mercy finally focused on a beauty mark on the woman's cheek and said, "I am pleased to make your acquaintance, Miss Pyke."

"Mrs."

Of course, she thought, the unkempt children must have been fathered by someone.

"Mr. Hartley promised to find us a better place to stay, and those rooms at the Red Lion are so noisy at night and the air is so stale. 'Tis not good for me 'ealth, yer ladyship. Nor for the little 'uns, neither. Shouting and carousing going on at all hours beneath us, and the mail coach blowing its 'orn right under the window. I can't get a wink o' sleep at night, and not for any good cause"—to Mercy's horror, the woman winked at her—"if you get me drift. I thought you could 'elp us find new living quarters, since that young man's bein' so bleedin' slow about it. He didn't want me going to his father, but I might 'ave to if things don't improve. I've me little 'uns to think about, ain't I?"

Aha. Mrs. Flick had mentioned Rafe keeping company with someone at the Red Lion. Molly had hinted that there could be another woman in Rafe's life, someone else he thought about.

Here then was the very creature.

But, no. Edward Hobbs, if he were there, would remind her not to let her imagination run away with her. For once, she would be calm and find out the facts without making any up.

"Mayhap you could visit, yer ladyship, and see the place fer yerself."

In her chair, Lady Ursula began to stir, and there was no chance now to learn more about the woman's predicament. "Yes…" she muttered. "Good day, madam." Mercy turned Lady Ursula's chair and headed for the door.

"I'll see yer again, then," the woman shouted after her. "Yer ladyship."

As the chair wheels tumbled rapidly across the floorboards, Mercy tried to make sense of this development. How had Rafe become involved with such a tawdry creature, who wore pearls in daytime and never washed the neck upon which they were displayed? She had many questions, but none could be asked while she was in Lady Ursula's company.

The next day, her inquisitive soul too restless, Mercy decided to pay a visit to Mrs. Pyke and find out more about her situation.

She found the woman not long up—dressed but with her hair still in curling papers—although it was noon already, and she was apparently not alone.

"Sakes!" the woman muttered, yawning and sleepy-eyed. "Two callers already so early in the day."

Mercy looked around the small room and at the three children ranging in age she supposed from a babe in a crib to a boy of four or five.

Her traveling gaze stumbled to a halt. There was Rafe Hartley, seated in a chair at the table. "Lady Mercy!" He stood at once, looking flustered.

"Mr. Hartley," she replied curtly.

They stared at one another for a moment, and she waited for his explanation, mustering every shred of her patience to do so. *Don't leap to conclusions.* She would let him explain what he was doing there with a woman he'd kept secreted away at the Red Lion. A woman whose existence he tried to deny after Mrs. Flick mentioned the "company" he kept there.

"I met 'er ladyship at the auction yesterday," said Mrs. Pyke.

"I see," he replied.

Mercy added, "Mrs. Pyke thought I might be of assistance to her."

"I see," he said again, squinting.

Was he trying to think of excuses? As if it mattered to her, for pity's sake. Mercy folded her hands before her. "I understand she is a *particular* friend of yours."

Pause. "That's right. A particular friend." He'd accused her of being a meddlesome busybody before, and now it seemed to her as if he was deliberately sparing with his answers, goading her.

She looked at the bosomy woman again. In her heart, she knew Rafe was not the sort of man to keep a paramour like Mrs. Pyke, but he clearly wanted her to suspect the worst. He had, only recently, boasted of having no trouble catching ladies' attention. Not that she was ever in any doubt of it. "Mr. Hartley, it is good of you to take an interest in the lady's affairs. I understand you found these accommodations for her."

He bowed his head. "Indeed. What else could I do for an old friend?"

Mrs. Pyke interrupted loudly. "These ain't the best lodgings I ever stayed in, by far. You told me we could do better, once we was settled in. But I've been patient, and I've got—"

"Little ones to take care of, yes, so I see." Lady Mercy glanced at the child in the crib and then turned her gaze back to Rafe. "Old friends? Have you known Mrs. Pyke for long?"

"A fair length of time." A slow smile eased across his face. "Mrs. Pyke is my friend from London. The lady I told you about. The lady of the velvet purse."

Mercy struggled to keep a solemn countenance. "Really? The lady of the velvet purse? Your benefactress?"

"She has fallen on hard times, as you see, and I would like to repay her for those many kindnesses."

She nodded gravely. "How very steadfast you are to an old friend."

"I am so to all my friends."

※

He saw at once that her lively imagination was at work in regard to his relationship with Mrs. Pyke. Her eyes were not the only bright shade of emerald in evidence. At first, he was annoyed with her for immediately assuming the worst—that he might be attracted to Mrs. Pyke. Clearly her regard for him was not as high as his for her.

But then he saw an opportunity for mischief.

For a woman who claimed to want him married off and out of her hair, Lady Mercy was showing remarkably little interest in finding that bride she'd promised, and he had warned her that he could take matters into his own hands.

Mrs. Pyke was listing her complaints about their current lodgings. "If we 'ad better rooms, yer ladyship, I know me 'ealth would improve. Something by that park, where it's right peaceful, would suit me."

"I'm sure Mr. Hartley and I can come up with a solution."

Naturally she thought she could take over, he mused. "It is good of you to offer assistance, Lady Mercy, but I must take care of these matters myself." He watched her gloved hands as they checked for—and found—dust on a chair back. "I promised Mrs. Pyke that I would do what I could for her and, as you know, *I* keep my promises."

For a further moment, she looked at him, and a dimple slowly appeared in her cheek. Then she turned to the other woman, ignoring his comment. "I know just the place to put you, Mrs. Pyke, under the care of a most obliging lady, where I'm sure you will be very comfortable."

Rafe watched her fingers twitching as she looked at the eldest child. No doubt she yearned to wipe the boy's dirty face and comb his hair. How would she ever manage with children of her own?

"Mrs. Pyke must come to the assembly ball," she said suddenly, "since she is your *particular friend* from London."

Aha! She'd fallen for it, hook, line, and sinker. He always knew he'd reel her in one day. "If you think she must."

"Oh, she must." Her eyes gleamed. "Mrs. Pyke, do you have a gown suitable for dancing?"

"I ain't been dancing in five years at least," the woman replied, obviously bewildered.

"Mr. Hartley said you do not go out much into Society. We must remedy that at once."

There was a sharp tone of defiance in her voice, as if she expected someone to stop her. Well, he wouldn't. She'd make a fool of herself over this and then have to beg for his forgiveness once she learned the truth. This would teach the meddlesome wench a long overdue lesson about her assumptions.

☙

When they left Mrs. Pyke's room, she said, "I wish you had introduced me to your charming friend much earlier." Mercy was enjoying every minute of this. He really thought he could pull the fleece over her eyes, trick her into believing Mrs. Pyke was his benefactress. "You must introduce her to your father at the ball. I'm sure he will be most pleased to meet one of your London acquaintances."

Some of the cockiness went out of Rafe's expression at the suggestion of his father meeting Mrs. Pyke. But even with his eyes narrowed cagily, he gave Mercy a smile just as sweet as the one she gave him. "Excellent idea."

She laughed. "I am so relieved you and I are friends and no longer at war. No longer looking to tease each other."

"Quite," he replied through his smile. "We shall have fun together at the ball."

"We most certainly shall." She paused. "I must say, Mrs. Pyke is exactly what I expected."

"She is?" They walked together down the narrow stairs to the courtyard of the inn. "Elaborate, if you please."

"She is a lady of obvious taste and refinement. Of knowledge and…wit. Just as you described her."

He said nothing.

"But tell me of this arrangement between you," she pressed. "The one you told me of before. You said marriage is out of the question for her."

"It is." His gaze clouded over, and she suspected he was trying to remember the things he'd said of his benefactress.

"I really think it is unfair of you not to consider Mrs. Pyke, now that you are in the market for a wife. You would make a fine couple. I had thought of Isabella Milford for you—as she is so *accomplished, demure,* and...*sensitive.* But now I think Mrs. Pyke is a better match. Much more"—she looked at him—"you. More suited to the earthy man of the soil."

Pressing a finger to his lips, he nodded. "Perhaps you are right."

"But you must make your choice with care at the ball. I have sent personal invitations to every eligible lady in Morecroft and beyond." She laughed again. "How will you manage, Mr. Rafe Hartley, with all these women vying for your affections?"

He stopped, allowing her to pass first through the narrow arch. "Oh, I'm used to it."

The laughter caught in her throat, and she swept by, biting her tongue.

"It's a relief to have you," he added. "At least I have one lady friend not after me for my body."

She shot him a quick glance as he caught up with her, but he pursed his lips in a tuneless whistle and walked at her side with a jaunty step, to all appearances completely carefree.

Lying hound!

Chapter 17

THE BALLROOM BEGAN TO RECLAIM ITS PREVIOUS glory, the layers of dust and cobwebs cleared away, fresh paint applied, dado mended, and mirrors hung to reflect light. Mrs. Hartley exclaimed that it was just as she remembered, perhaps even improved upon. Lady Ursula, who had to be helped up the stairs by her great-granddaughters but could not be kept away from the scene of the crime, declared the place looked like "a Southwark brothel."

No one bothered to ask how she knew what a brothel might look like.

"I take it you won't attend the first dances, then," said Mrs. Hartley.

"I shall not."

"Pity. I had hoped you might open them for us."

It was actually Mercy's idea to make the ancient lady feel included as a guest of honor on the first night, but she had let Mrs. Hartley make the final decision about asking her. Once the most important and consequential person in Morecroft, Lady Ursula still was exactly that. In her own mind.

She considered her answer for several ponderous minutes. "I suppose there will be cake."

"Of course there will be cake," said Mercy.

"I suppose, if I do not attend to give my blessing to this enterprise, no one will come."

"Without a doubt it will fail, unless you are there, Lady Ursula."

"Hmmph. I shall decide in due course." With that, she summoned her great-granddaughters to help her down the stairs again.

"Alas, she will hold this over our heads now," Mrs. Hartley muttered as soon as Lady Ursula was gone. "Never will one favor be so costly to attain."

Mercy patted her arm. "It was good of you to ask her. She'll come. You'll see."

"After she's made us leap like steeplechasers for the next few days."

"It will all be worthwhile."

Mrs. Kenton elbowed her way between them. "We have our work cut out for us there, don't we, ladies?"

We? Too annoyed for words, Mercy immediately walked away to where Isabella stood peering out of a window, pensively watching a fine drizzle of rain. "Are you quite well, Miss Milford? You look a little pale."

The lady forced a smile. "I am quite all right. I was just thinking...of dancing. It has been some time since I had the pleasure."

She followed Isabella's gaze into the damp market square below and spied Rafe dodging puddles, his head bowed against the rain.

"Mr. Rafe Hartley appears to be a very charming gentleman," said Isabella in her quiet voice.

It was tempting to point out that Rafe would not want to be called a gentleman; that the word, to him, bordered on an insult, as it suggested a person who did naught all day, but spent his time in worthless, even dissolute habits. But remembering they had called a truce, she kept that to herself.

"I wonder why Miss Robbins left him. That was her name, was it not?"

"I believe Miss Robbins wanted something different than that which she thought he could give her. However, I do not know for sure. It is not my business." There, she thought, that was fair. No one could possibly find fault with those statements or accuse her of being too opinionated.

"Yet, she must have led him to imagine she loved him." Isabella's eyes grew very round as she studied Mercy's face, searching for answers. "That was cruel, was it not? How can he excuse her? He must have such a forgiving soul."

Mercy hesitated. She did not want to admit her friend had ever been cruel, and the idea of Rafe being forgiving was very far from the truth. No one was so capable of holding a bitter grudge. Oh, this keeping of opinions to oneself was no easy thing.

"Excuse me," said Isabella, looking away again, one hand pressed to the cameo brooch that pinned her lace fichu at her throat. "It is no business of mine, and he seems adjusted to his circumstances."

"Yes. He is adaptable, to be sure. In appearances." She thought of him entering his father's drawing room a few nights ago, looking every part the gentleman of consequence. Her heart skipped a few beats whenever she thought of him in his blue coat.

Miss Milford was evidently enamored. At the bachelor auction, she had outbid all the other ladies for the first set with Rafe as her partner. He did not know yet, but he would doubtless be elated, since he saw Isabella as such a paragon of feminine virtues. But now he had saddled himself with the charming Mrs. Pyke while trying to tease *her*, she thought with amusement. How would he juggle all these ladies vying for his attention?

Mercy was glad not to be part of the unruly mêlée.

As Rafe crossed the market square and dodged puddles that filled wide, uneven dents in the cobbles, he looked up into the rain and found himself watched by two ladies from the second-floor window of the Red Lion. He raised his hat, and Miss Milford smiled in greeting. The Danforthe Brat turned away as if she'd not seen him.

He heard a horn and dashed aside just in the nick of time as the mail coach rumbled around the corner, splashing him with muddy rainwater from head to foot. Perfect. Just what he needed.

Emerging from the alley was Lady Ursula Hartley, bordered by his half sisters and closely followed by his stepmother, who rushed after them with an umbrella.

Rafe trotted across the square to join the little party. As usual, his great-grandmother ignored his approach, but his sisters greeted him happily.

He took the umbrella from his stepmother and held it for her. "Lady Mercy plans to stay longer, it seems," he remarked and inwardly kicked himself for raising the one subject he'd intended to avoid.

"Indeed. She can hardly leave until the assembly rooms are open. It was all her idea. Now, what do you have to wear for the ball? We must make certain you look your best."

He remembered how Mercy had looked at him in his blue coat and the pleasing sensation it caused to feel her blatant admiration. That, in and of itself, was perhaps worth making a little effort. Perhaps.

"Are you holding that umbrella for decoration or effect, young man?" Lady Ursula demanded, coming to a halt on the path.

He hurriedly raised it over the old curmudgeon and apologized for letting her feel any rain.

"That's better," she muttered. "If you have the height, you may as well be useful for something."

"Glad to find I am not completely without purpose, Lady Ursula."

"All men have a purpose. As Lady Mercy says, sadly women cannot populate the next generation without them."

It was the nearest he'd ever come to a conversation with his great-grandmother. Pity it had to include mention of his ex-wife, but he supposed it was inevitable that the two most difficult women he'd ever known should form a companionship.

Then the old woman added, "She reminds me that you are my grandson's only male offspring. There are not likely to be any further saplings produced. It seems I must acknowledge the fact that the Hartley name shall continue through you and none other." She cast him a quick, dismissive glance. "You have a strong, healthy, virile look about you at least. Although you should cut your hair, young man. Then perhaps I can better see what we have to deal with."

He thought his stepmother almost fainted. She gripped his arm to save herself from stumbling in shock. Thus Rafe Hartley's existence in the family line was formally acknowledged by the woman who had firmly refused to notice it for the past dozen years.

❧

Mercy had no ball gown with her, for there had been no expectation of needing one when she left London. There was little time to get one made, and so Mrs. Hartley suggested she lend her one from her own trunk.

"It is not as grand as any of yours, to be sure, Lady Mercy, but with a little new trim added..."

It was mauve lutestring with a high waist in the old style, short, puffed sleeves, and an appliquéd bodice.

"Of course," said Mrs. Hartley, holding the gown up to the window light, "it is quite out of fashion now. You may not want to wear it. Gracious, it must be...ten years at least since I wore it. I am surprised the moths have not got at it."

Mercy assured the lady that it was perfect. She could see the gown was once much loved, or it would have been cut up long before, the fine material used for something else. If only Molly were there to adapt the gown with her perfect eye for design and steady hand for quick stitching! Alas, they must manage without her skill. The Miss Hartleys were keen to help, but they favored an excess of decoration, and Mercy suspected she would end up looking like a performing poodle if she gave them free rein. Finally she settled for the approach of less is more. It was unusual for her, but on this occasion she felt it necessary to blend in rather than stand out. After all, she was not looking for a husband, was she? She had Viscount Grey. Let the other young ladies put their best foot forward. She would stand happily with the married ladies and chaperones.

As for Mrs. Pyke—her newest project—Mercy had enlisted the aid of Mrs. Kenton, whose figure was similar and who, naturally, was overjoyed to be of some use when asked to donate a gown.

"My friend, Mrs. Pyke, has fallen on hard times," Mercy told the lady. "In fact, I was hoping you might have a room for her to stay after the ball, while she remains in the county. I'm sure she'll be no trouble."

Mrs. Kenton could not comply fast enough, and found a dark blue gown that required only a little adjustment in the bodice. She also offered a chamber in her brother's house. "Anything we can do to help a friend of yours, Lady Mercy. Think nothing of it."

She was, in fact, so civil about it that Mercy felt increasingly guilty for thinking ill of Mrs. Kenton in the past. She might have certain oddities of speech, but she was not intentionally malicious. There yet remained the matter of the peacock-feather muff, however. That was harder to overlook.

Mrs. Pyke seemed to enjoy all the fuss being made over her. She was happy to stand for hours while the gown was pinned—as long as she was fed and watered at the same time. She even endured a lesson in applying less face paint, and suffered Mercy tugging at her hair with a brush and arranging it in a more sophisticated style.

The woman had evidently been coached by Rafe to answer none of Mercy's questions about how she came to be in Morecroft or what their relationship truly was. But Mercy had ways around that. She was confident that if enough marzipan was consumed, enough Madeira wine drunk, she would soon get to the bottom of it.

And thus she did. Having learned of Rafe's kindness to the Pykes, the commitment he made to his friend, Mercy couldn't understand why he kept it from her. Fool man. It seemed as if he wanted her to have the worst impression. Did he fear he might one day have to admit he had a sensible, serious side under that blithe, happy-go-lucky exterior?

Her heart warmed to him again, even as she tried to keep her emotions in their locked box.

She'd always known he had a generous spirit. Molly had often complained that he would give the last coin in his pocket to a beggar in the street, that he left himself vulnerable to those who would abuse his easygoing nature.

But it was that very vulnerability that made Mercy fret about him and want to help the man, even when he never appreciated it. Instead, he mocked her, and she kept coming back for more. Annoyed with herself, she stood before the mirror in her room and reminded the woman staring back at her to pull up her garters.

❧

On the evening of the assembly room ball, Rafe had been ready to leave for Morecroft, when one of his cows required immediate attention with a difficult calving. By the time he'd seen to the beast, washed, and changed clothes, he knew he was very late. He finally arrived at the Red Lion midway through the dancing and just as cake was served.

He made his way to his father, who was easily found, being a good head taller than most others in the room.

"You took your time, young man. The ladies who bid for a turn about the room with you are not very happy, to put it mildly. I have been forced to stand up in your place five times already, with women I barely know. Hardly a pleasure at my time of life." He looked Rafe up and down, clearly irritated by the garments he'd thrown on with haste.

Rafe explained about the newborn calf, and then quickly scoured the ballroom for Mercy.

"There you are at last." Mrs. Kenton was at his elbow, a tall black feather in her hair standing directly upright like a sentinel and twitching just under his nose. "My sister will be exceedingly glad to see you. She won the first set with you and has refused to dance with anyone else until you came."

Surprised, he looked down at her. "She did?" He had expected Mercy to outbid the other ladies. Disappointment and then crisp anger quickly followed on the footsteps of his surprise.

Mrs. Kenton took his arm and drew him aside in a conspiratorial fashion. "Mr. Hartley, you must excuse me, but I find it necessary, for my sister's good, to share with you a sad story. I know she would not wish me to tell you of it, but I believe you should be informed."

He waited. She looked up at him, that tall feather in her hair twitching like the raised tail of an excited hunting hound.

"Isabella is in much the same position as you, Mr. Hartley. She too has been treated abominably and had her heart trampled by a gentleman with whom she thought she had an understanding."

He waited, putting on his concerned face, not knowing what else might be expected from him. One never knew with women what reaction they required. Frequently he chose the wrong expression, or was accused of not listening. Tonight, he made an effort.

"She is a tenderhearted creature, and it wounds me to see her so depressed," Mrs. Kenton continued. "But since we came here, her spirits have lightened. I daresay you have much to do with it."

"Me? But I have barely spoken to your sister."

The lady laughed, shaking a finger at him. "You have charmed her, you sly thing. Now I do hope you will treat her well and not disappoint as another has done." She stopped then, seeing Isabella approach, and lowered her voice. "Do not let her heart remain damaged, Mr. Hartley. Of all men here, I believe you can fix it."

Isabella Milford approached and curtsied, her face shining with hope. He couldn't very well put her off. As they joined the quadrille just beginning, he apologized for his lateness and explained the reason.

"But do you not have men to help on the farm?" the lady asked.

"Yes. Although I like to do much of the work myself."

She seemed puzzled by this, her pretty eyes confused.

"There is much satisfaction to be had in it," he added.

Isabella was looking at his hand, and he realized, belatedly, that in his rush that evening, he'd forgotten his gloves. There was also some dirt visible under his fingernails. His partner graciously tried to pretend it went unseen. "It is most commendable, Mr. Hartley, that you do not rely on your other advantages, but choose to make your own way."

He thanked her but had no inkling what she meant by his other advantages. Over her head, he'd just spied Mercy Danforthe in rapt conversation with Sir William. There was something different about her, something not immediately obvious. What could that dull fellow be telling her that was so interesting? The man rarely put more than four words together, yet he kept her enthralled tonight.

Miss Milford must have tracked the path of his gaze. "My sister tells me you have known Lady Mercy for many years."

"Yes," he replied, terse. "Many."

Mercy was simply dressed this evening, he realized; none of her usual bright plumage in evidence. The Danforthe Brat almost looked like a normal woman, he mused, when she was not all "done up" and hiding behind her garments. She seemed smaller somehow. More accessible. He watched the little white flowers nodding in her hair as she agreed with something Milford told her.

"And are you acquainted with her fiancé?"

"Never met the man."

"Oh."

"I am hardly likely to meet him." He realized he

must have taken a misstep, for his partner was suddenly on his wrong side. In haste to correct his error, he stepped on her gown, and the sound of ripping stitches could be heard even above the music. She assured him it did not matter, when quite plainly it did. He apologized and paid careful attention to the dance after that. Remembering what her sister had told him, he tried to find cheering subjects they might discuss. It was clear that Mrs. Kenton assumed they should have much in common, but he could not find more than a cordial connection to Isabella Milford. She was pleasing to look at, she said all the right things, flattered him constantly, smiled on cue when he tried to be amusing. But something was missing.

As soon as the set was done, he escorted Miss Milford to her brother, so he could interrupt that cozy tête-à-tête.

Mercy's eyes surveyed him with extra warmth tonight, although he assured himself it must merely be the reflection of all the candles. "I am glad you found the time to join us, Mr. Hartley."

"Had a calving at home," he muttered.

"Sir William"—she turned to the stalk swaying at her side—"perhaps you would be so kind as to fetch me a glass of punch and some cake?" He obediently left her side to do just that. Isabella likewise hurried off to mend the tear caused by Rafe's clumsy boots. The moment he and Mercy were alone, she dropped her gracious manners and took him to severe task.

"Since you arrived late—without gloves and with your waistcoat buttons all in the wrong holes, I might add—it has completely made a mess of the bidding order," she exclaimed peevishly. Extracting a small folded card from her drawstring reticule, she almost threw it at him. "Here is the card that was made for you after the bachelor auction. As you see, half the dances are now over and done with. Those poor ladies were left to wait in vain. You will apologize to them, or a few may demand refunds."

Clearly she was in one of *those* moods, he mused. Something made her cross with him again and flustered. He suspected it went deeper than the fact of his lateness and his dress. Rafe calmly took the dance card she'd made and gave it a cursory glance. "My father tells me he stood up in my place."

"You are fortunate, Hartley, to have such a handsome and obliging father. If he was old and toothless, I daresay no one would have accepted him as a replacement. It was also very good of him to stand in for you, when he told me specifically that he does not like to dance with anyone but his wife. As for your stepmama, you must apologize to her also, for sacrificing the pleasure of her husband's company for most of the evening."

It seemed tonight would be one long apology, and he wondered why he bothered coming.

"I had a calving," he said again. "It was not a circumstance I could avoid. But I will thank my father and his wife, of course." Studying the card she'd pushed at him, he noted that her name was not among those listed. "You didn't make a single bid for me?"

"No, I did not. Why would I?"

"I took part in that silly auction only because I thought you would bid for me."

Her eyes glittered, full of reflected candlelight. "You know I am engaged. It would be improper."

"But we are friends now."

"Friends? Like you and Mrs. Pyke of the velvet purse?"

She was fishing to find out more. Good. He liked her curious; he liked to know she was thinking about him. "My relationship with Mrs. Pyke is quite different."

"You are the very limit, Hartley," she exclaimed. Rafe couldn't tell whether she was close to laughter or tears.

Mrs. Kenton passed, chattering away as she danced with a young man whose expression was one of pained politesse.

"There goes your mirror image," he pointed out.

"That woman is nothing like me."

"Really? Let's see." He counted on his fingers. "She believes firmly that meddling is her duty. She manages her brother's life to save him the trouble, and fancies herself a matchmaker. The only difference is she doesn't know she's annoying. You"—he leaned down to whisper—"do."

Her expression was quizzical, her lips pouting.

"Underneath it all you both have good intentions," he added, "just misguided methods sometimes."

He tried to take her hand, and for just a moment, he succeeded. Must have caught her by surprise. Curled around her slender, white-clad fingers, his own looked enormous, ungainly, the knuckles broad and scarred. Another reminder of their different worlds.

"There is good and bad in everyone, Mercy. No one is perfect. Not even you."

Her gaze sharpened, emerald sparks cooling. "*Lady*

Mercy, to you." After lending it to him so briefly, she now retrieved her hand.

Rafe sighed. "Lady Mercy. To me." She seemed determined that this was all she would ever be. The distance remained between them, carefully maintained by her despite his attempts to steer her closer.

"You are so sure I do not fit in your world," he murmured. "Yet you would be equally out of place in mine." Not that it mattered to him. He still wanted her there. "If you lived in my world, you might have to enjoy yourself once in a while, let down your hair and stop worrying about what others think."

She ignored him and looked away, searching the dancers for someone in particular. Someone else to save her from his company. His heart ached when she dismissed him like this.

Rafe shook his head and closed the card in his fist. "What were you talking of with Milford?"

Her left eyebrow curved in a sensuous arch. "He has just informed me that he plans to sell his property. You may soon have a new landlord."

That was no surprise. Milford evidently took on more than he and his pockets could handle when he purchased that pile of stones on the hill.

"Good riddance to him," Rafe snapped. "Perhaps we'll get a squire who takes more interest in the management of the place and doesn't spend three-quarters of the year away from it."

"Sir William has a seat in parliament that keeps him in Town so often."

He glowered at her, not liking the way she was so quick to defend Milford. "Exactly. Why purchase land here if he has no time for it? Men like him collect houses for a hobby. They never view them as homes to be lived in."

"I daresay he had hoped one day to spend more time here and make it his home. When he retired, perhaps." She shrugged. "But he has decided to sell up and relinquish the trouble to another."

"Hmph."

She looked up at him inquiringly. "And the meaning of that grunt?"

"I reckon Milford has pockets to let. That's why he's ready to sell. Mark my words, he's after your fortune, I shouldn't wonder. That's why he's all over you like spines on a hedgehog."

"It is indelicate to talk of money," she reminded him, pert.

"Just the truth. You're always a strong proponent of the truth." Except when it didn't favor her, he thought.

"Well, I believe his sisters' visit has prompted the decision to sell. Neither lady likes the country much—only the idea of it. Admiring a rustic scene on a willow-pattern plate is perhaps as far as they should have ventured. Sydney Dovedale is a little *too* rural for them. They much prefer the comforts of their brother's London home, and Mrs. Kenton is extremely fond, she tells me, of the tamer environs of Buckinghamshire."

"Is there such a difference?"

"Apparently."

"Well, Sydney Dovedale is too rural and remote for many folk." For Rafe, that was the attraction. He did not like crowds or busy streets where he had to adjust his stride to suit the speed of others.

"That will change in time." Mercy sighed. "New developments will come even to Sydney Dovedale. One day I shouldn't be at all surprised if even the smallest country cottage has indoor plumbing."

"I hear it never works properly for those who have it." He sniffed, digging his thumbs into his waistcoat pockets. "And who needs to bathe that often in any case?"

"You sound just like your great-grandmama!"

He did it on purpose to hear her laugh, to see her eyes light up. The pleasure he got from it never faded. Rafe was plucking up his courage to ask her to dance, when she raised her hand in an elegant gesture, and suddenly there was Mrs. Pyke at his side with feathers in her hair and too much punch on her breath. Efforts had been made to dress her up in dark blue silk, but the only thing about her not drooping was her bosom.

Mercy exclaimed jauntily, "You must find space on your dance card for Mrs. Pyke."

His friend's wife was tapping her feet to the music, which was loud enough at that point to prevent her hearing anything they said. There was a definite tilt and sway to her motion and a brilliance to her cheeks that went beyond the application of rouge. "Mrs. Pyke," he shouted, "have you been at the punch?"

She nodded merrily. "To excess, Mr. Hartley."

"Where are the children?" he demanded, annoyed. It wouldn't be the first time she'd forgotten the little Pykes.

"The children are in good hands," Mercy replied on the woman's behalf. "They are in the care of a good lady I hired for the evening."

"Oh, do let's dance!" Mrs. Pyke exclaimed, grabbing his sleeve and pulling on it. "Do let's!"

Rafe looked at Mercy. Her mouth was set in a firm pucker, her eyes stabbing at him like sharpened icicles. "Do dance with your particular friend."

Fine, he thought angrily. Now she'd passed her snippy mood on to him. "Mrs. Pyke"—he turned to the bouncing woman—"we shall indeed dance. What was I thinking to delay?"

Chapter 18

SHE KNEW HIS AUNT SOPHIE HAD GIVEN HIM DANCE lessons that week. Luckily for him, his partner was too dizzy, even before the dance began, to realize he steered her the wrong way most of the time. But he was trying. He had taken lessons in dancing. That he should bother was a surprise to Mercy, for he counted himself above all this. He might have mocked her for being proud and conceited, but he was no less discriminatory in his own way, scorning certain activities he considered beneath his trouble. Busy trying to convince her that he was Humble Farmer Rafe, he failed to recognize his own snobbery.

Lady Ursula had suggested she take Rafe's "improvement" on as another of her missions. "The boy plainly needs a knowledgeable eye cast over his clothing choices and his grooming," she had said. "We might at least see that he does not embarrass us on sight, even if the image is destroyed the moment he opens his mouth."

Mercy had agreed with a chuckle. "I always think

it a great pity men have to open their mouths at all. It would be much easier on us if they remained silent."

This—she was forced to admit tonight—was equally true of some women. And she followed Mrs. Pyke around the room with a pained gaze. Several other faces were observing the lady with wondering eyes. She was loudly laughing now, having slipped on a piece of cake and fallen into Rafe's embrace.

William Milford returned with cake and punch, but she had no time to enjoy either. A number of irate ladies headed directly for her. As head of the planning committee, they came to Mercy, ready to complain about the loss of the partner for whom they'd bid. Mr. James Hartley had saved many of them from a wallflower's fate in the absence of his son, but he was, of course, a married man, and so not the catch they'd hoped to win. Now, adding insult to injury, Rafe not only came late, he danced with an anonymous lady.

Mercy hastily directed them all to Mrs. Kenton who, she assured them, was responsible for the foolish bachelor auction in the first place. Let her take some of the blame. If the woman was eager to meddle where she was not needed, she ought to take the arrows as well as the accolades. Mercy certainly had.

And she had more than Rafe's lack of punctuality and a group of disgruntled ladies to worry about. Earlier that evening, Sir William had mentioned quite casually that he brought his sisters into the country entirely on the suggestion of Mrs. Hartley, who wrote to him very recently at his London house. It was wholly her idea, it seemed, that the ladies should come to Sydney Dovedale with him. She had wanted them, most particularly, to meet Mercy.

Mrs. Hartley, however, had always acted as if she had no hand in the ladies coming with Sir William—as if she barely knew them. It was all very strange. Did Rafe's stepmother think that she and Mrs. Kenton would be friends? Did she, like Rafe, think they had much in common? A horrifying thought indeed.

Glancing around the room, she saw Mrs. Kenton apparently badgering one of the young ladies into eating a slice of cake she plainly didn't want and advising another on drinking less punch. On all sides of the loud lady, people withdrew, trying not to catch her eye or likewise her criticism. Slowly, Mercy took measure of the wide space left around herself. Sir William was the only soul standing near, and he did so on the balls of his feet, ready to take flight. His nervous gaze constantly darted about, as if the room was on fire and he sought an exit.

She'd noticed a chill on her shoulders and now realized it was because no bodies were clustered around her, as they were around other people. Each time the doors opened to admit another person, and with them a blast of cold air, Mercy felt it directly, because there was no one nearby to shelter her. There were a great deal of backs turned. When she met an eye, it was hastily turned away and fastened intently elsewhere. In the past, she'd assumed it was natural deference— respect for her status. Now she wondered.

She swallowed with difficulty, for her throat was suddenly dry.

Had she been such a painful nuisance?

Mercy's blurred gaze found Rafe. At least he liked her.

She couldn't be so bad, if Rafe sought her company. He was honest about his likes and dislikes, and even though they quarreled—fiercely at times—no one made him walk over to her, did they? No one had made him call a truce with her.

Rafe. Thank goodness she was not completely without friends. Her gaze cleared after several more blinks and a hasty dab with a handkerchief. She observed him now with greater benevolence and forgiveness than ever before. Rafe.

❧

Aware of his father and stepmother watching in bemusement, he steered Mrs. Pyke toward them. Time to begin Lady Know-All's lesson.

"Father, may I introduce Mrs. Pyke of…" He glanced down at the woman wilting against his arm, cooling her face with flapping fingers in the absence of a proper fan. "From whence do you hail, madam? I forget the place."

She looked blankly up at him, lips parted, cheeks flushed.

"Where are you from?" he whispered urgently.

Mrs. Pyke seemed vexed by the question and then exclaimed, "I was born in Pillory Lane, weren't I?"

Well, that would do for now, he thought, amused. "Mrs. Pyke of Pillory Lane, London," he confirmed to his startled parents.

His stepmother was the first to recover and politely ask how Mrs. Pyke enjoyed the ball.

"I'm fair worn out," the woman replied. "Ain't been to a ball in ages."

"Perhaps some punch?"

Rafe interjected that he thought Mrs. Pyke had drunk enough punch, and his father gravely agreed. This left his stepmother temporarily at a loss for subjects. So Rafe said brightly, "Lady Mercy has selected Mrs. Pyke as a potential bride for me. Is that not thoughtful of her?"

While his parents looked on in undisguised horror, Mrs. Pyke slapped his arm and laughed. *"Sauce box!"*

Having left this news to ferment, Rafe gallantly led his partner back across the room, smiling broadly.

Within a quarter of an hour or less, the news was all over the room.

Mrs. Hartley rushed over to ask her what mischief she played to match Rafe with Mrs. Pyke. Mrs. Kenton approached her with the same question shortly after, but broached in less polite terms. "That frightful, common woman for Mr. Rafe Hartley? He tells us you selected her as a potential bride? This cannot be the case. I think he jests with me again."

Mercy looked over and saw him grinning at her. "Mr. Rafe Hartley is full of jests, as you've observed." He'd done it to irritate her, of course, make her look foolish. "I thought you liked Mrs. Pyke. You lent her a gown."

"I begin to wish I had not," the woman replied haughtily.

"But after all, despite Mrs. Pyke's lack of elegance and refinement, she is a victim of unhappy circumstances. As such, she should be an object for our concern, not our scorn."

"Well said," exclaimed Mrs. Hartley.

"But I did not know you had plans of this nature. What about Isabella? She is a much better match for Rafe Hartley."

"I'm not sure your sister is suitable for Rafe." Mercy grappled with the best way to word her objections without seeming to criticize Isabella. "His character is too strong."

His stepmother agreed that Rafe needed a wife capable of keeping him in line, not one who would permit him to rule the roost.

Mrs. Kenton's feathered headdress trembled fitfully. "I will not let my sister's chance for happiness be spoiled again, young woman."

"Again?"

Mrs. Hartley intervened with another cup of punch for Mrs. Kenton. Mercy, fearing the woman would throw the drink at her, attempted to smooth the waters. "I can assure you both," she said steadily, "Rafe is not going to marry Mrs. Pyke. It's just another of his pranks and an opportunity for him to make sport of me. Of us all."

Mrs. Kenton demanded to know why.

"I'm afraid it's what he does," his stepmother replied with a soft sigh. "He's always looking for ways to ridicule convention."

"Well, I must say!" Mrs. Kenton muttered under her breath, eyeing Rafe as he whirled his *particular friend* about the dance floor. "That fellow has gone down in my estimation, to be sure."

"I thought you enjoyed his lively manner," said Mercy.

"There's lively and there's impertinent. Mr.

Rafe Hartley, I see now, is in danger of becoming the latter."

Next came his father, who strode around the perimeter to complain to Mercy as if it was all her fault. "I thought that boy was settling down at last, finally growing up, serious about life. But now I see I was wrong. He's just as intent on mischief as ever."

"Mrs. Pyke is the wife of a friend," she explained. "Rafe has been helping them, that's all."

The subject of their conversation was spinning his colorful partner around the floor like a dust mop, enjoying the scandalized expressions around him.

"And why could he not tell me this?" his father grumbled fiercely. "To make me suffer, of course."

"Mr. Hartley, I'm sure he—"

"That boy will never change. He refuses my assistance, never heeds my advice. Everything in life to him is a jest."

"But he is so anxious for your approval, sir."

He scowled, adjusted his stance, put his hands behind his back. "I see scant evidence of that."

"He wants to make his own way in the world so you will be proud of him."

James gestured at the dancing fool. "And this is how he means to do it? He might at least have worn clean clothes and gloves."

"But those things are not important to Rafe, sir."

He sniffed. "I'm not sure what is these days."

Mercy looked up at James Hartley, who was impeccably attired, as always. Like her, she supposed he took comfort from the proper garments and could not understand how anyone else managed without them.

She was only just beginning to realize herself that it was not necessarily clothes that made the man. "You must remember, sir, your son's experiences of life have been very different from your own. He has learned to value other things. He must wonder why appearances matter so much to us. Actions are far more important to him."

James still frowned, watching his son escort Mrs. Pyke and her bosoms up and down the dance. "And his actions tonight? What are we to make of those?"

Mercy shook her head. "I fear this is my fault. He thinks he's teasing me, sir. He's making one of his points."

"Which would be?"

"That he is not afraid of rumor or other folks' opinions."

"Those things may not be important to my son, but they are to me. It's time he learned to consider the feelings of others."

Mercy replied, "I'm sure he does not mean to hurt you, sir, but sometimes getting any reaction from a parent is better than getting none at all." She knew this, because of her own trying relationship with Carver, the brother whose concern and attention she could capture only by running away.

Oh, Rafe was walking toward her with a very purposeful look on his face.

The prickly, overgrown hedge loomed again, and she raced toward it, wind whipping her face, tugging on her hair. Again, voices shouted warnings, urging her to slow down and take the gate instead. But she faced that hedge, put her head down, and gripped the reins.

It was not the fault of the horse out of control under

her. This was her decision, just as it had once been her mother's. She wanted to know what was on the other side of that hedge.

Her mother did not want the gate, because she preferred the thrill of adventure. Nothing would have stopped her that day. Mercy understood that now.

❧

When she saw him heading toward her, she turned her back and walked through the crowd at the edge of the dance floor. Rafe lengthened his stride, took a sharp turn, and blocked her path.

"People are watching," she exclaimed. "After the exhibit you just made of yourself—"

"She told me that you winkled it out of her. About Pyke's debts and why she and the children are in my care."

"Of course. As if I would truly believe Mrs. Pyke was your mistress!"

"But you kept up the pretense."

"Why not? You recently lamented the fact that I had lost my sense of fun."

Grabbing her hand, he hurried her through the small vestibule and into the gentlemen's cloakroom.

"Whatever is the matter now?" she demanded.

"This is more the fun I had in mind." He kicked the door shut behind him, and there in the dark, among the discarded greatcoats, Rafe kissed her, wrapping her in his arms, wanting to keep her in them forever. The need overflowed this evening, and it was too late for any attempt at good behavior. She pushed him back, whispering that they may have been seen, but he advanced again until they were both surrounded by coats, lost among them. Even when she cursed and struggled to get away, her slender arms in their long silk gloves seemed to be reaching for him. Her fingers made a pretense of slapping at him and ran teasingly along the broad slope of his shoulders. The warmth of her body, the soft curves undulating against his hard chest, only pulled him closer. And he ached for her.

Sweeping his hands down the sway of her spine, he reached her bottom and caressed it. She shivered. Her gasps tickled his cheek, then her rushed breath warmed his mouth, moistening his lips.

"Kiss me," he demanded, needing her surrender in the darkness.

"No. How dare you compromise me yet again?"

"Kiss me," he said again, his voice gruff, hard.

There was a small sound, like a mewl of despair. He knew the feeling.

At last came the kiss. An angry one, more complaint than submission. After a moment, as she began to withdraw from it, he deepened the kiss, made her give more, and he took it. She melted through the coats until she was against the wall. Her sweet perfume filled his senses, reminded him of the herb garden at his uncle's house, where he'd arrived as a boy of ten. He could almost hear the bees droning amid the chalky mauve flowers. Coming there to live, he'd finally known happiness for the first time in his life, begun to think he might belong somewhere. It was the scent of coming home.

Her fingers slid down his chest to the buttons of his waistcoat, where they worked quickly. Ah, she was eager. His kisses moved to her chin, her cheek, her ear, the side of her neck. Here the perfume was even stronger, and he could imagine her seated at a dressing-table mirror, dabbing the scented oil on her pulse points, leaving little clues for him to follow. She was probably undressed while she sat there applying her perfume, he thought, the image foggy in his mind. Perhaps she wore stockings. Yes, just stockings. He pictured himself standing behind her, watching in her mirror as he reached around to cup her breasts and fondle them. A shudder of desire rippled through his body.

"Rafe."

He licked her skin, let his tongue slip into the valley between her full breasts, where she was even warmer. Excitement lifted his cock, lengthened it.

"Rafe!" This time she spoke louder and pulled on his hair. "Rafe!"

Slightly annoyed, he looked up.

"There's someone tapping at the door."

Sure enough, as the blood stopped rushing quite so loudly through his ears, he heard the sound of a meek voice at the cloakroom door. "Mr. Rafe Hartley, sir. You're needed at the farm, sir. Bessie's calf-bed has come out. Young Will has been trying to get it back in, but it's a right mess, sir."

He set Mercy back on her feet and gathered his breath as best he could. "I'll come at once," he choked out.

In the darkness, he couldn't see her features, but he could hear her unsteady breathing.

"I must go," he muttered.

He kissed her quickly, just once more, while she stood limp against the wall. Then he left the cloakroom. As he followed the messenger boy down the stairs to the alley below, he made a hasty check of his clothes and discovered that Mercy had rebuttoned his waistcoat, putting the errant buttons back in their proper holes. Even in the dark, even in the heat of passion, she was anxious that everything be in order.

He mounted his horse and glanced upward at the glow of candles through the windows. Music still played, accompanied by the dancers' merry stomping. He only hoped Mercy would not find anyone else to dance with. With any luck, he'd left her in a knee-weakened state. It was damned frustrating that he had to leave her at all.

And it was bloody inconvenient to be in love with one's former wife.

Smiling haplessly, he steered his horse for home.

∽

It was, she supposed, a farmer's lot. Always there was some catastrophe with which to deal. She never had anything more trying to worry about than a wine stain on a crinoline.

Mercy waited a while before she exited the cloakroom, listening at the door first to be sure there was no one near. But if the messenger had been told to find Rafe in the cloakroom, someone must have seen them go in. It was a sobering thought. Once again, she'd flirted with scandal by letting him take her in there. Letting him kiss her that way. She had no excuse for it. Not a solitary glass of punch had passed her lips tonight.

She crossed the empty vestibule and reentered the ballroom. A few faces turned to observe her, and she thought she heard an odd snicker or two among them. Several fans fluttered a little too fast, and more than one gentleman cast her a knowing smirk.

This was very bad. She had forgotten herself with him again. This time in public.

Chin high, she walked to where Mrs. Hartley stood waving to her. Mercy's heart was throbbing, butterflies beating their wings in her belly, but even with that madness inside, when she caught her reflection in a mirrored panel, a calm, composed face looked back at her. No blush of guilt, just a sultry twinkle in her eyes that might reveal—to an observant soul—mischief afoot.

It was suddenly very dull without Rafe, as if some of the candles were snuffed, she thought, one hand slyly checking her curls and the little flowers nestled among them. He hadn't even stayed for half the ball, yet he'd made quite a stir, and now his loss was felt. It was his wicked charm, of course. That carefree manner that stopped at no boundary.

May he not ride home too incautiously, too hastily. Oh, what if he was thrown from his horse and lay injured on the dark road? What if he was set upon by robbers in the night? He could be dead already or minutes from it.

There she was again already, letting her imagination ornament a few facts into wild fiction, as Edward Hobbs would say.

Rafe could look after himself.

He couldn't, though, could he? That was just the problem. What was she going to do about him? About them?

This sneaking about would not do. It was a sure way to court scandal.

But she wanted him. Every pore on her skin, every hair on her head, yearned for his touch. Mercy could no longer pretend that her concern for him was merely that of one old friend for another. In his case, she was not the detached observer she'd intended to be. She was entangled, ensnared too deeply to find her way out.

She looked around for Mrs. Pyke and saw her sleeping in a chair under a sconce, a half-eaten slice of cake in her lap. There, a short distance away, was Mrs. Kenton, conversing with her weepy sister at the punch bowl. They both looked over at Mercy, and she knew, at once, they'd seen her go with Rafe into the cloakroom. It felt as if the entire room spun, and the floor cleared around her. Whispers of scandal floated in the air along with the dustbeams stirred by the dancers' feet.

She took a breath. And then another. Their next encounter, she decided in that instant, would be on her terms. No more hide-and-seek. No more games of chance. She, Mercy Danforthe, must take control of the situation before it got even further out of her hands.

Mr. James Hartley suddenly materialized at her side and courteously offered his services for the next dance. She took his hand, sincerely expressing her gratitude and feeling as if she would forever be in his debt.

"Mayhap, Lady Mercy, it is time you left Morecroft," he said, his tone kindly but firm.

She nodded her agreement, but what she had in mind was probably not what he expected.

Chapter 19

IT TOOK A WHILE TO GET THE COW SETTLED AGAIN, THE calf-bed back. When it was done, he went back to the house, stripped off his soiled clothes, and washed his chest and shoulders. He pulled on some clean clothes and sat by the fire a while, thinking about Mercy, trying not to imagine her dancing at the ball without him. Once again, they'd left the matter between them undone. He wondered if it would ever be finished, if they would ever find a way to bridge the weir.

He stirred up the fire as he felt a sudden brisk chill. But then he heard the door hinges, and he knew it must have blown open. He turned.

His mind was surely playing tricks.

A woman stood in the open doorway. A woman in an evening gown and long white silk gloves. She was shivering in the cold. "I know we don't belong together," she said simply. "And I know we should never have kissed, should never have thought of each other this way. But I want to make love to you. I want us to have the wedding night we never had. This is our chance, and we should make the most of it. We have a few hours until dawn. Will it be enough?"

She waited, watching him, hoping she hadn't just made a fool of herself.

Rafe stood with a poker in his hand, as if he might need to defend himself, she mused. "What made you change your mind, Brat?" he demanded, hoarse.

"Must have been the jealousy, country boy," she replied wryly. "Watching you dance with Mrs. Pyke."

Finally he put the poker back on its hook. "Shut the door. 'Tis damn cold out."

"I know. I rode all the way here in your step-mother's curricle. No coat." She held out her arms and walked toward him. "I must be mad."

Rafe raised his fingers to her hair and began slowly removing the little flowers. "Jealous, eh?"

"Yes. Jealousy and lust." She knew he wanted to hear her admit that she had faults.

He kissed her eyelids and then the tip of her cold nose. "I daresay everyone saw the lust in your eyes tonight, madam. It was quite blatant."

"Perhaps." She felt her heart skipping and dancing like a spring lamb. Perfectly ridiculous, and yet she couldn't stop it. "But here I am now."

He sighed. *"Women!"*

She tugged on his shirt and pulled it up over his head. *"Men!"* Mercy ran her hands slowly up his chest and examined the smooth planes, admiring the gleam of firelight across those gentle hills and valleys. "You are too beautiful, Rafe Hartley. So exquisitely created."

His eyes shone down at her, wickedly amused. "To you, I'm just a peacock-feather muff, my lady."

"Take me upstairs then, and I'll try you on."

He took a step back. "No," he said. "Right here. By the fire." He fell back onto the settle. "Undress. My lady."

Her rambling heartbeat echoed in her ears, but faded in and out. Rafe Hartley sat before her, arms tucked behind his head, thighs spread, eyes narrowed.

"I want you naked before me," he said.

She rather got the impression that, despite his claim of never planning anything, he'd pictured this moment for some time. The only thing not relaxed about his pose was the item between his legs, plainly to be seen jerking against his breeches and stretched almost to his navel.

Too late for shyness or an attack of nerves, she decided. Time for the Danforthe courage to be put to its greatest test.

She reached behind her neck for the little hooks at the nape of his stepmother's gown. Slowly, she began to shed her layers. All the way to her corset, chemise, and stockings.

At that point he instructed her to raise each foot to his thigh, and then he made much of removing the silk stockings for her while his rough fingertips stroked her calves.

"Turn" he growled.

"Why?"

"Turn."

Grumbling under her breath, she turned until her back was to him, and then his hands raised her chemise over her bottom. Warm air kissed her buttocks, and so did he. Then he spanked her. Hard. Just one cheek, but it smarted. She glared over her shoulder.

"That's for making me wait five years," he said, grinning.

She looked away again, wondering if he meant to spank her some more. She quite liked it but would never ask, and certainly would never admit it. The sting of his palm still heated her right cheek. But no more came.

She heard his knuckles cracking.

"I'll need your help with the corset laces," she said, beginning to enjoy the undressing far more than she expected. When she'd first set off in the curricle tonight, she had her mind set only on the moment of consummation, but now she saw there was more to this. Seduction, she thought suddenly. It had all been his up until that point. Now it was her turn.

She lowered herself to the edge of his seat and perched her bottom on the wood between his spread knees. "Undo me."

"Are you sure, my lady?"

Mercy frowned. "Yes. Make haste."

Several moments passed with nothing but the crackling fire to fill the silence. Then he hitched forward, and she felt his fingers on the laces. He was savoring her, she realized. Savoring the moment of her submission.

Well, as he said, she had made him wait five years.

His fingers tugged on her corset laces, much slower than before, each one slipping through his grip almost gracefully. She felt his breath on the nape of her neck and then the damp stripe left by a slow lap of his hot tongue. "Stand before me."

"But my corset—"

"Stand and face me."

She was still half-laced, but she obeyed his command. A curious first for her to obey any man, but she did. She wanted what he had to offer, and she couldn't risk one of their arguments now, not with her need at fever pitch.

While perched on the edge of the settle, he lifted her chemise until she was revealed to him, his face level with her naked womanhood, and then his tongue found her pearl again. His hands reached for her bottom, gripping her hard, fingers splayed as he pulled her against his mouth. A startled gasp flew out of her, and she held his head to steady her swaying body. Somehow her semiundressed state made it even more wicked, her half-unlaced bodice curled from her waist, the straps of her short chemise dripping from her shoulders.

What he did with his tongue was undoubtedly not within the rules…but whose rules?

Suddenly he sat back again and unbuttoned his breeches, his face turned to hers. His breathing was loud, hoarse, and his lips shined with her dew. "Come astride me, wench," he ground out as his manhood slid free, standing tall. Breathtaking in length and in breadth. Mercy had known what to expect; she studied as much as a girl could in these matters. But this was…shocking.

There was no going back. This was the point of no return, and he had readied her for it this time. No mistake, he'd gained experience in those years since their first wedding night.

∞

He held her waist and lowered her steadily onto his tall shaft. She cried out just once as he settled her there and thrust into the soft, welcoming warmth of her tight furrow. Her head rested on his shoulder, and she groaned his name. He waited a moment, letting her adjust to the state of fullness. For him, the glorious sensation of this possession was the greatest he had ever known. She was his at last. Slowly, he lifted and lowered her again, his heartbeat hammering away, painful in its intensity. He wanted to pound home in her, but he must restrain himself. Somehow.

"Mercy," he growled.

His wife.

He pulled her free of the corset, wrenching the last laces asunder, and then he suckled her breast through the thin chemise she still wore.

They had a few hours, she'd said. He kept reminding himself of that. No need to rush.

But the sweet friction of her body was more than his patience could stand. He would not last long. Not the first time.

With her pleading cries in his ear, he carried her up the stairs to his bed, her legs wrapped around his waist. Every step he took vibrated through the broad muscles of his thighs and into the woman he held connected to him by wanton pleasure and forbidden passion.

∞

Carnal knowledge. What an odd phrase that was. Cold words for a heated act.

She'd imagined her deflowering many times, not in fear like Miss Julia Gibson, but out of curiosity. After her engagement to Grey, she'd pictured a grand four-poster bed with his family crest embroidered on the counterpane, and she saw herself sit upon it, waiting in fine lawn and lace with satin ribbons tied all the way up to her throat. Adolphus would probably wear a long nightgown and a bed cap. It was one of those things she knew about him without asking. Not that it was the sort of thing she could ask her fiancé. He would think it very strange if she showed interest in his night attire.

Although she'd eavesdropped on several of her brother's sexual escapades, she expected nothing like that from Adolphus. For one thing, he had his health to consider, and too much exertion was out of the question. She expected the act itself to take no more than a few minutes. Adolphus was frugal with his time as well as his money, and he was not one for a great deal of unnecessary nonsense. All of this, Mercy had felt she could accommodate. But that was when she did not think herself capable of succumbing to lust, when she thought sex, for sensible, practical people like herself, was for procreation only. Recreational coupling was surely the domain of people like Carver.

Now she knew differently.

When Rafe took her to his bed that night, she thought the world outside that small farmhouse must have vanished completely, and everything she was so confident of before went with it. Time meant nothing. In his bed, there were no rules.

He kissed her from head to toe, lavished her with attention. Naked, they lay side by side, exploring each other, tireless, inexhaustible. It must be a dream, she thought, and wondered how they got there. She was seduced, a woman abandoning herself to passion, to fantasy. Until then, she never knew a man's hard body could be comforting, soothing to lie against and touch. She'd never experienced hands that could be rough on the surface and yet gentle in the way they held her. She'd never felt a simple caress in one tiny area of her body that reverberated all over it, made her heart miss beats and then make a new rhythm. A symphony.

He paused occasionally to ask if she liked what he did. Couldn't he tell? Then he would laugh as she dragged him to her for more—more kisses, more strokes, more licks of his clever tongue.

And in the supreme moment, when they were joined with his manhood inside her, she floated, crying out, and her fingers dug into the sweat-lined, flexing muscles of his back. The delicious sensations driving her body to a blissful peak were, she suspected, addictive. She needed that ultimate release—both his and hers—and yet when she felt it nearing and knew it could not be postponed another second, she wanted it never to end.

Eventually, as he lay spent beside her, his arm over her body, his breath blowing softly against her cheek, she forced herself back to reality.

"I must go," she whispered, although she did not know why it felt necessary to be so quiet. They were, after all, alone in his house.

"Stay."

But she slid off the bed and pulled on her chemise. Her skin smoldered from the lingering fire of his touch and, as the fine linen drifted down over her moonlit body, she felt the sigh of every pore and tiny hair. It was as if her body had slumbered, she mused, until Rafe woke it.

"I'll take you back," he murmured as he sat up and scratched his rumpled head.

Mercy swept her hair over one shoulder. It was dry now, but she had no idea how many hours had passed since she rode here in the rain. "We can't risk being seen together so early."

"But we'll announce our engagement this morning." He laughed drowsily. "May as well get the shock over with."

She froze and stared at him. *Engagement?* Had she missed something?

"My father will lecture me, I'm sure, but my step-mother will be delighted."

Mercy did not know what to say. She had gone to his bed with no intention of marriage, which made her a rotten little strumpet. Clearly they were at cross-purposes. The last thing she wanted was one of their arguments to spoil this moment of content between them, but she would have to set him straight at once with the truth.

"I am not going to marry you, Rafe." Again she saw a tall, overgrown hedge looming, her horse racing for it. This night she'd soared into the unknown. It was as if she had to do it, to learn what was beyond, to prove to herself that she was strong enough to keep control of her horse. That the same tragedy that befell her mama would not befall her.

Somehow she survived unbroken. But it was not a risk she could afford again. Once had to be enough. Her curiosity should be satisfied now, should it not? Last night she needed to be close to him. This morning, that same closeness began to terrify her.

"What?"

"I can't marry you."

While he was still digesting this statement, his mouth hanging open, Mercy took advantage of her chance and hurried out of the bedchamber. She rushed down the stairs to find the remainder of her scattered clothes. Keeping busy was one way to take her mind off troubled thoughts and dangerous doubts.

"Of all the rotten trickery, woman! You certainly are going to marry me," he shouted as he thumped down the stairs after her, completely naked and thoroughly distracting.

She was pulling on her stockings, balanced on one foot. "Do be sensible. This was very nice indeed, but it is only sport." She paused a moment and swapped feet to pull up the second stocking. "I'm sorry. Perhaps I should have explained, but I thought you understood what I wanted when I came here." As she fussed over the wrinkles in her stockings, she prayed he wouldn't see her fingers tremble.

He stood before her, knuckles on his hips, feet apart. "What *you* wanted?" His eyes were dark, confused.

"What we *both* wanted," she corrected. "Is this not satisfying?"

His anger mounted visibly in the movement of his chest, the tension in his shoulders. "I told you I wanted a wife."

"And I told you, many times, that we are not suited."

"What about this?"

"We cannot stay in bed forever. Sooner or later we have to go out into the world. And what will people say of us?" She stood straighter. "They will say you married me for my fortune, and that I married you to recover from scandal."

"Who cares what other people think?" he exclaimed, eyes ablaze. Suddenly he came toward her and gripped her by the arms. "For once in your life, Mercy, step out of that wretched cage in which you live. I may not be as rich as your viscount, but I have savings now, and they will grow. We can build a life here together. Take a chance."

This close and this naked he was a potent temptation, but she forced herself to face him bravely, calmly. "I have done so. To be here with you I took a great chance with my reputation." She'd wanted to prove her bravery to him, she realized. It was important, very important that he not think her a coward. "Last night can never happen again. I hoped we might get it out of our blood once and for all after five years of waiting."

He shook his head and drew her into his arms. She went limply, afraid of the tears she felt pricking her eyelids. For a moment, she allowed her brow to rest in the curve of his shoulder. He smelled of wood smoke, fresh grass, sun-warmed leather, and male sweat. So many scents detectable on his warm skin. Even a hint of her own fragrance. Good. She had left her mark upon him.

"Mercy, my love," he whispered against her loose curls, "I know you have always felt alone. I know you have taken care of yourself. But I wish you would learn to trust in another soul to do that. If only sometimes."

She sniffed. "I suppose by another soul you mean yourself?"

"Yes."

Hands to his firm shoulders, she pushed him back a few inches. "You? The man who was ready to marry another woman not so long ago? The man who charms every woman he meets? The man who firmly refuses to follow any rules? The man who has *just* decided to settle down after many years of wreaking havoc? I should trust you?"

A slow smile broke across his lips. "Yes."

"The man for whom a lady's engagement to another gentleman means nothing?"

"If I might remind you," he muttered wryly, "it was you who came here last night. You asked me to make love to you."

She faltered at that. "I suppose I did."

"You *suppose*?"

Irritably, she turned away and sought her corset and gown. "I cannot stand about arguing with you. Help me dress."

"Please."

"What?"

"Help me dress, *please*." He rocked on his heels, arms folded over his chest. Mercy wished he'd put some damn clothes on himself.

"Very well, then. *Please*."

"Better."

She turned her back while he laced her corset,

pulling on the laces with undue strength until she was quite without breath to speak.

"I'll teach you some manners after all, eh?" he muttered.

Stunned by the suggestion that she was the one who lacked manners, Mercy recovered speech enough to respond, "You want me to marry you and conform to your world, Rafe Hartley, yet you would never do the same for me. You speak of the cage in which I live, yet yours is no less confined."

He had no response to that, because it was perfectly true.

Once she was dressed, her shawl wrapped around her shoulders, she paused to look at him again. Still naked and apparently not in the least troubled by it, he stared back at her. There was only one word for that expression, she mused. Cocky. And scheming. Well, that was two words.

He had picked her lock. Why would he not look pleased with himself?

Rafe scratched his cheek, and she heard the rasp of fingers over stubble. "I'm disinclined to be used just for your pleasure and then tossed aside."

"And you got no pleasure from it?" she demanded.

His lip curled upward at the corner. "I did."

Mercy felt her face grow hot. He was not making it easy for her. But why would he? "Then you will be satisfied. As I must."

"Why must we?"

"Because I prefer the gate. I tried the hedge." She faltered. "I tried…"

When she thought of her mother, she remembered

mostly her bright hair and her laughter. Hard gusts of it that almost bent her double. Her mother was a fearless woman. When she took that hedge, it wasn't because the horse ran away with her; it was because she wanted to take it. She'd wanted to feel the wind pulling on her hair as if she was flying.

Oh, she liked taking the hedge too. Mercy was more like her reckless mother than she cared to realize. But the consequences...

Rafe unfolded his arms, one hand casually stroking his manhood which, although it stood now at half-mast, was still a magnificent creature of fine proportions. "Next time you need your fields plowed, let me know."

"Rafe Hartley, I shall never—"

"And when you're ready to marry me, we'll discuss further nights like the one we just shared. When you're ready to marry me."

At this stubborn repetition of something she'd already assured him would never happen, a tight spurt of annoyance ripped out of her. "I am not going to marry you."

"You'll never get another kiss from me, wench, until you say yes, admit you love me, and put an end to my suffering once and for all."

"Pass me your shotgun, and I'll end it for you."

"Ha! That's one thing o' mine you'll never get your wicked pixie hands on."

A moment passed. And then another. They faced each other, two old adversaries, squaring off their territories.

But the steel had gone out of her sword. She sighed. "I see we cannot have a civil conversation, even now."

"I'm not civilized, am I, according to you, Frosty-Drawers?"

Mercy left his farm that morning in a foul temper, but she had other matters to put in order, and for now she'd have to set this problem aside and return to address it later. With a fresh mind and when her heart was not so disastrously unsettled. On a passionate whim, she'd done the unthinkable with Rafe Hartley and given up some of her precious control. Now, in the cool light of a new day, the unthinkable must be thought about. She reined in her mental horse and likewise her racing pulse.

Marry him? It simply was not possible. Their worlds were too different. But the hankering for his company, his smile, his kisses, still remained. She did not know if she would ever be cured of it. Or if she could ever get Rafe Hartley back into the box where he belonged.

Chapter 20

"WELL, GOODNESS GRACIOUS, LADY MERCY, WE WERE not expecting a visitor so early." Rafe's aunt Sophie came to the door, still in her nightgown and surrounded by children, her hair in a long, honey-blonde braid over one shoulder.

Mercy tried to ignore the fact that she was in a ball gown, hoping that this would discourage any questions about it. "I decided to come and see what I might do to be of assistance here, Mrs. Kane. I've asked Mrs. Hartley to send some of my things by cart today. I do not mean to intrude. Please tell me if you think I will be in the way, but there is surely something I can do?"

She must have sounded quite pitiful—and looked it, shivering in a thin gown and white evening gloves.

Of course, Rafe's aunt did not turn her away. Mercy knew the kind lady would take her in, when she appeared like a stray waif on the Kanes' doorstep.

Fortunately, she could blame her trembles that morning on the cold air and her lack of long sleeves or a coat. No one, she was quite sure, would guess her in danger of anything more than a chill. But inside her, some wayward little imps—the ones she'd hoped to quell by her actions last night—were very much alive and dancing.

∽

Later that day, when Rafe visited his aunt and uncle, he learned of their new houseguest.

"Is it not very kind of Lady Mercy to offer her assistance?" his aunt exclaimed.

"Assistance?" It was difficult to imagine exactly what assistance the ice princess could give in that farm-house, so far removed from her usual environment. He wanted to be angry with her still for refusing to marry him, but when he saw her in his aunt's house, it was difficult to keep his temper raging. She had not told him her plans, of course, and he'd expected her to be back in Morecroft by now, making arrangements for her return to London. Instead, she stayed. Moved nearer, in fact. With one hand she pushed him away; with the other she tugged him close.

"Lady Mercy has offered to stay here and help look after the children while your aunt rests," his uncle explained.

A more vibrantly colored fish had never been seen so out of water. "Stay here? Where? There aren't enough bedchambers, surely."

"I share with the children," Mercy replied. "If a person is well organized, they need little space."

This, from a woman who grew up in a thirty-five-bedroom country manor and lived most of her year in a London town house that required, so he'd heard, a staff of twenty-eight to maintain it.

"I am very grateful for the extra help," said his aunt, shooting him a warning glance to hold his tongue.

Rafe did not know how he felt about this development. As long as she stayed at his aunt's house, he would see her every day. There was good and bad in that; pleasure and temptation. After all, he'd warned her there would be no more kisses until she accepted his marriage proposal. How was he supposed to keep to that vow if she walked by his farm every day?

He couldn't read her countenance. She wasn't the sort to stand there gazing at him with dewy eyes.

His uncle considered Mercy Danforthe to be all lace and petticoats. Like Rafe, he had a tendency to suspect the worst of those from the upper classes. He was probably thinking now that she would be more trouble than help, but his wife, of course, was too polite to refuse the offer when it came from Mercy directly.

Well, it would be interesting to see how she managed in that crowded farmhouse with very little in the way of luxury.

"I don't suppose you'll be staying long," he said to her.

"Just as long as I am needed." She flashed him a smile, and the appearance of those two dangerous dimples, while it might attempt to show innocence, warned Rafe of the very opposite. "I discussed it with Mrs. Hartley recently, and she thought it would be a very good idea for me to come here and lend a hand. I like to go where I am most needed, of course." Chin proudly raised, she added, "As Mrs. Hartley said, no one else is so capable of putting things in order."

Rafe groaned softly. His stepmama, the

mischief-maker. He should have seen her hand in this. "You didn't think to inform me of this last night."

"Don't worry," she said, dimples evident again, "I shan't cause you any trouble."

She already had, of course.

How calmly she'd stood in his house in the early hours of that day and refused to marry him. Even after the night they'd shared. He stared at her until he felt his uncle watching him, and then he looked away.

Mercy soon settled in at his aunt's house, and before too long had his cousins marching around the village in formation behind her like signets with a mother swan. That wouldn't last, he thought grumpily. Those wild imps would soon grow bored with the game and start playing up.

But the only complaint came from his uncle, who called in at the farm a few days after her arrival and spent half an hour relating a sad tale of how she burnt his supper every night and overboiled his egg every morning.

"Sophie tries to teach her how to cook, but the girl thinks she knows it all." He shuddered. "She likes to *experiment* with ingredients."

Rafe laughed. "Sounds like The Danforthe Brat."

"'Tis a good thing she won't have to cook when she marries. I'd pity that viscount if she did."

That curbed Rafe's laughter.

His uncle added, "I can hardly take a step in my own house without that young lady following behind, tripping me up with a wet mop. I don't know when she plans to leave, but I hope 'tis soon."

Since Rafe could not share his uncle's sentiment, he

stayed quiet. His heart wanted to believe she'd moved in with his aunt and uncle to be closer to him, but his head told him it was simply Mercy Danforthe taking control again, meddling.

Mrs. Pyke and her children had moved into Sir William's fortress on the hill, where they came under both Mrs. Kenton's eager care and Mercy's diligent attention. As Rafe commented to his friend's wife, she was in the lucky position of having two generous guardians now. However, Mrs. Pyke, who had previously complained that she did not get enough of anything, would soon be heard complaining adversely of too much. Rafe was relieved and amused that someone else took the burden upon themselves.

One day he caught Mercy leaving Hodson's shop with his little cousins in tow—each of them enjoying a mouthful of toffee, keeping them splendidly quiet and busy—and he stopped to congratulate her on this latest mission.

"Mrs. Pyke is fortunate to have your benevolent notice. Thank you for taking her under your wing."

"She is a sadly ungracious woman," Mercy replied with a hefty sigh that drew his yearning gaze to her high bosom and then her soft lips. "The moment I put a thought in her head, it falls out again. As much as she claims to find her life so hard, I rather think she enjoys it just the way it is and has no desire to change a thing about it. She cannot read, yet has no desire to learn."

He laughed. "Charity, given with no true understanding of the situation, is worth little. It can be used up and forgotten in the blink of an eye." For a moment, he considered putting his hands around her arms, there in the main street of Sydney Dovedale, and demanding that she marry him.

"If only her husband might be found."

"Pyke has gone into hiding from his creditors and, so I've begun to suspect, from Mrs. Pyke."

But Mercy looked very determined suddenly. "I shall write to Mr. Hobbs. He's very good at finding people and things." Her ringlets were less bouncy today, more wayward than usual, the heavy weight of her extraordinary hair pinned up in a more simple arrangement. He supposed it was difficult to manage without a lady's maid. Even her dress was muted, a simple printed cotton, more in keeping with her current surroundings. It was clearly Mercy's rare attempt to blend in. She probably did not wish to catch Mrs. Flick's eye again in her bright orange frock. Abruptly awake to the fact that he was staring at her dangerously curved shape under that gown, thinking of the corset he held for ransom under his bolster, he quickly cleared his throat and fumbled for a harmless, innocent subject in front of the children.

"How is my aunt today?"

"Improving vastly. Doctor Sharpe is very pleased."

"Good."

"I suppose you thought I wouldn't manage. That I'd be in the way."

He paused, looking at her thoughtfully. "I doubt there's much, my lady, that you could not do once you put your mind to it."

"Exactly." She was smug, pleased with herself.

"Except, of course, one thing."

Her smile faltered.

"The one thing that stumps your Danforthe courage."

She arched an eyebrow.

"Find me a bride that stays."

"Excuse me, Mr. Hartley. I must get home and start the supper."

After a brief hesitation, he stood aside and let her pass with the children.

Just then the door of the shop opened and Jammy Jim appeared in his apron. "Master Hartley, don't hover on the step. Come in and browse. We've some new gloves just in from Norwich, and you'll need some for the next dance at the assembly rooms. Lady Mercy laid some aside for you to try."

"Did she indeed?" he grumbled.

Jammy Jim chuckled. "Her enthusiasm is good for business. As is the reopening of the assembly rooms. Ladies don't buy the sort of folderols my wife gets in stock unless they have a place to wear them and be admired."

"Lady Mercy must be your best customer." He watched her hurrying away down the street.

"Lass can't seem to pass by without coming in."

She always was a spendthrift, but then she had money to waste. Her brother was one of the richest men in the country, and Mercy was rumored to have a fortune of six and a half thousand pounds. Although sometimes he heard it was ten. At other times it was only five thousand. That money, however much she had, was the most unfortunate thing about her, since it set her high above him.

"She knows what she wants when she sees it,"

Jammy Jim remarked, arms crossed over his chest as he leaned against the door frame. "And no price is too high."

If only that were true, thought Rafe. There was one price she would not pay. He wished she was penniless, a humble crofter's daughter or a shoeless wretch selling matches. Somehow he sensed she'd still be burdened with that damned pride.

"Handsome woman, that, eh?" observed Jammy Jim with a chuckle.

Rafe scratched his jaw. "I suppose some might find her so."

"I like a wench with a bit o' spirit and sauce."

"In moderate amounts, it might be tolerable."

"And a nice firm pair o'—"

"Why are you standing idle?" Jammy Jim's young wife made them both jump as she came to the open door and looked out.

"Idle? I'm talking to Mr. Rafe Hartley, woman." The shopkeeper straightened up.

"You look the very definition of idle to me. You promised to help me change the window display, lazy lump o' bacon lard. Make haste. I want Lady Mercy to see the new summer muslins when she next passes, and those parasols that just came in."

"All in good time, nag-a-minute. She doesn't need them right now. It could rain for the next dozen days. There's no need to get yourself in a tizzy, woman." He rolled his eyes for Rafe's benefit. *"Lady Mercy this, Lady Mercy that."*

"A young lady of exquisite taste," his wife exclaimed. "Not that you'd know."

"I've got taste, m'dear." He winked at Rafe. "Mr. Hartley and I were just discussing that very thing."

"I'm sure you were. I see it on your guilty face." She peered over her husband's shoulder. "How is your dear aunt Sophia, Mr. Hartley?"

"Much better, thank you."

"Lady Mercy's presence must be a great help to her."

"So she tells me."

There was a lengthy pause while Jammy Jim continued grinning, his wife's eyes grew wider, and Rafe tapped his foot upon the step.

Finally the woman nudged her husband again. "Well, go and get those items in the window, then. What are you waiting for, a sign from the good Lord?" When Jammy Jim sauntered off with a merry whistle, she quickly tugged on Rafe's sleeve to bring him inside. "You've known Lady Mercy from childhood, so I'm told."

"Yes."

"Such a fine young lady. We're very lucky to have her patronage here. She does a lot of good for this village."

"Hmmm."

"Now, what you need," the woman added, "is a new waistcoat. We have just the very bolt of embroidered damask—"

"Madam, I thank you, but embroidered silk is of no earthly use to me on a farm. It would be an extravagance I can ill afford."

"Oh." She looked crestfallen. "That is a great pity. Mr. Hodson just showed some to Lady Mercy, and she admired it so."

"Perhaps she will buy some for her fiancé," he muttered.

"We did suggest it, Mr. Hartley, but she said no. He would not suit it, she said. I rather got the impression she was thinking of another man. Someone else of her acquaintance. Someone with blue eyes to be matched by the blue thread woven through the silk."

Rafe's heart was beating too hard. She would not make him into another of her projects. Oh, no.

"There's been no word from Miss Molly Robbins?" she inquired casually.

"None."

"Such a sorry business, to be sure. What can that young girl be thinking of, to run off and leave you in the lurch? Miss Robbins always seemed so sensible."

"Yes. But I think I understand now."

The woman walked around her counter. "You do?"

"Her future was not with me. I could not have made her happy." It was hard to admit he'd been wrong and a woman had been right. But there, it was done. He was still standing, still breathing.

"Well…I suppose a woman knows when a man's heart belongs elsewhere." She opened a large crate on the counter and took out some bundles of packing straw. "We can't always love where it is easiest or painless. I mean to say, look at Mr. Hodson. Gets my blood up a dozen times a day, that wretched old windbag, but I wouldn't be without him. Not for all the sand in Egypt. When love hits a person smack in the face like a cricket ball, there's not much they can do about it, is there? Love doesn't always come where it's expected."

She was right. It didn't. If only Mercy could see that.

"Now, what you need, sir, is this." She showed him a parasol from the crate—a dainty thing with a pink fringe and a bamboo handle.

"I think I might be laughed out of the corn exchange, madam."

"Not for you! For Lady Mercy. Every lady likes gifts, and this is a practical one that will suit her completely."

"For Lady Mercy?" Uh-oh. Had it been so obvious?

Mrs. Hodson poked him with the tip of the parasol. "Courtship proceeds with gifts, young sir. Don't you think it's time you gave it a proper try?"

Rafe considered it. He wasn't much for presents. Had never given any to a woman who wasn't a relative. Not even to Molly. If she accepted a gift from him, what would it mean? There were, no doubt, rules about this sort of thing, as there were about everything in her world. But he'd known her since she was ten and witnessed her attachment to pretty, frilly things. Those *fancifications* he'd always disdained. When Mercy first came to Sydney Dovedale all those years ago, chasing after James Hartley, upon whom she had an amusing infatuation, Rafe's attention had been caught by the little girl's colorful and exuberant wardrobe. Her determination to remain clean and tidy had, naturally, caused him to try and get her dirty.

A dozen years on, and he was still trying to get her dirty.

He considered the parasol, picturing her with it. It was a foolish piece of frippery, but he supposed it did have a practical use. Like her, it wasn't merely decorative.

"You may count on my discretion," Mrs. Hodson

whispered. "No one but she and I will ever know who gave it to her. Won't she look a treat carrying it as she walks along the street? She will think of you every time she uses it. Of you and your blue eyes."

He looked around to be sure he was unobserved. "I'll take it."

Mrs. Hodson was artful in her methods. Once he had the picture in his mind of Mercy carrying a parasol he'd given her, there was no changing his mind, even when he heard the price.

Isabella Milford and her sister paid a visit to the Kanes' farmhouse soon after Mercy settled in. She knew they had never been before and probably would never have bothered if not for her presence, but Mrs. Kenton was her usual chatty self, lavishing half praise on the Kanes in her own indomitable style.

"Such a splendid orchard you have. I hear you make a very good jam, Mrs. Kane. I'm sure it is almost the same standard as that produced by our cook in London. But then Mrs. Gilkes is an expert jam maker and should not be compared to a novice. I do not know how she does it. I shall send you some when I return to London. This house is very tidy, considering you have so many children. It is no wonder you have no time for your own appearance." She laughed gaily, and poor Sophia Kane fumbled to adjust her lace cap, which had come askew. "Never mind, my good lady, we can work only with what we have. I think no less of you for a stained frock. I am amazed you are not worn away to a little gray thing from all the trouble I hear these children put you through! And two more away at school, I understand?"

"Yes," Sophia replied, covering the stain on her knee with one hand. "My eldest two boys are at boarding school."

"Gracious! And you with another on the way." She cast her disapproving gaze upon Rafe's uncle. "Dreadful."

"Mrs. Pyke and her children are enjoying their stay," said Mercy brightly. "They seem comfortable with you." She and Mrs. Kenton had formed a wary but civil pact while working together on the improvement of Mrs. Abby Pyke, and Mercy was making every effort to be useful without controlling. It was not easy, but she was determined.

"She likes the dinner we provide," agreed Mrs. Kenton, "although the place is a little too damp for her, she says."

For a woman born in Pillory Lane, Mrs. Pyke was peculiarly fussy about her surroundings. But she certainly knew how to get her own way. Mrs. Kenton had provided her with a full new wardrobe from her own castoffs, although Mrs. Pyke had been heard to suggest they were less than fashionable and the material not likely to wear well.

"Her children are not far removed from savages," Isabella offered quietly. Silent and apparently uncomfortable for most of their brief visit, she finally found the will to speak on that subject. "I hope Mr. Pyke shall soon return."

"I believe a great many folk feel the same," said Mercy with a smile.

Isabella had nothing else to say. She did not have

her sister's talent of always finding a subject, no matter where she was or with whom, and even if no one cared to hear it. Whenever Mercy caught her eye, Isabella looked away, as if she was caught doing something she ought not. The entire tenor of their friendship felt changed. When Mercy walked them to the gate, Isabella expressed a mild sort of admiration for her act of "charity" in helping the Kanes. But the admiration was mixed with blatant disgust for the farm surroundings.

"These folk live in squalor," Isabella murmured, looking around the yard with fearful eyes as if she expected wild beasts to pounce upon her at any moment. "I had not realized Mr. Rafe Hartley's family were so...so...vulgar."

Mercy did not know whether to be appalled or amused. "This is hardly squalor, Miss Milford." Evidently, just like Julia Gibson, this lady knew nothing—or very little—about life beyond her comfortable world. She would never have survived life as Rafe Hartley's wife. "This is how many people live. It is not a luxurious standard of living, to be sure, and they work hard to maintain what they have, but that is the way of it for many."

Isabella skirted a puddle, almost leaving her skin behind when the goat across the yard abruptly let out a loud "maah." Eventually she spoke again, but changed the subject, asking Mercy whether she'd heard lately from her fiancé, whether he was back yet from Italy. Mercy replied that she'd had no letter informing her of his return.

"The drier, warmer weather there must greatly

improve his health," Isabella remarked, waiting for Mercy to open the gate.

Her sister came up behind them and must have heard Isabella's last comment, for she added, "Adolphus is a martyr to his health. But then men are babies in general." She glanced over her shoulder with a last disapproving frown at the Kanes' crowded farmhouse. "When they are not being babies, they are making them."

It was much the same thought Mercy had about the male species, but she was not about to admit that to Mrs. Kenton.

"We are planning our departure in a few days and returning to London," the lady added. "Isabella has found the country very trying on her nerves. Only yesterday, she had an attack of panic when a flock of cows chased her as she passed a field."

"A herd of cows, Mrs. Kenton. Sheep and birds come in flocks."

"In any case, the beasts terrified her almost out of her wits. She is certain they were after her new straw bonnet. Therefore, we are returning soon to Town. If you would care to travel with us, Lady Mercy, you are most welcome. My brother's barouche box can fit four quite comfortably."

Mercy thought of going home. It must be faced, of course. "What of Mrs. Pyke?"

"She means to stay at the fortress. She is welcome to have the run of the place." Mrs. Kenton shuddered. "Once summer is over, it will be quite untenable, but it is up to her where she goes next. We will keep some staff here until September. If she chooses to stay on and keep house for us, I daresay William would agree.

Although a feather duster is as much as I've ever seen her use. She thinks herself above it."

So much for making Mrs. Pyke into a new woman, thought Mercy. How quickly interest was lost in that lady's plight. Rafe was right, she realized: charity with no true understanding behind it was worth little. Perhaps she could take Mrs. Pyke back to London with her, train her as a lady's maid now that Molly had other plans.

"Isabella will enjoy your company, if you travel with us," Mrs. Kenton added.

"I will give it some thought, madam. I have not yet made any plans for travel."

"Do, by all means." The lady paused, and after a brief check to see that Isabella had gone through the gate already and started up the lane, she continued in a lower voice, "I must apologize for Isabella's sullen mood. My dear sister has had a very difficult time of it. A broken heart is slow to heal. I had hoped she might find something new here in the country...a change of scenery, meeting new people, etcetera. But alas not."

"I am sorry, madam. I did not know of her broken heart."

"She was insistent that I should not tell you."

Mercy wondered why, if that was the case, the lady now chose to go against her sister's wishes. But Mrs. Kenton had more to say and was hedging her way toward it. She nervously checked again that Isabella was out of hearing, then she took a breath. "Young Mr. Hartley seemed a fine prospect for Isabella, but now that has fallen by the wayside. Any attentions he paid to my sister have markedly declined. But then, his fortune is not what we were led to believe, and Mrs. Pyke has told me of the shocking manner in which he earned his coin in London." She lowered her voice, looking scandalized. "With his fists! Not only that, but I had not realized his former fiancée was nothing more than a lady's maid!"

"Yes, Molly Robbins was my maid. And an excellent one. I was very sorry to lose her."

"I declare myself duly shocked." She pressed a hand to her ample bosom. "There I was thinking him a young gentleman of prospects and ambition. We were greatly misled by Mrs. Hartley. Imagine how very near my poor sister came to aligning herself with a man whose previous fiancée was a servant."

It was no surprise that Isabella hoped for a wealthy husband. Most marriages were conducted for financial or property gain, but Mercy did not think the lady could afford to be so circumspect as to turn her nose up at Rafe. Thank goodness, however, that she had.

Rafe deserved so much better.

The gate swung open with a rusty moan, and Mrs. Kenton passed through into the lane.

"My dear Lady Mercy"—she lowered her voice to a patronizingly hushed tone, her face grave—"I did not wish to raise the subject before his aunt and uncle, but I feel it incumbent upon me—as a member of your social mores and a woman of several years' more experience—to advise you, most strongly, against further dalliance with Mr. Rafe Hartley. People have begun to talk in a most unpleasant manner and to speculate upon your relationship with that young man. I heard from a good lady in the village that you were seen exiting his bachelor cottage unchaperoned and at very odd hours. While I know there must be a perfectly reasonable explanation, it is still unwise to flaunt convention and let anyone suspect the worst of you."

Mercy was shocked—not by the rumors, but that this woman thought it her place to lecture. "There is nothing untoward occurring between Mr. Rafe Hartley and myself. Not that it is any business of yours, Mrs. Kenton."

The other woman raised her head from its condescending tilt. "I am certain the rumors are false, of course. You are an engaged woman. However, talk can be dangerous if it reaches the wrong ears. I cannot allow my sister to be seen socially with a woman who has indulged in scandalous deeds, so I do hope this can be nipped in the bud. Even the hint of such reprehensible behavior can be detrimental to any young lady's reputation."

"I'll bear that in mind."

"I understand you were raised without a mother, and your brother has not perhaps been as diligent as he should." She smiled without showing her teeth. "It is not too late, however, to correct the error."

She caught her breath at the woman's audacity, and for that moment, words failed her.

"I mean only to advise," Mrs. Kenton added, the smile packed away.

"Naturally. Good day." She said it more firmly this time and then closed the gate.

Her opinion of both ladies was not improved by this visit. In the case of Miss Isabella Milford, she was distinctly disappointed. She'd hoped to find not just

another project, but a new friend. That was a less
attractive prospect now. As Rafe had said when she
told him of Sir William's plans to sell: *Good riddance.*

It was not until much later, as she read to the
children by the fire and readied them for bed, that she
remembered Mrs. Kenton calling Grey by his given
name, Adolphus. That was very odd indeed. She did
not think the lady was acquainted with him at all;
she'd acted as if the name meant nothing to her before.
Mercy knew she'd never mentioned his Christian
name in Mrs. Kenton's hearing. Perhaps Mrs. Hartley
or Lady Ursula had told them, she reasoned. That
would be a plausible excuse.

But she went to bed that evening with a nagging
doubt in her head, for both Mrs. Kenton and her
sister had mentioned his health, as if they had some
familiarity with it after all.

❧

The next day bloomed bright and breezy—perfect for
drying the laundry, not quite so perfect for struggling
with the damp linens she suspended over the line that
stretched the width of the yard. By the time all the
wet clothes and sheets were pegged in place, Mercy
felt as battered and windblown as a ship in a storm.
Fortunately, there was no time to daydream about
Rafe. She'd done too much of that lately.

Empty basket under her arm, she walked back into
the farmhouse, made certain the youngest children
were gainfully occupied with painting labels for their
mother's pickles and preserves, and then checked on
the lady herself.

A makeshift bed had been made out of an old settle, and this was where Aunt Sophie rested, on one side of the great inglenook hearth, a patched woolen blanket tucked around her, and a pile of books at her side.

"The baby kicks today!" Sophie exclaimed, one hand to her belly. "He gets less rest than I do now." She seemed thrilled by the imminent arrival of yet another handful. Mercy smiled politely and laid her hand on the woolen blanket as Sophie directed. The sudden jab of a forceful little punch took her by surprise, and she raised her hand again quickly. "One day you will know the sheer joy of holding your own babe in your arms, Lady Mercy."

"Yes," she murmured doubtfully, thinking of the pain and the mess to be endured. Not only with the birth itself, but for the rest of the child's life.

"Do you have much memory of your own mother? She died when you were young, did she not?"

Startled, Mercy quickly began gathering balls of spilled wool back into a basket. One of the little ones must have emptied it out again, as they liked to do. "She was killed in a riding accident, when I was five. My memories of her are scarce. I wish they were more." People did not ask about her mother. They were afraid to. Even Carver did not talk about their mother, and she often wished he would, because he must have many more memories than she had. Happier memories.

"Forgive me, my terrible curiosity, Lady Mercy. I should not ask about something so painful and private." There was a lengthy pause while Mercy continued searching for wool under the settle. Finally

Sophie lightened her tone and said, "You must look forward to the return of your fiancé."

"Indeed," Mercy muttered.

"Are you in love with him?"

Shocked again, faced by another question so brusquely and unapologetically set before her, Mercy clambered to her feet and stood with her hands full of wool balls, some unraveling, long threads falling to the flagged floor.

"Because to marry without love is a grievous mistake," continued Sophie. "I have seen it many times, and it brings no joy to anyone involved."

Her heart hammered away, her gaze fixed on the fluttering white sheets through the window. She was aware that one curly lock of hair now tumbled down the side of her face. "Viscount Grey is entirely suitable for me. I knew it the moment I met him."

Sophie's voice was gentle, full of concern. "How did you know?"

How did she know? Because he had not interrupted her when she spoke. He was quiet, unobtrusive, unchallenging. None of which was romantic. Mercy always thought she was too levelheaded for romance in her own life. She just liked to plan it for other people. That way she could remain detached, watch from a good distance, and never be touched by too much emotion herself.

"I did not mean to be overcurious," Sophie muttered. "Forgive me again. Goodness, my tongue does run away with me these days. That's what happens when I have too much time to sit about idle. My mind simmers away with questions I have no right to ask."

"Please, think nothing of it." In a way, she thought, it was nice to know someone cared. When she told her brother about the engagement, he had not asked her a single question about Adolphus or her feelings for the man. Edward Hobbs always went along with anything she wanted. There was no one else to show interest in her plans. No one to try and talk her out of them.

She had so few friends. Again the realization—already felt to some degree at the Morecroft dance—struck her hard, pummeling her already wounded spirits with brutal force. She had acquaintances who, in all likelihood, put up with her because of her title. Or they were afraid of her. She had Molly who, as she recently discovered, kept secrets from her and, as Carver pointed out, was really an employee hired to like her.

Rafe had been the truest friend she ever had. Even when he was her enemy.

"I am grateful to you, Lady Mercy," said his aunt quietly. "You have been such a ray of light."

Suddenly Mercy felt the need to sit. Still clutching a ball of wool, she lowered herself to the settle across the hearth. "I'm glad you're taking more rest. My mother had a miscarriage, you know, when she fell down the stairs once."

"How awful!"

"Yes." She wound the ball of wool tighter in her hands. "I had left a toy out on the landing by accident. She tripped on it. That's how she fell." She had never said those words aloud to anyone. It seemed as if they echoed.

There was a pause. Sophie sat up and reached across to take her hand. "And all this time, no doubt, you have fretted over it."

She looked up. "It was all my fault. When she recovered, my mother went hunting, and a horse threw her as she took a tall hedge. That's how she was killed. If she had not miscarried, she would never have gone out on a horse that day. Because of my carelessness," she added, "everything changed. Everything was ruined."

Sophie was silent for a moment, her fingers still laid over the back of Mercy's hand. Then she said, "Do you see this scar on my face, Lady Mercy?"

It was a thin mark across the lady's cheek. Molly had told her it was the result of a fall, but no one seemed to have more details than that.

"I jumped from a balcony," Sophie explained, "into the dark. Foolishly. My face hit a rusty nail protruding from a ladder. That's how I got my scar. Mr. Kane, you see, was an undergardener at that house, and he had left the ladder out by accident. When he heard what happened, he came to look for me, to make amends." She chuckled. "That's how he came here to Sydney Dovedale. It was fate, I believe. Not an accident at all. None of us know what fate has in store."

Was this meant to cheer her up? she wondered darkly. Oh, but it was a horrid thought. How could she control her world if fate could change it without her having a say?

"Mr. Kane thought it was all his fault, and he blamed himself for my scar. But how could he know I would jump? It was the one thing that brought us together. If not for that fateful night, we would never have met, never have fallen in love."

"But you jumped by choice," Mercy replied. "My mother tumbled over the ball I left out."

Sophie nodded. "Whether we jump or tumble, it is in fate's hands. Same with love."

Since moving into the farm and observing his aunt and uncle together, she'd seen how they loved and laughed. As Mrs. Hartley had said, no part of their life was too hard, because they lived it together. Mercy realized now that Rafe's stepmother had encouraged her to come and help Sophie, not only for the practical reasons, but for her own good too.

Chapter 21

RAFE HAD OFFERED TO TEACH HIS LITTLE COUSINS TO fish, and he took them all down to the shallow stream that meandered through a meadow on the border of his uncle's property. There, Mercy sat on the bank among the buttercups and watched as he patiently instructed the five children with rods and nets. She had forgotten to bring a blanket to sit upon. As Rafe drily pointed out to her, she would have to brave the ground insects and the possibility of a grass stain. For once, she did.

"Let me worry about the grass and my gown," she said crisply. "You worry about the fish. And don't let anyone drown."

It was the sort of place where accidents could happen, and with all those little children to watch over in close proximity to water, she felt more than an ounce of panic to be sure. But Rafe handled it calmly, self-assured as always, periodically scooping an overenthused child out of the stream. Unfortunately, there was altogether too much screaming, shouting, and falling in for much fish to be caught for dinner, but the children enjoyed the day immensely.

So did Mercy. A few weeks ago she would have felt lazy, sitting in the sun, doing nothing. She would certainly never have imagined it might be fun to watch five noisy little children getting their clothes wet and their feet muddy. The scene she observed was absolute chaos, and yet she'd never been more content, never felt such quiet pleasure in her heart.

At one point, as she moved to sit in the shade of an ancient willow, Rafe padded across the grass and retrieved a parcel from behind the tree trunk.

"It's for you," he mumbled uncertainly, tossing it at her lap.

Bemused, she untied the string, unwrapped the paper, and found inside a very pretty parasol.

"For the sun," he clarified unnecessarily. "So you don't get freckles."

She was moved. It was the first gift a man had given her that she did not pick out and wrap for herself. "It must have been expensive! Why would you waste your money on such an item?"

"I've plenty o' coin," he replied, chin up, eyes narrowed against the glare of the sun.

"But this is a fancification—the sort of thing for which you have no time."

"Do you want it or not?" he snapped grumpily.

"Of course I want it." She jumped up and gave him a kiss directly on the lips. It had to be the sunny day, she mused. This madness buzzing through her veins must be due to the heat on her head.

None of the children were watching, and she and Rafe were quite hidden under the bower of yellowy-green leaves that drifted in a gentle breeze. He had never looked more handsome as he did in his breeches and plain white shirt, and never had a kiss been so impatiently anticipated, at least by her. But when she kissed him today, he did not put his hands on her. His eyes remained open, watching her.

"Thank you for my gift, Mr. Hartley."

"Every time you use it, you'll think of me."

She nodded, her heart pinching.

"Marry me," he said suddenly.

Again he was asking her to take a risk. It was so easy for him.

"I have my own savings now," he added proudly. "And the farm is doing well. I know it's not so grand as—"

"Rafe." She placed a finger to his lips. "Best watch the children," she whispered.

"I won't ask you again, woman." He towered over her, hands on his hips. "And you'll get no more kisses from me until you make me an honest man."

Now that was a problem. Because she did want more of his kisses. Very much.

Head on one side, she peered up at him from under the fringe of her new parasol as it danced merrily. "So it's bribery, is it, Hartley?"

"That's right, Brat. You say 'yes,' and you get another kiss."

"I could just take one." She stepped closer, tipping her parasol back. "Try and stop me."

He kept his lips firm, as if to deny her the kiss she wanted. But Mercy knew he would not resist, and she pressed her mouth gently to his. Hands on her arms, he set her back a few inches, his touch once again kindling the fire inside her.

Mercy looked over to check on the children and pointed. "It looks as if you caught something."

His cousins were shouting in excitement, wanting him to see what they had in their net, so he trotted back to the stream, sunlight shimmering over the shoulders of his white shirt. Mercy stood in the sun and spun her new parasol, prouder of that accessory than she was of anything she'd ever carried. Each time Rafe looked her way, she gave it a little twirl, and the fringe shimmied, just like the lusty faeries living in her belly.

          ≈

When she returned to the Kanes' farmhouse, she was met at the gate by Mrs. Hartley, who came to deliver a letter that arrived for Mercy that day with the mail coach. She took it to the window seat, where she read in the light of the afternoon sun, away from the sticky fingers of her young charges.

> *Sister,*
>
>   *Grey drifted foggily into port yesterday and caught wind of unfortunate rumors regarding you and a certain farmer. It was all over White's last week, and Boodle's this. They are running a wager that your wedding will be called off. I have a fifty-to-one stake. Do come home and sort it all out, before your reputation is thoroughly trounced and I have wagered the family fortune to save your honor.*
>
>   *C*
>
>   *P.S. Do not wish to alarm, but Grey's old papa informed Hobbs in the early hours of this ante*

> *meridiem of intent to bring suit against us for breach*
> *of promise, and your farmer boy for some form of*
> *theft. Firstly, he suggested Grey settle the score*
> *with fists or pistols, but since I informed him of said*
> *farmer boy's skill at both, he changed his mind to*
> *an attack upon the pockets.*

It was time to go home and face whatever awaited her there. She refolded the note, her mind suddenly numb. All this time she had fretted about scandal, and now it was a reality that slapped her hard in the face. Yet she felt…calm.

"Mrs. Hartley, I think I must travel back to Morecroft with you this afternoon," she said quietly. "My brother requires me at home, and I must pack my things. I shall leave for London with Sir William and his sisters."

She remained as cheerful as possible in saying her good-byes to the Kanes and thanking them sincerely for putting up with her. To her astonishment, even Rafe's uncle seemed sorry to see her go and gave her a warm embrace before she left.

"You'll say good-bye to Rafe?" he said.

"I'm not sure there is time," she replied, feeling a sob caught halfway up her throat. She could not face him to say good-bye. Mercy knew she might weep, and that would make everything even harder. "I will try," she added when she saw the man's frown.

Mrs. Hartley drove the curricle out of the village. "We can stop by Rafe's fields. I'm sure he will be out there."

"I don't want to disturb him while he's working."

"Nonsense. You cannot leave without a word."

And so, with the afternoon sun beating down upon her, heart racing painfully, she was forced to say good-bye to Rafe by a plowed field with other men working around them and his stepmother right beside her.

He must have suspected something was amiss when he saw them at the hedge, waving. By the time he reached her side, he'd seen her trunk fixed to the back of the curricle too.

"I had a letter," she said, squinting against the sun. "I stayed too long."

Rafe ground his jaw and looked away from her. "Your brother calls you home, o' course."

They could not say everything they wanted to, with his stepmother listening and watching.

"I will return," she said suddenly.

He looked doubtful.

Mercy took a deep breath. "I promise," she added.

His eyes widened and then narrowed again. Of course, he'd accused her before of not keeping her promises, but this time she would not run away from her problems. She would face this scandal bravely, for she was a woman now, not a child or a silly girl afraid of shadows from the past. Afraid to let herself live.

"Will you wait for me, Rafe?" she whispered.

He shook out his fingers, his powerfully muscled arms hanging at his sides, restless. "What else can a humble fellow do? My lady."

❧

He watched until she disappeared over the horizon, a bright spot like a dying sunset.

Would she come back?

Could he trust her to keep this promise? She'd broken his heart before, and he swore then that he'd never believe another word from her bossy lips.

But he loved her. There was no getting around it now.

So he would wait.

⁓

The horses trotted along at a smooth pace, carrying her away from the village and from Rafe. For several miles there was no conversation. Mercy, with Rafe's parasol in her lap, was too full of ideas to speak, and Mrs. Hartley also seemed lost in thought.

Then, finally, Mercy forced herself to end the silence. "Mrs. Hartley, Sir William mentioned to me that you suggested he bring his sisters here to meet me."

"Did I?" The lady laughed. "I do not remember. Perhaps I did mention you were staying in Morecroft."

"Are they, in some way, connected with Viscount Grey?" She'd been thinking about Mrs. Kenton calling him Adolphus in such a familiar way, and of Isabella referring to his health.

Mrs. Hartley fumbled the reins. "My husband was most adamant that I not interfere. I promised him I would not." She sighed. "I thought perhaps it would come up in natural conversation between you."

Losing her patience, Mercy exclaimed, "Please do tell me, madam! I feel I have been kept in the dark about some matter that I should know. There is nothing worse than such a feeling!"

The other lady paused a moment, biting her lip.

"No one will know who told me," Mercy added firmly. "I mean to find out the whole truth when I get to London, but you may as well tell me now as much as you can."

Mrs. Hartley exhaled a heavy breath. "Very well. You do have a right to know, as I told James, but he thought things should take their natural course. Knowing how Mrs. Kenton chatters, we assumed she would——"

"Please, madam. Tell me what I should know."

"Viscount Grey paid court to Isabella Milford last summer in Buckinghamshire." As soon as she got the first words out, the others tumbled after, like pigeons newly freed from a cote. "I saw them together several times. She was with her sister, visiting friends at Hawcombe Prior, the village near Lark Hollow. Mrs. Kenton's husband was once the parson there."

"Yes, she told me."

"Viscount Grey was in their company quite often. I suppose no one but the two people concerned truly know what happened, and it is wrong, as James says, to speculate on these matters. But they seemed very attached. Perhaps it was all on one side."

Mercy stared at the road ahead, putting it all straight in her mind. "This then is the nobleman who broke Isabella's heart."

"I do not know that to be the truth." Mrs. Hartley shrugged, trying to make it all seem far less ominous, despite the fact that she'd sat upon this secret for several weeks and evidently longed to tell it. "Isabella appears to be a lady who fastens herself quite speedily to…ideas of that nature. Look how she affixed herself to Rafe while she thought him in line for a fortune and Hartley House. And as far as I can see, he never gave her any encouragement beyond a few smiles. It could be that Isabella, prompted by her sister's enthusiasm, was simply mistaken in Viscount Grey's regard for her."

It was no wonder then, Mercy thought grimly, that Mrs. Kenton had acted so strangely toward *her* and tried to give her advice. They must blame her for stealing Isabella's great prospect away. "But you said yourself, madam, *they* seemed very much in love."

"Oh, I am just a romantic." She groaned. "My husband tells me I see love affairs blooming just because I wish for them to be." And she tossed Mercy a sly glance. "I cannot help myself when I care about two young people."

Mercy struggled to readjust her neat cupboards. Isabella's many odd glances and gestures now made sense in a new way. She was not a meek, nervous creature, grateful for Mercy's notice, overwhelmed by her friendship. She was an angry, hurt woman trying to forgive the lady who stole away another man's affections. For the most part, trying to avoid her, in all likelihood.

Chagrined, she shook her head. Her pride had led her to assume too much, had blinded her to the facts that were right there to be found, had she only troubled herself to look or ask.

Now she had a mess to clean up at home, situations to confront and set right. Once that was done, she must prepare herself to take another hedge.

She knew what was on the other side of it now, and she was no longer afraid to face it. Or him.

Chapter 22

MERCY'S FIRST MISSION WAS A VISIT TO MOLLY
Robbins, who was already moved into lodgings
above the small shop she'd leased. Her former lady's
maid looked disgustingly happy and flourishing in
her new surroundings.

"Did you not, at the very least, think to answer
Rafe's letter?" Mercy demanded.

Molly frowned. "How was it to be answered,
my lady?"

"Pen and ink," she replied curtly, losing her patience.

"But, my lady, since it was a list of provisions he
required from the market in Morecroft, I did not see
any way to answer it."

Mercy stared. "It was *what*?"

"It was a list of items." Molly went to her dresser
drawer and took out the small folded square. "I kept
it, in case he needed it back." She passed it to Mercy,
who held it a moment, completely nonplussed, before
she unfolded the missive and read it.

Sure enough, it was a list of shopping.

He had never written a letter to Molly, urging her home to him. As she crumpled the paper in her hand, she remembered how he tried to take it from her when she found it on his mantel. She'd assumed it was for Molly. He'd tried to stop her taking it, but then gave up.

It must have amused him to no end. He did love his jokes.

"Wretched man!" she exclaimed under her breath. No wonder Molly had never answered it. All this time she'd thought her old friend callous and unfeeling for not answering Rafe's letter. "It seems I was wrong about so much."

"But you're never wrong, my lady."

Rather than respond to that, she strode to the window and looked out on the busy street below. "You are content here, Molly? You have all that you need?"

"Oh yes, my lady."

"My brother has agreed to finance your enterprise, has he not?" Unable to get a straight, sensible answer out of Carver, she now went directly to the source. "The truth, if you please."

Molly flushed. "He has, my lady. But I will repay him. Every penny."

She groaned. "I hope you know what you're doing." For once she was not going to give any advice. Let them figure it out for themselves. "And for pity's sake, after twelve years of friendship, I think we can safely dispense with the formality of my title. Can you not call me by my name?"

The other woman pondered this for a moment.

"I don't know that I can, my lady." She pressed her hands together nervously.

"You are not my maid anymore, Miss Robbins."

"True."

"Then I think you might address me as *Mercy*."

Molly's eyes grew wide and full. "But—"

"I'm sure you've called me worse than that, when I couldn't hear, Molly Robbins."

"Indeed I never have!"

Abruptly Mercy began to laugh. It rolled out of her until she thought the stitches of her corset might snap. "Come"—she held out her arms—"embrace me, Molly, for I have a very hard task ahead of me. You are my oldest and dearest friend and, prepare yourself for a shock of severe magnitude, but I think perhaps I should ask *your* advice for once."

"Mine?"

"I'm going to be married."

"I know. To Viscount Grey."

Mercy became serious now. "To Rafe Hartley. If he'll have me."

∽

"Lady Mercy, it was no easy thing to hear speculation and report of that nature, almost the very moment I set foot in England again."

She nodded slowly. "I am sorry you heard it and had any cause to be saddened on your return." Mercy made no attempt to deny the rumors. She sensed Adolphus came there that day because his father sent him. He generally avoided confrontation.

Eventually he managed a smile, sat forward, and

reached for her clenched hand, planting a friendly pat upon it. "But we are back together again now. I am willing to overlook the scandal, although it has offended my father to a great degree. Perhaps we can put this unfortunate incident behind us. And I see you looking so well, Lady Mercy, it quite lightens my heart."

How quickly he was willing to forgive her indiscretion, not even demanding to know anything about it, when she'd expected he might at least want her to tell him there was no truth in it. "The country air did wonders for me, sir. As Italy did for you, I think."

"Indeed." He set down the cup and saucer he'd held in his other hand. "Our time apart has now ended, and we can look forward to wedding arrangements. You must tell me, my dear, what you desire from me." He waited complacently to hear what she wanted, expecting direction. She could not see her face reflected in his eyes, only her fortune.

How very different from Rafe, she mused.

"Adolphus, have you ever met Sir William Milford and his sisters?"

A slight tremor disturbed the tranquility in his countenance, like tiny ripples on a lake surface. "Milford? The name has some familiarity." He hesitated. "Why?"

She slid her hand from under his. "I had the good fortune to become acquainted with Miss Isabella Milford in the country. Her widowed sister too."

"Oh?" He tried on another smile, but it was too tight for his face. Picking up his cup again, he took a few sips of tea.

"It was explained to me that Isabella had suffered a

disappointment in love, that she once thought she would be engaged, but that her lover changed his mind."

Adolphus swallowed. "Sometimes people do change their minds," he muttered.

"But he set her aside because he had found a bigger fish—or rather"—she laughed—"a bigger fisherman, for I was the one who set the hook for you, was I not? I made up my mind that you would do very well, and that was that." She'd never given him a chance. Once Mercy Danforthe made up her mind on some matter, there was no refusing her.

He looked at her oddly, probably wondering what she found to laugh about.

"You should have told me there was someone else," she said.

For a long moment, he did not reply. Finally he set his cup and saucer aside again, wiped his fingers on a napkin, and took a deep breath. "Would you have paid heed to me, if I did tell you?"

"Of course. I would never poach from another woman."

"But you are very—forgive me—but you are very self-assured, my dear. I was rather afraid to contradict you on any point. Once you set your mind upon marriage, I could not find a way to stop you."

She was not angry with him. Indeed, how could she be? She pitied Isabella Milford and was annoyed with herself for being so blind. It wouldn't be the first time her enthusiasm for the practicalities of an idea ran away with any other, more emotional considerations and made her disregard the feelings of another person.

"My father was most eager that I choose you over Miss Milford, for obvious reasons."

Those reasons being her wealth and position, naturally. She thought about this for a moment and then said, "My dear Adolphus, there is more to life than money. Is that all you people think it's about?"

He drew back, his bushy brows lifted in high arcs.

"Forgive me, Adolphus, but I find myself disinclined to marry you."

"Ah." He nodded. "I thought you might, my dear."

"We have so little in common."

"And I am considerably older." He was beginning to look relieved the more it sank in.

"So I think your father might be persuaded not to sue anyone."

He agreed fervently.

When he got up to leave, she almost pointed out that it looked like rain, but stopped herself. The man had eyes in his head, did he not?

A few days later, even his father was no doubt glad of the canceled engagement, for when Lady Mercy Danforthe refused to deny the rumors of her scandalous behavior in the country, the finer doors in London were no longer open to her. Hostesses who previously trampled one another to secure her attendance at parties and balls now gave her the cut. Her reputation, she was told by one matronly lady who dared visit, was in tatters.

And the cause of her great scandal? She'd been seen buying a watch and then *shaking the man's hand* in a street! Someone hinted that Lady Mercy was also seen, unchaperoned, riding with a man on his cart, but this was so heinous a suggestion that most people assumed it was rumor running away with itself.

"In time, Sister," Carver exclaimed jovially, "I daresay the general horror will die down, and you might show your face in public again."

Much to his surprise—and hers—she declared herself not particularly perturbed by the prospect of eternal expulsion. There was, after all, a great deal more to life.

Sitting at her writing desk, she composed a letter to Sir William Milford, inviting him, while he was in London, to join her for tea. If he could withstand the scandal of sitting down with a notorious hussy.

Then she penned another letter to Miss Julia Gibson, inviting her to tea on the same day.

There, almost all her obligations were now taken care of. Edward Hobbs had located the slippery Mr. Pyke, who was soon to be reunited with his wife and family in Sydney Dovedale, but the Pykes, apparently, would not remain there long. They were striking out boldly for the new world in America.

Hopefully, Mrs. Pyke would find that to her taste.

❧

One morning shortly after, while reading the engagement notices in the *Times*, Mercy was pleased to see a small announcement of Miss Isabella Milford's betrothal to Viscount Grey. But her joy was short-lived, for in that same issue she learned of several bank failures—an occurrence that was sadly not a rarity. This one caught her eye, when she read the name of the bank at fault, and her heart stalled. She knew Rafe was a shareholder there and had invested much of his coin.

She wrote a letter to Mrs. Hartley, enquiring into the extent of the loss, but for Rafe, she feared it was severe. He could lose everything. Despite that, he would never accept her help and would probably spurn his father's too. He'd been so proud of his savings, of the way he did it mostly alone, unaided by his father. It would be a crushing blow.

Four days later she received Mrs. Hartley's reply confirming the tragedy. But that was not the only post to arrive. With it came a short letter from Rafe. Even before she opened it, she feared to read the contents. Knowing Rafe, his pride would never let him marry her now he was penniless again. Sure enough, his letter released her of any obligation she might have felt to return and keep her promise. Rafe was leaving Sydney Dovedale and the life he'd begun to make for himself. Mrs. Hartley's letter had told her of his father offering another post with the family business, but Mercy doubted it would be accepted. Any attempt now to help him would be viewed as charity, and they all knew how he felt about that.

There was only one thing to be done.

She approached her brother in his library and told him of her plan.

"You're quite mad," he told her, as she knew he would.

"You know how I like projects, Carver, and I cannot think of a better one in which to invest my fortune."

"Yes, but your projects are usually people."

"So is this one. In a way."

He leaned back in his chair and studied her

thoughtfully. "This is about that farmer, is it not? That little bastard, Rafe Hartley."

"What if it is? Just as you wanted to *help* Molly," she pointed out drily, "I mean to help him."

There wasn't much he could say to that, other than, "I take it you've discussed this with Hobbs. And he agrees?"

"He does."

"Of course he does. Edward Hobbs would walk on fire for you." He sighed. "Then I suppose I must sanction this plan of yours, little Sister. By the way," he added as she was on her way out of his library, "I won my wager, you know."

"Which one?"

"That you would never marry Grey."

"I thought you placed a bet that I would. Isn't that why you called me home?"

Carver chuckled. "I called you home to prove that you wouldn't. It was time you realized it yourself." As he propped his feet up on the corner of his desk, a sheaf of papers were disturbed, and one floated to the carpet.

Mercy stooped to pick it up. "You are an insufferable cad, Brother." She handed the loose paper to him.

"And you're a scarlet hussy, Sister."

"Yes," she replied, "I am." That simple confession delivered, she walked to his door. "Now do tidy your desk. I won't be here to do it for you any longer." Nose in the air, she left him laughing again, but this time she closed his door quietly rather than slamming it. She was turning a new corner. They all were. She laid her palm briefly to his library door, wished him luck, and told him that she loved him. Just not out loud. Not with the footmen listening.

∼⁂∼

His father came out to the farm. This time, instead of hovering on the doorstep, he came all the way in. Rafe, expecting some lecture, instead found his father in a reflective mood.

"I know you and I have not always viewed life through the same eyes," he said as he swept off his hat and held it before him in nervous hands, "but, as Lady Mercy pointed out to me, that's because our experiences have been very different."

Startled, he could only say, "Yes, Father?"

"I suppose you will not take the post I offered."

Rafe felt stifled already at the thought of an office, a desk, and reams of paper, but he knew that if he found nothing else, he would have to take it. For now at least. "I wanted to thank you, sir, for the offer. I'm most grateful for the chance and yes, I…I will consider it."

His father's frown cleared. No doubt he had expected another quarrel and more resistance. Finally he set his hat on the table and said, "I am on your side, Rafe. I always will be. You may not wish to accept my help, but it is here for you. I will not judge. I will not say my way is better. You must do what pleases you. I should like you to know you can come to me in hard times as well as good." He paused. "I am your father, and—by God—proud of it," he added thickly.

James seemed to have ridden an hour in summer rain simply to tell him all this and get it off his chest. Whether he was sent by his wife or not, it was a gesture that could not be misread as anything other than one man's honest attempt to offer an olive branch. Rafe, try as he might, could find no fault with it.

"You haven't been at the wine already today, have you, Father?"

James frowned, and then slowly his brow cleared. "No, but I could make short work of an ale now, having got that all out." He looked around. "You've got a barrel, I assume?"

So the two men sat together in Rafe's little cottage and shared a mug of ale for the first time ever. All that time, he'd thought he needed to amass a fortune to please his father, yet in the end, it turned out that losing his money brought them closer.

"And I did hear some good news, Rafe. Sir William Milford has sold his property. You will have a new landlord," said James. "Perhaps you can negotiate better terms with the new squire to tide you over until the harvest is in and you're on your feet again."

This was indeed news of a more cheering nature. "But I thought you did not approve of me taking on a farmer's life, Father. Working the soil with my own hands."

James took a sip of ale and licked froth from his upper lip. "Rafe, my boy, the only thing I ever wanted was for you to be content. There has not been a day since I've known of your existence that I have not felt pride to call you my son. That I have not loved you and sought to make you as proud of me as I am of you."

There was nothing else for it, then, but to embrace. Stiffly, as men do.

But contentment seemed so far out of his reach

again now. He had lost more than his savings, of course. Not that he could explain this to his father.

He tried not to think about Mercy and her promise to return. The moment he realized he was ruined, he sent her the letter, so she need not feel guilty. It was impossible for him to think of keeping a wife now. Indeed, it was a good thing he was alone and had only himself to feed and clothe. These facts, however, did not stop the daydreams that haunted him. The yearning for what might have been.

The carriage that rattled through Sydney Dovedale two days later, carrying the new squire and owner of the fortress on the hill, was said to be very grand, pulled by four fine horses and driven by liveried servants. No one saw the passengers, but that didn't stop anyone from speculating. He was young and handsome, so it was said by a few of the unattached ladies who saw the carriage thunder by Hodson's around noon. He was old and gray with a face like a bulldog, so said Mrs. Flick, and—she added sternly—he didn't slow down for old ladies on the verge. In fact, if anything, his horses sped up when they saw her.

Rafe received a note that afternoon requesting his presence and so, wearing his best clothes, he rode up the lane on a plow horse, planning what he meant to say, hoping this fellow would be a man of reasonable temper.

He pulled the old bell cord at the door and waited.

When it finally creaked open, he was astonished to see a face he recognized. "Edward!"

"Young Master Hartley. Do come in."

At once his mood improved, although it was tempered by some uncertainty. "Your mistress has purchased this old place, Edward? I thought she was too ill to leave London."

"Oh, Lady Blunt's health has taken a turn for the better of late." Edward led him across the flagged floor of the medieval hall to a small chamber beyond. There were not many windows in the ancient building, for it had been planned during times of war and not used as a home for the first century of its life. Adaptations made to the fortress had been slight. It was almost as if the stones themselves resisted change. Just like some people, he mused.

But the small antechamber had a fresher atmosphere due, in part, to one tall, narrow window cut into the stone at some point in its history. Through this, a much-needed burst of light found entry into the fortress. Burning lavender in the fireplace helped sweeten the air, and two comfortable tapestry chairs sat beside a heavy oak table. In one of these chairs, the old lady he'd called his benefactress was apparently fast asleep, her head lolling forward, chin resting on her bosom, gentle snores disturbing the folds of her black lace veil. Her small feet rested on a worn tapestry footstool, and her gloved hands held a book in her lap, as if she were reading before she fell into her dreams.

Edward coughed loudly, and she raised her head. "Ah, there you are, young man."

He bowed. "Your ladyship, I am delighted to see you…" He would have said "so well," but since he could not see her face, it seemed foolish to make such a statement. She still kept to her black taffeta. Like a crow, perched on his fence, watching him. He sensed that this woman wouldn't be frightened by his scarecrow either, with or without the corset.

"I suppose you know why I sent for you," she croaked.

"I hoped, your ladyship, to discuss the terms of my lease. My bank recently—"

She waved a small, gloved hand wearily. "I am aware of all that. It is not in good taste, you know, to speak of money."

He nodded and looked down at her feet. They were tiny when close to his big, muddied boots. The rest of her was the same under all those black ruffles. He remembered how shocked he was when he felt her hand inside that glove on the one occasion when she gave it to him for a kiss. Very slight, delicate. But not as fragile as she looked.

"I am in need of a land agent. Sir William Milford has taken his away and left me with none. I should like you to take the post, if you feel up to it. The position, of course, will be that of steward *and* land agent, as Edward, sadly, cannot remain here with me but must return to Town."

Stunned, he looked at the lady in the chair. Why had this woman done so much for him? Still she strove for ways to help him. Why? All that she'd done for him went far beyond gratitude for saving her little dog from the wheels of a mail coach. "You wish to hire me?"

"That is correct. Why do you stare with mouth open? Is there some part of my speech that was not clear?"

"No. I mean to say—"

"You may keep your farm, if you wish. I understand

you have made it habitable, and this place"—she raised her hands, gesturing at the gray stone walls—"lacks the appeal of a home, for now. But I have plans to improve the building."

"You will live here, your ladyship?"

"That is the idea."

"But it is frigid cold in the winter and damp in the summer." He feared for her health in that place.

"Mayhap you can help me. I am told you have fixed your own cottage splendidly."

Again she showed off what she knew about him, through her "sources." He smiled. "I have, your ladyship."

"Made it for the bride who left you."

"Yes, I did."

"After all my efforts to see you settle. A great pity." Suddenly she sneezed. The book fell from her lap, bounced on the footstool, and landed on the stone floor by the hem of her black gown. Before Edward could spring to retrieve it, Rafe moved, bending forward. His little finger lifted her hem just half an inch while picking the book up, and there was the scarlet petticoat again that had so amused him before.

"Thank you, young man," she said, reaching for her book.

He looked at her gloved hand and then at the book. "A romance, your ladyship? I did not take you for a reader of romantic novels."

She snatched it from him with unladylike haste and then sank back to the chair as if the exertion brought her to death's door. "Will you accept the post, Master Hartley, or not? I haven't all day to wait for your answer." She sneezed violently.

His gaze moved again to the hem of her gown and the very slender flare of red beneath.

Red or orange? Or would she call it something else? "Mystery of the Orient," perhaps.

Finally Rafe looked at the lavender burning in the grate. His lips widened in a slow smile. His heart, which had been in a lethargic state these past few weeks, now perked up like a horse let out in the paddock after a day at the plow. "I accept the post, your ladyship. On one condition."

Her fingers wrapped nervously around her book. "Condition?"

"You must come to the Morecroft assembly rooms tomorrow, above the Red Lion in the market square. We have monthly balls, you know, and they are very popular. I should like you to meet my family, and in particular, my father, since you are the reason I returned here to heal the rift."

"I'm afraid that is out of the question at my age. I do not go to balls. Ever."

Rafe eyed her thoughtfully. Of all the rotten tricks. To make him take her advice so slyly—and her damned money too.

Charity, whatever she called it.

"If you do not come," he said carefully, leaning down to whisper against her veil, "it will be out of the question for me to accept the post, your ladyship."

He heard her breath change, become shallower so that it barely moved the veil anymore. Tasting her scent on the lace, he licked his lips.

"Do we understand each other?"

The only reply she managed was a low complaint

about the inconvenience of going out at her age, and something about spores in the air.

"I'll come for you at six o' clock, your ladyship." He straightened up, nodded to Edward, and left the chamber.

She thought she could get away with it, did she?

Of all the filthy, interfering ideas! His benefactress for months in London, and now she planned to do the same here. That wretched, meddling woman.

But as he mounted the plow horse, he felt laughter rumbling through his chest, fighting its way out past his anger and wounded pride. Despite his letter releasing her from that promise, she just couldn't stay away, it seemed. He was, as he'd said to her once, her lavender.

Somehow he'd get that woman to admit she loved him, despite the class difference and every other obstacle she tried to lay between them. Women! Never could say what they wanted and be done with it. A man had to guess, and if they guessed wrong, it was their fault.

She must be using her entire fortune, he realized, just to buy that old ruin and keep him on his feet, but she would never have done that without her brother's blessing. Did that mean the past was finally behind them?

Only one way to ensure that. Bury it once and for all, and all the grudges with it. Start fresh. That went for him too.

∽

Disguising herself again was the only way Mercy knew to make him accept her help. If she went to him as herself, he would have laughed scornfully and thrown the money back in her face. Besides, she left Sydney Dovedale under such a bower of suspicion and scandal that returning as Lady Mercy, she felt, would not be wise. As Edward Hobbs pointed out, she could not hide away behind a wig and widow's weeds forever, but she replied that she would get away with it for as long as she could. At least until Rafe was back on his feet and flourishing. His happiness was all that mattered.

Now he insisted, in some quirk of foolishness, that she attend the assembly-room dances. If she did not, he would not accept the post she offered. Stubborn ox! He would never change.

On the other hand, she wasn't sure she wanted him to change. Not too much, in any case. He was really quite perfect as he was.

The next evening, she refused to sit around waiting. He would probably be late.

But to her surprise, he was prompt. Even a little early.

She'd expected only a minute attempt to dress up on his part, yet he wore a completely new set of clothes—black tailcoat, ivory neckcloth, emerald-green waistcoat, finely embroidered. The only remaining sign of old Rafe were his boots. He refused to wear shoes for dancing. Since he'd made such an effort with everything else, Mercy didn't feel it right to complain.

"I thought we were taking my carriage," she warbled uncertainly, when he offered her his arm to walk outside.

"I borrowed my father's, your ladyship. I hope you approve."

It was polished and shining, the horses stomping proudly in gleaming harness. Even Edward Hobbs, who was never impressed, managed to look less grieved by the idea of a night out. He held the carriage door open while Rafe helped her up. She'd brought her cane, thinking to keep him at a distance with it, if need be. He noted it, clearly, a vague smile playing over his lips. Mercy thought she still had him tricked with her masquerade, but occasionally there were glimmers of doubt. He was altogether too cunning.

Edward took the seat beside her, and Rafe sat opposite, smiling deviously. "You are comfortable, your ladyship?"

"Quite so, young man."

"Excellent." His smile widened until it became quite wicked, and she had an awful pounding in her heart. She felt Edward glance at her, but she kept her face turned to look through the carriage window. Being summer, it was still light out, fortunately, and there was much to see, much to focus on. "I had hoped you might put aside your widow's weeds tonight, your ladyship."

"I never wear anything else, young man," she replied in subtle outrage at the suggestion.

If he had guessed her identity, why did he not say? No, he must not have realized, she decided. He was simply being Rafe, arrogant and getting his own way. He really did want her to meet his father. She would have to be very diligent to save herself from exposure. If Rafe knew she was behind this, he would never stay, never accept the position of working for her. Rather than let her help him, he would go back to the law and be desperately unhappy, cutting off his nose to spite his face. He might even go back to fighting for a living. She couldn't bear to think of that.

"You have been very good to me, your ladyship," he said suddenly. "I cannot imagine what would have become of me without your advice and friendship during those dark days in London. You have helped so many people with no thought for your own gain."

She hesitated, fingers clasped around the head of her cane. "It was my pleasure, young man, to have you as a friend."

"And it was my pleasure," he grinned slowly, "to have you."

Mercy thought her heart would stop, but somehow it kept beating out a strong rhythm.

෴

The assembly rooms were packed on this warm summer evening, but he located his parents and quickly steered his guests through the mob. He kept his hand under her elbow, because he had the distinct impression she might try to run off at some point in the evening. But this woman wasn't going anywhere again without him.

"Father, I'd like you to meet the lady who has purchased Sir William's property and lands. She and I became acquainted in London. Lady Blunt, my father, Mr. James Hartley."

His father curiously eyed the little woman in the excess of black taffeta and lace. "Honored to meet you, your ladyship."

"And I you," the figure whimpered behind her lace.

He tightened his hand around her arm. "This is my stepmother, Mrs. Hartley, and my great-grandmama, Lady Ursula."

Both women looked intrigued but also rather relieved that this acquaintance was an improvement on Mrs. Pyke. Rafe had mischievously told them nothing about his guest that evening, other than the fact that she'd offered him a post and he was considering it. They were all happy to hear that he might stay in Sydney Dovedale and find employment there. Even Lady Ursula managed to agree that the country was a healthier place and that she would like to see him succeed there.

"Lady Blunt," she exclaimed in her loud voice, "you must sit with me here out of the rabble. My grandson will fetch us some cake."

"Forgive me, Great-grandmama, but I have asked Lady Blunt to dance."

They all looked taken aback at the idea of a young man dancing with such an elderly lady bedecked in widow's weeds. The disguised troublemaker at his side attempted to pull away, but he took her cane and gave it to Edward, who was too surprised to argue. If she wished to continue the charade—which she clearly did—she would have to rely on him to hold her up. Before she could take the cane back from the other man, Rafe drew her rapidly into the dancing crowd.

Faces turned to watch in morbid curiosity as he hauled the supposed old lady about in a waltz. He almost stepped on her feet.

"Have you taken leave of your senses?" she gasped.

"I fear so, your ladyship. More so than ever. I put them into the hands of a meddling young woman, and she ran off with them. Along with my heart."

"You are intent on murdering me, you young blackguard. Put me down at once. I am an aged cripple. Am I not due some respect? To be treated thus—"

"Be silent, woman. You give me a headache again."

That quieted her squawking. She stared up at him through her veil, and he spun her around in the dance while everyone watched, wondering what on earth reckless Rafe Hartley—he with the ever-curious taste in dancing partners—would do next.

They were about to find out.

❧

"I wanted this to be a very public declaration, my lady," he said softly, one arm stealing around her waist, holding her close, "because I am weary of secrets, of veils and hiding. I am weary of pretense and charades and keeping up a front to please others."

She couldn't breathe. He held her too tightly. Everyone was watching.

"As you once said to me: 'Facing your problems is the answer. Running away from them is not.'"

"Young man, I—"

He bent his head closer. Even the musicians watched so intently that they began to miss notes. "I love you," he whispered. "You are going to marry me, and that, madam, is all there is to it. With all the scandal you've caused, who else would have you but a reckless rogue?" He lifted her veil and kissed her full on the lips.

The music stopped. The kiss did not.

Mercy had no will to fight it. She had missed him intolerably, and the relief of being in his arms outweighed the scandal they were causing there and then.

Someone cried out in shock. There was a sudden cacophony of something falling to the floor. A fainting, perhaps. At least they knew it wasn't his great-grandmama, because Lady Ursula's voice could be heard clear as a bell in the awestruck room as she bellowed, "Well, it seems it's never too late after all for a little romance. Which of you vigorous, young fellows wishes to dance with this old curmudgeon and sweep me off my feet in the same manner?"

And thus, on that warm summer's evening, the Morecroft assembly rooms bore witness to a number of formerly inconceivable phenomena. Lady Ursula Hartley would hobble through her very first "indecent" waltz, Mr. and Mrs. Hodson lasted an entire set without arguing or threatening to beat each other about the head, Edward Hobbs was actually observed smiling, and Lady Mercy Danforthe was seen to pass several untidy chairs without once stopping to straighten them. But most remarkable of all, two hotheaded, stubborn young people finally found words to declare their love for each other, and the roof did not cave in.

Epilogue

Autumn 1835

THE BABY SCREWED UP ITS TINY FACE, HOWLING LOUD enough to bring down the church walls. Gathered around the font, his proud parents, Sophie and Lazarus Kane, looked on happily as the parson held the baby and dripped water on that furious, wrinkled brow. Standing nearby, the godmother tapped her foot and glanced surreptitiously, once again, at the watch face on the slender pink ribbon she wore.

Suddenly they heard footsteps, and everyone turned to see Rafe running down the aisle in a stained shirt.

"You're late," Mercy exclaimed under her breath.

"I am aware of it, woman."

She began to think he'd be late for his own funeral. Work always came first for him and always would. But he took her hand, hastily assuming his role as godfather to his uncle's youngest child, and the ceremony continued without a hitch. With his hand in hers, she no longer cared about the time. Indeed, it was difficult to concentrate on a solitary task when he squeezed her fingers gently and she felt his warmth and vitality at her side.

Afterwards, as they all left the church and emerged into a crisp November day, golden leaves and pine needles crunching at their feet, he whispered a dare in her ear.

"Last one home's a lackwit."

She took him up on it, of course. How could she not accept a challenge? He rode home on his plow horse, and she raced him on her new stallion, delighting in the fresh bite of air on her cheeks. He beat her—somehow he cheated, she had no doubt. When she got to the gate, he was waiting, and he was barely out of breath.

"I was thinking," he said as he watched her dismount.

"Oh dear, not again."

"It's about time we had one of our own, Mrs. Hartley."

She patted the horse and handed her reins to the groom. "I assume you mean children."

"A strapping son."

"I cannot guarantee the sex of the child."

"Why not?" He followed her into the Great Hall, and his long stride almost caught her up. "I thought you could control everything."

She whirled around and held her riding quirt to his chest. "If I had control, I would most certainly have a girl."

"What use would she be?" He screwed up his face and held out his arms. "There's more than enough women about already. No, no, you'll give me a son, and that's an end to it."

"Men! You can do nothing without us. A man without a woman is like a candle without a wick."

He grabbed the end of her quirt and tossed it aside. "I'll show you my wick, wench."

"Or a...a door without a latch."

"Here's my latch, Bossy-Drawers."

She turned and ran up the stairs. He chased after.

"A woman without a man," he shouted, "is like a flower without a bee."

Mercy slammed the bedchamber door and held it shut. "A girl is best. A daughter is always superior."

"A son is actually useful. A daughter is merely decorative. A boy earns his weight in gold. A girl"—she opened the door suddenly, so that he tripped forward, since he was leaning on it with all his strength—"spends it."

"Of course another girl to adore you would be too much, I suppose," she muttered, hands on her waist.

He closed the door and turned the key in the lock. "Now that's a point. I suppose she would look up to me. And I'd have the very great pleasure of turning every lad away from our door when he comes to pay court."

"And if we had a son, I would have a chance to raise at least one young man with a proper appreciation of the female gender."

Slowly, Rafe grinned and advanced toward her warily, as if she might bolt again. "So we are decided then."

"Yes." She beckoned him closer. "Twins."

"Twins, Mrs. Hartley?"

"Twins."

He squinted, pretending to consider, so she slid her arms around his neck and drew him down for a kiss. "If you can manage it," she whispered.

His blue eyes flared with the challenge. "Best get to work at once."

As they tipped sideways onto the bed, she murmured, "Rafe, darling?"

"Hmm?"

"Do mind my gown. It's very fine silk."

With a low growl, he rolled over and silenced her with another kiss. Before too long, that very fine silk was discarded on the floor in any case, and soon assaulted by his rough cord breeches, his torn shirt, and his muddy boots. The silk gown bore this indignity with remarkable aplomb and, unlike its mistress, came out of the encounter quite unscathed.

Discover a new LOVE

Are You In Love With Love Stories?

Here's an online romance readers club that's just for YOU!

Where you can:
- **Meet** great *authors*
- **Party** with new *friends*
- **Get** new *books* before everyone else
- **Discover** great *new reads*

All at incredibly BIG savings!

**Join the party at
DiscoveraNewLove.com!**

About the Author

Jayne Fresina sprouted up in England, the youngest in a family of four daughters. Entertained by her father's colorful tales of growing up in the countryside, and surrounded by opinionated sisters—all with far more exciting lives than hers—she's always had inspiration for her beleaguered heroes and unstoppable heroines.